O9-BTN-197

RECEIVED

OCT 04 2012

By_____

# THAT'S
# NOT
# A
# FEELING

No Longer the Property of
Hayner Public Library District

HAYNER PUBLIC LIBRARY DISTRICT
ALTON, ILLINOIS

OVERDUES 10 PER DAY, MAXIMUM FINE
COST OF ITEM
ADDITIONAL $5.00 SERVICE CHARGE
APPLIED TO
LOST OR DAMAGED ITEMS

HAYNER PLD/ALTON SQUARE

# THAT'S NOT A FEELING

## DAN JOSEFSON

Copyright © 2012 by Dan Josefson

This is a work of fiction. Names, characters, places, and incidents either are the product of the author's imagination or are used fictitiously, and any resemblance to actual persons, living or dead, businesses, companies, events or locales is entirely coincidental.

Epigraph is from THE PHILOSOPHY OF ANDY WARHOL by Andy Warhol. Copyright © 1975 by Andy Warhol, used electronically by permission of The Wylie Agency LLC, and in print by permission of Houghton Mifflin Harcourt Publishing Company.

All rights reserved.

Published by
Soho Press, Inc.
853 Broadway
New York, NY 10003

Library of Congress Cataloging-in-Publication Data
Josefson, Dan.
That's not a feeling / Dan Josefson.
p. cm.
ISBN 978-1-61695-188-7
eISBN 978-1-61695-189-4
1. Teenage boys—Fiction. 2. Suicidal behavior—Fiction. 3. Boarding schools—Fiction. 4. Friendship—Fiction. I. Title.
PS3610.O6657T53 2012
813'.6—dc23          2012018508

Interior design by Janine Agro, Soho Press, Inc.

Printed in the United States of America

10 9 8 7 6 5 4 3 2 1

F
Jos

b20100930

*for Julia*

*Beautiful jails for Beautiful People*
—Andy Warhol

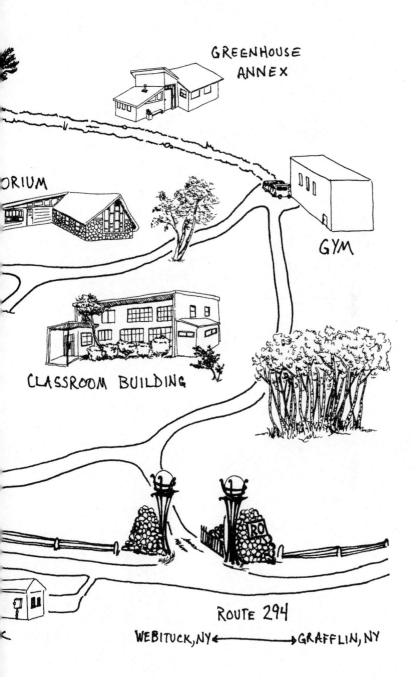

# PROLOGUE

**Upstate New York, late August**

No one noticed the evening's approach until the long shadows cast by the mountains began to merge in the grass. Alternative Boys stood on the Dirt Pile, digging away at it with their shovels and tossing the dirt toward the adjacent woods. Only when Roger woke to the growing darkness did he order the boys down and tell them to hurry back to the Mansion for supper. I'm losing it, he thought, and rubbed his face with his hands. He followed as the boys crossed Route 294 in a clump and then stretched out into a loose line to pass through the school's iron gate. The gate hung between two stone pillars; on the right pillar a sign read THE ROARING ORCHARDS SCHOOL FOR TROUBLED TEENS, WEBITUCK, NY. The Mansion they headed toward was built on a slight eminence and sat in an angle of light. Most of the boys rested the shovels on their shoulders or dragged them rasping along the gravel driveway. William Kay and Andrew Pudding soon fell behind; they were swinging their shovels at each other like swords.

They walked face-to-face, Pudding shuffling backward up the drive, William laughing wildly as the heavy wooden handles met overhead with dull clacks. Roger was glad the two of them rarely had energy for anything other than this sort of idiocy. Pudding was short and solidly built, with a round, babyish head. William was skinny and mean. If they set their minds to it, they could do plenty of damage.

It was the time of evening when everything recedes into its outline, when it feels as though there's more than enough time and space for every conceivable thing to happen. Roger called for William and Pudding to quit playing and hurry up. He told the boys in front to wait for their dorm mates. But his voice died on the air, and no one was listening.

Alternative Boys rounded the curve beneath the weeping beeches at the top of the drive. In front of them stood the Mansion, an enormous white farmhouse augmented by a jumble of disconsonant additions. Before the boys could reassemble to climb the steps together, Roger called out, "Freeze." They stopped where they were. "Hands out, gentlemen." Alternative Boys dropped their shovels and held their arms out straight, each trying to reach the boy closest to him without moving his feet. They wiggled their fingers and stretched. The boys in front were close enough to form a jagged line that connected them all. William and Pudding could reach each other but were separated from the rest of the dorm.

"You've drifted," Roger said. "Hold hands."

Leaving their shovels where they lay, Alternative Boys formed a circle and all held hands. The sun had tipped farther back behind the hills, and an orange band of sunset light, followed by shadow, slid up the trunks and lower branches of the trees until only the highest leaves held light any longer. "Now," Roger said, "what's going on with you guys that you can't stay grouped?"

The boys rolled bits of gravel under the soles of their sneakers or stared over the heads of the boys on the opposite side of the circle. Eric Gold was visibly upset. He had thick eyebrows and a wide, flat nose and, in the week and a half he'd been at the school, hadn't made any friends. "This is bullshit," he shouted. "You can't hand-hold me. You don't even know me." The other boys found this very funny, but those on either side of Eric tightened their grips to keep him from doing anything that would get them into more trouble.

Roger cleared his throat. "I know that if you're letting your dorm mates fall behind, you're either not paying attention to them or you're not willing to confront them. That's all I need to know." Roger adjusted his hat, a green felt cowboy hat, and scratched at his beard. "Has anyone explained the idea behind grouping to you? William, could you tell Eric what 'group' stands for?"

"Goats remember only. . . ," William began.

Roger sighed. "Pudding? Want to help your friend?"

Pudding looked at William and back at Roger. "Gee, I recently . . . ordered . . ."

"Pudding," Roger said.

". . . underpants . . ."

The other boys reacted with embarrassed silence. "I'm not hearing anything," Roger said, "to convince me that if I were to unhand-hold the dorm right now I wouldn't get taken advantage of again." The pink, gilded clouds of the reflected sunset faded in the picture windows of the Mansion. Shadows had risen from the valley floor to where the boys stood; the sparse woods darkened.

"Han," Roger asked, "could you please help us out?"

Han Quek hesitated, unsure which would be worse: spending more time holding hands in a circle or playing along with Roger. He decided quickly. "'Genuine relationships occur in uncomfortable proximity.'"

"Thank you. You see, Eric? This isn't about punishing anyone. It's about bringing the group closer together. And when you're out of arms' distance, when you drift, you're denying real intimacy by fleeing togetherness. So, Pudding, why were you having such a tough time being close to the people in the dorm today? Why are you and William isolating?"

"I wasn't isolating," William said. "I was genuinely trying to hit him with my shovel. *Genuinely.*" William's pale skin and blond hair looked even lighter in the darkness.

Pudding laughed and tried to kick William, but they were holding hands, and Pudding couldn't turn to kick him properly.

"No, really," William said. "Is there anyone here who doesn't think Pudding ought to get hit with a shovel? Raise your hand." Holding hands, no one could. "See? Pudding's the only one who doesn't think he should get hit. He's the one isolating. You should ask him why he's isolating."

"I did," Roger said. The clouds were melting away into the dark, but he was willing to wait. Roger believed in following the school's process, which could take time. He was calm and prepared to be completely rational and, if necessary, thoroughly unreasonable.

Pudding said that he hadn't seen the other boys getting ahead of him because he was walking backward, and as Roger began describing the difference between an explanation and an excuse, someone flipped a light switch inside the Mansion. The picture window in front of Alternative Boys ceased reflecting the shreds of sunset and opened now onto the Meditation Room. It hovered above the boys like a lit stage. Frances, one of the school's therapists, had entered the room with Nancy Ormsbee, a student in New Girls. The boys watched Nancy and Frances sit down in the oversize wicker armchairs beside the glass-topped table.

All of a sudden it felt late. The day was lost, and the boys sensed there was no time left for anything. They would hurry to change for a late dinner of cold cuts and corn chips and caffeine-free store-brand soda, and go to bed.

It was one of the last days of Summer Session, and every dorm was on retreat. Roger didn't like that Alternative Boys could see Nancy at therapy. She had only been enrolled three days ago and had already run away once; the police brought her back. Roger allowed the dorm to be un-hand-held. They returned their shovels to the Mansion basement, then went upstairs where they changed from work clothes to school dress and waited their turn for dinner. Bit by bit, darkness seeped into the corners of the valley. The birds that had spent the evening flitting from branch to branch flew deeper into the woods to sleep.

One at a time the dorms walked to the back of the Cafetorium to pick up dinner trays, then brought these back to their quarters in the Mansion. Regular Kids, Alternative Girls, Alternative Boys, New Girls. When they were all back inside, New Boys exited the Cottage where they lived, got their food, and returned.

Later, lights around campus were turned off one by one until only the windows in the upper floors of the Mansion were lit. Then these, too, went out, one after another down the hallways as dorm parents entered each room to administer nighttime meds and say good night. Finally the floodlights illuminating the front of the Mansion were the only lights left on.

The valley was quiet. Deer stalked windfall apples in the orchard on the east side of the Mansion. Their heavy lips slid over the apples, and they broke the cool skins with their teeth. These were crab apples, small and sour, but there were too many deer in the valley, even in late summer when their numbers had been thinned by trucks hurtling down the interstate; they ate what they could. The deer stopped and looked nervously over their shoulders. They froze not at any sound but at an intensification of the silence that pealed like a bell.

On less quiet nights, the wind racing down the hills would rattle the Mansion's dusty window screens and whistle in the branches of the trees. But tonight the sky weighed down directly on the valley and on the school in its center. The students were left awake, their visions curling in on themselves like fiddleheads. Voicelessly they went through the same exhausted speeches that they recited on other sleepless nights: the monologues to their parents about all the reasons it had been a mistake to send them to the school; the rants they would let loose on Aubrey if they could get away with it; or just the stories they would tell with studied indifference, collapsing onto an old couch in a friend's basement, about what a fucked-up place it was they had just escaped. We moved our lips through these febrile daydreams and could not sleep.

We were fourteen, fifteen, sixteen years old, although there was a tired joke at the school that Aubrey would accept a six-year-old as long as someone paid his tuition. Maybe I shouldn't say "we" quite yet—the day I'm describing is the day before I arrived at Roaring Orchards. My story here and in what follows is based on what I saw and what I was told, by students and occasionally by members of the faculty. Students and faculty had very different experiences of the school, but we had one thing in common: we would all rather have been somewhere else. But we stayed, or many of us did, most of the time. We all stay except for those who don't, as Aubrey sometimes said. Nancy Ormsbee was one of those who didn't stay.

In her top bunk in her room in New Girls, she inched toward the edge of her mattress, freezing at each squeak of the metal springs. She climbed over the footboard, lowered herself off the bed. Nancy crawled across the carpet and braced herself against the wall beside the door. Then, as she had done earlier that week, she gently slid the plastic mattress, on which her roommate Laurel slept, away from the door inch by inch, taking time between each little push to let Laurel readjust in her sleep. When there was just enough room, Nancy turned the doorknob until she felt the spindle pull the latch from the post. She opened the door and squeezed out, keeping the knob turned and only letting it spring back when she had carefully pulled the door shut on the girls asleep in their room. She stole a pair of sneakers from Alternative Girls and slipped out of the Mansion into the dark.

Nancy took a deep breath and sprinted across the lawn to where the school vans were parked beside the gym. She opened the back doors of the newest-looking one and felt around in the dark for the jack. With it she returned, her hands shaking with adrenaline, to the Mansion.

New Girls' med closet was a room off their lounge. Nancy set the jack beneath the doorknob and worked the lever. She winced at the sound of wood cracking and held still. She didn't seem to have woken anyone. She pumped the jack again, and the knob bent, the metal growing paler while the old wooden door gave way. When the bolt cracked loose, Nancy entered and quickly went through the girls' allowance envelopes, taking the money saved in each. She was about to leave when she turned back and grabbed the packet with the next morning's meds. She ran back downstairs and outside.

Before she disappeared from Roaring Orchards, Nancy took one last look back at the Mansion. The floodlights in the flowerbeds lit the building but distorted it as well. The eaves and the gingerbreading above the entrance cast magnified shadows over the white façade. It reminded her of a person holding a flashlight under his chin in the dark. And then she left the school forever.

The Mansion sat in the center of the valley, surrounded by trees unstirred by any wind. The moon had risen, alone in the dark sky but for the haze around it. They were a pair, the moon alone in the sky, the Mansion alone in the valley, each snug in its socket like an eye and a tooth.

# PART ONE

## Roaring Orchards

# 1

**Tidbit tried to** remember what she had just been thinking of. She was at a loss. She stared at her hand digging idly in the soft earth and tried to focus on the flutter she still felt beneath her ribs. It had been a worry, that much she knew for sure, and not a worry about anything far off but about something that was going to happen soon. She wasn't sure of anything else, except that she would recognize it if she thought of it again.

A drop of sweat rolled across the bridge of Tidbit's nose and into her eye. She squinted, rubbed the eye with a dusty fist. The morning heat was stunning. Tidbit had taken a couple of extra Dexedrines after breakfast, ones she had hidden away in her pillowcase. Her skin tingled and her heart pounded. Her mind dissolved in the heat like a sugar cube in a glass of tea.

Already she regretted the pills. Tidbit had wanted a quiet day and now she was locked into countless swells of hollow enthusiasm. She had given Carly Sibbons-Diaz two pills in exchange for Carly taking her turn doing dishes. They'd been woken up early for a candor meeting when it was discovered that Nancy had run again, and Carly thought the pills would keep her from being exhausted all day. But she hadn't wanted to take them alone.

Tidbit crawled along under the juniper bushes, inhaling the sugary scent of the evergreen leaves. The juniper shook with the movement of all the other New Girls, who were searching for the razor blade Beverly Hess had dropped somewhere in the shrubs that ran along the front of the Classroom Building. Tidbit should have been looking for it, too. But she was sure that the blade wasn't lost in the dirt any longer, that either one of the other girls had grabbed it or Bev had never dropped it in the first place.

Like every morning for the past two weeks, the girls had carried brushes and the aluminum ladder and all the gallon cans of paint from the upper equipment shed to the Classroom Building, where they were repainting the window frames. Recently they'd gotten bored and begun to see how much paint they could get on the windows themselves, letting paint drip from their brushes or spray across the glass from bent bristles. The previous day, Tidbit had basically painted over an entire window.

So this morning when they got to the Classroom Building, their dorm parent Marcy told them to drop everything. While New Girls were rubbing away the pink indentations that the wire handles of the paint cans had left on their palms, Marcy opened up the fanny pack she always wore back to front around her belly and took out enough retractable razors for all of them to use. She told them that today they were to scrape off all the paint they'd gotten on the windows.

"Look at how this looks!" she'd said, flapping an arm in the direction of the building. "This is careless, sloppy work, and it takes *out* of the community when you're supposed to be putting back in."

Careless? Tidbit thought, sweating in the dust. How could Marcy have believed one of them covered an entire window by mistake? She just didn't want to waste a day getting the girls to admit they'd done it on purpose, then figuring out who did what and what the repercussions would be. So Marcy pretended no rules had been broken, and the girls went along. But scraping paint off the windows got boring quickly; the girls did soon get careless; and no one was surprised when Bev announced that her razor had fallen out of its holder and into the junipers, though Marcy did say, "I can't believe this shit." She collected all the retractable razors and sent the girls to find the missing blade.

Tidbit crawled into a spot large enough for her to lie down, between the stems of two bushes whose branches had grown into one another overhead. She could see the Mansion's front lawn and the valley beyond it. The sun hung over the hills, dripping heat. A brown Oldsmobile Cutlass she didn't recognize was driving up the school's gravel driveway, making a buzzing sound.

It parked in the carport next to the Mansion, facing the girls. A scream escaped it as a door opened and a woman climbed out and was silenced when she swung the door shut. New Girls stopped what they were doing to look out across campus at the car. The scream erupted again as another door opened. A man exited the driver's seat slowly, and again, like in a cartoon, the scream was gone when he closed the door. The couple climbed the front steps and, after taking one long look back, entered the Mansion. It was an intake.

Tidbit couldn't tell whether she heard muffled screaming still coming from inside the Cutlass. Another dazzling wave of energy was seeping through her. She stared at her hand drawing circles in the dust. Tidbit used to tell me how much she hated her hands. Except for the bloody parts where she bit them, they were completely pale, even at the end of the summer. Worse, they were so swollen that her knuckles just looked like dimples, and they trembled from the lithium. It was what it did to her hands that made Tidbit want to get off lithium. But Dr. Wahl always said maybe.

Tidbit turned to see Carly Sibbons-Diaz crawling toward her in the narrow space between the wall of the Classroom Building and the back of the shrubs. Carly squeezed into Tidbit's space beneath the junipers and collapsed next to her.

"Hi, Tidbit," she said. "Found the razor?"

"Nope." At home Carly had worn her hair dyed black, but no one at the school was allowed to use dye, so in the weeks since her intake her blond roots had begun to show in a thick stripe down the center of her scalp where she parted her hair. Everyone said it made her look like a skunk, but up close, Tidbit thought, it didn't really. "How're you feeling?"

"Okay."

"Anything yet?"

"Nah. You?"

"My vision's kinda messed up," Tidbit said. "I keep seeing tiny, tiny little blackbirds hopping from branch to branch in these bushes, but when I look they're not there." This wasn't exactly true, but when she said it, it felt sort of true. "You see anything like that?"

Carly just sighed and looked where Tidbit was looking, at the brown Cutlass by the Mansion. She thought she saw a silhouette move inside it. Carly edged forward so she could see the car better. Maybe the Dexedrine was messing with her vision. "You think Bev just took the razor blade?" she asked. "Is she a cutter?"

"Everyone's a cutter," Tidbit said. "Have you seen her belly?"

"Did she do that to herself?" Carly spat in the dirt. "Shit. She didn't do that with a razor, though—"

Tidbit held up her hand to quiet Carly.

She heard something from inside the car now, a distant wailing. There was a thud, then another, a banging that was getting louder and slowly gaining speed. The sunlight reflecting off the windshield trembled with each thud, and with each Tidbit could just make out the sole of a shoe hitting the inside of the glass. Then two soles, kicking the windshield together until the shatter-proof glass began to spiderweb. Finally the kicking became bicycling, one foot after the other. The girls could hear the screaming with perfect clarity as two gray-green sneakers kicked the crumpled window away.

After a few moments, a group of staff members and Regular Kids ran out of the Mansion. They opened the front doors of the Cutlass, which I hadn't bothered to lock, dragged me from my parents' car, and held me down on the ground until I stopped yelling. It took five of them to hold me, though I'm not all that big. Then they led me up the Mansion steps and inside.

"Holy shit," Carly said. "Finally something cool happens at this fucking place."

"Yeah, yeah, yeah," Tidbit said.

**I was deposited,** alone, in the Reception Room. I wasn't sure where my parents were at that point, but I assumed they were on the tour I'd agreed to come up for. All I wanted was to get it over with and go home. I was anxious to know what these people were telling my parents. I'd only agreed to come in the first place because it had calmed them down.

In the Reception Room, there was a table with flower vases, one a pyramid glazed light blue, the other round and yellow, both holding white flowers. There was a Persian rug on the floor, bookshelves standing against one wall, and a small fireplace. In the back corner of the room there was a baby-grand piano.

Above the mantel hung a portrait of a man, who I soon learned was Aubrey, sitting on a horse. Either the proportions were off or the horse had unusually long legs. Aubrey wore some sort of uniform with epaulets and gold braids hanging from the shoulders. There was a curved sword hanging from his belt. Aubrey stared straight out of the painting with a blank look on his face, his eyebrows raised in a way that made him seem both a bit doubtful and as though he were inviting the viewer to be impressed. The horse, with Aubrey on its back, stood in the foreground of the painting, at the near edge of a large field. Visible in the distance, between the front and back legs of the horse, a building burned.

I could hear the creak of floorboards and the murmuring of voices on the other side of the Reception Room doors. The doors were heavy and slid out of the walls to meet in the middle. There was a crack between them through which I could see a few of the students and faculty members who had dragged me out of the car and into the Mansion.

They had said strange things when they were holding me down outside. "It's all right, we'll keep you safe," and "Just let it all out," like they were encouraging me. That had scared me more than the fact that they were restraining me. They seemed disappointed that I didn't struggle more. I assumed that now they were standing guard outside to keep me from bolting, but there were windows in the Reception Room that I could have gotten out of just as easily.

I took a closer look at the painting. The burning structure was a barn. There were more horses near it. One reared up on its hind legs; one lay in the grass to the side of the building. This second horse was black and on fire, and there were other horses sticking their heads out of the barn, their throats and faces framed by swirling brushstrokes of black smoke. The trees behind the barn were in the grip of a wind evident nowhere else in the painting. Their branches swung out and upward so that the gray-green undersides of the leaves showed against the darkening gunmetal sky. The paint itself was thick and, especially in the little scene with the burning barn, looked wet and greasy. I could see how each flame rising from the barn or from the body of a horse was laid on by the soft tip of a paintbrush.

I turned toward the entrance when I heard the doors being dragged open. I was ready to tell my parents that I'd changed my mind about the tour, that these people were crazy and we should just go home. Aubrey walked in first, followed by one of the kids who'd held me down outside. This was clearly the man from the painting, but in front of me he seemed almost orange, his tan was so deep. Aubrey was short and had a paunch that the figure in the painting lacked. He wore a dark gray suit over a light gray shirt and around his neck a light, mint-green scarf. I stepped to the threshold to look for my parents in the Great Hall. Aubrey grabbed me tightly by the arm and led me back into the Reception Room. In his other hand he carried a small gift bag.

"Where's my parents?"

Aubrey didn't say anything, just sat down in a flower-patterned armchair and removed a fork and a plastic container from his small bag. The container held a small salad. I looked to the kid for help, but he was watching Aubrey remove a silver pepper grinder from the bag and grind pepper over his salad. Next he tucked the corner of a striped pink napkin over his scarf and into the collar of his shirt. He began eating.

"Benjamin," Aubrey said with his mouth full of food, "this is . . ." He looked up.

"Tyler," the kid said.

"Tyler," he said, and swallowed. "He's in Regular Kids and works in the dorm you'll be joining, Alternative Boys. Your dorm parent Ellie will be here soon to take you to meet the other boys, but in the meantime I've asked Tyler here to look after you."

I felt blood rush to my face and a burst of pain behind my eyes. The fork, I thought. I should grab his fork. "I'm, I'm just here for a tour," I said. "Where's my parents? They said I only had to come for a tour." My throat felt almost swollen shut. My skin itched. The true facts of the situation were slamming up against one another in my head.

Aubrey stuffed a huge forkful of salad into his mouth, and after trying once or twice to talk through it he looked up at Tyler and gestured for him to explain.

"Your parents decided to enroll you," he said. "They'll send your stuff up. Until then, you can borrow what you need from other boys in the dorm."

I bolted through the open doors and into the Great Hall but stopped when three students who'd been leaning against the furniture stepped in front of me. I shouted over their heads into the office adjacent to the Great Hall. "Mom! Dad!" I turned back to Aubrey. "This is fucking stupid. Where are they?"

Aubrey put his bowl of salad down on the floor next to him and stood up. He pulled a wad of money out of his pocket and pulled a few dollar bills from the silver money clip. He handed them to Tyler. "We don't use that word here. It's a violent word." Then he sat back down and picked up his salad.

"Your 'rents left already," Tyler said.

*'Rents?* I just looked at him.

"They thought it'd be better to avoid a scene. You can call them this weekend and see them next Parents' Sunday."

Aubrey nodded to the people who had been standing guard, and they all left. Then he gestured with his fork for Tyler to take me away, absently waving in the air the endive and chunk of radish he had just speared.

As Tyler led me into the Great Hall, I felt the need for some drastic action but had no idea what to do or what the repercussions might be. If my parents were really gone, it wouldn't do any good anyway. But what if I were being lied to again? What if my parents were hidden somewhere? There was a chill in the enormous room and the smell of furniture polish. A tall, narrow dinner table with spindly legs and an inlaid top slid by as I followed Tyler past it. From a cavernous stone fireplace I caught the smell of cold ashes.

Tyler stopped next to an enormous couch. "We'll wait here for Ellie," he said. He gestured for me to sit down, and he dropped into an armchair. After a while, presumably done with his salad,

Aubrey walked from the Reception Room to the Office. "Behave yourself," he called to me. Tyler picked up a magazine.

**Outside, Marcy was** yelling at New Girls to all come out from the bushes right away. Tidbit felt a diffuse foreboding, and as she emerged from the junipers she finally remembered what her worry had been. Marcy was holding Tidbit's glasses by the end of one ear-piece and swinging them around in a circle. Her posture suggested a cool disappointment in her dorm's behavior, not at all unanticipated. But when Marcy spoke, a bare wire of fear shook in her voice.

"I don't think you girls realize what a serious situation you're all in," she said. "Last night you let a girl who you should have been taking care of run away for the second time with all your money and meds. And now I have no choice but to assume that this razor blade isn't missing but that one of you has it, and you're hiding it, and God knows what you're—." Marcy pointed the glasses at Tidbit. "How the hell do you think you're going to find a razor blade lost in the dirt without your glasses? Tell me exactly, Tidbit. I'd really like to know."

"Well, I just—"

"You know what, don't even bother. I'm just so sick of all of you right now. Really, physically sick of you." Marcy's head bobbed when she was angry, so that the cluster of keys she wore on a string around her long neck rattled. "You know where I found these?" she asked, stabbing Tidbit's glasses in the air in front of the girls' faces. "Tidbit, where would you guess I found your glasses?"

"Bridget had them?"

"That's right, Bridget had them. And why don't you tell every-one what Bridget was doing with your glasses when I saw her."

"Burning ants?"

"Yes, Bridget was using them to burn ants. So that's at least two people not looking for the razor. Plus, really cruel. I just can't believe you, Tidbit. For a week all you've talked about every meeting is how you've decided that you're going to be good, that you want to get out of here and you're going to follow the pro—"

"But there's a huge anthill right next to the wall of the Classroom Building!" Bridget Divola interrupted. She was hopping up and down. "If we don't do anything, I think they're going to invade the building." New Girls stared at Bridget. At twelve she was younger than the rest of the girls. She was pudgy and had a bowl haircut that made her face look like a doorknob with eyes. In the silence that followed, Bridget pinched a large black ant off of her thick elbow. Folding Tidbit's glasses shut, Marcy looked as though she might cry.

"Now this is the deal," Marcy finally said. "Lunch is in three hours, and I'm not allowed to make you skip lunch. But I can't take you into the Cafetorium when one of you might be hiding a razor blade. So if you haven't found it in two hours, we're going to go back to the dorm, and you're all going to be strip-searched before we go to lunch. Do you all understand?"

A dull flame of rage flickered through the dorm and was smothered. After waiting for someone else to take the lead, Laurel Pfaff said, "You can't do that. It's punitive. You're not allowed to punish us all just because a few people aren't looking."

"It's not a punishment," Marcy said, more confident of herself as the girls got more upset. "It's a consequence. It's the only way I can make sure that all of you and everyone else on campus are safe. If you have a better idea, I'd be glad to hear it."

The girls knew nothing would come of arguing. At the school one thing followed from the last like the logic of a bad dream, the drawer you don't want to open even as you watch your hand reach toward it. Only Laurel persisted.

"But what if none of us has it?" she said. "What if the razor's just lost in the bushes? Then you're humiliating all of us because Bev and Bridget and Tidbit can't manage to do a single thing right."

"I don't have any razors!" Bev shouted. Despite the heat, she wore a maroon velour dress that bore at least a half-dozen food stains, which were dull against the general glinting of sun off the velour. She was almost bald, having the habit of pulling out her hair.

Tidbit wasn't really following. She clenched her teeth and endured another surge as more drugs spilled into her brain. The whole thing made her sleepy. She stared at a young Japanese maple tree past the far corner of the Classroom Building, vaguely aware that a fight was starting among the girls. The maple had a thin trunk and perfectly smooth branches. Tidbit watched the branches of the tree stay still as the purple leaves swayed in the heat. Bridget had been so happy when Tidbit had given her her glasses.

There was a time when I thought that I was in love with Tidbit, but I realize now it was more than that. Tidbit was my friend when no one else would be. I don't mean for that to sound sentimental; I'm writing all this down so I can forget about her, so I can stop thinking about the school. All I want is to lay something down between myself and the things that happened there, even if it's nothing but a screen of words. There's an insect I read about called the western spittlebug, *Clastoptera juniperina*, whose nymphs protect themselves by chewing up juniper stems and spitting out little bubbles until they've covered themselves in foam. The foam keeps the bugs from being dried up and burned by the sun. That's really all I'm doing by writing this.

Tidbit turned and watched her dorm mates. They seemed so far away. Bev lunged at Laurel, who looked terrified. Marcy got hold of one of Bev's arms and as she was twisting it back accidentally stepped on the hem of Bev's dress. Bev tumbled hard onto her side, Marcy falling on top of her. "Girls, some help here," Marcy called. As New Girls hurried forward to help restrain Bev, Marcy saw Laurel. "Not you," she said to her. "You stay away." Tidbit slowly walked closer.

The girls held Bev facedown, one of them sitting on her ankles. Bev was reduced to yelling and spitting. After some time she quieted, her breathing interrupted only occasionally by a loud grunt.

Marcy leaned her face closer to Bev's.

"What's going on with you, Bev? What are you feeling right now?"

"Can I roll over?"

"Not as long as you still need to be restrained."

"Please? It hurts!" Bev struggled against the girls holding her down but soon gave up.

"You can turn over when I can trust that you've calmed down, sweetie."

Bev tried to turn her head, but her chin scraped against the pavement. "I'm calm. I promise."

"I'll believe that when you show me you're honest enough to talk about how you're feeling."

Bev huffed loudly. Tears and snot glistened on her cheek. "I feel like a piece of shit," she said.

"That's not a feeling," Marcy said, sounding bored. "You're not a piece of shit, and you certainly can't feel like one. We've been over this before."

"Ugghh! I feel like killing someone."

"You might kill someone, you might not. But you can't *feel* like killing someone. Think of the list of feelings."

Bev was quiet for a moment.

"I feel very, very, very angry."

"Okay." Marcy nodded to the girls to ease up. They let Bev roll onto her back and then held her again, more gently now. There was a deep blankness to Bev's expression at times like this, when she was struggling to make sense of something that had just happened or was happening. Her dark eyes were vacant and her cheeks slack, like a large damp flower past its bloom. Damp wisps of hair stuck to her head. Her chin was pebbled with red abrasions.

"What are you angry about?" Marcy asked her.

"Everyone thinks I stole a razor."

"Have you checked that out? Or are you a mind reader?"

Bev wasn't sure whether she was meant to laugh at this. She smiled at Marcy, but getting no smile back she stopped.

"Well? Do you want to check out whether they think you have the razor, or do you want to stay angry?"

Bev looked up at the girls standing in a circle looking down at her. "Do you guys think I have it?"

There was a mix of shrugs and nods and shaking heads.

"See?" Marcy said. "Not everyone thinks that."

New Girls' attention was drawn away by the sounds of footsteps rounding the corner of the Classroom Building. Four of the school's five teachers were on their way into the Classroom Building to plan classes for the coming semester and to finish grading papers and tests from the last one. Only Spencer, a tall, balding blond whose belly pressed against his T-shirt, stopped to see if he could help.

"Well, ladies, what's going on here?"

Marcy didn't much want his help but was in no position to say so. "Bev got violent. We're trying to work it out."

"In a wiggle, huh?" Spencer leaned forward, his hands on his knees. Sunburned skin was peeling from the tops of his ears. "Bev," he called down at her in what he imagined was playful mock anger. "What are you doing down there? You got your nice purple dress all dusty."

"Hi," she said.

He stood up straight and turned to Marcy, squinting in the sunlight. "Anything I can do?"

"She's going to need to sit in a corner when she gets up. Could you get a chair?"

"Sure." He looked around. He noticed that Doris, the supervisor of the Teachers' Group, was leaning on her cane at the entrance to the Classroom Building, waiting for him. "I'll be right back with it." Spencer nodded to the rest of the New Girls. "Girls," he said.

Before he could go inside, Doris asked him what was going on. Doris was obese. She had a handkerchief she used to wipe the sweat from her face. When he explained about getting a chair, she reminded him that the teachers had a day off to schedule classes and weren't supposed to be working in the dorms. She looked over to where Bev lay on the ground. "Just be quick," she said.

New Girls were still talking about Bev's feelings when Spencer brought out a chipped green plastic chair with a white desk attached. The metal legs shone in the sunlight. The girls' discussion came to an end with a point that Carly Sibbons-Diaz made.

"At first I thought maybe Bev did have the razor," Carly said, "but then I realized: if she was hiding it anywhere on her body, she'd be all cut up by now. But she isn't."

This sounded absolutely crazy to Tidbit, and she felt a rush of fear, thinking that Marcy would figure out that Carly was on drugs and they would both be caught. But everyone else seemed convinced. Marcy let Bev up; Bev dusted off her dress and went to sit in the chair, facing the corner of the Classroom Building. Marcy sent the rest of the girls back into the bushes.

As time passed, the few New Girls still looking for the razor blade gave up and waited for Marcy to lead them back to the Mansion to be searched. They sat talking to one another quietly or drew elaborate pictures in the dust. By the time Marcy said it was time to go, many of the girls had fallen asleep beneath the bushes. Those still awake crawled around and woke the rest.

# 2

The Classroom Building was a cinder-block structure in moderate disrepair. Thin wool carpeting and dingy linoleum covered the floors, and the whole building somehow seemed much larger than it was. Doris, Spencer, Dedrick, and June sat in the Teachers' Lounge. Over the large window on the east wall, a torn and twisted set of bamboo blinds were lowered to keep the sunlight out. But the string that held the left side of the bamboo slats together had gotten tangled in the pulley at the top, leaving the blinds hanging at an angle. They cast a yellow shadow across the room.

In addition to Doris being supervisor of the Teachers' Group, Aubrey had recently made her the assistant director of the school as well. In her short time as an administrator, Doris had learned that the fewer decisions she made, the less she would be held responsible for. But avoiding making decisions as the teachers' supervisor meant that she had to get the other teachers to do things themselves. This she found extremely difficult, especially with Spencer and Dedrick. She had always been baffled by clever young men, which is what she thought they were. There seemed to be some tacit understanding that underlay their banter. Doris had no idea what this was, but it didn't seem to involve helping her get things done.

She could see Dedrick was about to start. The flip side of

Aubrey's belief that faculty members should be role models for the students was, Doris thought, that they themselves weren't all that different from the students.

"Spencer," Dedrick said, "what's going on with your dorm?"

"They're not really my dorm until classes start," Spencer said. He was looking out the window. "I'm still with New Boys, at least until they're done with Building Bridges." He sat down on the couch under the large window.

"Building Bridges. How's that going?"

"The bridge is done. All they have left to do is the sign."

"No, I mean the emotional bridges between the boys. How's that going?"

"Fuck you," Spencer said and laughed.

"Where's Brenda?" Doris asked. "How is it that she's late again? Having a day like this is a favor Aubrey does for us. It's an insult to him."

Doris wasn't the best person Aubrey could have chosen to be his assistant director. Some people thought he wanted someone who would defer to him, but I think he was trying to teach us something. Not anything about fairness or about giving an unpromising candidate a chance, but something about power. If Aubrey had picked someone competent, it would have rendered his power invisible. The person who deserved the job would have gotten it; events would have been following their own logic. Only by choosing someone inept, by being arbitrary, could Aubrey remind us that he answered to no one.

"There's plenty of stuff we can do until she gets here," Spencer said. He tore open a bag of pretzels with his teeth and placed it on the coffee table in the middle of the room.

"That's not the point," Doris said, "but you're right. We'll have you do the beginners math class again. But we need a new name for it."

"We just gave it a new name this semester."

"Yes. We have to come up with a new name every semester. If the students' educational consultants look at their transcripts and see that we have them in the same class twice, they think we're not following the individual educational plans. So what did we call it last semester?"

"God, I don't remember."

Dedrick laughed and let some pretzel dust spray from his mouth. "You don't remember the name of the class you taught?"

"I think," June said, "it was something about humble beginnings."

"*That's* right," Spencer said. "Humble Starts and New Beginnings." He turned to Dedrick. "See."

"So," Doris asked, "any ideas?" She had a yellow legal pad in her lap.

Spencer thought for a moment. "How about Mathlab?"

"I don't know. We had a Mathlab once but the students started calling it Methlab."

"Math on the Run," Dedrick suggested.

"No."

"How about Make Mine Math?"

"Fun with Numbers."

"Guys," Doris said.

"Counting Without Fingers."

"Don't Step on the Math, Man."

"Gentlemen, this isn't helping."

"What?" Spencer said. "I thought that last one was pretty good."

There was a knock on the open door. "Good," Doris said, "now we can get started." But she grabbed hold of her armrest and turned herself around to see that it was not Brenda but Ellie in the doorway.

"Hi, teachers," Ellie said, "can I crash your party?"

"Sure," Dedrick said. "How come you're not with your boys?"

Doris excused herself. She was going to call around and try to find Brenda. She pushed past Ellie on her way out.

"Huh? Oh, they're working on the Dirt Pile with Roger," Ellie said, looking after Doris as she went.

Ellie walked across the room and climbed onto the arm of the couch that sat beneath the window. She untangled the string from the slats but was too short to reach the pulley mechanism at the top. She wore a long, narrow black skirt and a small blue T-shirt. "What are you guys doing?" she asked as she tugged at the string to even the blinds.

"We need a new name for beginner's math." Spencer watched her stretch to reach the top of the blinds. "Any ideas?"

"I always sucked at math," she said.

"Sort of long for a class name," Spencer said.

"I don't know," Dedrick said. "We should ask Doris."

"Oh!" Ellie cried as the blinds crashed to the floor behind the couch. A thick ray of dirty light flooded the Teachers' Lounge. The whole room seemed suddenly airless and tight, brimming with dust motes. Ellie jumped down off the arm and collapsed onto the couch next to Spencer. "I hate this fucking place."

Ellie was blond, with eyebrows so pale they were barely visible. Her nose was round, and her eyes were a light, light gray. Every boy she knew fell in love with her at least a little. She waited for some response to what she had said, but the teachers had retreated into themselves. They all hated working there, and they all stayed for what they believed were bad reasons. They made fun of the kids, and they made fun of the place, but they rarely said more about it than that.

Dedrick asked, "You thinking about leaving?"

"Every day. And then I think maybe it's just that I haven't had a weekend off since July." She laughed indifferently. "All the new staff showing up and then quitting. That guy in the overalls last week, he didn't even stay a full day."

Spencer picked up the folder of papers next to him on the couch and began reading through them. The other teachers found things to work on, too. Ellie picked up a Styrofoam cup and filled it with pretzels. She leaned back on the couch and put her feet up on the lime-green table. It occurred to her that all the furniture in the lounge was upholstered or painted various shades of green.

"Hey, you want to hear something funny?" Spencer asked. "For the final essay for my social studies class last semester, I had them write an analysis of some piece of advertising. Listen to this: 'Cereal boxes use colorful characters to try and convince parents to be their children's breakfast.'"

"Nice," Dedrick said.

"Whose is that?" June asked.

Spencer flipped the page over. "William Kay."

"I'd believe," Dedrick said, "that his parents became his break-fast. They might yet."

"Is he one of your serial killers?" June asked.

"I'm not sure. He's probably on the list," Spencer said. "Do you remember?" he asked Dedrick.

Dedrick shook his head. "Check," he said.

"What's that?" Ellie asked.

Dedrick explained as Spencer got up and grabbed a green spiral-bound notebook off a shelf: "We found this list of attributes that most serial killers share. Awkwardness around the opposite sex, intelligence, bedwetting, starting fires, some others. We've been keeping a tally as we find stuff out about the kids."

Spencer flipped to the middle of the notebook. "We have William down for cruelty to animals, but that's it. He's probably not smart enough to be much of a serial killer anyway."

Spencer put the green notebook back on the shelf, between *Bridge to Terabithia* and *Tristes Tropiques*, which is exactly where I found it fifteen years later. This was only a few months ago, when I had returned to wander the campus for no reason I understood. The school had been closed down for some time and was abandoned. In the Classroom Building, the walls were cracked, and tiles had fallen from the ceiling. I roamed the rooms and hallways, and browsing the stacks in the Teachers' Lounge I saw the notebook on the shelf.

The pages were stiff and had yellowed. In them I saw names I hadn't thought of for years, and some names that I'd thought of every day since the one I've been describing, when I first arrived at the school. It didn't even occur to me to look for my own name until I had read through the notebook and hadn't seen it. There were short essay assignments stuffed between the pages as well, maybe the papers the teachers were grading that day. Putting down the notebook, I found that I was sitting on the floor and that outside the light had begun to fade. In my mind's eye I saw the teachers, sitting around the room the way they must have once, and I suddenly understood exactly what it must have been like. I found a pencil, and right there, on the floor of the Teachers' Lounge, I began to write this book.

I looked up Dedrick soon after and wrote him a letter to tell him about the project I had begun and to ask him a number of questions about his experience at the school. I was surprised when he wrote back at how happy he was to hear from me—surprised that he remembered me at all. Dedrick told me all sorts of things about what his life was like now, but neither answered my questions nor said anything at all about his time at Roaring Orchards.

Doris returned from her phone calls. "Someone's gone to look for her," she said. "Apparently Brenda's spending some time with the girls in Zen Gardening, dragging logs out of the woods to chop for firewood. In the meantime, let's talk about electives. Dedrick, we need an English elective."

"Didn't I just do one like two semesters ago?"

"Yes, but several of our pupils completed the state requirements since then."

Spencer folded one of his exams into a paper airplane and threw it toward the open door. It veered left, crashed into the wall, and fell. He said to Ellie, "Dedrick taught this class about unreliable narrators, and it was a disaster."

"The kids were always on so much medication that, well, it wasn't a very high-functioning situation. Bev Hess drooled on her desk all through *Diary of a Madman*."

"Is she on your serial killer list?" Ellie asked.

"All the theorists are," Dedrick said.

"So," Doris said, "for this semester?"

"You should teach a class called Books Spencer Can Reach from the Couch," Spencer said. He reached up and without looking knocked a number of books from the shelf beside him. They tumbled down, some landing in his lap, some bouncing off the arms of the couch and landing on the floor.

"Guys, we really need to get this done today."

"Doris, we'll change the name," Spencer said.

"What've you got?" Dedrick asked.

Spencer began reading off titles and tossing the books one at a time across the room to Dedrick. "Aristophanes's *The Birds*, *Famous Monologues from TV Teleplays*, Kropotkin's *Fugitive Writings* . . . *Walden*, *The Long Goodbye*, *New Science*."

"Whoa, whoa," Dedrick said, struggling to catch or dodge the flying paperbacks. "That's enough."

"You really think this will make an okay elective?" Doris asked.

"I definitely do," Dedrick said.

"Because the Alexander Academy just gave us a box of brand-new books. Maybe you could use those?"

"Can Spencer reach them from the couch?" Dedrick asked.

"Oh, well—"

"I'm just kidding, Doris. Sure we'll use them. What did they send?"

"It was a big box, but I think the only book was *The Decameron*."

"They sent us a big box with one book in it? What, like a joke?"

"No, there were about two dozen copies."

"Well, fine," Dedrick said. "I'll add it to the syllabus."

"So what should we call it?" Doris asked.

"Cooking with Butter."

The phone rang in the atrium. "That better be Brenda," Doris said. She waited to see if anyone else would go to answer it. When no one did, she got up out of her chair and went.

"What's up with her?" Dedrick asked.

"With Doris?" June said.

"No, with Brenda."

"I think she just got really close with those girls over the summer," June said. "She had them put on one of her plays as an activity."

"Sucker," Dedrick said.

"I think it's sweet."

Doris returned. "Ellie, they need you in the Mansion. You've got an intake."

"Oh, great." She struggled up out of the couch and said, "Sorry about the blinds. Am I a part of this meeting or can I just go?"

"I think we need to consent," Doris said.

"This is my consensus to leave the meeting."

"Agreed."

"Agreed."

"Agreed."

"Agreed."

# 3

**I don't know** how long I'd been sitting in the Great Hall by the
time Ellie arrived to collect me. I had worked myself into such
an intense state of sadness and anger that she had to shake me to
get my attention. I didn't understand how my parents could have
left me, and I didn't know what to do. Tyler got up, dropped his
magazine on the chair, and wished Ellie good luck.

"You ready?" Ellie asked, and without waiting for an answer
took my hand and led me to the Office.

The secretaries all turned and smiled brightly at me. On one
of their desks I saw my book bag sitting dejectedly, half collapsed
over itself. They must have gone out and come back in again, I
thought. I had left the bag in the car. My parents had found it there
when they went to leave and brought it back in before leaving
again. It was a stupid thought. The image of my mother running
back into the Mansion, shaky on the steps, while my father waited
impatiently in the car behind the crumpled windshield, and then
her stealing out again. But they must have.

It was a paltry thing. But it was dizzying, too, and all I had. I
looked down into the long, deep drawer of a filing cabinet that was
open beside me. It was only when I felt a tear fall and graze my
wrist that I realized I'd begun to cry. When I told myself that this
was absolutely the last thing I should be doing, the sobs swept from

me beyond my ability to control. The Office ladies' lipsticky smiles faded in the flickering, aquatic light of their computer monitors.

Ellie rubbed my back and waited for me to cry myself out. I imagine she was relieved that this crying jag of mine and whatever might follow it were happening in the presence of the ladies in the Office, that it hadn't begun when she was alone with me. When with long heaving breaths I swallowed my last sobs, she patted me gently and grabbed my book bag off of the desk.

"C'mon," she said and led me out of the Office. I looked pleadingly over my shoulder at the secretaries who only raised their smiles, which now barely hid what seemed a profound but passing worry. I followed Ellie back into and across the Great Hall to the foot of a wide wooden staircase next to which, through bleary eyes, I saw an enormous, brightly painted rocking horse with a coarse woolly mane. I don't know how I had missed it before.

"Keep up with me." Ellie took my hand in hers. We climbed the staircase, which turned elegantly and then turned again. Ellie led me through doorways and around corners, and I quickly got lost in the maze of the Mansion. The higher floors were hotter and smelled of dusty wool carpeting. The walls were white, though scuffed and dirty near the floor.

At one point we walked down a corridor with doors open on both sides to small bedrooms. Each door had a page torn from a spiral notebook taped to it, on which were written three or four girls' names. The names appeared in bubble letters, imitation graffiti, or in letters with teardrops running down their sides to suggest melting wax or dripping blood. Then the signs stopped, and the doors were blank. The hallway was narrow enough that Ellie had to walk on ahead of me.

My book bag was slung over her shoulder and swung briskly across her back with each step. Her blue T-shirt didn't quite reach the top of her skirt, the waistband of which seesawed slightly with her hips as she walked. I slowed down to increase the distance between us, to see how far ahead she would go. When she rounded a corner and passed out of sight, I stopped, opened a door on the right, and slipped into a room. I quietly closed the door behind me.

What little light there was came through a window high on the wall, its curtain drawn. I stumbled down two wide steps that led into the room. There was a shadowed futon against one wall of the room, and opposite that there was a desk with a computer on it. I walked quietly around the room once, letting my eyes adjust. I froze upon noticing that there was someone asleep on the futon. I stepped closer. It was a heavy, middle-aged woman with dark, curly hair. She would later be introduced to me as Frances, and for my first few months at the school, she was my therapist, until for some reason I was switched. She snored softly.

I quickly returned to the door and listened. Not hearing anything, I opened the door and almost bumped right into Ellie.

"What were you doing in there?" she asked.

"I fell behind," I said. "I thought you went in there. What's that room for?"

"No, I went around that corner." Ellie gave me a long, dubious glance. "That's one of the therapy rooms. If someone had been in there you and I would both be in a heap of trouble."

"How do you know no one was?"

I thought I saw Ellie's mouth soften into a tiny smile. "Because," she said, "I don't hear any trouble. Alternative Kids aren't allowed to walk around alone. Only Regular Kids are. Come on. You always have to be with a staff member, and when you're with the dorm you'll always need to be within arms' length of the other boys."

"Arms' length?"

"It's part of Aubrey's system. The point is to develop honest relationships. That's a big step in dealing with whatever it might be you're dealing with."

I nodded. I wondered what it was I was dealing with. Ellie explained some other things as well. I would be in Alternative Boys. Most new students started in Alternative Boys or Alternative Girls. Those were the middle dorms. New Boys and New Girls were lower functioning, she said. Regular Kids were higher functioning. If I got violent or tried to run away, I would be sent down to New Boys. To get into Regular Kids I had to follow the process, though Ellie was a bit vague as to what exactly this entailed. Students could only graduate from Regular Kids.

"But if I'm new, shouldn't I be in New Boys?"

"Oh, no," she said. "There are some New Boys who've been here forever."

Ellie directed me around the corner and through a door that led into a kitchenette. The kitchenette was attached to a good-sized lounge furnished with three large couches. These were arranged around a small square table. The thin carpeting was worn to strands in parts.

We walked through the lounge to a hallway with bedrooms on either side. The loose-leaf signs on these doors had boys' names. Eventually I would learn that all the dorms in the Mansion had this same setup: a hallway along which were situated a number of bedrooms and one large shared bathroom. Each dorm's hallway ended in a lounge, and off the lounge was a kitchenette. The exceptions— at Roaring Orchards there were exceptions to everything—were Regular Kids, who had more spacious rooms spread across one of the Mansion's upper floors, and New Boys, who didn't live in the Mansion at all but in a converted trailer called the Cottage.

Ellie walked into one of the bedrooms and tossed my book bag on the lower bunk of one of the two bunk beds in the room. "This room'll be yours," she said. She dropped an extra pillow from one of the other beds onto a blue plastic mattress that lay on the floor between the two bunk beds and said, "That'll be your bed for now.

We'll get you some sheets, but I don't think you'll need a blanket yet. If you do there are some up in the attic to use until your parents send the rest of your stuff."

I nodded and nodded and couldn't think of anything to say. I didn't really believe that I would spend the night here, let alone that this room would ever come to feel like mine. At the same time, I didn't know what could keep that from being the case. The only color in the room came from the quilts and pillows on the four beds. I felt exhausted. "Where is everybody?" I finally asked.

"Alternative Boys are out on a Reciprocity Detail across the street, working on the Dirt Pile. We'll head over there once we go through your things." She sat down on the bed next to my book bag, unzipped it, and began removing things. She pulled out a CD player tangled in the wires of its headphones, a stack of jewel boxes, half a Milky Way bar still in its wrapper, a plastic alarm clock, a crumpled soft-pack of Camel Lights, a few grimy bills, a six-pack of Welch's grape soda with two cans missing, a torn book of matches, and my black sweatshirt. She folded the sweatshirt carefully. "Well," she said. "You can keep the sweatshirt and the alarm clock. But the rest—money, music, food, smokes—that's all off-limits."

"The alarm clock's not mine."

"What?"

"I mean it's not mine. Why would I carry an alarm clock around in my backpack?"

"Your parents must have put it in there. When they got your bag out of the car."

"Yeah. They must have brought it up." I held out my palm, and Ellie handed me the clock. The black cord was wrapped around it. The clock was covered in thin sheets of plastic meant to look like wood. "Could I have one of those sodas before you get rid of them?" I asked. "You can have one, too." That was stupid. They weren't really mine to offer any longer.

"We should probably get over there."

"To the Dirt Pile?"

"Yeah. I guess we could split one of these first." She pulled a can from its plastic ring and sat back on the bed, propped up by a pillow. She pulled the tab and took a long swig.

"It's warm," she said, handing me the can.

"It was in the car."

We passed the can back and forth in silence. Ellie used her feet to move my things out of her way so she could stretch out her legs. On the bed she looked like a high school student herself.

"How long have you worked here?"

"Too long." After a moment, she laughed. "It's not that bad here. You'll make some really good friends." She looked at me for a while. I don't know what she thought.

Ellie left the sweatshirt and scooped the other things up. She put the rest of the grape sodas in the refrigerator in the kitchenette, then looked around for a moment. "I don't have the keys to the med closet," Ellie told me, walking across the lounge to a gray metal desk, "so I'm just going to put these things in the desk. We'll lock them up later. Don't tell anyone this stuff is here, okay?"

I followed Ellie around corners and through doorways. We went down a long flight of stairs in the back of the building and onto a landing then down more stairs until we ended up in a damp basement lined with washing machines and dryers. In a back part there were large wooden folding tables leaning against one wall and spiderwebs up in the corners. A short staircase led us outside and onto a wide white porch with peeling paint. I wasn't sure where we were in relation to the part of the school I had seen. The Mansion's layout didn't seem to make any sense. Directly in front of us was a buckled macadam parking lot. Past that, a garden path led to a fountain.

Ellie took my hand again and led me around the porch to the

front of the Mansion. We walked down the hill and cut across
the lawn to the stone pillars and iron gate at the entrance to the
school. There was an old weathered fence at the edge of the lawn.
Some of the crossbeams had fallen from their posts and lay angled
against the grass, which smelled like it had just been cut. Ellie led
me across Route 294, the main road that ran past campus into
Webituck. We walked toward a long, low building covered in red
shingles. In front of the building was what I assumed must be the
Dirt Pile.

Seven or eight boys stood on it, each holding a shovel and digging away at the dirt, tossing shovelfuls into the thin copse of trees
behind it. Behind one of the boys, who was fat and drenched in
sweat, a bearded man stood shouting, "That's it, Pudding, there
you go! Keep digging now!"

When the man saw Ellie approaching with me, he called to the
boys to climb down off the dirt and to get into a circle. The boys
did, leaving a space for us. We joined them and completed the
circle.

"Boys," Ellie said, "this is Benjamin. Benjamin, this is Alternative Boys. And this," she said to me, "is Roger. He's a supervisor."

Roger reached across the circle to shake hands. "Glad to know
you," he said. His eyes were watery, and his face splotched red.
"Now, boys, why don't we go around the circle and introduce
ourselves. Tell Benjamin where you're from and what got you sent
here. Who's gonna start?"

A thin boy with a mop of platinum-blond hair began. "My
name's William. You wanna see my dick?"

"Goddamn it, William." Roger sounded less angry than tired.
"That's not funny. He's new. He doesn't know you're joking."
William was so pale I could see the blue veins in his neck.

"You think I'm joking?" William said, unfastening his belt.
"I'll really pull it—"

"Stop being an asshole and tell him why you're here."

William laughed and fixed his belt. "I'm from New Hampshire. I got sent here for taking a bunch of roofies when I was already on probation for beating up a kid. I ended up staring at a wall for like two days. They sent me here from the hospital."

"William's here as part of his probation," Roger added, as if William had been too humble to mention it himself. He nodded to the next boy in the circle, who had thick dark hair and a nose that looked to have been smashed flat.

"I'm Eric," the boy said. "I just got here, too. Like two weeks ago. It sucks."

"Eric," Roger said.

"I'm from Baltimore," Eric said. "I skipped school a lot."

"I'm Carlos," said the boy next to him, who was very short and very skinny. "My parents sent me here because I wasn't taking my meds during the day in school when I was supposed to, but most of the time I just forgot." He looked at Roger, then back at me. "Sometimes I on purpose forgot. They sent me here so people would watch me closer."

They continued around the circle. I couldn't keep track of much of it. The boys were from all over, but mostly the East Coast. Someone had been sent to the school for chasing his father around the house with either a fork or a hammer, but I couldn't remember his name. Someone's parents were afraid that he was going to hurt his sister. There was a large boy named Zach. Could there have been two Zachs? Someone else messed up his parents' car by either scratching it with a fork or hitting it with a hammer, whichever the boy who had chased his father around hadn't used.

The fat boy whom Roger had called Pudding when they were shoveling dirt was still catching his breath when it was his turn to speak. He introduced himself as Andrew Pudding and said he'd found ten thousand dollars in a safe in his father's office and had spent all of it. The boys around the circle began to smile, and one of them said, "Tell the new kid what you spent it on," and Pudding stared at me, sighed, and said, "I took cabs a lot of places." Alternative Boys all laughed, but Pudding kept looking at me. A boy named Han said he'd been sent to the school for not being a good-enough driver, but the words were barely out of his mouth before everyone was yelling that he was full of shit, that no one got sent there for that. Han shouted over them that parents could send kids to the school for whatever reason they wanted and that Aubrey was perfectly happy to take tuition from people whose kids had no other problem than that they couldn't drive well, but the boys were not convinced.

When it got around to me, I said, "I'm Benjamin. My parents just left me."

"That's what they did to me, too!" Pudding shouted from across the circle. "I hate that! They tell them it'll be easier that way but it isn't true, and then they tell them everything you're going to say before you say it so they won't believe you!"

"Yeah," someone added. "And as soon as they're gone Aubrey'll call all the other parents and tell them to call your parents to tell them how happy they are that they sent their kids here and about how well we're all doing."

"Yeah," said Pudding, waving his shovel. "And look at us!"

Roger stopped things there. He told us to get to work. The boys climbed back up onto the pile of dirt and began scraping and shoveling, all except for me and Pudding, who waited next to Roger. "Go on ahead and get to work without me," Roger told him. "I've got to talk to Ellie for a minute. Don't let me catch you slacking."

Pudding wandered around to the side of the Dirt Pile where Roger couldn't see him and sat down with his back to the rest of the dorm. I followed him, since I didn't have a shovel. Pudding was pulling something out of his pockets and stuffing it into his mouth. I sat down next to him. "What's that?" I asked him.

"Pancakes. Don't tell."

Pudding didn't offer me any, he just kept pulling pieces of pancake from his pocket and eating them. The boys on the Dirt Pile above us were throwing shovelfuls of dirt in the direction of the woods with a slow, regular rhythm. Some of the dirt they tossed made it to the trees, the rest landing back on the pile or somewhere in between. Roger called out that he was leaving and that we should listen to Ellie. Soon after that, Pudding turned to face the boys up on the Pile.

"Hey, could you please watch where you're throwing that dirt?"

"Okay," someone called. Clumps of dirt rained down directly onto Pudding and me. One shovelful hit me in the back of the neck, getting dirt down my collar. A small rock clipped me in the temple. Pudding stood up and started yelling, and when another shovelful got him in the face, he ran at the pile and grabbed for someone's ankle. I took a step back and looked up to see that it was William's ankle Pudding had hold of, and despite his hitting Pudding in the shoulder with his shovel, Pudding wouldn't let go. Then William's green eyes flashed in his gaunt face, not with anger but with glee, as he wound up and swung the shovel like a golf club, hitting the side of Pudding's head so hard that *I* almost fell over. More amazing than that strike was the fact that Pudding seemed unfazed. He dragged William off the pile and fell on him.

The other boys ran down from the top of the Dirt Pile and circled Pudding and William until Ellie got there, at which point they pulled the two boys apart. Pudding picked up his glasses and began cleaning the lenses on his shirt. William was smiling, some blood running from his nose. He pointed at Pudding's waist and said, "Hey, what's that?"

A piece of pancake was sticking out of Pudding's pocket. "Nothing," Pudding said, stuffing it back in.

"Bullshit, nothing," William said. "That's a pancake. You've got goddamn pancakes in your pockets again." The rest of Alternative Boys were crowding closer to get a better look.

"Empty your pockets, Pudding," Ellie said.

"This is ridiculous," Pudding said, taking a step toward Ellie. "William starts a fight and throws dirt and belts me in the head with a shovel, and it turns into a debate about pancakes. This is why our dorm is always getting put on restriction, Ellie, because you let people distract you from focusing on the central issues."

Ellie's gray eyes darkened a touch. "So you're saying you did take pancakes from breakfast and stuff them in your pockets?"

"No, what I'm saying is that if someone gets violent with a shovel, that should get dealt with and not ignored to discuss pancakes. And if I did, it wouldn't be against the rules anyway."

"Empty your pockets, Pudding."

Alternative Boys were in the middle of arguing about whether it was or was not against the rules to take food from breakfast and if so whether pockets were an appropriate place to keep it when someone shouted that Han was running away.

I turned to see him sprinting past the Dirt Pile and into the sparse woods behind it. Han was short and heavy and ran close to the ground with his arms pumping wildly at his sides. He tossed his shovel high over his head and picked up speed, his flannel shirt flying loose behind him as he went.

"Shit!" Ellie said as the boys all dropped their shovels and started chasing after him through the trees. She ran after them, and I jogged along behind her. The dorm followed Han through the woods onto someone's front lawn and then onto Route 294. Ellie stopped when they got to the road and grabbed me. "Go to the Mansion and find Roger," she said.

"He should be in our dorm going over paperwork. Tell him that Han ran."

She turned back to follow the boys running down the road as I called out, "But, wait, how do I get to our—"

"It's just right where we were before," she yelled over her shoulder. "I've got to go."

I stopped and watched Ellie and the dorm chasing Han. They were a clumsy bunch, some running on the road, some on the grass to the right. The pack slowly thinned to a string, the boys behind struggling to keep up. I waited until I could just make out the last of Alternative Boys disappearing over a slight rise in the road.

# 4

When I saw they were gone, I looked at the road stretching away from the school in the opposite direction. By the time anyone realized, it would be almost impossible for them to find me. I wondered what they would do, whether they had people who looked for runaways, if they would get the police involved. My parents would worry. The road ran straight as far as I could see, trees overhanging both sides. It would serve them right.

I wandered across the road. The Mansion stood atop the hill in front of me, across the green field. A high, peaked roof sloped steeply down, into which was set a series of gabled windows. I couldn't see them from where I was, but I remembered the wraparound porch, painted white, and the slate steps that led up to the building. Near me in the grass, two wasps were chasing each other in quick, erratic circles. Their legs hung loose with an obscene indifference as they zoomed around, bumping into blades of grass.

Staring up at the Mansion, I felt I had stepped out of a game I'd been involved in for as long as I could remember. I knew I should run, but I felt rising within me a new fascination. The sinister, oddly decorated rooms; the gingerbreading above the entrance-way; the winding stairs and hallways leading endlessly inward. I looked down at the wasps in the grass and, feeling as though a fog had cleared, I thought, It's fine, I can always leave later. It was the same mistake I always made: I thought that feeling would last.

I climbed over one of the fallen crossbeams of the fence onto campus. *You go first, I'll follow you*, I thought with a sick, giddy smile. I headed left around the hill on which the Mansion stood, rather than going to find Roger directly. The lawn led into the midst of a few enormous old-growth pine trees. These were far apart, the ground beneath them covered with dry needles. A wooden sign nailed to one of the trees read ENCHANTED FOREST. There weren't more than a dozen trees, and from anywhere among them I could still see Route 294.

I followed a rutted gravel road that led around campus. There were small houses on either side. A wooden sign in the shape of an arrow pointed down the path to the left and read simply, FARM.

Straight ahead was a field overgrown with gorse and thorns. A rusted backstop, the only sign that the field had once been a baseball diamond, had collapsed on one side and looked as though it were in the process of lying down in the grass. I saw a group of girls working among the trees behind the backstop, dragging logs out of the woods on sleds.

It was amazing to think that I might never have seen these things. I knew, although I didn't quite believe, that I had tried to kill myself. Twice, I remembered. It didn't seem like the kind of thing you would forget, but sometimes I did. The first time was with pills, and that had started the hospital and everything. The locked room with nothing in it but a red rubber playground ball that was so upsetting because I had no idea what it was for. The second time I had tried to hang myself, which hadn't come close to working, but they started looking for places to send me. As I looked out at the rusted backstop being warmed by the sun, it was hard to imagine that I had done anything as violent as that. If it had worked, I wouldn't have been there. I would have just disappeared, and the field would be there, the sunlight pouring down and the girls dragging logs out of the woods, but I never would have seen it. *I'll go first, you follow me.* Just like it would all be there the next day, if I had run away right then.

The gravel road ran through an orchard of small crabapple trees. Another wooden sign sticking out of the ground identified this as the North Orchard. The grass here was hummocky and rough with weeds, and last fall's leaves lay decomposing in corners of the fields, caught up in furze and briars. I followed the road toward the back of the Mansion, to the edge of the garden I had seen with Ellie.

There was a path of large slate stones that had begun to sink into the ground, lined on both sides by box bushes. Halfway across the garden the path widened to a circle, in the middle of which stood a fountain. To my left was a small gazebo. As I approached the fountain I noticed a small pond to my right, under the wands of a willow tree, which was identified by a sign nailed to a post in the ground as the Ornamental Pond. A toy bridge, painted maroon and green, traversed the pond.

The fountain in front of me consisted of three marble bowls, one above another. Each bowl brimmed with water that trickled down from the smaller bowls above to the larger ones below. In the top one there sat a statue of a large curly-headed child who held a large turtle in his lap. The turtle's front legs reached resignedly over the edge of the bowl, and on one of them it rested its square head. Around the base of the fountain was a flower bed. Summer was over, and most of the flowers were gone or wilted, but a few late-blooming chrysanthemums and daylilies weathered the heat, bright and bored.

I hurried across the small parking lot into the Mansion. It was too strange that they'd left me alone; I had the feeling I was being tested. From the foyer I took the stairs down into the laundry room and up the back staircase Ellie had led me down. I realized that I didn't know how many floors to climb. On the stairs I could hear people moving around the Mansion but couldn't tell from the sounds just where they were.

I guessed I should take the stairs all the way up. They ended at a door that opened into a dark room, which was incredibly hot and smelled like sawdust. I pulled a chain hanging from an exposed lightbulb, and the bulb flickered and lit up. The room seemed to be some sort of an attic, maybe the attic Ellie had mentioned. There were dark green file cabinets stacked in one corner and odd pieces of furniture scattered around. On top of the file cabinets were some folded blankets. My nose itched, and sweat rolled down my face. I went to return to the staircase, but the door had locked behind me.

I made my way across the attic, stumbling over some rolled-up rugs and things, and found a door on the opposite side. This one opened onto a staircase identical to the one I had climbed. I ran down the stairs and opened a door one floor down. There was a huge room with deep, pink wall-to-wall carpeting. Thick, vertical stripes covered the wallpaper. I let the door close and ran down another flight of stairs. The door here opened onto a small kitchenette that led to a lounge.

Relieved, I saw the desk, but no one was there. "Roger?" I called. "Roger?"

A thin, anxious woman wearing a bunch of keys on a string around her neck marched into the lounge, closing the door to the hallway that led to the bedrooms. "What are you doing in here?" she asked. She seemed angry, but she was whispering. "Who are you?"

"I'm new," I said. "Ellie told me to find Roger and tell him that Han ran away."

"Keep your voice down. Roger's not here. Han Quek?"

"I don't know his last name." I was whispering now, too. "He got sent here because of his driving. I need to find Roger."

"Did you check Alternative Boys?"

I looked around. "This isn't their dorm?"

The woman looked at me suspiciously. "No," she said. "This is the girls' wing. I'm Marcy, by the way. Hold on." She grabbed the receiver of the phone on the desk and dialed two numbers. Marcy watched me as the phone on the other end rang and rang, nodding her head impatiently. She hung up. "When did you get here?"

"This morning."

"And you're walking around by yourself why?"

"Ellie told me to go tell Roger."

She laughed bitterly. "You just wait here. Don't go anywhere. I'll find him."

"Thanks," I said. Instead of leaving directly through the kitchenette, Marcy headed back into the hallway she had come from, closing the door loudly behind her.

Marcy walked into the large tiled bathroom where New Girls were. Carly was getting undressed, handing her clothes one piece at a time to Kelly, one of the two Regular Kids whom Marcy had called to help with the searches. The girls who had already been searched were separate, in the shower room, so none of the girls waiting could hand any of them the razor. Tidbit told me about this all months later, when we had become friends and could joke, still somewhat uncomfortably, about how we had first met. Kelly went carefully over the hems, cuffs, waistband, and pockets of Carly's clothes, then folded them and placed them in a neat pile on the floor. Jenna, the other Regular Kid, sat next to Kelly and kept an eye on the New Girls waiting to be searched. She wanted to make sure they didn't stash anything anywhere. Kelly and Jenna were dressed alike, in slim tan pants and black button-down shirts. Regular Kids always looked better than the other kids on campus.

Aubrey took them all shopping with the school credit card at the beginning of each semester.

Once Carly had taken off all her clothes, Kelly had her raise her arms, turn completely around, crouch down, and then stand up. Carly stared into a corner of the bathroom as she did what Kelly told her. Kelly checked Carly's mouth, ran her fingers through her hair, and looked behind her ears. When she was satisfied, she smoothed Carly's hair. "Your natural color's coming back in. It's pretty." Carly said nothing, just took her clothes to go get dressed in the shower room. Tidbit was next in line.

"Kelly, Jenna," Marcy said, "I've got to go take care of something. Please just finish up the searches and take the girls to lunch if I'm not back by then."

"Who was yelling?" someone called from the shower room. The tiled walls made the voice echo strangely. "It sounded like a boy."

"You guys don't need to worry about that. Girls who've already been searched stay in the shower, and all of you listen to Kelly and Jenna."

Marcy left. When she passed through the lounge, I was where she had left me, staring at the desk.

Kelly began to go through the routine with Tidbit, having her take off one piece of clothing at a time. Carly, dressed now, sat down in the entrance to the shower room, where she could see both Regular Kids. The floor of the showers wasn't quite even, and there were always puddles of standing water. Carly crossed her legs and called to Jenna and Kelly, "Hey, what do you guys enjoy more about this: getting to see us all naked or getting to order us around? Or is it a combination, you get off ordering us around when we're naked? And telling us we're pretty."

Kelly and Jenna continued doing what they were doing.

"I mean, it's one thing when Marcy's here making you do it. But now that she's gone, why would you keep this up if you weren't enjoying it?"

"Carly," Kelly said, without looking away from Tidbit, "if you actually wanted to have a conversation about this, we could. But you're not asking honest questions. You're just trying to start a fight."

"Did you ever think," Jenna added, "that maybe we want to keep you guys from hurting yourselves? We were both in New Girls once, too, you know."

Kelly looked at Jenna as if to tell her not to waste her time. She folded the last of Tidbit's clothes and asked her to raise her arms, then turn around.

Carly shook her head. "You two are a couple of sellouts. I'd rather stay in New Girls than become a RO-bot."

"You can stay in New Girls as long as you want," Jenna said.

Kelly asked Tidbit to crouch down. Tidbit stared at her for a moment. "You know you're looking for a razor blade, right? How crazy do you think we are?" But she crouched down anyway.

"You never know," Kelly said. "All right, you can get dressed."

Before Tidbit could take her things, they heard the squeak of the showers being turned on and the sound of water splashing in the shower room. Jenna and Kelly turned but couldn't see any of the girls in there. "Hey, turn off the water," Jenna called, but there was no response. "I said turn it off!"

"Go see what they're up to," Kelly said.

Jenna hurried into the shower room while Kelly and the other girls waited and listened. "Goddamnit, why'd you girls let her do this?" they heard Jenna shout. "Kelly, you better come in here. Bev's dress is all wet. She says she was trying to wash off the dirt that got on her hands when they put her in a wiggle."

"Shit," Kelly said. "She's skirted, isn't she? Now we have to find a dress."

Kelly told the girls waiting to be searched not to move. She went into the shower room to help Jenna. When she was gone, Laurel grabbed Tidbit by the arm and nodded in the direction of the lounge. Tidbit hadn't gotten dressed yet. "Go see if it's the new kid," Laurel whispered. "Go welcome him to Roaring Orchards."

Tidbit looked toward the shower room where Kelly and Jenna were. She shook her head. "You're just pissed still about the strip searches. We're already in enough trouble."

"Exactly," Laurel said. "It won't make any difference at this point."

Tidbit had meant everything she'd been saying recently about following the rules and working on her issues. But it would be funny. She could always start following the process tomorrow. The other girls looked at her expectantly.

"I'll hide your clothes," Laurel said. "So if Kelly comes back she won't notice you're gone."

All Tidbit knew was that thinking about it, thinking about anything, was the last thing she felt like doing. She looked back once toward the shower room. Then she slipped silently out of the bathroom.

When she was gone, Laurel grabbed the neatly folded pile of Tidbit's clothes and took them to one of the stalls. She rested them on top of the tank behind the toilet. From her pocket she carefully pulled a razor blade. She hid it on the floor behind the toilet and rejoined the girls who hadn't yet been searched.

**I turned when** the door opened and took a step back when I saw Tidbit. She was short, with a thick waist and large breasts. When I caught myself staring, I quickly looked around to see if anyone else was there. Turning back, I thought it was strange that she walked toward me normally, as though nothing were out of the ordinary. I assumed girls walked differently when they were naked, and it briefly occurred to me that it was because all the naked women I'd seen were in photographs, where they generally wore high heels.

She leaned her hip against the desk and looked me in the eyes. She wore glasses with round, red frames. "You're new here, right?"

"Yeah. Yeah, I got here today."

"I saw you kick the window out of your parents' car."

"Oh. I didn't think anybody saw that."

"I was under some bushes. And then them dragging you in. What's your name?"

"Benjamin. I'm Benjamin."

"I'm Tidbit. Here, look at this." She turned around and held her hair away from her nape to show me a tattoo on the back of her neck. My eyes followed the curve of her spine down to her waist and hips before looking back up to see what she was showing me. It was a homemade tattoo in blue ink that said, simply, TIDBIT.

"Can you see it?" she asked.

"Yeah. The tattoo."

"My friends did it."

"Here?"

"No, at home." She turned back around.

"Is that why you got sent here?"

"No."

"So what are you here for?"

Tidbit stared at me. "I have a self-afflicting personality," she said.

I nodded. The pulse of blood in my skull had slowed to a drowsy thump. Her face was sweet, not too pretty. A soft, round forehead, a wide nose. There was something about her that seemed restless and oversensitive. The frames of her glasses cast a rounded shadow across her cheek. "Aren't you worried about getting into trouble?" I asked.

"Why? We're not doing anything."

"I know."

"So, did you meet Aubrey?"

"For a minute. He didn't say much." I was struggling to return her gaze. "Is he nice?"

"Nice? No. He's fucking crazy." Tidbit picked a pencil up from the desk and began playing with it. "My first day here, he bit me."

I followed Tidbit's eyes down to look at the pencil in her hands, stole a glance at her breasts. "What?"

"Well, I bit him first." She laughed.

"Still."

"I know," Tidbit said, looking up. "It's part of his philosophy."

I felt like we should be talking about something else. "He was okay with me. He just ate a salad."

"Here's all you need to know about Aubrey: at breakfast once, he came out of the bathroom with this long strip of toilet paper hanging out of the back of his pants. It was like a tail, it reached all the way down to the ground, dragging through the Cafetorium behind him. Of course everyone was terrified to tell him because who knows what he'd do. And I know some of the teachers and dorm parents saw because they were careful not to step on it. But nobody said anything. When Aubrey finally sits down in his arm-chair at Campus Community and sees it you know what he says?"

I shook my head.

"*I have never felt so alone.*"

We heard the sound of people climbing the stairs on the other side of the kitchenette. Tidbit grabbed my arm. She leaned close and whispered. I felt her hair against my cheek and the hot rush of her breath and it wasn't until she had run back into the hallway and closed the door behind her that I pieced together what I thought she'd said: "Don't tell them anything. Make something up."

Jenna and Kelly were still in the shower room when Tidbit snuck back into the bathroom. They were having a meeting with the girls who had already been searched about why no one had been paying attention to Bev and about finding a dress she could borrow now that her velour one was soaked. The rest of the girls were where Tidbit had left them. Laurel pointed to the stall where she had put Tidbit's clothes. Tidbit got them and dressed quickly.

"Well," Laurel asked her, "who was it?"

"The new kid," Tidbit told her. "His name's Benjamin."

"Yeah? What's he like?"

Tidbit pulled her shirt over her head. "A lot more freaked out than he was about three minutes ago."

**When Marcy finally** returned to get me, it wasn't Roger who came with her but a teacher who introduced himself as Spencer. Spencer took me downstairs and across the Mansion to my dorm. On the way he told me about what had happened with Han. As Alternative Boys and Ellie were gaining on him, Han had run up to someone's house and tried to get them to let him in. "But before the woman in the house could open her door," Spencer said, "three or four Alternative Boys tackled him off of her stoop and right into her azaleas." It was clear that Spencer found this hilarious. I'm relatively sure he had invented the part about the azaleas—no one else who told me the story ever mentioned them.

"Anyway, the rest of the dorm shows up and puts Han into a wiggle and totally tears up this woman's garden." He looked over at me, to make sure I was properly awed by the story. "The woman, the one who lives there, of course has no idea what's going on. Or maybe she did. She called the police and they sent like four cars and the paddy wagon. Who knew the Webituck PD even had a paddy wagon?"

We walked across a landing that overlooked the wide wooden staircase leading down to the Great Hall. Spencer said that after checking the boys' stories and calling a few probation officers, the police had decided to charge only Ellie. Roger had gone down to the station to bail her out. Alternative Boys were now in a candor meeting, which Spencer said stood for claiming any negligence or dishonesty in our relationships. "You probably don't have anything to say since you just got here," he said. "But if anyone broke any rules with Han or knew about him breaking rules, or knew that he was planning to run, that's when they have to admit to it. Then everyone needs to confront Han about running away."

Spencer opened the door to Alternative Boys' kitchenette, from where I saw the boys sitting on the couches in the lounge. Han sat on a plastic chair facing the corner of the room, wearing a sheet draped around him like a toga. Pudding slid over on his couch and patted the space next to himself for me to sit down.

"Hey," Spencer said, "you're back!" He was talking to Ellie, who was sitting at the desk where she had put my things earlier.

Ellie nodded. Her head rested in the palm of one hand, her elbow on the desk. She glared at some paperwork in front of her.

I went to sit next to Pudding, but Spencer stopped me. "Hold on," he said. "You can leave your shoes over there." He pointed to the corner of the lounge, where the rest of the boys' shoes were lined up in pairs. "Students don't wear shoes in the Mansion or the school building. In New Boys or New Girls, shoes get locked up, but not in Alternative Boys or Alternative Girls."

"See, we're trusted to be in the same room with our own shoes, Benjamin," Pudding said. "You should feel honored."

I put my shoes with the others and sat down next to Pudding. Each of the boys had a piece of notebook paper that he was either writing on or staring at.

"Hey, who's this?" asked the other grown-up in the room. He was a short black man with a goatee and an eyebrow ring.

"Dedrick, meet Benjamin," Spencer said. "He just got here today. Benjamin, Dedrick."

"It's not always like this," Dedrick said. "Well, it's usually a little like this." He handed me a piece of notebook paper. "Write down any fibs you've got."

"Fibs?" I asked.

"God, Ellie," Spencer said, "didn't you tell this poor kid about fibs? What were you talking about the whole time you did his intake? Your credit card debt?"

Ellie didn't look up. "Screw you, Spencer."

"Jeez," Spencer said.

"That's an f-word substitute!" Pudding was already up out of his seat and pointing at Ellie. "'Screw you' is definitely an f-word substitute! I heard it! She owes three dollars." He was smiling wildly and looking around for support.

"Sit back down," Dedrick said, putting his arm gently over Pudding's shoulder. "You've got more fibs to write."

"No, we can't do anything until she pays three dollars. Everything stops. And I already wrote all my fibs."

"No, you didn't," Dedrick said. "I can tell you still have fibs from the way you're acting."

"It's true," someone called out from one of the other couches. "You're acting like an asshole."

"No," Pudding said, more serious now. "Everything has to stop until she pays. That's the rule. Even for staff."

"God, Pudding." Spencer was across the room, where he was collecting and reading the pages the boys had been writing on. "She just went to jail. Could you show a little sympathy?"

"Yeah," William said. "You're being a real screwhead."

"Sit down, screwface!" someone else shouted. I thought maybe this was Zach.

Pudding was smiling. "Those are all f-word substitutes! That's verbal rape! Aubrey even said so. I feel so molested!"

"You wish," someone said.

"And so what if Ellie went to jail," Pudding added. "We're in jail every day of our lives."

"Every day of your lives," Dedrick said, pushing him back onto the couch.

**When things quieted** down, Dedrick offered to take me aside to answer some of my questions. He led me into the kitchenette, where he could still see what was going on in the lounge. Fibs, Dedrick said, were functioning intimacy blockers. "It's like if you have a secret, if you broke a rule or you know someone else did and you haven't told anyone."

I looked at him, waiting to hear anything that might be helpful.

"They're called intimacy blockers because if you're keeping a secret from someone, about something you did or that somebody else did, whichever, then you're not in an honest relationship with them."

"Okay."

"So, what else do you want to know?"

I looked around the lounge. I didn't want to sit back down. "How come Han's wearing that sheet?"

"That's to make it harder for him to run away again. It's called being sheeted."

"How long's he going to sit in the corner?"

"Until Aubrey allows him back onto campus officially. Han needs to call him and ask to be allowed back. But in a little bit we'll let him join the meeting for his friends to confront him."

I nodded again. "Can I have one of the Welch's sodas in the fridge?"

Dedrick looked at me curiously, then checked the fridge. "How'd you know about these?"

"I brought them with me. Ellie put them in there."

"Oh. Well, no, you can't have one right now. What're these, grape?" Dedrick took a soda out and opened it.

"I need to talk to my parents," I said. "I didn't get to talk to them before they left, and I'm sure they didn't mean to leave me here. I was supposed to just take a tour."

Dedrick took a swig of his soda, then opened the fridge back up and got one for me. I opened mine and took a long drink as soon as he handed me the can. "If you thought you were only here for a tour, why'd you kick through your dad's windshield?"

I felt my face flush and shook my head. "You know about that?"

"Word travels pretty fast here."

"My parents didn't know about this place."

"They didn't leave you here by mistake, Benjamin."

I leaned back against the counter and had another big pull of grape soda. "I just need to talk to them. Can you let me call them?"

"Not until they've done a New Parent Orientation, which they'll probably do the next Parents' Sunday. I'm not sure when that is, but there's one every few months. Ellie'll call them to let them know how you're doing."

"No, no," I said, "no, that's too long." My back slid down the face of the counter until I was sitting on the floor. I pressed the palm of my empty hand against the cool tiles. "I don't want to run away or anything, but I need to find a way to talk to them, just once, to straighten things out." The sweet soda stuck in my throat.

"Are you telling me you're planning on running away, Benjamin? Because if you are, there are—"

"I don't mean that, it's just—," and I leaned over and vomited grape soda on the floor. It came up twice, forming a sticky, gray pool on the linoleum I hovered over, heaving and spitting out strings of bile. The sight of it made me heave again, but nothing else came up. Grape soda and half a Milky Way bar were all I'd eaten that day.

"Shit," Dedrick said. "You're going to have to clean that up. Wait here. I'll get a mop and bucket."

While he was gone and I was wiping spit from my chin, the door to the kitchenette swung open and then shut. Then Tyler, the Regular Kid who'd informed me earlier that my 'rents had left without me, stumbled in carrying a large cooler. He dropped the cooler and looked down at the vomit on the floor. "Did you do that?" He looked around. "Where is he?"

"I got sick. Dedrick's getting a mop."

"No, I meant Han," he said. "You're going to have to clean that up."

"Uh-huh."

Dedrick returned with the bucket and mop. "Oh, hi, Tyler." Dedrick took him to where Han was sitting in the lounge. Then he returned to tell me to clean up quick. "You don't want to miss this," he said.

As I mopped up my mess, I could hear Tyler screaming. "What the hell were you thinking? You are such a goddamned coward! I'm so hurt that you'd just leave, just throw me and everyone else here away like garbage." This went on for a while, as I finished cleaning and then dumped the dirty water down the sink. I entered the lounge to see Tyler still leaning over Han. "There are so many people in this dorm who care about you, or who want to care about you, and you just shit all over them. Again and again. And people give you more chances and you just pull this same crap!"

Tyler paused to catch his breath and wipe away the tears that were running down his face. Han didn't look at him. He simply leaned forward in the corner, his elbows on his knees. Ellie got up and took the paperwork from the desk where she was sitting. She walked out of the lounge and left the dorm through the door at the other end of the hall.

Tyler paused once to ask why Han was wearing jeans under his sheet.

"Oh," Dedrick said, "he was arguing about it and we just wanted to get him in the corner."

"Well, that's not okay," Tyler said. "You're the dorm parent."

"Actually, I'm a teacher. But I get your point."

Tyler started up again, and laid into Han for several more minutes. When he was done, he turned and asked Spencer, "Has the dorm had a chance to confront him?"

"Not yet, no."

"Well, we should start. Han, you need to go and take off those jeans. Could you take him, Dedrick?"

Dedrick nodded and led Han down the hall to his room. Tyler pulled Han's chair out of the corner and put it next to one of the couches. "Now it's really important that you guys be completely honest with Han in this meeting. I understand that you're angry with him and that can be difficult to express, but he's at a tough point right now and needs to know exactly how you all feel. You've just gotten rid of all your fibs so there shouldn't be anything interfering with your ability to be honest. I know that it can be weird to feel totally clean like that, but it should help you tell him how you were affected by his running."

"We haven't had lunch yet." This was Carlos. "Can we eat first?"

"We can't do anything until we finish this meeting," Tyler said. "And we can't finish the meeting until Dedrick, Spencer, and I feel like you guys've been honest with Han. So no, you can't eat first. Try to focus."

Dedrick returned with Han and sat him down in his chair. "So who wants to go first?" Tyler asked.

No one said anything for a long time. On the ride up to the school I'd been lying across the backseat, and from the angle where I lay I could just see the side of my mother's face in the rearview mirror. I spent a large part of the trip looking at her that way, until everything else just sort of receded, the way at night, if you stare at one star, it gets brighter while the rest of the sky goes dim. There was only that image, her cheekbone and chin. She could have been anyone, just another person sitting in front of me.

"We can sit here all day," Tyler said. "Carlos, why don't you start?"

"I really don't care that he ran," Carlos said. "I mean, we could have gotten into a lot of trouble, but no one did. Except Ellie."

"First of all, talk to him, not me," Tyler said. "And try to go a little deeper, Carlos. I see you guys palling around all the time. And he abandoned you. You both hate this place? Fine. But he was going to leave you here by yourself. How did it feel when you saw him take off? Honestly."

"Honestly? I was proud of him. I wish I'd run, too. I'm sorry you got caught, bro."

"That's bullshit! I don't believe that for a second. Is there anybody here who's not so codependent with Han that they're willing to tell him how they really feel, or are we going to be here all day?"

"I think the same thing as Carlos said." I think this was Eric. "So I don't think it's bullshit."

"Even if every one of you all say the same thing," Tyler said, "that doesn't make it the truth. There's no way that your friend leaves you and you feel proud. That's retarded. And we can't end the meeting until you all begin to deal with this. And there's something else you're not considering."

He turned to Han, who had been patiently following the discussion, awaiting its inevitable conclusion. "I think that what Han desperately wants to hear is that you guys are angry that he would run. He acts like he doesn't need anyone, but think about it. If he really wanted to get away without getting caught, he could have. It's not that tough. But here he is, which shows that he didn't really want—"

"No, there you're definitely wrong," Eric said. "He was really trying to get into that lady's house. You should have seen him banging on her door."

"Yeah, he was not playing around," someone else said.

Tyler rolled his eyes. "Right, but he could have run at night. He ran in the middle of the day, right in front of everyone. If he had waited until night he could have gotten away."

"But Roger has us all sleeping in the lounge, with trusted people sleeping in front of the doors." This was Eric again.

"Oh, come on," Tyler said. "Everyone knows all you have to do is slide the mattresses about six inches away from the door. The door in the kitchenette hardly even—"

"Tyler," Dedrick interrupted, "I don't think that's exactly—"

"My point," Tyler said, "is that slower people than Han have made it off campus. Pudding ran and stayed away for two and a half days, and he only got caught because he was bumming cigarettes in front of the police station."

"It's true," Pudding said. He smiled, proud to have been singled out for this qualified success. "I'm a pretty slow runner. But Han might actually be slower."

Han laughed. "No screwin' way I'm slower than you," he said.

"What the hell did you just say?" Tyler said. "That's an f-word substitute."

"See!" Pudding shouted.

"Han," Spencer said, "you're not supposed to say anything until the end of the meeting."

"And you owe a dollar," Tyler said. "You know you can't say 'screw.'"

"Stop it! Will you all please stop it!" William, the skinny kid who'd tried to show me his dick at the Dirt Pile, was standing, his face red. "Will everybody please shut up!" He turned to Han. "I can't believe you're sitting here joking with Pudding. Remember that other time we were all laughing together? When we had that art project due for Brenda's class, and we snuck the big bottle of rubber cement into our room? We were all passing it around, huffing it and laughing our asses off. And you passed out while you were huffing and spilled rubber cement all over yourself, and the next morning you woke up glued to your sheets? Don't laugh at that! Don't laugh while we're sitting here at a candor meeting you caused. If you had your way, we'd never have another thing like that to laugh about because you'd be gone." William's white T-shirt hung down from his knobby shoulders as he yelled at Han. His hands were balled into fists. William punched himself in the thighs as he spoke, except when he paused to brush the hair out of his eyes or hike up his jeans.

Alternative Boys were stunned out of their torpor. We all sat up straight. The meeting, it seemed, had entered a new phase. I noticed that Zach, the large boy sitting across the circle from me, was surreptitiously pulling hairs out of his nose to make himself cry.

By the time William had finished, Zach's eyes were full of tears. He got up and started yelling at Han about how bad things were in juvenile detention. If you think the cells we were in this afternoon were something, he told him, lockup was a million times worse. And that's where Han was headed if he kept pushing people away. No one there had ever told Zach how much they cared about him, and they wouldn't do that for Han either. He was angry at Han for making him remember all that, he said. He was angry that Han took what he had at the school for granted.

After him, the other boys in the dorm took turns voicing their anger at Han, even those who had previously claimed not to have any. I didn't know whether I was supposed to take a turn but was too amazed to ask. I just sat there and watched, and no one bothered about me. When they were finished, Tyler told them how proud he was of them. He asked Han whether he had anything to say before returning to the corner.

Han said only, "I acknowledge everything you had to say. I'll try to take it in."

Tyler nodded. "This is my consensus to end this candor meeting."

"Agreed."

"Agreed."

"Agreed."

"Agreed."

"Agreed."

"Agreed."

"Agreed."

"Agreed."

"Agreed."

Afterward, we had fish sticks for lunch.

# 5

**Ellie found herself** wandering around the campus, walking faster and faster. The Incident Report, she saw, was still in her hand. Shaking her head, she marched to the Office and dropped off the form. It sailed into the tray marked INCIDENT REPORTS, immense and anonymous. She hated this place. God, if she had left the school last night, she thought. But she hadn't. Ellie marched out of the Mansion, blind as a fist.

At the police station they had separated her from the boys, whom they had put in two cells while they figured out who everyone was and called the probation officers of the boys who had them. Ellie was interviewed in a room close enough to hear the boys goofing. The officer taking her statement had paused to listen to Pudding yelling that he was going to make Carlos his bitch, was going to trade him to Zach for a pack of cigarettes. Ellie had stared at her hands, and then, like an idiot, she laughed. Another officer sat in the back of the room, but he didn't say anything the whole time. The officer who interviewed her, Officer Sotelo, had long gray hair she wore piled on top of her head. She had seemed disinterested and cold, but when she told Ellie that they were charging her with assault and reckless endangerment, the policewoman had suddenly glowed with elegance and wisdom.

Ellie felt a damp chill rise up from the road. She was walking down the school's driveway toward the teachers' apartments. A dry brown leaf spiraled down the air and fell by her foot. Ellie wondered why she had wanted the policewoman to understand her, to like her. She knew she should relieve Spencer and Dedrick, but she couldn't bear being alone with the students right now. She needed to be around people. As she descended the hill she felt a raw wind against her skin. While no one was paying attention, autumn had broken summer's back.

It was because, Ellie thought, the policewoman had been exactly right. She *should* be charged for what she did. That was what infuriated her most. She hated the things she had to do at the school, which is exactly why she had been thinking of quitting. Of course that was worse than useless to her now. The policewoman was simply free to say what Ellie could no longer afford to admit.

Ellie was devising a plan as she hurried down the drive. The police were out to make a case against the school. That much everybody knew. When kids ran away, the police brought them back because they had to, but there were always stories of officers telling the kids to run away again after they turned seventeen, when they wouldn't be brought back. Ellie was sure that if she could help them bring a case against the school, the police or DA or whoever would be willing to drop the charges against her. She could tell them plenty of things that might shut Roaring Orchards down. She just had to figure out how to make a deal with them.

Across the road ahead of her, she could see the lights on in June's apartment. June was kind and treated everyone fairly, which was an infuriating quality in a friend, Ellie thought. Especially at a place like Roaring Orchards, where you often needed a friend to reassure you that yes, what someone just said was crazy. But it was June's good sense that Ellie needed right now.

Ellie wondered about the fact that the school had paid her bail. She certainly wouldn't be able to keep working here once the people found out that she had turned state's evidence. Is that what it was called? Ellie was beginning to feel a little better. She would just have to come back to Webituck maybe for witness prep and then to testify, she thought.

Ellie was almost running now, across Route 294 and down to the teachers' apartments, which were in the building covered with faded red shingles I had seen beside the Dirt Pile. It was referred to as the Paddock and resembled an old motel. June would help her sort it all out. Ellie banged on the door. But when June opened it, Ellie saw Doris and Brenda behind her, surrounded by piles of papers and oak-tag posters. The teachers had moved their meeting down there. Doris stood anxiously and then sat back down.

"Oh, sorry," Ellie said. "I didn't know you guys were still meeting." Shit, she thought to herself.

"Yeah, but come on in anyway." June gave Ellie her most sympathetic look.

"No, really, I don't want to interrupt."

"It's no interruption," Brenda said, leaning back in her chair. "We were worried about you." Brenda's long dark hair was messy, and she wore a shapeless red cardigan sweater. Ellie was often struck by how beautiful Brenda was, in her carefully cultivated dishevelment.

"Ellie," Doris said.

"Yes?"

"Did you happen to seen Dedrick or Spencer? No, it's just that we sent them a while ago to cover your dorm and, I know you've had a rough day but"—she gestured to the sprawl of papers behind her—"we do need them here. This is our day to get things together for the semester."

The four women nodded in silence for a moment.

"Yeah, well, I was going to head back up there in a minute. I just needed—"

"Of course, whatever you need. But when you see them."

June rubbed Ellie's shoulder.

"Sure," Ellie said. "I'll send them down." She smiled at the teachers and let herself out.

As she walked across the flagstones that ran along the front of the Paddock, Ellie thought she would figure out the details of the plan herself. She would think of something to give the cops that would send everyone back home. The kids, the faculty, everyone. She wondered if she should pack up her apartment now and leave, just disappear. She could go straight to the police station to speak with the officer who had interviewed her. Ellie heard a tapping on a window and someone call her name. She stopped, but she didn't know where it had come from. A lightbulb lit up over one of the doorways, and Roger swung open the screen door to his apartment.

"Hey," he said. "How are you feeling?"

"Fine," she said. "Good."

"Good." He seemed to be waiting for her to say something else.

"Thanks for before. For bailing me out."

"Sure," he said. "You'd have done the same for me."

"Okay. Well. Thanks again." Ellie turned to leave. She had only gone halfway up the Paddock's drive when she stopped and called out, "Hey, Roger?"

His screen door swung open again.

"Can I talk to you about something?" She wasn't sure this was a good idea. Roger was a true believer in the school. But she felt reckless, like she had made up her mind, like she was already gone.

"Sure," he said. "Come in."

Ellie hesitated, but only for a moment. Inside she sat on Roger's blue sofa and told him about her plan to make a deal with the police. She told him about the policewoman, too, Officer Sotelo, and how powerful she had seemed simply because she was free to tell the truth. That's all she wanted to do, Ellie told him, to tell the truth. And if the police might be willing to drop the charges in exchange for that, shouldn't she at least find out? Hearing herself talk about it, Ellie felt she wasn't making the best possible case.

Roger laughed nervously. "Do you want something to drink?"

"Okay."

Ellie watched Roger move through the kitchen. She was surprised to see him pull a bottle of white wine out of his refrigerator. Drinking wasn't exactly against the rules, but it wasn't something she expected of him. She studied the one painting in the apartment, of a three-masted sailing ship in gold on black velvet.

Roger returned to the sofa with a couple of glasses of wine and a box of Ritz crackers. He had been trying to think of something to say that would calm her down without seeming like something meant to calm her down.

"I know just what you mean about this place." He sat at the other end of the sofa and passed her a brown tube of crackers. "I can't tell you how many times I've wanted to sue this place for workman's comp. My elbows are all kinds of messed up from six years of putting kids in restraints." He pulled his sleeves up to show Ellie, but they just looked like elbows to her. "Every time I've spoken to Aubrey about it he puts me off. He tells me that if the kids respected me more they wouldn't get violent in front of me. That they don't get violent in front of him. Talk about blaming the victim."

Ellie ran her finger around the rim of her wineglass. Her hair hung down in front of her face. For a moment Roger lost the thread of his argument.

"My point," he said, "is I'm glad I never sued because the times I feel that angry are few, far, and in between. The school has great lawyers. Aubrey's got these really expensive guys from the city who, like, come up for a day and totally outclass the local yokels they're arguing against."

"Well, right," Ellie said, "I mean, it'd be great if they could get the school off. If the prosecutor drops the charges against me, and I testify, and still nothing happens to the school. Then everyone wins."

Roger sighed. "Your plan sounds like a movie. I know you want to get this resolved all at once, but I wouldn't be honest if I didn't tell you I thought it was a bad idea. If you go against the school you'll be out of a job, and you'll get stuck paying for your own lawyer. You'll be all on your own."

Ellie wasn't responding, and Roger felt he might have gone the wrong way, but he found he couldn't stop. "I think you've just got to stick this one out. Trust Aubrey. This isn't the first time something like this has happened." Roger had no idea why he was nervous. "The school never loses. They'll drag the whole thing out until it's just not worth it for the town to continue. You'll be fine. You'll see."

Roger leaned over and brushed Ellie's hair out of her face. Her cheeks were wet with tears, and she trembled slightly. Roger felt himself grow hard so suddenly that he had to shift his position. He slid closer to her. Roger couldn't tell whether she had noticed. He rested his hand on hers for a time, and she didn't pull away. When Ellie felt his fingers at her waist she covered his hands with hers to stop him, but she didn't follow through. She felt his beard against her cheek. It was softer than she would have thought. Then he was kissing her neck, and Ellie laid her head back on the armrest of the sofa. She felt for the first time all day that she could really think. And this is what she thought:

She had left her real life behind somewhere. And she was being carried farther and farther away from it. It didn't distress her. She felt lighter being rid of it. Her real life was a heavy glass box with nothing inside. This was what she needed, she decided—to get as far from that as she could and toward a life she cared about less. Roger was running his hands over her T-shirt, squeezing her breasts. She almost laughed. She was excited to see how it would feel to live a life other than her real life. It was like leaving the house with no money in her pockets.

Roger kept hesitating, as if to give her the chance to change her mind. But for a time she let him continue. She kissed him until her jaws ached, then sat up slowly and said good night. Ellie left, and she promised herself that she would stop thinking of things as being either good or bad. She would only think of what would carry her into a world cheaper and more free, toward a life that would burn like paper.

**That night, Tidbit** lay in bed talking with her roommates. They were reminiscing about Anna and Aurora Li, twins from Texas who had left the school long ago. There had always been some confusion about why they were there, something about an abusive cousin who may or may not have died, the girls' stories changed constantly. One or the other of the twins claimed she dreamed of him regularly.

"But remember Aurora," Tidbit said, "the frail one who always walked around with one eye open and one eye shut? Was that Anna or Aurora? After she left, I heard from her therapist that if she opened that eye, all she could see out of it was a church."

As they spoke, Tidbit opened the window beside her bed to retrieve her stuffed animal. On cool nights she used to wedge him between the metal screen and the windowpane to get him cold so she could warm him back up before falling asleep. He was once a teddy bear, but Tidbit had loved all the fur off of him. She covered him in white felt with two holes cut out for his eyes. When his felt cover got dirty Tidbit would add another layer of white felt on top. She had done this so many times that his arms had turned to poorly defined nubs and his belly stretched down to his feet. Even with the new coats of felt there was always a gray spot on the back of his head where she drooled on him in her sleep. As a bear his name had been Bear, but now she called him Burn Victim.

Bev was watching Tidbit from the top bunk on the other side of the room. She tugged at strands of her hair and laughed at Burn Victim returning from the cold. Bev's laugh was an exclusively verbal gesture; she didn't smile and she didn't shake. She simply said, "Huh-huh-huh," like a laugh in a book.

"Are you laughing at Burn Victim?" Tidbit asked, hugging the doll to her chest. She turned it around, looked at it. The doll's black plastic eyes were scratched and dull. "Why would anyone laugh at Burn Victim? He's my silent witness." Hugging him to her again beneath her covers, Tidbit felt the cold dissipate in her arms. "Yes, you are my little silent witness, aren't you? Yes you are."

Bev laughed again, "Huh-huh-huh."

**Upstairs in his** rooms Aubrey slept curled beneath his covers, his thick gray hair mussed as it always was. He dreamed that his ex-wife lay beside him. Aubrey was a short man, and she had stood a full head taller than he. When they slept she had held him in her arms, her large square hands holding his shoulders or spread across his chest. But in Aubrey's simple dream he was taller than she, and it was he who held her in his arms and in his strong, square hands.

**As for me,** my first night at the school passed without incident. I was exhausted and glad that my dorm mates kept their distance, whether because I was an unknown quantity or simply from lack of interest. I don't remember now exactly who else was in that room— those sorts of arrangements never lasted long at Roaring Orchards, with students getting shunted from one dorm to another so often. But I do remember the plastic mattress on the floor, cool through the thin sheets, and the smell of the dusty wool carpet inches from my face. And when I try to re-create that first night I have a strange sense, a feeling that I could not have possibly had then: that despite the terrors of that unfathomable new place, lying in a room with four other kids, hearing them breathing and shifting as they slept, I seem to remember feeling somehow protected.

**The chairs in** the Campus Community Room were made of carved cherrywood and had cushions of green-and-blue-striped silk. There were enough to run along the entire perimeter of the room. After my first breakfast at the school—cold eggs, soy bacon—I followed the available faculty and those students not cleaning the Cafetorium as they walked in for the daily Campus Community meeting. Upon entering I saw that Zbigniew, whom I had not yet met, had taken his shoes off to climb on the chairs so he could water the plants that hung above them. He was in his fifties. He had short white hair that he clipped himself and deep wrinkles that radiated from his dark eyes. The plants were in plastic pots or crocheted baskets, and they hung from the aluminum grid that held up the ceiling's acoustic tiles. Stuck into the dirt of one pot was a plastic hummingbird on a wire. Zbigniew took care not to spill water on the seats.

Everyone found seats around the room: faculty in the chairs, the students on the floor near their dorm parents. It was Monday morning, and it seemed to me that everyone was mildly excited. I soon learned that there was a giddy energy at the beginning of every Campus Community meeting, since you never knew what was going to happen or to whom. I followed Alternative Boys and sat next to Pudding at Ellie's feet. The only armchair, at the end of the room, was reserved for Aubrey. He came in last, flanked by the Regular Kids, who sat in chairs on either side. Aubrey wore a blue suit, the jacket of which had a banded collar. A yellow scarf hung loosely over his shoulders.

Zbigniew hurried to finish with his watering before the seats beneath the last plants were filled, climbing up onto chairs and hopping down again in his socks around the last corner of the room. He was in charge of maintenance and would leave before the meeting began. Campus Community meetings could last five minutes, or they could go on for hours. But by simply pulling on his boots and waving his watering can in a simple gesture of good-bye, Zbyszek, as he liked to be called, could momentarily suspend everyone's fractiousness and anxiety.

"Zbyszek likes when we see him working early in the morning," Aubrey said, catching Zbigniew by the wrist as he was crossing toward the door. Aubrey held him gently, his dry thumb against Zbigniew's pulse. "He likes it," Aubrey continued, "because then he can take the rest of the day off, and as far as we know he's been very busy."

Everyone laughed. When he had let him go and Zbigniew had closed the door behind him, Aubrey said, "Now he can write home, and in a week his whole village will be crowded around his letter about how horrible his American boss is." Aubrey cut this round of laughter short. "You shouldn't dismiss country people. They possess a great wisdom."

The room waited while Aubrey removed a plastic container of frozen yogurt and then a bottle of vanilla extract from a small pink gift bag with yellow polka dots. He balanced the plastic container on his knees as he shook a few drops of vanilla onto the yogurt. After screwing the top back on and replacing the vanilla, he fished around in the bag for a moment before sending one of the Regular Kids back into the Cafetorium to get him a spoon.

Starting at his immediate left and going around the circle Aubrey asked each Regular Kid and faculty member if he or she had anything to share. They gave news about their dorms, who had been moved up or down, or mentioned personal things like how many days it had been since they had had a drink or smoked a cigarette. Or they simply said good morning and let him pass on to the next person.

When he got around to Roger, who was sitting next to Ellie, Roger reported to Aubrey and everyone else what had happened with Han Quek.

"At this evening's meeting we'll probably more appropriately place him down into New Boys."

"Mmm," Aubrey said. "And why's that?"

Roger looked around the room and laughed as though it might have been a trick question. When he realized that it wasn't he explained, "Because he broke one of the bottom lines of the dorm. He ran away."

Aubrey nodded and moved on.

"And Ellie, how are you this morning?"

"All right," she said.

"Ellie had a rough day yesterday," he said.

Aubrey asked her about reports he had heard from some Alternative Boys that the police had been a little rougher with them than necessary.

"I don't know about that," Ellie said. "They questioned me in a different room."

"Well, try to remember." Aubrey ate a spoonful of yogurt and said to Alternative Boys sitting on the floor, "Any of you boys who saw or experienced something like that should sit down with me at lunch and we'll discuss it." Then Aubrey handed his breakfast to one of the Regular Kids next to him, stood, and walked to the green chalkboard behind him. He searched for a suitable piece of chalk. He drew a big circle. "This is the campus," he said. "Three sides are fenced. The fourth is bordered by woods. Now. No faculty member is to chase a student past the boundaries of the campus. Is that understood?" He turned around. "Questions? Good."

Aubrey returned to his seat and took back his food. He resumed calling on people around the circle. Some he asked questions, to some said good morning. Aubrey was now up to Spencer, who was sitting next to Marcy.

"Good morning, Spencer."

"Morning."

"You have anything for us?"

"Nothing." Spencer smiled.

"Marcy's totally going to get it," Pudding whispered in my ear.

Aubrey placed the top onto the plastic container that had held his breakfast. He crossed his right knee over his left, exposing a long expanse of shin, and said, "You know, I had a funny conversation with Mr. and Mrs. Ormsbee over the weekend." He leaned down to put the plastic container of yogurt back in the pink gift bag. "Nancy's parents?" There was a lilt to his voice as though he were looking forward to relating this anecdote. He removed a cotton napkin, sat up, wiped his mouth.

"They had already been told that Nancy had run away, again, but I felt that I should call to express my apologies. Again. But I couldn't because *they* were so busy apologizing to *me* over and over and over, I could barely get a word in. I was hearing how embarrassed they were at what a problem their daughter was, how much trouble she had put us through, how understanding we all were, and so on. Can you imagine?" He shook his head and chuckled. I looked at Marcy as everyone laughed, and she looked relieved.

"I had to stop them," Aubrey said. "I had to ask them to stop a few times. I mean, I was calling to explain myself, to discuss the fact that we had lost their poor daughter twice in three days. And they were so enmeshed that they were apologizing to me. I had to explain to them, very slowly"—he looked at the Regular Kids sitting on either side of him, who were cracking up—"I had to explain to them that they should be angry, not sorry. That I was the one who should be sorry. 'Oh, but Aubrey,'" Aubrey said in a high voice, "'she promised after the first time. She promised that she wouldn't run again and you were so kind to believe her.' *I didn't believe her,* I said. *I don't believe any of these kids. They're a bunch of goddamn liars.* Even if on occasion one of you tells the truth by mistake, it isn't anything I can count on." Aubrey winked at Alternative Girls sitting on the floor. There was general relief around the room that Aubrey was taking this so well, and the students' spirits rose on the breath of his laughter.

"'Oh, but Aubrey,' her dad said, 'she was so ungrateful when you were the only school willing to accept her.' *You paid me to accept her,* I told him. *That's how it works. It's my job.* It was almost impossible for me to convince the Ormsbees that this was our fault, not Nancy's and not theirs. And by our fault, of course I mean it was Marcy's fault."

There was a pause and then an uncomfortable shift in the room as Marcy, red faced, moved to respond. But Aubrey continued, "Andrew looks like he has a question."

Surprised to be called on, Pudding swallowed a few times. I felt nervous myself having Aubrey look in my direction. I could almost feel Pudding thinking carefully beside me. "Well . . . if you're saying it's not Nancy's fault that she ran away," he said, "how come when someone runs they have to be cornered?"

"Because sitting in the corner isn't a punishment," Aubrey said. "Look at Han Quek. He felt he needed for whatever reason to get away from his dorm. So he ran. But the road isn't safe, and we're responsible for his safety, which Ellie understood, so she brought him back. But at the same time we respect what Han is telling us by running, that what he needs right now is to be alone, to not be a part of the school. So we create an off-campus place for him, where he can have what he's telling us he needs. And we feed him and we give him a bed to sleep in and so on. And when he decides that he wants to come back onto campus, he calls me, and we talk about it. In his case, Han's run away what, six or seven times now? So he'll really need to convince me that he wants to come back, and that might take some time."

Aubrey arranged his scarf over his shoulders. "Now, Marcy, what are you doing about this? Why should I trust that there'll be any girls left in your dorm when I wake up tomorrow morning?"

Marcy ran her hands over her thighs and looked as though she were about to recite something she had prepared. "Well," she said, "I probated myself yesterday afternoon with all the other dorm parents. I have a plan of things that I need to work on before—"

"That doesn't tell me anything about why I should allow students to be supervised by you tonight."

"Well, I'm going to—"

"You were at this meeting?" he asked, turning to Roger.

"Yes."

Aubrey slammed his hand down on the armrest of his chair and jumped up. "I don't understand how you can sit here and tell me that I should entrust students to this woman! Because that's what you're telling me." He looked around the circle. "You're all supposed to be holding each other accountable, but you'd rather massage each other's egos than do your job taking care of these children. You're all supposed to be teaching the students to value themselves above all things, and you're showing them exactly how little you think they're worth. Somebody loses one of them, and there aren't any consequences. Ellie's courageous enough to put herself in legal jeopardy to protect one of her students, and Marcy can't be bothered to wake up to check on a girl we all know is in crisis! How on earth can you leave Marcy alone with a dorm right now? She can't control them. Twice now she's lost a girl who couldn't even have stolen ice cream from the kitchen.

Do you realize that? Why not?" He looked fiercely around the room. "Who's going to tell me why Nancy Ormsbee was so harmless that she couldn't even have so much as stolen a scoop of goddamned ice cream from the school?"

He looked around at the bewildered faces.

"Who'll tell me? Why couldn't she steal ice cream?" Aubrey had quieted some now, his voice scratchy from shouting. He looked slowly back and forth across the room but seemed poised to jump again.

Tyler, from Regular Kids, said, "She didn't know where the freezer was."

"Yes, yes, yes!" Aubrey said, hopping up and down though his feet didn't leave the floor. His scarf floated gently around him. "That's exactly right! The students are the only people in this room who'll tell the truth! She couldn't steal ice cream because she was only here two days and didn't know where the fucking freezer was!" Aubrey took his money clip from his pocket and threw some dollar bills on the floor. "And now this poor girl, who was entrusted to you, this girl who couldn't so much as steal ice cream, she's now stalking through God knows where with pockets full of drugs, money, and a goddamn fucking tire jack!" He dropped some more bills on the floor and sat down. "Tonight New Girls all sleep in their lounge, and the dorm staff will wake-shift them. Roger will draw up the schedule."

More quickly now, Aubrey went through the rest of the circle. A girl from Regular Kids picked up the dollar bills he had dropped. No one had much to say. It was stuffy, with too many people together in the room for too long. And there was a comfortable exhaustion in the feeling that the worst had passed. We felt we had survived it, and we students were surprised and flattered that Aubrey saw us as innocent. We shifted against one another at our dorm parents' feet in sugary somnolence.

Aubrey didn't pause to chat with anyone until he got to Doris, who was fidgeting nervously.

"Good morning, Doris."

"Good morning."

"How is planning for the semester going?"

"Everyone's been doing a very nice job, Aubrey. We had a little interruption yesterday, but we'll be ready to start classes on Wednesday."

"Doris, you are an enormous woman," Aubrey said.

All the drowsiness went out of the room. I already knew that Aubrey could be cruel, but I didn't see what he had to gain from picking on someone as theatrically vulnerable as Doris.

"You're an enormous woman, Doris," he repeated, "with very tiny feet."

Everyone looked down. Her feet were crossed at the ankles and tucked beneath her chair in what seemed to be black ballet slippers. Even Doris leaned over to look at them. It was true. They were tiny.

# 6

**A**ubrey's new dictum that faculty couldn't chase students off campus had an unintended but easily foreseeable consequence. Over the course of the autumn there were an increasing number of footraces to be seen between faculty and students. These began at various points on campus and terminated with the student and faculty member on opposite sides of the fence by Route 294 if the student won or in a heap somewhere before that if the faculty member did. No one could think of a way to prevent it. As the season progressed, dorm parents and teachers escorting their students across campus took to walking slightly to one side, between their dorm and the nearest fence, to give themselves a head start.

This gave students sitting in their classes in the Classroom Building something new to think about. I rarely thought about anything other than getting home, but even those who had reconciled themselves to being at the school were never more than half devoted to whatever was going on in front of them. So if anyone spotted a chase across the front lawn, the whole class would run to a window to watch. In this case it was Ross Salazar running. Pudding was the first to spot him, and he wasn't even sitting near the window. But he was up in an instant, and everyone else was close behind. I stayed in my seat for a moment but eventually joined the others. I hadn't met Ross, but even from the second-story classroom where Dedrick was teaching our English elective, Cooking with Butter, I could tell he was small and not very fast. But New Boys' dorm parent Jodi was even slower. Jodi was tough, and she never spoke more than was absolutely necessary. She always wore a baseball cap with her short blond ponytail sticking out the back of it, and she was running so slowly that it stayed on her head. We watched Ross pulling away little by little, and we moaned collectively as he tumbled where the lawn dipped down toward the road. This allowed Jodi to catch up. She collapsed on top of him, and then the rest of New Boys arrived and helped her put Ross into a wiggle.

I had been at the school for a couple of weeks at this point, and things had only gotten more difficult. Even on the rare occasions when something did amuse me, I made sure not to let it show lest anyone realize that maybe I wasn't as miserable as I claimed to be. I don't know what I hoped to gain by this—it was plain by that time that no one would show me any mercy on account of my being unhappy. It wasn't even clear that anyone had noticed.

Dedrick walked to the window. He peered over our heads. "They're on restriction," he said. "You're not supposed to look at them."

"We couldn't tell they were from a restricted dorm until we saw Jodi," Zach Strohmann said. "Who was that, Ross Salazar?"

"Of course they were from a restricted dorm," Dedrick said. "Otherwise they'd be in class, not out there. Don't be an idiot." Zach laughed and Dedrick sat back down at his desk. "This is just what I was talking about. Boccaccio's intr—do you all think you can find your way back to your seats? Bev, you can sit back down on the floor." We slowly turned from the window and sat down. Identical paperback copies of *The Decameron* lay on the half-desks attached to each of our chairs. "Hey, why are all your books so beaten up? They're brand new."

We looked down at the curled covers of our books and said

nothing. Finally Bev Hess, sitting on the floor in her long dress, said, "Maybe we were trying to roll them up and smoke them."

"Bev?" Dedrick said. "I can't tell if you're serious. Did you try to smoke your book?"

"No, it's just something my friends at home would probably say."

"Aren't you like eleven?"

"I'm thirteen. No, fourteen. No, wait, yeah, I'm thirteen."

"What did you do to get your furniture popped anyway?" Dedrick asked her.

Bev looked surprised. "I don't know," she said.

"She knows," Carly Sibbons-Diaz said. "She was arguing with Marcy and stood on a couch with her shoes on."

"What are you, trying to get every limit set on you at once?" Dedrick smiled at her and counted off on his fingers: "You're skirted, your furniture's popped, are you going to get cornered next? Or roomed?"

Bev smiled at him.

"Can you be sheeted and skirted at the same time?" someone asked.

"Hey, Zach," Pudding said, "remember when you got logged?" He turned to the room to explain. "Zach hit someone with a log but said it had just slipped, so Roger made him carry a log around all the time so he'd learn how to hold it without it slipping and hitting someone."

Zach smiled. "Yeah. I even had to carry it to my court date."

"Remember?" Pudding said. "And Roger said, 'Don't take the log into your own hands, you take it to court.'"

"Bev, do you have to sleep on the floor?" Dedrick asked.

"I pull my mattress off the bed. Marcy said the mattress isn't furniture."

Dedrick nodded and stared out the window. "Where were we?

Oh yes!" He slapped a hand on his desk. "I was just saying that Boccaccio's introduction, his description of the plague in Florence, even though it's a short bit at the beginning, is in a way the center of his whole project. I mean, this perfect ten-by-ten grid of stories—this book is all about trying to impose a kind of insanely paranoid order on all the external and internal forces of chaos." He glanced over our heads at the clock on the opposite wall. "And just as I'm making that point you all run to the window to check out the latest bit of chaos going on outside. Proving, among other things, that the age of irony is truly dead, at least here at the Roaring Orchards School for Troubled Teens. As if we needed reminding. Anyway. You'd all be right at home in fourteenth-century Florence."

The other students laughed at this. Dedrick was considered very funny. "What are you guys laughing about?" Dedrick asked with a smile. "I just called you a bunch of panic-driven medieval nincompoops." They laughed harder. They laughed at most of the things he said. "Hey, Pudding," Dedrick said.

Andrew Pudding giggled with anticipation. "What?"

"Don't be an idiot."

Pudding burst out laughing and doubled over. The students cracked up. Even Bev said, "Huh-huh-huh." All except for me.

"Okay," Dedrick said, "what I want you all to *try* and do now is to make an outline of Boccaccio's introduction. Summarize what he's talking about paragraph by paragraph. Then we'll see whether we can *espy*"—he drew this word out—"any pattern."

"Does this have to be in complete sentences?"

"Who asked that? Pudding, was that you?"

"No," Pudding said. Then he asked, "Does spelling count?"

"Pudding, why don't you just drool on the page instead of writing? Really. I mean it."

The laughter died down, and we got to work. When the bell

rang the students crowded around Dedrick's desk holding out small squares of paper. As he took and initialed them he told us to finish the summaries for homework. When their first-period check sheets were signed, everyone else left for their second-period classes. I waited.

I stood across from Dedrick, staring down at his desk. I tugged my sleeves down over my wrists. I scratched nervously at his desk, and Dedrick stared at my hand. "Could I ask you a question, Dedrick?" I was almost whispering.

"Sure, Benjamin."

"What do I need to do to graduate? I mean, is there a way I can just pass the classes I need to and go home?"

Dedrick let out what I'm sure was supposed to be a good-natured laugh. "Well, you can complete all your classes, but to graduate here you also need to work your process. Or at least you need to do a really good job of faking it. It's not exactly something you can rush." Dedrick looked up at other students entering the room for his next class. "Try to take it slow," he said. "Things'll get easier."

I'd begun to cry. "So there's no reason to work hard at my classes? I mean, if it's not going to help me get home?"

"Doing badly will certainly keep you from going anywhere, Ben."

"Benjamin."

"Benjamin. But there are also things other than classes you need to address before leaving. This isn't an ordinary school."

I nodded. I was starting to shake, tears falling faster now. I knew I should probably just leave, that the students arriving were looking at me, that this wasn't going to do me any good. "I haven't gotten any letters. From home."

Dedrick must have found this all a little ridiculous. I could feel his patience running out. "That must be tough," he said.

"But I've written to them. Do you think their letters could be lost someplace?"

"Well, have you talked to your dorm parent? You know mail gets inspected, right? Maybe . . . who's your dorm parent, Ellie? You know what, I'll ask her about it. Okay? But you probably need to get to your next class, don't you? Otherwise no early graduation for you." I could see Dedrick smile at me, but I kept staring down at the desk. Well, fuck him then, Dedrick must have thought. I gathered my things and walked unsteadily out of the classroom.

Next door, Spencer's math class, Humble Starts and New Beginnings, had just let out, and his history class was about to begin. I bumped into students from both as I made my way to my art class. I was beginning to believe that there was a conspiracy aiming to keep me at the school. One aimed at me, personally, and I thought I saw the signs. The fact that no one could explain how the place really worked; Dedrick's suggestion that my parents' mail was being kept from me.

Of course, what was actually keeping me at Roaring Orchards was that I was being lulled to sleep by the rhythm of the days there, days that repeated endlessly and were filled with routines that even then had begun to ensnare me in their impenetrable mysteries. As we walked out of the dorm in the morning, we would all stoop to pinch pieces of lint and litter off the carpet and would drop them in a wastebasket Ellie held out for us as we went through the door. Before lunch, we all threw our backpacks into an enormous pile in the Cafetorium lobby and afterward had to disentangle them and each of us find our own. With dinner every night there were bags of soft bread.

When Spencer couldn't find a reason to send his history class to the library, he worked with them on building a scale model of Fort Ticonderoga out of Popsicle sticks. In June's science class, since they couldn't use fire or anything huffable, they were grow-ing lima beans in cups, the beans pressed against the clear plastic by wet paper towels. The students spent each class period drawing a new picture of how their plants had changed. Every chance I got I looked in at the bean plants growing in her classroom, their pale leguminous elegance stretching beneath fluorescent lights. I had no idea how ardently I would remember these things.

In my art class, which was called Expressions, we were making papier-mâché masks. Brenda insisted that the masks reflect our innermost feelings. She was skeptical of my mask because I had added a bird's beak to it. She wouldn't criticize it directly, since she probably worried it might indeed reflect my innermost feelings, and I'm sure I seemed pretty fragile just then. But she had asked me several times to explain why, exactly, a beak. She was more impatient that day because Tidbit had begun trying to fashion a duck's bill to add onto her mask.

Tidbit had been in Expressions with me since classes began, but she hadn't said anything more than hello. She acted as though it was no big deal that I'd seen her naked, as though she hadn't whispered in my ear. I wondered if maybe the fact that neither of us mentioned this meant that there was something between us, like a secret, or if it meant that there was nothing between us. But of course there was nothing between us. We acted like we didn't know each other because we didn't know each other. But maybe the duck's bill was a gesture.

Brenda dropped the rolled sheets of oak tag she was carrying onto a table. "I don't understand this," she said. "I'm willing to give you guys some leeway since I really want you to *own* these masks, but I'm not willing to let them become a joke." She looked around the room. The students looked at one another, wondering.

"These beaks!" she said. "Tidbit, what's with this? I'd like to know just where you got the idea to add a beak to your mask."

Tidbit didn't look up from her work but answered evenly. "Well, when Benjamin added a beak to his it made me think of

Sheila Baird. Do you remember her? Bairdypants? Her parents withdrew her like a year ago, but when she was new she used to fall asleep all the time. In the middle of class and everything. Not like Bev, but still a lot. I don't know if her meds were off or if she was depressed or what. We were in Alternative Girls then, and Jodi was our dorm parent, and Jodi said she didn't want other faculty members to have to keep waking Sheila up. She said she was our dorm mate and it was our responsibility to be aware of her and keep her awake, so she set this limit where if anyone outside the dorm had to wake Sheila up, everyone in the dorm who was there had to stand up and sing that Sammy Hagar song 'Eagles Fly.' Like as a consequence. And after Benjamin's mask made me remember that, I couldn't get that song out of my head. 'Eagles Fly.' And I thought maybe there was a reason it was there. Like thinking about eagles flying was a sign that I was feeling good about myself. And I thought that was something I could represent on my mask."

Only now, after having glued the top and bottom parts of her bill together and carefully wiping off the excess glue, did Tidbit look up. Brenda looked skeptical. "So why a duck's bill?" she asked. "Why not an eagle's? Beak, I mean."

"There are these ducks on the pond near my mom's house? I guess I was thinking of how they fly south in the winter and then come back. Like they have two homes, and they go where they need to be to take care of themselves. Like how I have a home there, but this is where I need to be now, and it's a kind of home, too. I guess I could really relate to that, you know?" Tidbit looked right at Brenda without cracking a smile or even blinking. There was nothing Brenda could do, though Tidbit might as well have just spat in her face. This was what, even then, I was beginning to love about her.

Brenda was relieved of having to respond by Pudding, who

called across the room. "Those ducks' issue," he said, "was they were looking for a geographical solution to an emotional problem."

"Shut up, Pudding," Brenda said.

# 7

**A** freakish snowstorm hit the school in late September, dumping almost two feet in the valley. The trees hadn't yet lost their leaves, so their branches held more snow than they could support. As we woke and hurried to take care of our snow jobs, we heard enormous branches snapping under all the weight. They sounded like rifle shots, followed by the muffled fall of the branch and its weight of snow against the snowy ground. I tingled with excitement at the almost constant crack and thud from every direction, the world falling to pieces.

There was so much snow that every dorm was late to breakfast. None was allowed to eat in the Cafetorium. We all had to carry trays of food up to our quarters in the Mansion. In the Cafetorium, Aubrey and a few faculty members quietly ate poached eggs. Even Regular Kids had been late. But after breakfast Aubrey canceled classes for the day so that we could clear more of the campus of snow. He had Floyd, the cook, keep the hot chocolate machine working, and over the course of the day Aubrey personally went around and sent one dorm at a time into the Cafetorium for a break.

**Aaron arrived on** campus just as the sun dropped through the low-lying clouds. It warmed him through his driver's side window despite the snow and the cold. He pulled into the driveway, made his way past the stone pillars and the open iron gate, and parked next to a red Subaru wagon in the small carport by the Mansion. Getting out of the car, he thought that the school looked different under the snow. He checked to make sure his car was locked and climbed carefully over the packed snow on the Mansion steps into the Office, where Doris had told him to meet her. Aaron happened to arrive on the same day that my parents made an impromptu visit to the campus, one that I wasn't told about for quite some time.

The receptionist, Hazel, told him that Doris was in a meeting, but that he was expected and she would be with him shortly. She opened a drawer and pulled out a form attached to a clipboard. She handed it to Aaron with a pen and pointed him toward an armchair across from her desk, beside the entrance to Doris's office. There was something clipped about her tone. Hazel always acted as though she were playing along with some sort of farce but wanted you to know she didn't buy it for a second.

Aaron filled out the top half of the form, then clicked the pen shut and looked around. Hazel was going through a pile of messages and throwing most of them into a round wire wastebasket at her side. She was old, and her white hair was done up in a perm. Aaron must have wondered whether he would become friendly with her, if he would joke around with Hazel when he passed through the Office. Beyond Hazel's desk there was a large open space with five or six desks, one secretary sitting at each. Occasionally a phone would ring, and someone would answer, "Hello, Roaring Orchards School for Troubled Teens, how can I help you?" and then efficiently shoot the call across to some other desk.

At the far end of the Office was an open doorway that led into the Great Hall, but Aaron couldn't see much of it from where he sat. While he was looking, Doris walked through the doorway, and Aaron began to get up when two other people followed her into the Office. Aaron sat back down. One of the people with her was a tall, stooped man with a large bald spot and thick glasses. A short, frail woman was with him. Her long, black hair was frizzy and streaked with gray. Her face was pale, and the left half of it was entirely covered with a white bandage. A long piece of medical tape stretched from her forehead to her chin affixed the bandage to her face, along with another that went from her nose to the edge of her left ear. She kept wiping at the corners of her right eye and the right side of her nose with a balled-up Kleenex. Her hand was also bandaged. Over her arm she held a dark blue ski jacket that would be much too large for her. It had a red stripe across the chest. These were my mom and dad.

It wasn't until years later that my parents told me they had come to the school that day. I only learned that my mother had burned herself falling asleep smoking when they visited the next Parents' Sunday.

They spoke with Doris quietly, just inside the Office, and although Aaron couldn't hear them, he could tell from the way they were gesturing and looking that my dad wanted to go back into the Great Hall and that Doris was trying to talk him out of it. My dad half turned toward the doorway and looked back into the Great Hall for a long time without saying anything. He said something to my mother, but she was searching in her purse for another tissue and shaking her head back and forth. My dad nodded and let Doris lead him and my mom to the main doors, next to which Aaron was sitting.

As he shook hands with her, my dad said to Doris, "Couldn't you just tell him for us that his mother is all right?"

"What I've been trying to explain is that he never got the letters about the accident in the first place," Doris said. "We thought it would be too upsetting, on a number of levels. So you don't need to worry."

My mother's mouth moved, but she didn't say anything.

"That's why there's no need right now to show Benjamin that you're okay. You must be aware that our dorm parents read all incoming and outgoing mail. To make sure nobody's sending drugs or making runaway plans. But since you've come to campus at a time other than Parents' Sunday," Doris said, "we have another problem. That you'll have to solve with Aubrey or with the other parents in your area. But I'll tell you, they're much tougher about this sort of infraction than he is."

My parents were silent. "You'll give it to him?" my dad finally said. Doris nodded. He opened the door and held it for my mom, who was trying to fold the big ski jacket. She was standing almost directly in front of Aaron, who might have noticed, in that pause, that under the edges of her bandage her skin was red and raw. My mother shook Doris's hand awkwardly and passed her the jacket.

"I'll come up with something," Doris said. Then, after she had closed the door, she turned to Aaron. "Hello again," she said. "An unsanctioned parental visit. I shouldn't be much longer. Why don't you wait in my office? You can finish the form in there." She gestured with the jacket to a door to his right.

Doris left Aaron in front of her enormous desk, surrounded by store-bought Thanksgiving decorations, and went to bring me my jacket. I was outside shoveling snow, wearing two shirts and a hoodie, when she showed up and told me the jacket had come for me in the mail. I asked her whether there had been a note or anything, but she just shook her head and said she had to go.

Aaron took a closer look at the decorations. There were orange, brown, and yellow streamers taped to the walls and other cardboard shapes taped to the windows, facing out. It was early for Thanksgiving, Aaron thought. He took a moment to remember the date. It was still September. Maybe some of these were for Halloween. Aaron wondered whether the students were involved in preparing the campus for holidays. Was that something they enjoyed, or would they resent it? He had seen some students when he came up for his interview, but there's no way he could imagine what we were really like.

Doris's office had built-in bookshelves that held some framed photos of Aubrey with groups of students and family and friends. The rest of the shelves were taken up by a series of bright blue binders. Aaron thought of Hazel at the reception desk and of a waitress she reminded him of at Johnny-O's Club Andy, a little bar where he'd spent most evenings the past few months. He used to feel so comfortable in that shitty place that he often got panicky at the thought of leaving at the end of a night. It sent a shiver of fear through Aaron. He hadn't even known how bad off he was. He was terrified that this job wasn't going to work out. On Doris's large oak desk stood a turkey with a glossy cardboard face and a spherical body made of colorful tissue paper.

Aaron heard the sound of Doris's cane against the wood floor as she approached and realized he'd forgotten about the form he was supposed to fill out. She entered and stood in the doorway, her cheeks red from the cold. "As soon as it started snowing, they headed up here to bring him a jacket. Talk about overidentified." Doris laughed, and Aaron laughed, too. He had no idea what she was talking about. "Shall we get going?"

"I haven't finished this," Aaron said, tapping the clipboard with the pen.

"Oh, that's all right." Doris took the clipboard from him. "I don't think you need to worry about this right now."

Aaron followed her to Hazel's desk. "Do you mind," Doris asked, "if he fills this out next week along with the tax forms?"

"All right," Hazel said, "but the last two people left before they gave me any paperwork, so I don't have contact numbers or anything. One of them put us down as a reference, God knows why, and I didn't know what to say when they called me. What kind of person puts down for a reference a job he left the afternoon after he got there?" Hazel shook her head and put the clipboard back in a drawer. "The same kind of person who leaves a job the afternoon after he gets there."

Doris led Aaron out of the Mansion and past his car. "You can unpack this evening. I'd like to show you your apartment and introduce you to the dorm you'll be working with. You'll be living in the Greenhouse Annex, a charming little space." Aaron was wearing his nice pants and shoes and hoped that he was dressed all right for working in the dorm. His shoes were new and still squeaked when he walked.

From the hill where the Mansion sat, Aaron could see the afternoon light reflected across the gentle slope of the snow. Brief tapping and scraping sounds floated through the air. Groups of students clustered together in front of the various buildings, shoveling snow. Doris led him down toward one of the buildings. Aaron noticed that the sounds of the students' work were badly synchronized with their movements; the sound took some time to travel to him through the cold air. The effect was slightly disorienting. He turned away and focused his attention on the blue shadows cast by the trees and the hill across the snow.

Doris stopped and drew Aaron's attention to Aubrey, who was walking their way. He was wearing an enormous parka with a fur-lined hood. He was rubbing his hands together and smiling.

"Doris, who's this you're shepherding around my campus?" He held out his hand, and Aaron shook it.

"This is Aaron, the new dorm parent I was telling you about. Aaron, this is Aubrey."

"It's an auspicious day to start, Aaron. Something about this strange weather's made our students briefly content to behave like the children they are. It's really wonderful—those two magical words, 'snow day.' You should see how excited they are when I invite them to come inside for hot chocolate."

Aaron looked at Doris, and when she laughed politely, he did, too.

"Doris is answering all of your questions, I hope?"

"Oh, yeah. Yes, absolutely."

"I'm glad. I have a tremendous amount of faith in Doris. She has a great personal power, Aaron, but she doesn't acknowledge it. Some people find that sort of humility a virtue, but I think it's her only flaw. When she finally chooses to be as strong and insightful as she actually is, she'll be a force of nature." Doris was leaning on her cane. Whether she was blushing or her face was simply red from the cold, Aaron couldn't tell. Aubrey grabbed Aaron's arm gently just above the elbow. "She'll take this place over when I'm gone. I've poured everything into this place, my whole life. So you can see that I must feel she's special."

Aubrey turned and began to walk with Doris and Aaron, still holding on to Aaron's arm. But he stopped almost immediately. "Doris told you how she started working here?"

"No, she hasn't." Aaron smiled at Doris as though she had been keeping something from him.

"Doris and I had known each other for years, from this weight-loss group and that one," Aubrey said as they strolled. "Whatever it was, we were there, trying to slim down. I wasn't always this size—if you think Doris is big, well, that's nothing. I was enormous. I didn't start losing weight until I began the process that is now the basis for how Roaring Orchards works. And when I did that, the weight just disappeared. It's really remarkable; there are some students here on campus who've done the same thing, they'll tell you.

"I hadn't seen Doris in months. Then one afternoon I'm at the Price Chopper over in Grafflin, and there she is, in the produce section. I had lost all this weight, but it never occurred to me that Doris wouldn't recognize me. But she didn't. I passed by her once or twice to be sure. Not even a second glance. So I walked over quietly with my basket and stood next to her, just like anyone else at the supermarket, except that then I leaned over and looked into her shopping cart and I took something from it and put it in my basket. Doris started like she didn't quite believe her eyes. When she turned away I did it again; I took a look at another couple of things in her cart, considering them, and put some of them in my basket. Doris finally said something, like 'Excuse me, sir.' I looked at her for a long moment and burst out laughing. That's when she figured out who I was. She was so relieved. And I told her she should come here, to work with me. And it's turned out wonderfully."

They walked toward the Annex. On the way, Aubrey told the story of how the building Aaron would be living in had been converted from a greenhouse. Before founding Roaring Orchards, Aubrey had been working at another school but had gotten fired. And all the parents, Aubrey explained, immediately withdrew their kids from that school and gave Aubrey two years worth of tuition or whatever they could afford so that he could buy Roaring Orchards. The kids spent the first year and a half fixing up the place, and converting the old greenhouse had been one of their first projects. "Then we all moved in there so we could start fixing up the Mansion," he said. "So don't mess that place up—it's got some real history." At that, he said good-bye to Aaron, gave Doris a hug, and walked off toward the Mansion.

Me and the rest of Alternative Boys were shoveling snow outside the Greenhouse Annex, and we stopped to let Aaron and Doris enter. When they had, Spencer shouted at us to get back to work. Doris led Aaron into a large, bare room with blue carpeting and a wood-burning stove in one corner. We had cleaned it out the day before as a Reciprocity Detail. There were two unpainted wooden doors on one wall, and one on each of the others.

"This will be your apartment for now," Doris told him. "You might have to switch when you get a permanent dorm, but we'll try to avoid that. Your room is the one straight across. In the other two rooms here are, let's see, well, one's empty. It used to be Sheldon's, who taught English. In fact, I remember he specifically asked to live here, rather than in the Paddock where most of the teachers are. So that's the empty one, and . . . oh yes, Zbigniew, who is in charge of maintenance and runs our Reciprocity Detail, he's in the other. You'll like him. The bathroom is right there." She pointed to a door. Where the doorknob would be, there was a hole cut in the door. Aaron walked across to his bedroom and opened the door. A large box spring with a slightly stained mattress sat on a metal frame in one corner of the room. The walls were light yellow, and there was a large window on the back wall that had a view of the trunks of pine trees behind the building. The window didn't have any blinds or curtains. Aaron looked around, trying to imagine where his things would go, but he didn't have much stuff, and he couldn't really think of what it all was just then. "Let's go meet Alternative Boys," Doris said.

They headed back outside, to where we were shoveling. "Aaron, this is Spencer," Doris said. "Spencer teaches math and history and works with Alternative Boys when their dorm parent Ellie isn't around."

"And sometimes when she is," Spencer said.

Doris seemed a bit confused, then annoyed. "Yes, and sometimes when she is. Spencer, Aaron's just arrived, and I'm going to leave him with your dorm, at least for the afternoon."

Spencer shook Aaron's hand roughly and said, "Good to meet you, Darren."

"Aaron."

"What's that?"

"Aaron."

Doris left and Spencer had us stop our shoveling to meet Aaron. "Aaron," he said, "this is Alternative Boys. You'll get all their names later. Guys, this is Aaron. Now you show him you can act like a group of gentlemen and not a bunch of slobbering imbeciles. Eric, that's not funny. Wipe your chin. All right, enough. Finish shoveling while there's still light."

At that, William dropped his shovel. It rattled against the ground. He waited a beat, then asked Aaron, "You wanna see my dick?"

"Oh, William, cut the bullshit," Spencer said. William laughed. His scrawny frame looked funny in his puffy down coat. "Now all of you get to work." As the boys went back to shoveling, Spencer asked Aaron about himself and explained a little about the dorm and the school. "Some of the staff here are all right, but we get some real wackos, too. You'll figure out which are which pretty soon."

I noticed Aaron looking at me. I realize now that it must have been because he recognized my jacket and had seen my parents. He had been working there about fifteen minutes and already knew more about my life than I did. "Who's that?" he asked.

"That's Benjamin," Spencer said. "He's pretty quiet as long as you don't let him get overly emotional. Not a wiseass, is the point. Listen, there are a couple of phone calls I need to make about something. Would you watch these guys while I go inside for a second? I'll be right back."

Aaron stammered, trying to find a way to refuse, but Spencer saw his hesitation and said, "Don't worry. Kids in this dorm aren't allowed to get violent or run away." He walked up the hill toward the Mansion.

Aaron put his hands in his pockets and turned to face us. We kept working at clearing the path to the road that ran around campus but traded quick looks as people decided what to do. Aaron noticed but must have hoped he was imagining it. Not a minute passed before William marched up to Aaron, held out his shovel, and said, "Well, get to work."

Aaron looked at him and nodded, laughed through his nose. But William just waited, looking up at him. Aaron rocked back on his heels. William held his shovel out to Aaron again. He was almost trembling with excitement. I kept my head down.

"Get to work, I said. Come on." William swung his snow shovel and hit Aaron in the shin, hard, with the edge of its metal face. Aaron hopped backward. It must have hurt a lot. He was trying not to wince.

"What do you mean?" he asked William, and looked from him to the rest of us, who kept shoveling, some laughing, most pretending to be unaware of what was going on.

"What do I mean? Take a shovel and get to work. You think we're the only ones who should shovel snow? Get to work, get to work, get to work!" With each of the last of these, William swung the shovel again, catching Aaron in the shins all three times. Aaron held out his arms to try to push William back, but the shovel was long enough to reach him.

William turned around and went back to shoveling snow. The pain in Aaron's legs made him hop up and down on his toes. He bent down to rub his shins and check if they were bleeding into his new pants and saw that the bottom of his right pant leg was torn. But there was only a little blood.

We finished shoveling the walk quietly, and by the time we were done it had begun to get dark. Aaron followed us back to the Mansion basement, where we left the shovels, and then up to our dorm, where Spencer was sitting at a desk in the hallway talking

on the phone. He waved thanks to Aaron, and when he didn't ask
how things had gone outside, Aaron didn't tell him.

**For dinner Aubrey** decided to allow everyone back into the Cafetorium, though he was not there. Ellie had returned, and Aaron
sat with us, too. He was happy to meet her, but she seemed distracted; she asked him his name twice, and he was still pretty sure
she hadn't gotten it. Other than that, his first dinner at Roaring
Orchards went relatively well. It was fried chicken, everybody's
favorite, and since I was waiter I had to get up half a dozen times
to get more from the kitchen. The only incident occurred when
Pudding stuck his knife into the edge of the lazy Susan in the
middle of the table. The next time someone turned the lazy Susan,
the knife revolved with it and knocked over a few plastic glasses of
water. Ellie hardly seemed to notice.

After dinner Doris asked if anyone had any announcements.
Kids who were following the program raised their hands and when
they were called on stood and announced things like "It's been
twenty-three days since I got violent" or "I haven't eaten sugar for
four days." Aaron joined in the light applause after each announce-
ment. In the Campus Community meeting after dinner Aaron was
briefly introduced. Afterward, Doris sent him with New Girls for
the evening. She said she wanted him to move around between
dorms as much as possible the first few days so he could meet
people and get to know how the school worked.

That evening, Aaron sat with Marcy and watched her girls do
their homework in the lounge. They sat on couches or on the floor
around the low table in the middle of the room. Bev stood by a
bookcase. The girls worked diligently, and when they spoke they
spoke in whispers. Aaron was impressed.

When the girls had been working for a while, Marcy got up and
motioned for Aaron to come along. In the kitchenette, she began

filling little paper cups with water. "These are for their nighttime meds," she said. She showed Aaron the med packet and the notebook where he would have to check off each dose administered when he came to be in charge of a dorm. "We'll give these once they're in bed, but I like to start getting things ready beforehand."

He looked back into the lounge where the girls were still working. Aaron watched one girl slide off a couch and sit next to another by the table to ask her something about a page of homework. They both leaned over the page and made marks as they discussed it quietly. "That girl over by the bookcase," Aaron asked Marcy. "The, uh, bald girl in the dress? Is there something going on with her that I should know about?"

A strange, delighted smile appeared on Marcy's face. "That's Beverly Hess. She's so funny. They've been lowering her meds and it's like she's coming out of a fog, for the very first time. She's actually very sweet, but she also has episodes now that she's not so heavily medicated. She's standing because she and I got in this argument. It was so stupid—I think it was about whether Grand Forks or Bismarck was the capital of North Dakota, I don't even remember who was arguing which. It was for someone's homework, and it turned out Bev was right. She knows all sorts of obscure things, actually. But she got really heated and climbed up on the couch so she could yell in my face, so I popped her furniture."

"Popped it."

Marcy herself seemed to come out of a reverie. She laughed. "It means something's forbidden. If your furniture's popped, you're not allowed to use furniture."

"Is there a handbook or glossary or something I'll get?"

Marcy shook her head. "Aubrey doesn't allow anything like that. It's important to him that Roaring Orchards remain a flexible place and that it's able to adapt to the needs of the students. Sometimes he says that there aren't any rules here at all, just the school's philosophy. And that if you understand that and if you're honest about your motivations, you can do whatever you think is right."

"What *is*, like, the school's philosophy?"

"It's hard to put it all into a sentence. I mean, it has a lot to do with the kids learning to make themselves the most important person, you know? In their lives? Because they can't be good to others until they're good to themselves. And there's a lot about responsibility, about taking responsibility for everything in your life. Personally, I'm not really at a stage yet where I entirely understand it. Aubrey actually believes that before you're born you choose who your parents are going to be, so you're even responsible for that."

"Really?"

"It's like, if they do bad things, you shouldn't complain because you're the one who chose them. So you can take responsibility even then, for the things you choose to let happen to you."

"Oh," Aaron said.

He followed Marcy back into the lounge, where she told the girls to put their work away. They closed their books and collected their papers. They placed them neatly on the bookshelf. Then the girls all sat down on the couches, except for Bev, who stood. Closer to her now, Aaron could see that Bev wasn't entirely bald. A few wisps of blond hair swirled against her temples like down.

"All right," Marcy said, "I know Bev wants to work out her furniture, and I have something to bring up. Anything else?" No one said anything, so Marcy began.

The thing she wanted to discuss was an issue from that morning, when they had breakfast in the dorm. Marcy said that after breakfast she had found three empty envelopes of juice mix in the trash, but she only remembered the girls making one pitcher of juice. "Maybe I'm wrong about that, but I don't think so. Did you guys drink three pitchers of juice this morning or just one?"

New Girls said nothing. "Well, if it was just one," Marcy said, "I'd like to know who made it."

After a pause Tidbit said that she'd made it. "But I know what you're going to say," she said, "and it wasn't a yummy. Yummies have a lot more mix than that."

"My understanding," Marcy said, "is that a yummy is when you use more juice mix than you're supposed to use. You're supposed to use one packet per pitcher. You're telling me you used three?"

"Yes, but that doesn't make it a yummy." As she spoke, Tidbit repeatedly swept her dark hair out of her face and pushed her red glasses up the bridge of her nose. The argument went on for some time. Aaron gathered that yummies were popped. They were popped because students had used them to self-medicate, altering their moods with excess amounts of sugar. Most of the dorm members agreed with Tidbit that a pitcher of juice was only a yummy if it contained the absolute maximum amount of juice mix that would dissolve in it. They claimed that this would take about seven envelopes if you used hot water.

"The point here," Marcy said, backing up, "isn't so much whether you've broken a limit, Tidbit. I'm not interested in getting you into trouble. But limits exist for a reason, not just to keep you from doing certain harmful things. They are also so we can all see what's going on inside you by how you behave. I don't understand you, Tidbit. You've been talking such a big game about wanting to be good and follow the process, and then you always somehow find a way to undermine whatever progress you might have made. And with stupid things like this. Why do you think you're doing that?"

Tidbit hugged her knees. "I don't see what that has to do with anything," she said. "How was I undermining myself if I thought using three envelopes of mix was okay?"

"Let's move away from exactly how many juice packets you did or did not use. That's not really what this is about. You know you'd be safer using just one. Why didn't you?"

"But I don't think I knew that," Tidbit said. "Juice just tastes better with more mix. I didn't think I was breaking any rules."

"Girls?" Marcy said, turning to the dorm. "What do you all think about this?"

"Whatever," Tidbit said.

"Well, to tell the truth, I feel set up," Bridget Divola said. "I had no idea that the juice was a yummy when I drank it, and I feel like Tidbit made me act out even though I didn't want to." Bridget was chubby and had a bowl haircut. Aaron thought she was adorable.

Tidbit pushed the hair out of her eyes and sat up straighter. "You've got to be kidding."

"I'm not kidding. You all know I'm addicted to sugar, and even if you're not interested in following the process, there are some of us who are." Tidbit just glared at her, so Bridget continued. "You know what this reminds me of? Remember that one meeting where you told us about how when you and your mom were feeling really stressed and crazy she would take stuff out of the refrigerator and you guys would paint all over the kitchen walls with peanut butter and ketchup and toothpaste and stuff? Like you'd both just laugh hysterically and go crazy, making a mess? To deal with the stress?"

"That has nothing to do with this," Tidbit said. "And I said that in a meeting, so it's confidential."

"Well, this meeting is confidential, too." Bridget looked briefly at Aaron. "And I think it does have to do with it. Because you're acting out in the kitchen. With condiments. It's like, maybe if that's how you bonded with your mom, then maybe you—"

"This is why people don't talk in meetings. And you're not addicted to sugar, Bridget. You're just fat." Tidbit pulled on her hair so that it hung down in front of her face. "God, this is such bullshit. Stupid shit."

"Tidbit," Carly Sibbons-Diaz said, "I really don't think that's—"

"How come you're getting nasty if it isn't true?" Bridget said. "I don't think you'd—"

"I'm getting nasty because you're a bitch. This is why your sister killed herself. She couldn't stand listening to another word out of your fat mouth."

No one said anything for a long time.

Then Laurel Pfaff said, "God, Tidbit." Bridget sat perfectly still, her cheeks pink and shining.

"Okay," Marcy said. "I think you girls need to sit for a while with what happened here and think about it." Marcy's voice sounded calm and satisfied.

"I think Tidbit needs to apologize," Carly said.

A number of girls agreed, but Marcy wanted to move on. "Now Bev," she said, "you ready, hon?"

"Yes." Bev blinked. She faced the dorm. "I got my furniture popped for standing on a couch and arguing. Marcy, I'm very sorry I stood on a couch and fought with you about"—Bev suddenly looked worried—"I don't remember what we were fighting about."

"That's okay," Marcy said. "Did you get your furniture popped for arguing?"

"No?"

"So what did you get it popped for?"

"Oh, for standing on the couch in my shoes! Which is taking advantage because furniture is a privilege!"

"Okay, Bev," Marcy said. "But what are you going to do if you get upset like that again? To make sure that you don't act out?"

"If I get upset like that again I'll talk about being upset instead of acting out."

"Good." Marcy could barely help beaming at her. "And how are you feeling now?"

"I feel like I should get my furniture unpopped."

"You're almost there. But 'like I should get my furniture unpopped' isn't a feeling. Check the poster."

Bev turned to a sheet of oak tag taped to the wall. On it someone had written in green Magic Marker:

The seven feelings
1. Happy
2. Proud
3. Confused
4. Frustrated
5. Scared
6. Angry
7. Sad

Bev thought for a moment. "I feel proud. I feel proud that I did a good job working out my furniture. Is it unpopped?"

"It is," Marcy said.

The girls made room on the couch. Bev sat down.

**Later Marcy suggested** that Aaron stay to observe bedtime. While the girls were brushing their teeth, he followed her as she walked back and forth between the kitchenette and the girls' bedrooms, placing the appropriate number of cups of water outside each room. When all the girls were done in the bathroom, they separated into groups of roommates. Marcy gave them ten minutes to change for bed, journal, say their prayers. Whatever they needed to do, she explained to Aaron.

Aaron followed Marcy down the hall as she visited one room at a time. He stood in the darkened doorway and watched as she sat on the edge of one bed after another. First, she gave the meds.

She checked each yellow envelope before administering it, making sure that the contents matched the label. Then she poured the pills onto the girl's tongue and watched as she drank the cup of water. Then Marcy looked inside her mouth. Then they talked for a minute before Marcy moved on to the next girl. For the girls in the top bunks, the process was the same, but instead of sitting, Marcy stood. And instead of rubbing their backs and giving them a hug good night, she smoothed their hair.

When she had finished with the last room, Marcy pulled out the next morning's med packet so she could show Aaron. "Eventually, you'll know which pills are which," she said, "but until then you should probably give meds along with someone who does. Because Kavita—she's the nurse—she's been known to make mistakes."

Marcy dumped the contents of several envelopes out on the counter. She separated the pills with her fingers and named them for Aaron. Klonopin, Prozac, Dexedrine, Paxil. Effexor, Haldol, lithium. Trazadone, Mellaril, Ritalin, Thorazine.

Aaron said good night, and she told him how to get back to his apartment. "I haven't even unpacked yet," he told her. When he was gone, Marcy cleaned up around the lounge. With her hand, she collected the crumbs from the counter of the kitchenette and dumped them in the sink. She ran the water, splashing it around and waiting for the crumbs to dissolve and get washed down the drain.

# 8

Over the next days the early snow melted away and fall resumed its course. New Boys and the few students on Reciprocity Detail cleaned the debris from the storm, the fallen branches still flush with leaves. Autumn from that point on proceeded differently. The colors when they came seemed muted, and the drying leaves curled against their branches and clung to them longer. Husks of dead bees collected behind the Mansion's heavy curtains; tiny white spots of mold appeared on the windfall apples in the orchard.

Dedrick decided to give us a day off from Cooking with Butter to help decorate the Classroom Building for Thanksgiving. He took us to the atrium, which was just a wide lobby with large, potted plants, and dropped an assortment of Magic Markers onto the floor. The heat hadn't been turned on yet, and the large cinderblock building was drafty. Dedrick gave each of us a poster to draw on. He said we should trace our hands to make turkeys and include Thanksgiving messages.

"But try to make them look as retarded as you possibly can," he said. "Misspell things, write with your left hand if you need to. Pudding, you just write the way you always do."

"Ha-ha," Pudding said.

Everyone thought the project was hilarious, though I did my

best to seem morose. Laurel Pfaff carefully made all her Rs face the wrong way, and she drew a big turkey, which she colored in like an American flag. Zach Strohmann drew a crow and beneath it wrote, "Yeesturday we R reeding a Turgee." Bev covered her poster with an assortment of dark squares. When I asked her what they were, she told me they were brownies. Dedrick heard her answer. "Brilliant!" he said.

Seeing us as objects of fun let the faculty imagine we were somehow protected, I think, as comic figures are able to survive all kinds of harm. I never minded that the staff amused themselves at our expense, although I'll resent forever the fact that I was so indifferently educated. In part that was my own fault—by the time I got to Roaring Orchards, I was pretty much a lost cause intellectually. What little I know now I've mostly taught myself, and it's come complete with an autodidact's insecurity and pedantry. Looking back I can see that the teachers had plenty of reasons of their own to be angry, and that they were occasionally funny, too. Toward the end of the period we ran around the building taping the posters to the wall.

"Are these going to stay up for Parents' Sunday?" Pudding asked.

"God I hope so," Dedrick said.

**Walking to lunch** with Spencer and June, Dedrick asked them about something that had been on his mind for a while. "What the hell is going on with these *Decamerons*?" They were passing the shelves in the hallway of the Classroom Building where students left their shoes while they were in class and where they left their books when they went to lunch. Among the math and history textbooks lay badly worn copies of *The Decameron*, their covers curled and bent. "Almost every copy I see is dog-eared and torn, the spines are broken, chunks of pages are falling out all over the place. I don't get it. They were all brand-new about two months ago."

June stopped to pick up a copy. There were pages that had fallen out and were now stapled together and stuffed back into the book. The spine was curled, and the pages that hadn't fallen out radiated from it like spokes on a wheel. "Maybe these are just really cheap editions," she said. "Where'd we get them?"

"Someone sent them, I think," Spencer said, taking the book from June. "Maybe they knew there was something wrong with them." He flipped through the pages only to have a clump of pages fall to the floor. Spencer picked them up, put the book back together, and placed it back on the shelf. "No, it's probably just that our kids don't know what to do with books."

Pudding and I overheard this on our way out. We couldn't help laughing, but just looked down and kept walking.

**The closest any** faculty members came to discovering why all the copies of *The Decameron* on campus were in such bad repair came during a candor meeting that Alternative Boys held because of me in the middle of one night that fall. At two thirty in the morning, I got caught with my alarm clock going off. I'd hidden the clock beneath my pillow, hoping it would wake me and no one else. But William Kay, in the bunk across the room, heard the alarm and saw me, startled, wake and scramble to turn it off. I think he might have seen me set it and stayed up to catch me, either because he thought it would be funny or just because William was a jerk. Maybe the alarm just woke him, and he was annoyed. Whatever his reason, William began shouting that I was running away, although he knew that wasn't what was happening.

He woke the other students, who woke Ellie, who pulled an oversize tan sweater over her pajamas and called Alternative Boys into a meeting to figure out what was going on. The boys dragged their blankets with them and curled up on the couches. I sat down angrily.

"I wasn't running away."

"Then why did you have your alarm wake you up at two thirty in the morning?" William was the only person who seemed entirely awake. He was bouncing slightly on the couch, his skinny arms sticking out of his T-shirt, his white-blond hair hanging in front of his eyes.

"Don't be a dick, William," someone said groggily. "You know why."

"None of us know why until Benjamin tells us," William said, "and you have to admit it looks really suspicious." He smiled. "So, why were you getting up when everyone else was asleep?"

Ellie leaned back in her chair. "William, just lay off, all right? Benjamin, you set your alarm for the middle of the night?"

"Yes."

"Why?"

I just looked at the carpet.

Pudding sat up and wrapped his blanket around his shoulders. "Oh God, will you just tell her so we can all go back to sleep? We've got to wake up in a few hours."

"Pudding, what are you talking about?" Ellie was uncomfortable being the only one not to know what was going on. She tugged on the sleeves of her sweater and crossed her arms.

"Do you want to tell her or should I?" Pudding asked me.

"Shut up," I said.

"Pudding, will you just answer my question?"

"He was going to whack off!" Pudding said. "You think any of us want to do it as soon as we get into bed, when everyone can hear? You were just waiting for everyone to be asleep, weren't you? So you could do it in peace?"

"No." I was, but wouldn't say so.

"I don't know why you set your alarm clock instead of just staying up like a normal person," Pudding said, "but we all know what you were doing, so you might as well just say it."

"Yeah," William said, "because, personally, if that's not why you were getting up, I'd assume you were going to run away, which means you can't stay in this dorm."

"I'm just saying that I wasn't going to run. I swear, Ellie. You can go check my room—I didn't pack anything. How could I be planning to run without at least setting aside clothes to change into? Go ahead and see if you don't believe me."

Ellie sat up. "It's the middle of the night. You don't get to choose what you feel like being honest about and what you don't. Now, is what they're saying true? You were getting up to masturbate?"

"I wasn't going to run."

Ellie let out a cry of frustration and stomped her feet against the carpet. She stood up. "You guys figure out what the fuck is going on with him. I'm going to go pay for that f-word and search his room."

From that point on, I refused to talk. Whether the other boys tried to convince me that there was nothing wrong with masturbating, or tried to goad or threaten me into talking, they didn't get me to say a word. It's embarrassing to remember now. I don't know why I wouldn't talk. I'd like to think I was bored with the dorm and that was just my way of getting sent to New Boys. Or that I just didn't want to take back what I had initially said.

Ellie returned to the lounge and stood talking quietly to Roger, who had emerged from her bedroom. It was the first time we realized, with some shock and disappointment, that they were sleeping together. When she rejoined our meeting, Ellie said it didn't look like I had been preparing to run, but she wasn't satisfied. "If your dorm mates and I have reasonable questions about what you were up to, and you can't tell me or aren't willing to talk about it, then you can't be trusted to stay in this dorm. Do you have anything you want to say?"

I glared at her.

"Then it's my consensus that Benjamin be more appropriately placed to New Boys."

"Agreed."

"Agreed."

"Benjamin, this is stupid. You should say something."

I didn't.

"Agreed."

"Agreed."

"Agreed."

"Agreed."

"Agreed."

"Agreed."

"Agreed."

"Agreed."

Ellie helped me throw my things into two garbage bags and that same night escorted me to the Cottage where New Boys lived. Along with the clothes and toiletries my parents had sent, I packed my blanket, bedsheets, and pillow. Hidden in the last of these were my two favorite novellas from *The Decameron*: one told by Fiammetta on the third day of the book, *In which Catella dotes on Filippello Sighinolfo, and consequently finds herself in a dark room at the public baths. Here she addresses herself to the wrong party, one Ricciardo Minutolo, with unpredicted results*, and a second, shorter tale in which, *At Pietro's request, his friend Don Gianni sets about transforming his wife into a mare; but when Don Gianni comes to the hard part, Pietro ruins the spell*, which was the last story told on the ninth day, by Dioneo. I'd torn these stories from my copy of the book and folded them into fourths when no faculty members were watching. They had been the inspiration for my furtive assignations with myself over the past few weeks. Previously, I had simply stayed awake until the boys in my room were asleep. But that night I'd been tired, so I tried to get some sleep and wake up using the alarm.

In the absence of pornography, *The Decameron* had been a welcome discovery for the students in Dedrick's Cooking with Butter class. Word quickly spread to the rest of the students on campus, and we were soon slipping copies back and forth, dog-earing our favorite stories or tearing them out to keep. Passages were copied by hand into journals and into notes that were folded, a name carefully printed on the outside, and passed from hand to hand. If faculty members had known to look, they might have found pages from *The Decameron* smuggled into restricted dorms, stuffed under mattresses, or hidden at the bottoms of drawers full of T-shirts or underwear. As the season wore on, boys and girls who ran away took their favorite parts with them, so that the box of books that had arrived at the beginning of the school year was slowly dispersed, piece by piece, to distant corners of the campus and around upstate New York.

# 9

**M**y first night in New Boys I didn't sleep. It was after three in the morning when Ellie brought me down to the Cottage. She had called Jodi, who let me in and tossed the garbage bags with my things onto one of the couches in the large living room. Jodi was wearing gray sweats and a Pittsburgh Penguins ball cap and didn't say a single word to Ellie, to me, or to the other boys, who began cursing impressively when she turned on the light in the Cottage's only bedroom so that I could make my bed. They held their pillows over their heads and complained to Jodi as if I weren't there. By the time they turned their attention to me and started threatening what they would do to me if I didn't finish making my bed and turn off the goddamn light, I was done. A line of Christmas lights was hung around the perimeter of the room near the ceiling but wasn't plugged in.

I knew the boys in that dorm only by reputation, and it was in part those reputations that kept me awake my first night there. But I was also kept from sleep by an awareness of a long-held confusion slowly disappearing. I lay at the back of my bunk, my back pressed against the cheap fiberglass wall, and tried to pay attention to this unworking of my mind. For as long as I could remember, I had suffered under the delusion that if I were only good enough, or quiet enough, I would somehow be allowed to return to a time in my life when things were all right. All right with myself, and all right with my family, and I would be able to proceed from that moment on. But that night I understood that an iron gate had been shut behind me, that each passing day was another gate slamming shut, and that there was no way back and never would be.

New Boys were off restriction when I was sent down. This was a dorm with no bottom line, where you could do whatever you wanted and wouldn't get kicked out. Yet somehow they had all been good enough long enough that they were allowed to be part of campus. I could feel the tension it caused. My new dorm mates, especially the ones who had been in New Boys for a while, knew something catastrophic would happen before long to ruin it, and there was a sense that the sooner it did, the sooner they could stop worrying and things could get back to normal, which wasn't too bad. New Boys were watched more closely and had fewer privileges than other dorms, but the boys mostly did what they were supposed to and otherwise left one another alone. There was always the potential for an eruption of violence, but there wasn't the pettiness and dishonesty I'd grown used to in Alternative Boys.

For the time being, I was glad I could still go to classes. In Expressions, we had finished our masks and lined them up on a shelf, and we were now working on still lifes. The assignment was to paint an assortment of inanimate objects in a way that conveyed one of the seven feelings. Brenda had also decided that to make the classroom a special place, she would give us a password each day that we would need to remember to get into class the next day. It was dumb, but I didn't mind lining up and having to whisper the new word into her ear each day. Her dark, messy hair smelled like apples and mint.

We didn't have many of the objects that we wanted to paint so most of us were painting from memory. There had been a number of requests to do still lifes that portrayed other feelings than the seven included on the posters in each dorm's lobby. Brenda felt that these had resulted in some useful discussions but had said no. I was painting a vase and seashells that were supposed to demonstrate that I felt proud. When Brenda asked what I was proud of, I told her that if I could get the things in my painting to look right, I'd be very proud of that. She tried to explain that our paintings were supposed to express something we felt, not something we hoped to feel, but the other students pointed out that there was no way anyone could possibly feel the same thing every day we worked on our paintings and that my project sounded fine to them.

Tidbit's painting showed groceries in her kitchen at home, and it was pretty good. When it was her turn to explain her painting, she said she wanted it to look like the groceries had just been put on the counter. In the still life it was late afternoon. There was a paper grocery bag with some things sticking out of the top and next to it a bunch of bananas and a few cans and a bottle of club soda, which must have been the toughest part because clear things are so hard to paint. The counter was a drab green, and there were darkly stained wooden cabinets in the background. Tidbit told me later that she could see it all in her head. She wanted the painting to be dark and for it to look like the groceries were standing out from the darkness. The brighter parts would be the bananas and where the cans and soda bottle caught the light. The feeling she had chosen to express was number 5, scared.

No one in her dorm had talked to her much since the meeting when she'd been so horrible to Bridget. An itchy nausea swept through Tidbit when she thought about it. She had no idea why she did things like that. She really was trying to be good. It was like some kind of voodoo the school did. Trying to be good there turned you into the most awful person in the world.

Tidbit was like me, I think. Not in most ways, but in this: she had no idea what was wrong with her. Sometimes she felt that whatever it was must be so large and diffuse that she couldn't get her head around it; other times it seemed it was some tart, nasty thing right at the center of her. Or not quite the center. Just off center enough that she was always twisted and sweating and stumbling off in the wrong direction.

One afternoon, just a few days after I had moved down to New Boys, I watched her as she was painting. She wore brown corduroy jeans and a yellow T-shirt and was working on the cans in her picture. One was beans and one was soup and one was corn. Tidbit used a tiny brush to try to get the gradations of shadow around the curved surfaces just right. She added highlights to their tops. She looked happy with how the cans were coming out, but as soon as she took a step back she seemed to feel her mind cloud again with anger. The cans were perfect, but they didn't rest on the counter so much as float above it. She couldn't tell why. And the bananas were good too, but the perspective or something was wrong. It looked like they were about to pitch forward and roll off the counter into her lap.

Ever since Bridget had brought up how Tidbit and her mom used to mess up their kitchen, Tidbit couldn't help imagining the parts of the kitchen her painting didn't show, where she and her mom might be smearing stuff on the walls and laughing wildly. She never should have told the dorm; it was like Tidbit had failed to follow the advice she gave me my first day: don't tell them anything. Not just because there were people who would store it up to use against her—she still thought that was what Bridget had done, and she knew that was what she had done to Bridget. But because now the memory wasn't just hers and her mom's anymore; it was everyone's.

This was something Tidbit and I talked about a lot when we got to know each other better. It was like the opposite of a fib. Aubrey said that the problem with breaking the rules was that you kept it secret, and then the secret kept you from being close with the people around you. That's why it was a functioning intimacy blocker. But the part they never admitted to was that the secret, for as long as you kept it, made you that much closer with the few people who knew it. And the worse the secret, the closer you were. This was the closest Tidbit had ever come to articulating something I had always felt: that getting better would be a betrayal.

Tidbit mixed a green so dark it was almost black and tried to anchor the cans and bananas where they sat by putting in shadows. She painted the shadows darkest where they touched the objects and made them fade slightly as they stretched away. She was careful to make the shadows stretch right up to the edge of the shapes. Tidbit took her time and tried to make the shadows look smooth.

But again, when she stepped back she felt she'd made it worse. The parts were still okay, but they were stuck in a painting that had been ruined. The shadows didn't look like shadows. They looked like things, like dark shapes floating across the surface of her painting. They obliterated the illusion of space and barred Tidbit from the kitchen and the few things she had gotten right.

Tidbit took her paint knife and slashed at the canvas. Just a little at first. I was engrossed with watching her do it—she had to poke the canvas a couple of times before it tore. Tidbit was holding the paint knife so tightly her hands shook. I felt proud of her as she began to tear the thing apart; I have no idea why. She grabbed the top of the canvas so the easel wouldn't tip and cut it into ribbons thick with paint. The other students heard and were startled. They stood back, scared at first but amused when they understood what Tidbit was doing. She stabbed the canvas again and broke the frame. I'll admit that I started to get a little frightened for Tidbit. Even more so when Brenda ran out to the hallway and screamed for help.

■ ■ ■

**Like I said,** New Boys' time as an unrestricted dorm was destined
to be short. The end came soon after Tidbit got dragged out of
Expressions, and a few days after William Kay got sent down to the
dorm. Someone had told about how he'd hit Aaron with a snow
shovel on Aaron's first day, and he got more appropriately placed to
New Boys for violence. I'm not sure who told or what William had
done to make him mad, but it was a pretty big deal. The faculty
felt that Aaron should have said something sooner. William told
me the story the night he got to the Cottage. After lights out, Jodi
let us plug the Christmas lights in for a few minutes and talk, and
William was excited about the fact that no one had much sympathy for Aaron. "They were all like, 'Think of what you've put that
poor kid William through. All this time, he's been living with that
fib, and you're the adult, and you're blah-blah-blah.' The whole
fucking faculty," William said, "was blaming that poor fuck for
getting hit with a shovel. On his first day here. But they still more
appropriately placed me."

Everyone took William's arrival for an ominous sign. It was clear
he was going to start a fight with someone; it was just a question of
when and with whom. Jodi tried to keep things calm, but we had
all basically accepted that we wouldn't be off restriction much longer. Then one morning, for the first time since the dorm had been
allowed to rejoin campus, we were late for breakfast. We had to
pick up our food and bring it back to the Cottage to eat, and, as if
we needed anything else to upset us, when we got to the back door
of the kitchen Floyd greeted us with a big smile and said, "Well,
well, well, the bitches of the campus." And then when we were
about to leave with our food, he said, "Have a good day, boys. And
have lots of sex," which he knew students weren't allowed to do.
So things were already shitty when, for some unfathomable reason, all through breakfast Ross Salazar, who'd tried to run away a
couple of months ago as I'd watched from Dedrick's class, decided

to make them worse. Ross kept blaming Gary Gudzenko for making us late in the first place and just wouldn't shut up. And he
wasn't wrong. That morning, Gary had refused to get out of bed.

Gary could easily have passed for thirty. He was closer than anyone else at the school to being a professional criminal. That didn't
simply mean that he came to violence more easily than the rest of
us, including William, although he did; it also meant that he didn't
take things personally. He'd been sent to the school for stealing
cars, and he was there as a condition of his probation. He passed
time at the school the way a convict might pass time in prison: he
laughed easily, defended himself when he had to, and otherwise
simply waited out his sentence. I liked Gary a lot. He was stupid
but almost never started a fight.

Gary hadn't wanted to get out of bed that morning, and neither Ross Salazar's warnings about getting put on restriction nor
Han Quek's insistence that he was hungry meant much to Gary.
Ross continued to hammer away at him over breakfast, when it
was clear even as Gary was sitting at the table that he would still
rather be in bed. After Gary finished his waffles, he reached across
the table and flicked Ross's nose. Ross shut up immediately. Gary
flicked him again. Ross was holding back tears. Then William got
up, left the kitchen, and returned carrying a closet rod from one of
the wardrobes in the bedroom.

I don't even know if he managed to hit Gary three times before
Gary got the closet rod away from him and went to work. It was
upsetting. It was like William had broken some sort of code that
only Gary understood, and Gary calmly went about beating the
hell out of him. He might even have been smiling. I stood perfectly still, like I was paralyzed or scared that if I moved he might
notice me. When I told my therapist Frances about this later, she
asked, "Have you reacted that way in other stressful situations?"
Which was a good question, but I hadn't really seen anything like

that before. I knew that Ross paged Roger and then called the phone in the Cafetorium. I heard him tell whoever answered to send as many people as possible.

At some point I revived enough to run to the opposite side of the couch from where William and Gary were. From that point on, I kept the couch between me and them, circling slowly as they moved and then as Jodi and the rest of the dorm struggled to get Gary onto the carpet. Roger arrived and helped take Gary down. Then through the window I saw Aaron and a number of boys from Regular Kids sprinting from the Cafetorium. A few of the boys tripped and fell at a dip in the lawn, but Aaron kept his feet. He seemed elated, surprised to suddenly be at the head of the pack, running across the grass still wet with dew.

Roger and Jodi, with the help of Han Quek, held Gary down on the floor. Aaron slammed into the front door of the Cottage before opening it and coming in. He leaned over, hands on his knees, and tried to catch his breath as the Regular Kids entered and kneeled on either side of Gary, who was now calmly lying there, looking at the ceiling. Jodi went to the med closet and came back with two bottles that she placed on the floor.

William was jumping up and down, shouting. "Make him take it," he said, "he has to. You've got to make him." William's face was scraped and bruised. He was bleeding badly from a cut over one eyebrow, and part of his mouth was swollen. But he seemed happy, shouting and smiling, occasionally wiping blood out of his eye or off his lips. His bright blond hair was damp and stuck to his forehead. I was amazed to see him jumping up and down after the job Gary had done on him. William was holding his side. He showed me the bruises later. His T-shirt was stretched out of shape, one sleeve torn off at the shoulder.

Jodi saw Aaron and said, "Could you go get a couple of med cups from the kitchen and fill one of them with water."

Aaron nodded. "One with water."

"Yeah."

Aaron stood up straight. He found the sleeve of little paper cups on the kitchen counter. He took two, filled one with water from the sink, and then put them down next to Jodi.

"You can't give me anything," Gary said. "I'm completely calm."

"Are you going to stay calm?" Jodi asked.

"No, I'm going to pound the shit out of that little shit."

"Then we can give you your Thorazine. And if you don't take it, we'll force it."

"You can't force meds on a perfectly calm person," Gary said.

"If you take the pills, we won't have to."

"Fuck you."

Jodi shrugged. Resting upside down on top of one of the bottles she had brought from the med closet was a plastic measuring cup. She measured out a dose of liquid Thorazine and poured it into the empty cup Aaron had placed beside her. She pinched Gary's nose shut. Gary grunted and tried to twist out of the restraint. He was almost able to turn onto his side before the boys pushed him back down.

"You're going to take Thorazine one way or another," Roger told him. "Either calm down and take the pills or Jodi's going to pour that down your throat. And you know how awful it tastes. It's your choice."

Gary said through clenched teeth, "Fuck you. I was perfectly calm before you brought that stuff out here. And I was perfectly calm before that skinny little faggot attacked me with a fucking closet rod. And I swear to fucking god that I will kill you if you force that shit on me. I need to request it if—." In the middle of his speech, Jodi tried to pour the Thorazine into Gary's mouth, but most of it spilled across his cheek. Gary winced and spat over and over.

"Ha-ha, you stupid fucker," William shouted, leaning on Aaron's shoulder. "How's that taste, you dumb motherfucker?"

Jodi twisted to look up at Aaron. She looked exhausted. "Could you pour another dose in this cup? And get William out of here."

Aaron picked up the bottle and poured some more Thorazine into the cup, but by that point, Gary had agreed to take the pills. Aaron put the cup down by Roger and led William to the corner of the room.

He sat him down in a plastic chair and asked what had happened. William told him about taking the closet rod out of his wardrobe. "He's so much bigger, it was my only chance," William said. "He actually started it. He flicked Ross. Twice." The adrenaline had worn off and he looked a little frightened. There was blood in his teeth.

Roger sat on the floor with Gary until the Thorazine kicked in. Then he led him to a chair in another corner, across the room from William. He told New Boys to clean up the dorm. Aaron noticed that Jodi had the closet rod sticking out of her back pocket. The Regular Kids left to go to class.

"So William just went at him?" Aaron asked Jodi, not knowing what to say.

"Yeah." Jodi shook her head. "That kid loves getting himself beat up."

Aaron laughed. "Maybe we should put him on a structure where if he does what he's supposed to, he gets a punch in the gut. You hear that, William?" he called. "If you keep acting out, no more punches." Suddenly unsure whether that was an appropriate thing to say, he smiled vaguely at Jodi. Aaron had developed a strategy for dealing with all the inscrutable issues that came up over the course of a day. There were so many rules and concepts, and everyone had strong opinions about everything. So Aaron maintained a persistent amusement. A haze of fun permeated his reactions to everything he heard and colored everything he said. This way, if he misunderstood or said something wrong, misused a term or offended someone, there was nothing he couldn't easily qualify, treat as a joke, and backpedal away from.

There was a white blur in the back of the room, and when I turned I saw that William had bolted from his corner and was raining punches down on Gary. Gary was trying to bat him away, but the Thorazine made him too slow. It was kind of amazing. It took Aaron, Roger, and Jodi to pull William off of Gary. Aaron held him around the stomach and lifted while Jodi and Roger pried open William's hands, which were grabbing at Gary's hair and face. As they finally dragged him off, William got a good kick at the back of Gary's head.

Aaron tossed William back into his chair, and Jodi told him to stay there. Aaron wiped off some of William's blood, which had gotten on his neck.

"Eww, what the—," someone said from behind them.

We all turned to see Han looking down at a paper cup in his hand. He looked up at Aaron and Jodi.

"Han, don't you goddamn tell me you just took Gary's dose of Thorazine," Jodi said.

Han kept working his tongue in and out of his mouth. "I thought it was a cup of water for his pills," he said.

"Bullshit you did, you little liar," Roger said. "Shit." He stared at Han for a long while. "It's not even worth arguing with you about it now. Go lie down someplace. But you're in a truckload of trouble once that stuff wears off."

Han Quek sat down on the floor where he was. When Aaron and Roger left, he was lying on his back on the torn wool carpet, his knees raised to his chest. He rolled from side to side, waving his hands slowly in front of his face and watching the traces.

▪ ▪ ▪

**Aaron wasn't sure** just where to go when he left the Cottage. He wandered into the Classroom Building's atrium, where he heard the teachers in their lounge. Aaron peered in. They were all looking out the window in the back of the room. He walked over to where they were standing and tried to see, over their shoulders, what they were looking at.

"What is it?" he asked.

Dedrick turned and told him, "An owl. Up there, on the electrical wires."

"There must be something wrong with it," Brenda said, "to be out during the day."

Aaron leaned down and looked up to try to see the owl, but he couldn't. He left the Teachers' Lounge and the Classroom Building, stepped outside, and with his hands thrust deep in his pockets walked around to the back of the building. As he rounded the corner he saw the owl sitting perfectly still on the black wires. Aaron took a few steps closer and looked up at it. It was light brown with a white, heart-shaped face.

Aaron must have been aware that the teachers were somewhere behind him, watching him look up at the owl, but after what he had seen this morning in New Boys he felt he had the right to stand here, singled out. The teachers didn't know about the fight yet, but they would hear about it later, and they would understand why Aaron had needed to take a step outside. He thought they might be impressed that he hadn't felt the need to tell them about it immediately. He thought they might notice that he seemed different.

Aaron took a step closer. The bird stirred. It flew to a spot on the wires a little farther from him. Aaron followed deliberately, away from the Classroom Building and the teachers. He tried to think about the owl, about whether it was sick or if it felt confused to be out in the daylight. But his thoughts kept turning to himself and to us boys. There was something primitive about what we had been doing to ourselves and one another. Each one of us, Aaron thought, was doing the very first thing that came into his head. He looked over his shoulder, back at the Classroom Building, which was a way behind him now. Then the owl took off again and flew farther than Aaron could follow it, and when he got tired of standing out there he turned and went inside.

**Doris made her** way down to New Boys' Cottage carrying an armload of phonics workbooks. It had rained that morning, and the warm air smelled of wet pavement. Doris was careful and stopped to rest frequently. She thought of the novel she had just been reading. There was a woman in it who was obese and who walked with a cane. Doris had never read a book with a character who in any way resembled herself, and it had come as quite a shock. Doris couldn't help imagining herself in the role of this character, whose name was Eunice and who was rich and lived in Morocco. She drank gin all day and hired a young Moroccan prostitute to be her companion. Usually Doris preferred scotch, but making her way down to the Cottage she would have loved a glass of gin.

Doris hadn't liked how the book ended. Eunice had been by far the most interesting character, but she had disappeared from the story about halfway through. It was strange, Doris thought, how the story just dropped her and moved on. Doris arrived at the Cottage. Jodi let her in, and Doris sat down to catch her breath.

While we finished the breakfast dishes Doris went through the workbooks she had with her. The previous day's fight had ended our brief sojourn on campus, and New Boys were once again on restriction. It was surprising, though, how quickly things were calm again. Doris had work from the other teachers to hand out to us and a checklist of homework she was supposed to collect. For herself, she was going to spend the period working with Han

Quek and Gary Gudzenko on their English. She looked forward to her sessions with them. Supervising the teachers and assisting Aubrey was baffling and exhausting work, but the Cottage was quiet and she was confident that she could help the two boys read.

Jodi told Doris that we just had to use the bathroom and then we would get to work.

"Fine, fine."

"And I'm going to leave you with them for a while again. That's not a problem, is it? You know there was an incident yesterday." Jodi was neatening up the bookshelves and not paying much attention.

"These boys? No problem at all," Doris said and laughed. "They're good boys." Doris knew we weren't entirely good boys, but she had never had any problems with us. She always told us she thought we were one of the most pleasant dorms to be with. Doris "enjoyed our society" was how she put it. That seemed a bit generous to me, but I knew what she meant. The intricate rules of the dorm, enforced by Jodi, somehow took the place of formal manners so that there really was something old-fashioned and polite about how we behaved with her and with one another. Not always, but sometimes.

In the bathroom, we took turns, four of us sitting in the doorway while the rotating fifth used the toilet. This way we were technically still grouped since we were all in the same room. When I had my turn, I took my time. Those were the only moments of the day I could be almost alone. The toilet was next to a window; I leaned my elbows on my knees and watched the pink-striped curtains move in the breeze from an air vent in the floor. In that morning's meeting, Jodi had tried to get William and Gary to talk about what happened the day before. She was wearing her Phoenix Suns hat, which she once told me was her favorite. She asked whether William had any resentments or if it had scared Gary to see how easily he could hurt someone. But they said they were fine, and they really did seem to be, so Jodi dropped it.

That was what I liked about New Boys. Maybe that's why I had let myself get sent down. In Alternative Boys, they were always trying to get me to talk in meetings and to begin following the process. It's not that I had any secrets; I just didn't have anything to talk about. And thinking about myself that way made me uncomfortable. I didn't like the feeling of separating myself in two: the Benjamin who was doing the thinking and the Benjamin that was being thought about. It made my head fuzzy and reminded me of the way I used to think about killing myself. Me killing myself. The made-up song I hummed to myself when I used to think about it: *You go first, I'll follow you, I'll go first, you follow me.*

In New Boys, Jodi's only concern was with keeping us from getting violent or running away. No one bothered much about what I was or wasn't thinking. For a moment the vent blew the pink curtains aside, and I saw two birds pecking at a squirrel that had gotten onto the bird feeder outside the window.

We finished in the bathroom. Han chased Ross around the living room with an open plastic garbage bag, threatening to catch him in it. "But see how well behaved you are," Doris said. "When Jodi told you to stop, you stopped. And apologized."

We took our school things from the shelves and got to work. We said good-bye to Jodi. Doris handed out the work the other teachers had sent down and realized that she had nothing for me and nothing for William, because he had just been moved down to New Boys.

Doris told us that for that period we could just read books. Gary had a copy of *The Decameron* from Dedrick's Cooking with Butter class, but William wanted to read that. I took Ross's *Daniel Deronda*, which he'd been assigned because he'd been at the school so long that he'd finished all his academics and no one knew what else to do with him. Doris said she would talk to my teachers about making sure they sent assignments to the Cottage.

Han and Gary sat down with Doris, and they spent some time talking. There was some sort of mix-up that led to Doris working with the boys on English as a second language. While it was true that Han and Gary had each spoken another language before learning English, they both spoke English as well as any of the other students at the school. Which meant far from perfectly but much better than Doris believed. They were happy to play along until they were found out and forced to do something more challenging than phonics worksheets.

Doris asked Han how he was adjusting to his move down from Alternative Boys. Did he regret trying to run away? She asked if he was making friends with the other boys. Then she asked Gary if he was helping Han. How was he helping?

They did some reading work next, which went fine until Doris chose to work on some irregularly spelled words. Han got stuck, or rather he pretended to, on "iron."

"No, I know it looks like it would be pronounced 'i-ron,' but it's an irregularly spelled word. We say 'i-urn.'"

"I-ron."

"I-urn."

"I-ron."

"Can you help him, Gary?"

Gary moved his finger under the word slowly. "I-ron," he said.

A bird flew into the Cottage through the window. It was just a shadow flickering in the corner of Doris's eye until Ross jumped off the couch screaming.

We all jumped up and began running around, some of us away from the bird and some trying to catch it. William had a broom and was swinging it through the air. I grabbed the garbage bag Han had been chasing Ross with and held it open.

Doris sat where she was and told us to calm down, though she was not remotely calm. She had picked up her cane and was holding it tightly. The Cottage had low ceilings, and the bird was flying into walls. If it came at her she could hardly move out of its way in time. "Boys, listen to me," she called again and again. Finally we did. "Everyone sit down a minute. Let the bird rest."

We sat down, and soon the bird alighted on top of the bookshelf, its head twitching.

"Good, now quietly open all the windows."

"More birds'll fly in!" Ross said.

Doris shook her head. "No more birds will fly in, Ross, I promise. Now open them." She pointed with her cane. She was less sure of her next idea, but she was enjoying the sense of authority we had granted her. "Now let's prop open the front door and do the rest of schooltime on the porch." She stood up. "Will someone please carry my chair? Take your work." Doris stood aside as we collected our things and dragged chairs out onto the small porch. It was cool outside, but the sun was shining. I read to myself from *Daniel Deronda*, and William read *The Decameron*. Han and Gary filled out phonics worksheets. Ross was drawing with colored pencils. From time to time we heard the bird moving around the Cottage. Doris looked around and enjoyed the breeze, and before too long the bird flew out the door, over our shoulders, and into one of the pines across the gravel road.

When she walked back to the Classroom Building, enjoying a well-earned sense of exhaustion, Doris said out loud to herself, "No one ever said it would be easy." But at the same time she was glad. We had had a little fun.

# 10

**A**ubrey had been away for a few days and had missed the meeting where New Girls announced that they had cornered Tidbit for the painting incident in Expressions. During the first Campus Community meeting he attended once he returned, he made them take it back. "I don't understand why you're always so eager to put everyone in the corner," he said. He wore a black turtleneck sweater tucked into gray pants that were belted high around his paunch.

"Every time anything happens around here," Aubrey said, "someone ends up in the corner. I have no idea where that comes from."

Marcy hurried to explain herself. "Tidbit knows the rules," she said. "She sliced up a painting, which is campus property, and destroying property is violence. Tidbit knows the consequences for breaking the rules. She's the one who made the decision to act out. We can't send her to another dorm because we're the lowest functioning girls' dorm, but my girls don't have to be scared that they're going to be attacked every time they confront—"

"Those are just arguments. This school is not a place!" Aubrey slapped his hand against his armrest. "That's one of the things I'll be talking about to the new parents on Parents' Sunday in a couple of weeks. Roaring Orchards is not a place. It's a *series* of places. That's what makes it different from other schools and hospitals.

We assign students to different places on campus based on where they need to be. Tidbit is in New Girls because she demonstrated to us that she needed to act out. So we put her in a place to do that. And now that she does it you want to punish her? It doesn't make any sense."

"I'm not sure I understand what you want me to do," Marcy said. "Shouldn't there be any consequences for Tidbit? She destroyed her painting, and she had to be held down for ten minutes before she was calm enough to be let up. What are we supposed to do?"

"That's an honest question," Aubrey said, "and the honest answer is that I don't entirely know." He looked around the circle. "But she's had her chance to act out, and I think she's done enough, so I'm going to move her up into Alternative Girls."

There was some grumbling from Alternative Girls.

"What about Laurel Pfaff?" Aubrey asked. "Isn't she in that class as well?" He had turned his attention to a plastic container of yogurt he was eating.

"Laurel Pfaff?" Marcy asked. "She wasn't really involved in this."

"Well, that's part of the problem, isn't it?" Aubrey said. He looked down at Laurel, sitting on the floor. "How long have you been here, Laurel?"

"About four years," she said quietly.

"What's that?"

"Four years," she said, louder this time.

"And you're embarrassed about that?"

"A little."

"Bullshit," Aubrey said, eating a spoonful of yogurt. Everyone waited as he swallowed. "You're completely humiliated, aren't you? And maybe you should be. To still be in New Girls after all this time? Girls who you think are so inferior to you come here, move up, graduate, and you're still where you were."

Laurel nodded. She looked at the floor and her back shook.

"Well, you're not going to go anywhere until you get used to the idea that *you're not better than them!* Do you understand that?"

Laurel nodded again.

"Now, what about the letters you were going to write me?"

Laurel looked up. "I wrote them," she said.

"Well, are they not getting sent? Because I only got two."

"No, I wrote two, but I thought . . ."

Aubrey turned to the rest of the room. He put his container of food down on his armrest. "A couple of months ago, almost a year ago now, Laurel sent me a letter asking for help. She was very frustrated that she wasn't moving along through the school, her dorm mates had begun referring to her by a nickname that she didn't like." He raised his eyebrows. Students around the room giggled. "A nickname I won't mention since I'm the one who popped it. And so on. I was very impressed by your letter, Laurel, as I told you at the time. I was moved that you thought of me when you wanted help. So I sat down with Miss Pfaff and we talked about how she could move ahead. And I put her on a structure where she would write me a letter each week telling me whatever she wanted to tell me. And I got two letters."

"No, you just said to write anytime I needed to, not every week."

The room was quiet. "So I'm lying about this?"

"No," Laurel said. "No." She paused. "I just don't remember you saying to write you every week. I thought it was just when I wanted to write. I misunderstood."

"You misunderstood."

"Uh-huh."

"You thought that I just wanted you to write whenever you felt like it, and I'd be there when you needed." He waited for an answer, leaning out of his chair toward Laurel.

"Well, kind of." She was crying.

"Does that sound like the sort of arrangement I'd make with a student, Laurel? Especially with a student as perpetually manipulative and selfish as you?"

"No."

"But that's still how you *remember* it?"

"Well—"

"Good. At least that's honest." He sat back in his armchair and picked up his breakfast. "The next step is for you to remember our conversation correctly. Marcy, I want Laurel to stay in her room until she better remembers our talk. Then she can figure out what she wants to do about it."

"She's roomed?" Marcy asked.

"Correct. Next."

Aubrey went around the rest of the room quickly. When he got to Aaron, Aubrey asked to be reminded of his name.

"Aaron," Aaron said.

"And how are things going, Aaron?"

"Fine."

"Good. Don't steal any of my suits."

Before everyone left, there was a story that Aubrey wanted to tell. More and more lately, he said, he had to go to the bathroom in the middle of the night. "Two times, three times, four times a night," he said. And it was strange, he told us, waking up so many times. It began to make the line between sleeping and waking less clear, especially since some of his dreams were now about waking up to pee. He was animated and smiling through this performance, encouraging the faculty members and students to all laugh along with him at the ridiculousness of his situation.

"And last night," he said, his voice rising to a hilarious pitch, "at one point I actually fell asleep on the toilet. Because when you have to wake up to pee four or five times a night, you start to pee sitting down. And of course the only thing that eventually woke me up was that I had to go to the bathroom again! But because I didn't realize that I was already in the bathroom, I walked back to my bedroom and figured out where I was just in time!" The room was roaring with laughter.

"But it made me realize something very strange," he said through his own laughter. "We say 'going to the bathroom,' but where is it we're going? I mean, you say you need to go to the bathroom. So you walk into a particular room called the bathroom. But even once you're in the bathroom, you still need to go to the bathroom. And even when you're doing what you do, you're *still going* to the bathroom. And when you're done, you've gone to the bathroom. But you're never there. It's like a place you're always going toward, but you never get to. And then you claim to have returned from where you never were. I'd never thought of this before."

And though the students laughed at his story, what we understood was that Aubrey was sick and that he wouldn't be with us much longer. Somehow he had felt that telling this story would hide rather than expose the fact that he was dying, but we all understood right away. Even if we didn't know that we knew, even if we would have reacted with some disbelief had someone told us *Aubrey is going to die*, at some level it would have accorded with what we now understood. Aubrey hadn't meant to say anything because he didn't want his students to worry. But we didn't worry. We just knew.

# PART TWO

## Down the long green hill

# 1

**P**arents' Sunday was dreaded as much as it was anxiously awaited. Everyone had a scheme, whether it was to convince our parents that the school's program wouldn't work for us or that it had already worked so well that we could safely return home or some equally transparent ploy. All these plans invariably melted away in the face of the physical presence of our parents themselves.

Laurel Pfaff stood at the window of her room, as she had for much of the past two weeks. It was a late autumn day, and the trees clustered across the broad hills on the opposite side of the valley were bright with dying leaves. Marcy usually came in at some point in the morning to make sure that she was awake and out of bed, but Laurel was sure she had other things to worry about today and didn't expect her.

The first week she was roomed, Laurel had schoolwork to keep her busy, but when she hadn't made any progress Marcy began taking away distractions. First her journal, then her schoolwork, and finally any contact with other members of the dorm. Now Laurel only saw Marcy when she brought meals, and her therapist once a week. Occasionally, other staff members passing through the dorm would stop in to check on her, but Laurel had begun to realize that people were forgetting she was there. Three times already, Marcy had forgotten to bring her a meal, and Laurel had to wait until Marcy returned to the dorm to remind her.

Laurel looked out at the cars lining up at the school gates for Parents' Sunday. She had already seen the cars of the new parents roll onto campus a couple of hours ago for the New Parent Orientation. The other parents' cars were outside the gates along the shoulder of Route 294, waiting for ten o'clock when they would be allowed onto campus. Any parents spotted on campus before ten would be sent away immediately. Laurel's watch was in the other room with her things, so she couldn't tell how much longer they would have to wait. It was disorienting, never knowing what time it was.

Laurel was restricted to her room whether or not her parents showed up, but she hadn't been able to find out if they were planning to come. She didn't even know if they had been told that she'd had been roomed for the past two weeks. Laurel had wanted to write to tell them, but by the time she thought of it Marcy had taken her things away.

The cars outside the gates began honking, and Laurel knew it was almost ten. A few moments before they could drive onto campus each Parents' Sunday, the excited parents all began to honk their horns. After half a minute of honking the cars began to pull forward through the gates. The line continued, rolling slowly on its way to the Mansion. Laurel looked carefully for her mother's car as the parade moved along. But then, her mother was always late.

Tidbit's mother, on the other hand, was on time. She parked along the shoulder, outside the gates, and checked on a cat asleep on the backseat before getting out of her car. She walked past the gates, brushing aside wisps of long gray hair that the wind had blown across her face. She passed beat-up sedans and new SUVs, with parents getting out alone or in pairs, some with siblings of their Roaring Orchards students, some without.

She walked up the stone steps and into the Mansion. Doris was greeting parents and offering refreshments, but Ms. Lasker headed straight through the Great Hall and up the stairs, familiar enough with the complicated path to New Girls' dorm that she ignored the handwritten signs posted to direct parents through the building. She jogged up the stairs, watching her step, and when she got to the lounge she was surprised to find out that Tidbit had moved up to Alternative Girls.

When she made her way there, Tidbit was waiting for her. She hugged her tightly.

"What'd you bring me?" Tidbit asked, pointing to a small brown bag in her mother's hand.

"Oh," she said, looking down at the bag, which was folded at the top. "This is for you. I didn't know you got moved up. That's great." She handed the bag to Tidbit.

"Candy!" she said, looking into it. "Really good candy. You went all the way by the mall."

Her mother mussed her hair. "Short," she said.

"My hair or me?"

"Both."

Tidbit turned to her mother. "Did you bring Fatface?" she asked.

"He's in the car."

"Hold on." Tidbit went and found June, who was covering Alternative Girls, to tell her she was going out. She put on her shoes. When Tidbit returned, her mom was speaking with the parents of one of the other Alternative Girls. Tidbit held out the bag of candy and asked, "Do you want anything from in here?"

"Sour peach," her mom said, taking the bag. She took a candy from inside and offered the bag to the couple.

"Are there any of those candy corns?" the man asked. He had a loose face that was marbled red like a beefsteak.

"No, I don't think I got any candy corns."

"Aw, hell," he said, leaning over and looking into the bag. "Give me one of those strawberries."

"Let's go see my Fatface," Tidbit said, kneeling down to tie her sneaker. Although neither Tidbit nor her mother would have admitted it, they both knew that the best part of their visit had just passed. Only their anticipation was perfect, and they understood each other well enough to see, with equal parts relief and disappointment, that nothing much had changed. Ms. Lasker put the bag of candy in her purse and fixed her purse on her shoulder. It pained her to see Tidbit trying so hard, to hear the dead spot in her voice while she was trying to sound chipper.

Once they had exited the Mansion, Tidbit stopped suddenly. "Wait," she said, "I just thought of something. I can't go off campus because I'm on Reciprocity Detail. And pets aren't allowed on campus."

Her mother looked down at her. "Can you play with him by the fence?"

"Yeah, I guess that'll work." They walked down the lawn to where the car was parked. Tidbit stayed on the near side of the fence.

"I'll get him," her mom said.

"I can't wait to see him," Tidbit said.

Her mother followed the fence to the gate and got the cat out of the car. She brought him to the fence opposite Tidbit and put him down. Fatface rubbed his cheek against his shoulder a few times, then lay down, stretched, and showed her his belly. Tidbit reached through the fence and petted him.

They played like this for a while. Tidbit's mother had brought one of Fatface's toys, a plastic wand with a little stuffed pillow tied to the end of a string. Tidbit leaned over the fence and swung the pillow back and forth, and Fatface jumped to chase it. The pillow had a little bell hidden in it. Tidbit's mother watched them play. A breeze lifted some fallen leaves and then dropped them where they had been.

Laurel continued to watch through the window for her parents. She was hoping that they weren't planning to come this Sunday, but of course as soon as she thought that, she saw their Mercedes wagon pull through the gates. She couldn't see where it parked, so she just sat down on her bed and waited.

A few minutes later, a tall woman with long chestnut hair, wearing black slacks and a gray sweater, entered the Mansion. She held her purse tightly to her front. "Excuse me," she said to Doris. "Hello." She smiled and paused for a moment, expecting to speak with her, but when Doris turned to welcome other parents, Mrs. Pfaff began following the signs up the stairs to New Girls. She entered the dorm by the kitchenette and walked into the lounge, looking around uncertainly. Families were sitting together on the couches or standing around and talking, and after circling through the lounge twice, she found Marcy and said, "Excuse me, I'm looking for Laurel?"

"Oh, Mrs. Pfaff. Hi. I wasn't sure whether you were coming or . . ." Marcy always tried to look as busy as she could on Parents' Sundays so she wouldn't have to make any small talk. Parents made her nervous. A pink coral pin Mrs. Pfaff was wearing caught her eye. This was the conversation she had most been dreading. "I tried to call, but I couldn't get in touch with you."

"Oh? I must not have gotten the message. Did you leave a message?"

"Well, what I meant was that I tried to get a chance to call, but I didn't find the—"

"Is something wrong with Laurel? Where is she?"

"No, no, Laurel's fine. But she's roomed right now. Restricted, that is, to her room. That's what I had wanted to call to tell you about. Of course, you're welcome to have a short visit with her, but she's really not supposed to be spending time with people right now. Of course, she sees her therapist, and I give her her meals and meds, but other than that. She's restricted. To her room. So she has time to think."

"She's in her room?" Mrs. Pfaff said, blinking. "What? You mean right now? Or all the time?" She tucked her hair behind her ear, exposing a tiny earring. "What did she do?"

"Well, Aubrey had put her on a structure where she was supposed to write him letters and she said she didn't remember—"

"She's roomed for not writing him letters?"

"It wasn't so much the not writing as not remembering what Aubrey had said. She said he had said something different."

"I don't think I understand." Mrs. Pfaff looked at her.

For a moment, Marcy must have wished she were a little more like Mrs. Pfaff. It was as if all she had to do was imagine the world the way she assumed it must be and blink her bright eyes, and no one would tell her anything different.

"The rooming," Marcy said, "was Aubrey's limit. Because when he reminded her that he had told her to write him once a week, I think it was, she said he had never said that. And then she said she didn't *remember* him saying that. So Aubrey told her to stay in her room until she could remember their conversation."

"And how long ago was this?"

"About two weeks."

Mrs. Pfaff felt a brief swell of vertigo, then settled again more firmly on her feet. "You can't be serious. That's unacceptable. If she doesn't remember, how is leaving her in her room going to help her remember? I'm not paying tuition so that my daughter can be locked up staring at the walls. I could do that at home."

"Mrs. Pfaff, I—"

"No, I'm going to need to speak with Aubrey about this. Where is he?"

"Aubrey?" Marcy had to think for a second. "I think he's still in the New Parent Orientation. Downstairs, in the Reception Room."

"I'd like to see Laurel first." She was breathing deeply now, her chin tilted up a bit.

"She's right down the hall," Marcy said, glad to have survived this part of her day. She led the way. They found Laurel sitting on her bed, staring at her bare feet. Her mother ran in and gave her a hug, kneeling beside her.

"Sweetie, are you all right?" Mrs. Pfaff ran her thumb across Laurel's face where a tear would have been if she had been crying.

"I'm fine," Laurel said, looking at Marcy and then back at her mother. "Where's Dad?"

"Julie's soccer team had a game in Lakeville he had to take her to. Laurel, why are you letting them keep you in here? Why don't you just remember what Aubrey told you?"

"I'm trying to remember it, but I haven't been able to yet. Sometimes I think I'm getting pretty close, but other times it feels like the memory's getting fuzzier and farther away. It's hard, but I'll get it, Mom. Don't cry."

Marcy left them there and headed back to the lounge to see about the rest of the girls and to sneak into her apartment for a while if she could. At the end of the hallway, she ran into Bridget and her parents. Bridget's younger brother was with them Her father was a short, blurry man with red cheeks like Bridget's and only a small bit of dark hair left on his head. Her mother was taller and thickset, with hair that might once have been the color of Bridget's in a long braid down her back.

"Hello, Marcy!" Bridget's mother began. "Bridget says the girls have decided to let her off campus today. Is that right?"

"It is," Marcy said, happy to give someone good news. "She's been taking good care of herself, and the rest of the dorm decided that she's earned their trust to go off campus." Marcy looked at Bridget's father, who seemed skeptical.

"So what's the rules?" he asked.

"We know the rules," his wife told him. "Now, it's okay for us to take Bridget to buy some clothes? She says she needs clothes, and I want to get her a haircut." She grabbed a handful of Bridget's hair and lifted it, as if to convince Marcy.

"Shopping's fine," Marcy said, "but the girls get haircuts on campus. The point is for all of you to have a nice afternoon together. So you can go for lunch, do some shopping, go for a walk, whatever you like. One of you has just got to be within arms' distance of Bridget at all times, and she's not supposed to go back to your hotel room."

Bridget's father nodded through all of this while her mother beamed at Bridget, one hand on her shoulder. Bridget's brother watched Marcy as she talked. He looked terrified.

After Bridget's family left, Marcy had a few moments to herself. The girls whose parents hadn't come were sitting quietly in the lounge. Marcy pretended to rearrange books in the bookcase and was about to head into her own room when Mrs. Pfaff returned.

"You know, she's really very upset," she said, "and I can't say I blame her. She doesn't like to show it, but still. A person would go crazy sitting alone in a room like that."

"Laurel's not going crazy," Marcy said.

"No, she's not. I agree with you there, she's certainly not. Now, I'm going to speak to Aubrey about this, even though Laurel asked me not to. She was afraid it would make things worse."

"No, I think talking to Aubrey would be a very good idea. I don't see how things could get worse." Mrs. Pfaff narrowed her eyes slightly. "What I mean is, I'm sure that Laurel wouldn't be punished for your speaking with him about this."

"Yes, well, I should hope not."

**In the Great** Hall there were large flower vases full of orange and violet lilies. Refreshments were being set out by the parents who usually helped on Parents' Sundays, some of them parents of former students who had graduated from Roaring Orchards, some the parents of children who had run away from the school and were still missing.

I was sitting at a table in the Great Hall with the other students whose parents were in the orientation. We hadn't seen our parents yet; the orientation had begun before we were sent down to the Great Hall. Tyler from Regular Kids was watching us. He sat sideways in an armchair, his legs dangling over one of the arms, and flipped through a glossy magazine. We just waited and wondered what Aubrey was telling our parents.

Mrs. Pfaff came down the stairs and smiled at Tyler. He asked if he could help her with anything.

"I'm just waiting to speak with Aubrey," she said.

"He's still in the orientation. They should be almost done. You're welcome to go in if you'd like."

Mrs. Pfaff decided that she would. Tyler's eyes lingered over her as she turned away and pushed back one of the doors to the Reception Room. She squeezed into the room and took a seat toward the back as quietly as she could. With the door open, I could see a bit of the room and hear what was going on inside. Aubrey was speaking from a large armchair in a front corner of the room to about a dozen parents, who sat on couches and chairs arranged to face him. He leaned back in the chair and crossed his legs. He was wearing a light gray suit, a green sweater, and no socks.

"The point I'm trying to make," he said, "is that in most of

your families, the child that you've sent to us was the most powerful member of the family. Which was a problem for you, but it
was an even bigger problem for your child. Because what a child
wants is to be a child, and what does it mean to be a child? To have
limits. And too often in your families, your children were denied
the opportunity to be children, because you didn't set those limits.

"And what we do here is as simple as that. We set limits, and
we hold your children to them, we hold them responsible. Think
about that phrase for a moment: 'hold them responsible.'" Aubrey
was up on his feet now, pacing back and forth across the front of
the room from the armchair in one corner to a baby-grand piano
in the other. With his arms he made a cradling gesture. "Why do
you think that's how we say it? Because that's what your problem
children have been craving, being held, being held responsible.

"You know, when pupils here get violent, when they try to
hurt themselves or someone else, we have a structure that we call
a wiggle. I recently got into an argument with another faculty
member who was confusing restraints with wiggles. A restraint is
an emergency response that simply serves to keep a student from
hurting herself or others. But rather than simply restrain a pupil, in
a wiggle we use their energy as an opportunity. 'Wiggle' stands for
a 'wonderful invitation to grow and gain a limiting experience.'
Because that's what children are asking for when they act out.
They're asking to be limited. There's nothing scarier for a child
than feeling all-powerful. So in a wiggle we hold them, and keep
them safe, and talk to them about what they're feeling." Squares of
light shone through the windows on the north side of the Reception Room and fell at Aubrey's feet.

"Now you should all notice, too—I expect that by now you all
have noticed—that when the most powerful, dominant member
of your family is sent away, this also creates a problem for you
at home. There's a void, and the impulse is to see that void as a

problem and to fill it with worry. To worry about your child. But the void should also be an opportunity for you, to fill it with adult activities that can replace all the time you used to spend catering to childish demands. Here at Roaring Orchards, we end each Parents' Sunday with a cocktail party in the Mansion for all the parents, and it's a time for us to all enjoy being adults together. And a time to role-model adulthood for the pupils. Because it's important that they're aware that there are certain things that are appropriate for us that are not appropriate for them. And although you'll never get them to admit it, knowing this makes them feel safer."

Aubrey leaned against the piano. He pulled a handkerchief from his pocket and blew his nose. "Some of you, when you took a tour of the grounds, asked me about a fountain we have in the back garden. You know the one I mean? The top of the fountain has a statue of a large infant playing with a turtle in his lap. And I always tell parents that I'll explain it at the orientation. The statue is based on the myth of Zeus and Aliaphone." He walked to the window and looked out. "You can just make it out from here," he said, and turned back to the parents, whose eyes were trained on him intently.

"Aliaphone was a gorgeous water nymph who used to splash around in her father's pond. And Zeus, as often happens in these stories, noticed this nymph and began to pursue her. Aliaphone was young and innocent and did everything she could to evade Zeus's advances. He appeared to her in all sorts of disguises, and Aliaphone wasn't seduced by any of them. But there came a day when he had cornered her, and all she could do was call to her father for help. So her father turned her into a turtle, and whenever Zeus would try to molest her, she could now simply retreat into her shell." A man in the back of the room laughed loudly at this. Mrs. Pfaff kept watching Aubrey.

"Well, one day, a young child approached the turtle Aliaphone.

He had golden curls, and he seemed curious and friendly. Slowly, as the boy showed himself to be harmless, Aliaphone began to trust him. She came out of her shell and played with the child. But of course this was only another of Zeus's disguises, his most ingenious, and he took his chance, in the form of this infant, to have his way with Aliaphone." In the silence Aubrey stepped slowly to the center of the room, his hands clasped behind his back.

"My point," Aubrey said, "is that inside each of your children is a god." He paused, looking each of the new parents in the eye. "That's the truth. But it means we must be *more* vigilant, not less! So go out there, and enjoy the day with your children, and don't you dare let them intimidate you." Slowly the parents shook themselves loose from his spell and stood. The man who had laughed at Aubrey's story clapped his hands and smiled at the woman sitting beside him, who applauded briefly as well. Two Regular Kids pulled the doors all the way open, and Aubrey led the parents out to the refreshments.

It was the first time I'd seen my parents in about three months. I was furious and relieved. They were awkward, at once energized by Aubrey's talk and cautious toward me. My dad smiled and slapped me on the back. I gave my mother a hug. I didn't yet know she had been burned, but parts of her skin were pink and waxen, and there was a tightness to her face that let me know something was very wrong. I had planned to stay angry at them, to refuse to talk at all, but seeing them, I knew I wouldn't.

**When it was** our turn to thank Aubrey, my father told him it had been a great speech. "Really gave me food for thought," he said. He thanked Aubrey for looking after me and said he could tell just by looking that I was doing better.

"Is that true, Benjamin? Are you doing better?" Aubrey asked. It was the first time he'd spoken to me since my intake.

"Um, I don't really know."

"Well, I-don't-know is probably a good place for you to be right now. Are you planning to take your parents somewhere off campus?"

"I, I'm in New Boys—I didn't think we were allowed to leave campus."

"Oh, that's right," he said. "I'd forgotten Benjamin switched dorms. Something about an alarm clock." Aubrey turned to Mrs. Pfaff, who was standing beside us. "Mrs. Pfaff," he said, "have you met the Greihls?"

She was standing a few feet away, watching the other new students and their parents leaving the Great Hall. "No," she said, startled, "I don't believe I have."

"I'm sure you're here to speak with me about Laurel," Aubrey said.

"Actually, I am," Mrs. Pfaff said, and paused.

"We don't have any need for secrets here. I'm sure the Greihls would benefit from hearing the concerns of a parent who's been involved with the school for some time. Mrs. Pfaff's daughter Laurel," Aubrey explained to my parents, "has been restricted to her room."

"For two weeks," Mrs. Pfaff added. "If we're going to be frank, I've got to tell you, I'm a bit confused and not at all happy to hear what's been done with her."

"And why not, may I ask?"

"Because it's a waste of her time, and I don't see how sitting in a room trying to remember a conversation about writing letters—"

"Mrs. Pfaff, you're going to be unhappy with me, but I've got to tell you something. This is not about Laurel. Laurel is a liar, and a pretty good one, which is why she's here and not at home. It would make sense for Laurel to be upset about being roomed, and I imagine she is, but there's no reason as far as I

can see for you to be upset. You're not restricted to your room."
He paused. "Why do you think you're letting this make you so
unhappy?"

"Mr.—"

"Please—Aubrey." Only a few parents sat on the couches, and
the Great Hall felt enormous. I remembered my first day, running
in there from the Reception Room, shouting for my parents. Now
they were here, right in front of me, and we were politely listening
to someone else's problems.

"I'm upset, Aubrey, because she's my daughter, and she doesn't
know what to do about getting out of her room. And I'm not paying tuition for—"

"Mrs. Pfaff, I think it's much simpler than that. You're upset
because you're too closely connected to Laurel, which isn't good
for either of you. You're insulted that your daughter is being treated
like everyone else because you feel that you're special and that your
daughter must be special, too. And of course you're right. But neither of you is more special than anyone else."

"The situation you've put her in is abusive and totally unreasonable. She has to wait for her dorm parent to bring her meals, and
if they forget she doesn't get any. She told me this has happened
several times."

"Mrs. Pfaff," Aubrey said, taking her hand. He waited a moment
and raised his thick eyebrows.

"Michelle," she said.

"Michelle. If you believed for even one second a word of what
you just said, you would have taken Laurel right out of the Mansion the moment you were told she'd been roomed. Because
you're a good mother, and if you believed that Laurel was being
abused or starved, you wouldn't have left her upstairs and come
down to talk to me about it. You would have gotten her the hell
out of here as fast as you could. Am I right about that?"

Michelle stared at him. His eyes were dark, and he seemed entirely calm.

"But you didn't take her home. You left her in her room, because you know that's where she needs to be right now. You're embarrassed that that's what she needs when you see all these other children allowed to roam around campus with their families. But that's what Laurel decided. I'm sorry she did that to you, but she's the one you should be angry with, not me." Aubrey blinked. "But you came here to have a nice day," he continued. "That's a lovely pin, by the way. Is it coral?"

Michelle looked down at her pin. "Yes," she said, but she was shaking her head. "What you have to realize—"

"I don't need to realize anything," Aubrey said. He straightened the cuffs of his suit jacket. "You need to take Laurel home. If you know better than we do what she needs, then every moment she spends here is doing her a disservice. Not to mention the past four years. You know where she is. Her things are already in bags."

She wasn't going to take Laurel home, I realized, and only upon understanding this did I sense how much I'd been hoping she would. Mrs. Pfaff suddenly seemed ugly to me, an object of pity. She wasn't going to take Laurel home because she didn't want to.

"That's not what I mean," Michelle said. "It's not that I don't trust you. I'm just trying to understand—"

"It seems to me that understanding is exactly what you're trying very hard *not* to do. I'm finished talking about this. Shall I tell, um . . . Laurel's dorm parent to get her things together?"

"No."

"Good. You're here now, and there's no reason to let a beautiful day go to waste. If Laurel's trying to make sure that no one can be happy unless she is, then the best thing you can do for her is to enjoy yourself without her. Then maybe next Parents' Sunday she'll take care of herself so that she can be with you. The way

Benjamin here is set to enjoy the day with his parents. Wouldn't it be nice to know that that was something she worked for, rather than something she made you work for?"

Michelle sighed, defeated, and tucked a damp lock of hair behind her ear. I was thrilled to find myself in such close proximity to Aubrey's philosophy. Glinting obscurely somewhere within what he'd said was a key to the secret that kept me there.

"You know what I think you'd enjoy? You're heading down to the New Boys' picnic, aren't you?" Aubrey asked my parents. They looked at me and I nodded. Aubrey called over to the parents sitting on the couch, "Cynthia, are you planning to go to the New Boys' picnic, too?"

A woman with short, curly hair twisted her head around and stood up. "Sure am," she said.

"I'd like you all to take Michelle here with you," he said, leading her by the arm toward Cynthia. "Her daughter got herself roomed for Parents' Sunday, and this lovely lady has no place to go."

"Oh, dear. I am sorry. These kids get themselves turned around every which way, they don't know what they're doing. My Ross was doing great in Regular Kids for four months before he got sent down to New Boys. I'm sure she didn't really mean to do this to you."

"Don't apologize for her, Cynthia," Aubrey said. "You and Mr. and Mrs. Greihl just take care of Michelle. And bring her back here for the cocktail party this evening. Your job is to teach your new friend to enjoy herself by the end of the night."

"Aye-aye, captain," Cynthia said. She picked up her purse and put on her jacket and led Michelle and the rest of us through the Great Hall and outside, explaining about the picnic as she went. "Now what you have to understand is that these boys are *always* on restriction. If it isn't one thing it's another, so instead of waiting until we got to campus to find out if maybe, by some miracle, they got off restriction, we just accepted that the boys were going to have to stay within fifty feet of the dorm." To our right a marshy field was crowded with weeds and cattails. An assortment of bird feeders hung from a wooden arch. "So us gals and guys put our heads together and decided we'd save time if we each brought some food and had ourselves a potluck right in the Cottage. This is three years ago, when Ross was in New Boys for the first of many, many times."

Cynthia stopped next to a neat old-model Camry and began rooting through her purse for the keys. She wore a red jacket two sizes too big. Cynthia opened the door and pulled out a large bowl covered with tinfoil.

"Potato salad," she said. "And what did you do to get sent to this fine establishment, young man?"

"You'd have to ask them," I told her, nodding toward my parents.

Cynthia laughed and said to my parents, "I really should know by now: if you want a straight answer, ask a parent; if you want denial and attitude, ask a New Boy."

When we got to the Cottage there was a gray-haired man outside placing meat on a portable grill. A woman sat on the open tailgate of a station wagon beside him. They both wore shorts and flip-flops. "Ed! Naoko!" Cynthia called, and ran over to hug them, holding the bowl of potato salad in front of her. She placed it on the tailgate, and when we caught up, Cynthia was saying, "I almost didn't recognize you!" as Naoko stood and struck a pose, one hand on a jutting hip, the other arm straight up, bent at the wrist.

"She lost ninety-three pounds," Ed said proudly. Michelle, my parents, and I were introduced to William's parents, Ed and Naoko Kay, and we all took turns shaking hands.

"He lost forty pounds, too," Naoko said, patting Ed's still substantial belly.

Thin blue smoke drifted from the barbecue, and the air was filled with the smell of grease burning off the grill. There was a slight chill, and after standing a while, shifting my weight from foot to foot in the grass, I saw New Boys approaching.

"Sorry we're late," Aaron called. "I just had the boys out clearing away some deadfall and—." He stopped to separate Ross and Han, who were slapping each other. "We'll just drop this equipment in the shoe closet and get ready for lunch. I'm Aaron." He looked each of the parents in the eye as he shook hands. The boys were all carrying tools, a couple of handsaws and an ax. Cynthia and Naoko waved to their sons, who waved back with the tools they were carrying. I was surprised that William looked embarrassed.

"You take your time, Aaron," Ed called out. I wasn't sure whether I should join the dorm or stay with my parents, so I just stood still. Michelle was looking off toward the Mansion. I thought about the conversation between her and Aubrey; I wondered if Laurel knew, the way Aubrey had, that no matter what, her mother wouldn't take her home.

"Michelle's daughter is stuck in her room," Cynthia explained to the others.

Naoko gasped and placed her hand on Michelle's arm. "That's such a shame," she said. "You know, William's a real wrecking ball, but I'm glad we don't have a girl. They can be such little bitches." She rubbed Michelle's forearm, then let go. I couldn't tell whether I heard a slight southern accent in Naoko's voice. Cynthia led us all into the Cottage, carrying the bowl of potato salad.

Inside, Han was chasing Ross around a long table carrying an open, empty garbage bag, both boys laughing. They swerved to avoid Michelle and Cynthia, who called out "Rossie!" Ross stopped, got bumped into by Han, rubbed his nose, and gave his mother a hug. William was sitting on one couch reading a paperback, and Gary was dusting a bookshelf in the back of the room. A pretty woman, heavily made up, was setting the table and singing to herself in what I thought sounded like Russian.

"Gary," she said, "come help your mama."

"Can't you see I'm doing something?" Gary said.

"His such a lazy boy."

My parents and I sat on the other couch in the living room, quietly. They looked at each other and then told me about my mother's accident. There hadn't been much permanent damage; the burns were healing well. She told me she was a little woozy from all the antibiotics she was still taking.

Cynthia introduced Michelle around. Ross took the opportunity of his mother's momentary distraction to turn and flick Han, who resumed chasing him. Han's parents hadn't come that Sunday.

"I saw that," Aaron yelled from the kitchen, which was adjacent to the living room where we all were. "Any more of that and nobody gets any potato salad," he said, and the whole room laughed. "But seriously," Aaron said, "I'll put you two in the corner, Parents' Sunday or not."

Aaron administered meds ostentatiously, as if to make sure that everyone saw that he knew what he was doing. Ed brought in a few trays of hot dogs, burgers, steaks, and sausages. Everyone was very nice. Varvara, Gary's mom, was unable to get over her amazement at Aaron's ability to spend so much time with us boys. "My Gary, his so lazy," she said many times, as if that were his biggest problem. She wore a large T-shirt with the image of a panda bear on it, decorated with rhinestones. "Your daughter," Varvara said to Michelle at one point, "she must be very beautiful."

Ed and Naoko talked at great length about how they had managed to lose the weight and seemed unable to keep their hands off each other. "Now we look like a family," they said to William.

My family was more quiet. My parents answered everyone's questions politely but didn't say much more than that.

But mostly we ate. Varvara had brought sweet potatoes and whole ears of corn that Aaron boiled in the kitchen, and there was bread and a deli platter from the school kitchen. The other boys talked and argued quietly among themselves, and the parents talked when they weren't eating, but mostly, they ate. I wondered, Don't these people realize where they are? Time seemed to pool here like still water and gently knock or tap against the living room windows, but not so anyone would notice. If this afternoon were to last forever and lunch were never to end, Ed and Naoko and Varvara and Aaron, and the rest of New Boys for all I knew, would be perfectly happy to spend eternity eating barbecue and talking about whatever it was they were talking about; I could no longer tell.

After lunch was done and the table cleared, each family found a place around the Cottage where they could talk quietly or sit sullenly and wait out the remainder of the afternoon. William and his parents sat together on a bed in our bedroom, while Varvara commandeered a couch with Gary. Cynthia and Ross went for a walk in tight circles around the Cottage. My father and I waited while my mother went to the bathroom to apply some lotion to her scars. Then we all sat at a picnic table just behind the dorm.

"You don't understand," I said. "This place is awful. They're making it look good today, but this isn't really what it's like. Some of these kids are really criminals, like Gary in there. He beat William with a closet rod. I'm scared *all* the time." I'd spent many nights thinking about exactly what I would say to them when I had the chance, but now I didn't remember what I had decided. I was just talking.

"Gary seemed very nice to me," my father said. "And you don't seem much the worse for wear."

"Well, what about that girl Laurel stuck in her room?"

"I don't know about that. But I trust Aubrey. He makes a lot of sense. And they seem to know how to take care of you here."

"They don't," I said, and pounded the picnic table for emphasis. I turned to my mother. "Why didn't you write me? I didn't get any letters from either of you."

She seemed stung. "I, we, we did write," she said.

"Well, I didn't get any letters. They must have kept your letters from me. Is that the kind of place you want me to be? Where they don't let me read your letters?" I was crying and I didn't care. "This place isn't going to do me any good. I hate it, it'll just make me worse. I promise you, it will. It's going to make me worse."

"Benjamin," my father said, "that's exactly what they told us you would say. It's what all the kids say when they get here, and a lot of them do get better."

"Just because they told you I'd say it doesn't mean it isn't true!" I pounded the picnic table again, at first to make a point but then faster and faster so that it lost all connection to what I was saying and continued into the silence that followed.

My father sighed. "Aubrey said that you'd say that, too." He put his hand on my shoulder. "Boy, have they got your number here." We sat like that for a while. "Now, I think we've got to get you back, because we're supposed to go to some kind of cocktail thing at the Mansion, isn't that right?"

"No," I said. "Let's just go home. We could just leave. Please. Take me home."

My father smiled and mussed my hair. "You're going to be all right."

When Tidbit had tired of playing with her cat, she went back to the dorm while her mother left to pick up some Chinese food. Then they went and sat in the garden together, eating noodles and fried rice under the willow by the Ornamental Pond. Talking

was never a problem for them. They talked about Tidbit's grand-
mother, about the house, about Fatface. Her mother wanted the
whole story about getting moved up to Alternative Girls, so Tidbit told her.

"It was like a gift," she said. "Even when Aubrey moved me, he
didn't say that I'd earned it. But that makes me even more feel like
I don't want to waste it, you know? I really want to make the best
of this chance." Tidbit looked over at her mother, who was leaning
back on her elbows, her long legs crossed at the ankles.

Her mother closed her eyes. "It's funny, isn't it, how all it takes
sometimes is for someone else to really believe in you?" Her head
tipped back in the sunlight.

The word "believe," coming from her mother, gave Tidbit the
shivers. When their bikes had been stolen from their garage years
ago, her mom had spray painted on their neighbors' garbage cans,
I BELIEVE, because she had been sure one of them had done it.
Another time her mom had killed Tidbit's pet snake because she
believed that they should work to love no one but God. Tidbit
came home to find her snake cut into pieces, its blood congealed in
the sand in the terrarium. At least those are the stories that Tidbit
told me.

"It isn't so much that he even believed in me," Tidbit said. "I
think it's that he was like 'I don't know if you'll be able to deal
with this or not,' and that's what makes me want to prove to him
that I can follow the process. And I have been."

"How are the other girls in the dorm?"

"They're kind of mean. Well, no, not mean, they just don't
like me much. I think they resent that they didn't get a say about
me getting into the dorm. But I'm on Reciprocity Detail all day
anyway, for slashing the painting, so I don't see them that much."

"Like what do you do for that? What kind of work?"

"It changes. I fill up the bird feeders some days and feed the animals on the Farm. About once a week I mop the rooms in the Classroom Building. It's nice to get to be alone here. That's one of the good things about Alternative Girls not liking me much. It makes it easier being honest with them in meetings. This way I can just focus on me and what I have to do for myself."

Her mother nodded. She had heard this from Tidbit before, everyone had, but she didn't mind. It was nice to hear. Tidbit would figure things out eventually. She herself had no idea anymore what Tidbit needed. Or rather, over the years she had had so many ideas, tried so many things for her that didn't work, that she no longer trusted any ideas she had.

Only when they were walking back to the Mansion did Tidbit ask her mom what she had been studying lately. Her mother's religious ambitions had mellowed since their most extreme point, though not to the level of relative normalcy she remembered from when she was little. Her mom was drawn to particularly kooky strands of Judaism. But it was what her mother most enjoyed talking about, so she asked.

Tidbit's mother had joined a new *chavurah*, she said, because the old one had gotten too traditional. From what Tidbit could gather, this meant they had acquired a building and were no longer meeting in members' living rooms. But her mom liked the new one. She was part of a prayer group and was studying kabbalah. She told Tidbit about a favorite new thing she had learned, about a part of the soul called the *tselem*.

"Well, it's not part of the soul exactly," she said, "it's separate. It's not the soul and it's not the body, it's called the subtle body. It's kind of like the personality, but not quite that. *Tselem* is like a sleeve that fits around the soul. If it wasn't there, the body would be destroyed by the soul's radiance, which makes such perfect sense if you think about it. I mean, there would have to be something there, right, to keep the body from burning up?"

Tidbit kicked leaves out of her way as they walked. After hugging her good-bye upstairs in Alternative Girls' dorm, her mother pressed the paper bag of candy into her hand.

**Marcy's respite was** coming to an end. Soon parents would be dropping their daughters back off in the dorm, and she would have to defend herself or the school against whatever accusations the girls might have made over the course of the day. If any of the girls or their parents broke any rules she would have to deal with it. She leaned back on the couch and rubbed her eyes. When she opened them, Beverly Hess was standing in front of her in a green gingham dress. Bev and the other girls who hadn't had any visitors had spent the day quietly in the dorm.

"What is it, Bev?" Marcy asked. It occurred to Marcy that maybe Bev hadn't been working to get unskirted because she just liked wearing dresses.

"I have a fib I need to turn in."

"Well, it's good that you want to turn it in. What did you do?"

Bev looked around to make sure no one else would hear. She whispered, "I licked soap."

"What?"

"In the shower. This morning. I licked the soap."

"Well," Marcy said, "I don't think there's a specific rule against that, but it's not very good for you. If you felt guilty about it, it's good you turned it in. Why did you lick the soap, hon?"

Again, Bev looked around. She leaned toward Marcy conspiratorially and told her, "It smelled good."

**Left alone, Michelle** wandered out of the Cottage and walked around the campus. The sun sat low in the sky, and the dimming light lent everything an edge of speed and harshness. Two young children ran by laughing sharply, out of breath but continuing their game. Michelle found a small piece of blue yarn in the grass, and decided to make a little bouquet to give Laurel before she left. She gathered some witchgrass and scattered buttercups and tied them together. Michelle checked her watch and realized that the hours for visiting were almost up. She took her little bouquet and headed quickly back to the Mansion.

She hurried to New Girls' dorm. The lounge was crowded with families saying good-bye, and it again took her some time to find Marcy, who was sitting in the hallway talking on the phone. She shook the wildflowers in the air and pointed to Laurel's room as if to ask, *Is that all right?*

Marcy shook her head and covered the bottom half of the receiver with her hand. "We're kind of in crisis mode right now. Bridget's parents took her back to their motel, and now she's refusing to come back to campus." She went back to talking on the phone, but later, when she noticed Michelle still standing there, she took the flowers from her and waved good-bye.

Michelle figured she should find Cynthia rather than go to the party alone. That seemed to be what Aubrey had told her to do. She wandered back in the direction of the Cottage. She found Cynthia standing by her car, wiping her eyes. She laughed when she saw Michelle.

"Those boys," she said through her tears. "They're just so sweet." Cynthia took a dress draped in a plastic dry-cleaning bag from the hook over the backseat. Together she and Michelle walked back to the Mansion.

**Zbigniew, Dedrick, and** Spencer had all had a quiet day off. They got some Chinese food, rented a movie, and were now going for a walk outside, watching as parents said good-bye and then headed to the Mansion for another one of Aubrey's parties. The sun had dipped below the line of hills and would soon, when it passed the horizon, spray yellows and pale pinks against the undersides of the clouds.

"Who's that?" Zbigniew asked as they watched Michelle and Cynthia approach the Mansion.

Spencer shrugged. They watched Jenna and Kelly from Regular Kids carrying a crate of oranges and a crate of limes from the Cafetorium into the Mansion. Behind them, in the parking lot, a young boy of about six or seven was walking bent over, his hands scraping along the ground in front of him. The parking lot was lit at night by two bright lights, one in each corner. The boy had found a large frog, which he was shepherding in the direction of the small woods to the side of the parking lot. Just pressing the frog forward with his hands cupped, so that it would jump in the right direction. The boy cast two shadows, one from each of the lights, as he moved toward the edge of the parking lot.

"Felix," a voice called out, but it was impossible to determine from where. "Honey, let's go." It was a woman's voice and called with a lilt.

"Just a minute," the boy with the frog called back.

"Felix, we've got to get Zach back to his dorm. We can't be late."

"I've just got to free this frog. It's in the parking lot. It could get smooshed." He was almost at the edge of the woods.

A deeper voice responded this time. "Felix, it's my ass if I'm late. Let's go."

Felix looked back over his shoulder, then scooped the frog up in his hands. He took one big step and hurled it overhand toward the trees, where it disappeared in the shadows. Felix ran back to his parents.

Spencer was laughing. "Did you see that?" he asked.

Dedrick chuckled. "An existentialist frog," he said, "condemned to be free."

Zbigniew added, "His *dasein Geworfenheit* forever."

Inside, the sounds of the party had begun.

**All this time,** I had been back in the Cottage growing more agitated. Aaron encouraged us to have a relaxing evening. Things were always emotional on Parents' Sunday, especially in dorms with new students, he said. I wondered where he'd gotten that. He'd hardly been at the school six weeks. William got back to his book, sitting sprawled out on one of the couches. Ross and Gary were sitting on the floor, trying to remember as many details as they could about a movie they had both seen before being sent to the school, a horror movie called *Pedestrian Crossing*. I had the other couch to myself. I sat, alternately crying and writing in my journal. The form my writing took was to hold a pen in my fist and tear through as many pages as I could, scratching back and forth with the pen.

Aaron tried two or three times to talk with me, to get me to calm down. Finally he figured that I would just have to get it out of my system, that I would tire myself out. "At least you'll sleep well," Aaron said, "and you'll wake up much better tomorrow." Again, I wondered who was feeding him that shit.

It wasn't until we had been sitting around the dorm for a couple of hours that Aaron noticed that Ross and I, who had both gone outside to spend time with our parents, were still wearing our shoes.

"Everybody up," he said. "Benjamin and Ross need to put their shoes away."

"Can't you let them drift?" William asked. "I'm in the middle of reading."

"Nope," Aaron said. "Parents' Sunday is over. You guys need to be arms' distance."

"Shit," William said. "C'mon." We all stood and followed him to the back of the living room to put his book on its shelf, then all went to the other end of the room and waited while Aaron unlocked the door to the shoe closet. We walked in and everyone waited as Ross and I untied and took off our shoes.

The shoe closet in the Cottage was a lot bigger than the ones in the dorms in the Mansion, and unlike those, it was used for general storage as well. It stretched back, long and narrow, along the side of the trailer. On its deep wooden shelves were a number of pieces of luggage, an incomplete set of encyclopedias, a pair of stereo speakers, and a bunch of old sports equipment from when Roaring Orchards used to compete against other high schools in the area. It was on these shelves that Aaron had told the boys to leave the tools from that morning's Reciprocity Detail, the saws and ax.

After putting my shoes next to those of the other New Boys, I looked at the tools laying there on the shelf. I picked up the ax. I didn't do anything with it at first, just held it in my hands, feeling the weight of it, the smooth wooden handle against my palms. The rest of the boys, when they noticed, took a step away and watched me carefully. I was amazed by the power of simply holding it. There wasn't any way for them to tell how far I would go. I might put the ax right back and laugh at them for getting scared, or I might swing it at one of them. They hadn't seen me like that before. They hadn't seen me let Roaring Orchard's rules just roll off my back like rain.

I shook the ax back and forth a bit to better test its weight. I nodded at the other boys to take another step back, and they did. I gave the ax a test swing against the wooden shelves that held the sports equipment. I hadn't swung hard at all, and still the blade embedded itself two inches into the plywood.

"What was that?" Aaron called as the other boys ran out of the closet. "Who's in there, Benjamin? Benjamin? What are you doing in there?"

I took some wider swings at the shelves. I snapped through one of the posts so that a shelf of encyclopedias collapsed. A few volumes slid to the floor. Aaron had begun yelling, telling me to come out right away. I took a swing against the wall, and the ax put a deep gouge in it. Aaron was threatening to come in, but he sounded scared, and I didn't think he would. I was surprised to be so confident about that.

There was a power box on one wall of the shoe closet, and I tapped it a few times with the ax. I had a brief thought about getting electrocuted as I took a deep breath, but I swung anyway. Raised the ax and swung hard at the box. Sparks went everywhere, and then I saw I had split the metal cover of the box and mangled whatever was inside. I swung again and once more, Aaron shouting just outside the closet. My last swing killed the lights in the Cottage. I was sure now that no one was coming in after me.

Aaron and my dorm mates asked some questions through the doorway, but I wouldn't answer. Then I heard Aaron on the phone to the different dorms, asking them to send down whatever extra staff was around. Most of the Regular Kids were unavailable because they were preparing food or serving drinks at Aubrey's party. Apparently Doris was dealing with Bridget and her family, who were still at their motel. But even when Brenda and Dedrick and Ellie had joined Aaron in the dark Cottage, they had no better idea of how to proceed. No one was willing to come into the closet, not as long as I wouldn't respond and they couldn't see me. Brenda and Dedrick thought they should get Aubrey; Ellie thought they should bring my parents down from the party to talk with me. Aaron worried that it was his fault the ax was in the dorm at all. When I heard mention of my parents, I hit the wall a few more times with my ax, hitting something that gave off sparks. I guess I was secretly hoping my parents would find out about what I was doing.

They decided to get Aubrey. "I'll go," Aaron said. "It's my dorm, it's my fault, I'll tell him about it."

"Yeah, but maybe you should stay with them," Ellie said. "Because it's your dorm." They talked about this and decided that Dedrick would go.

The scene at Aubrey's cocktail parties was always odd. Parents dressed casually for Parents' Sunday, but many who had been to Aubrey's parties before had brought a change of clothes. So there was a strange mix. There were new, suspicious parents in barn jackets and jeans, wondering just what it was they were supposed to be doing and how long they were expected to stay. And there were the old hands in formal wear, already tipsy and waiting for the Regular Kids to go to sleep so the party could really begin. Aubrey always opened up the empty rooms in the Mansion to people who didn't want to drive back to their hotels, and if there were more than would fit in those rooms, the couches in the therapy rooms all converted into beds as well.

Dedrick found Aubrey in the middle of a circle of parents all in suits and dresses. Aubrey had put on a tuxedo. The only one in their circle dressed less formally was the woman he had seen before, with Spencer and Zbigniew, the pretty one they hadn't recognized. She wore a pink coral pin on her gray sweater. Someone in the circle was telling an elaborate dirty joke, and Dedrick waited in the corner for it to be done. When it was, he approached Aubrey and tapped him on the shoulder. Aubrey turned fiercely and took Dedrick into the hall, reminding him that faculty members were not invited to these parties.

Dedrick explained the situation in the Cottage.

"And none of you feel you can deal with this?" Aubrey said.

Dedrick shook his head.

"Don't tell anyone here about this," Aubrey said. "I'll take care of it."

Before leaving, he smiled and told Cynthia that he would be right back and asked her to see to anything his guests needed. He left the Mansion gracefully and then began storming down toward the Cottage. "That goddamn little pissant son of a bitch," he said as Dedrick jogged next to him to keep up. Aubrey took off his jacket as he walked and tossed it to Dedrick. He began working on his bow tie. "Little fucker," Aubrey said and muttered under his breath so that all Dedrick could make out was something about anyone having a good time without him. Aubrey only stopped when Dedrick asked if he wanted him to go and tell Benjamin's parents. "Don't you dare bother those poor people," Aubrey said, and resumed walking to the Cottage.

I could sense the small crowd of New Boys and faculty members moving away from the door to the shoe closet when Aubrey arrived. He waited a moment for his eyes to adjust to the dark, then walked to the open door. He began unbuttoning his shirt. "All right, Benjamin, you little bastard. This game is over in about two minutes. I'm coming in there after you, and if you want to fight, you damn well better be ready to kill me with that ax. Because I'll tell you right now, I fight dirty. A clean fight simply doesn't make any sense to me."

He handed his tuxedo shirt to Ellie and stood at the entrance to the closet in his sleeveless undershirt. My eyes were well used to the dark, and I could see him in detail. He had a solid paunch and flabby arms. Tufts of white hairs sprouted from his shoulders. Then he lurched into the closet, and I let him take the ax from my hands. He pushed me out and, with the ax in one hand, asked, "Is there anybody in this room I can trust with this thing?" He looked directly at Aaron.

"I'll take this and the other tools to the Mansion basement," Ellie said, reaching for the ax and finally twisting it from Aubrey's grip. She gave him his shirt, which he put on and carefully began to button.

"No, Dedrick, you put those things away. This beautiful young lady has to help me with my bow tie."

**Bridget's mother returned** to their motel room. She had been out at the pay phone speaking with Doris. Bridget was sitting on the bed, playing checkers with her brother.

"Doris says this is it, Bridge. If you don't go back to campus now, that's it. We have to take you home with us. That what you want, hon? 'Cause we will."

"I dunno. I miss you when I'm there." Her brother made a move, and she kinged him.

"I miss you, too. We've gotta decide, though; we've got to come to a decision."

Bridget looked up. "Mom, how tall was Casey? When she died?"

Mrs. Divola was somewhat taken aback. "How *tall* was she? I don't know that, hon. Too damn short. Where's your father? Where'd he go?"

"He's in the bathroom, Mom," Bridget said. When her mother rolled her eyes, Bridget said, "He's allowed."

"What? He's making noise in there?"

"No! God, Mom." Bridget's brother laughed and she glared at him. "Not 'loud.' '*A*llowed.' As in he's allowed to go to the damn bathroom without asking permission. Oh, hell," she said. "Just take me back to the school."

# 2

**A** **few nights** after the autumn Parents' Sunday, Tidbit shook Carly Sibbons-Diaz awake.

"Let's go smoke."

Carly woke slowly and said through a yawn, "Tidbit? What are you doing here?"

"I missed you guys. Alternative girls are so horrible."

Tidbit climbed down from Carly's bunk and checked the pack of cigarettes in her back pocket. She had taken them from her mother's purse during Parents' Sunday. Tidbit carried Burn Victim under her arm. Carly woke Bridget, who moaned and punched her pillow.

"We're going to go smoke," Carly whispered.

"No," Bridget whispered back, as loudly as she could. "What's Tidbit doing here? You get sent back down already?"

"Just visiting," Tidbit said. "C'mon, we've all got to go."

"No."

"If we leave you here and you get caught without your group, you'll get put in the corner," Tidbit said.

"I'll just tell about your smoking. And sneaking out of your dorm."

"You'll still get into trouble for not turning us in right away," Tidbit said. "And when the rest of the dorm finds out you told, you know what they'll do, so just come on."

"Unnngghhhhaaa," Bridget said. "You're such a bitch, Tidbit."

"Thanks for the confrontation. I'll try to take it in."

Bridget punched her pillow again and climbed out of bed. She didn't smoke, but she did like the prospect of moving through the dorm in the dark when no one knew what they were up to. She climbed down to get Bev ready.

The girls always found Bev almost impossible to wake up. Bridget sat down on her bed and gently pulled back the covers.

"Oh God," she said, "she's sleeping in her jeans. Who forgot to help her change?"

"Obviously, everyone forgot," Tidbit said. "Why's she even wearing jeans?" She came over and grabbed Bev under her arms and swung her around. Bridget grabbed Bev's legs, and they lifted her up while Carly took her pillow. They began to carry Bev to the bathroom, but Tidbit stopped just as she got to the bedroom door. Bridget didn't see her stop in the dark and almost bumped into her, folding Bev in half so her bottom bumped against the floor.

"Be careful," Carly hissed. "You'll hurt her."

"Sorry," Tidbit said. "I forgot Burn Victim on Bev's bed. Could you grab him?"

"Shit. Why do you always want him with you?" Carly asked, looking through Bev's sheets. She found the doll at the foot of the bed, his black plastic eyes like raisins pressed into his white face.

"Yeah, you don't want him to smell like smoke," Bridget said.

"I have to take him," Tidbit said. "He's the silent witness."

"God," Bridget said.

"Should we get Laurel?" Tidbit asked.

"She's roomed. We'll get in a lot of trouble." Bridget shifted her grip on Bev's legs. "Come on, she's getting heavy."

"But I haven't seen Laurel in forever."

"None of us have," Carly said. "Okay. I'll get her." She stuffed Bev's pillow under Tidbit's chin and went to Laurel's room.

Tidbit and Bridget walked quietly down the hallway carrying Bev. In the middle of the night, the shadows in their dorm seemed to stretch through the entire Mansion. The bathroom was cool and large. Tidbit and Bridget laid Bev carefully on the tile floor in front of one of the stalls, her head on her pillow.

The truth was that Bev slept enough during the day that she slept lightly, if at all, at night. But when the girls had to use the bathroom at night, or someone had cigarettes, Bev pretended to stay asleep so they would pick her up and carry her, which she enjoyed. She also liked eavesdropping on their conversations and being able to drift off to sleep on the tile floor when she wanted.

In Laurel's room, Carly shook Laurel awake with a hand over her mouth.

"Carls," she said when Carly removed her hand. "You running?"

"No, we're just going to smoke. Tidbit snuck down from Alt Girls. You wanna come?"

"That's so nice," Laurel said, getting up. "Sure." She hadn't seen Carly in weeks and noticed that her hair was mostly all blond now, and longer. When the barbers came to campus, Carly wouldn't let them trim the ends, which were still black.

They found Tidbit and Bridget standing in the shower room, beneath the small window high on the wall. "It's so good to see you guys," Laurel said. "It's good to see anyone."

"Laurel The Pfaff," Tidbit said.

Laurel stopped. "Call me that again, I'll have Marcy in here in about two seconds."

"Relax, Laurel," Carly said. "Have a smoke."

"I'm just saying," she said. "Don't call me that. It's popped."

Carly lit one of Tidbit's cigarettes and then passed it around the circle. One at a time, the girls blew smoke up toward the window. A shower dripped, and the sounds echoed strangely off the tiles at night. The girls' whispers swirled around them.

"Hey, Bridget," Tidbit said. "Try a drag."

Bridget had been doing everything she knew of to show every-one how angry she was at being woken up, but of course she wanted to smoke, or would want to if she knew how. She tried to keep her voice even. "Maybe in a minute," she said. But when the cigarette made its way around the circle to her, she held it and looked at it. She put it in her mouth and sucked.

"Oh hell, you don't even know how to smoke," Carly said. "You're not inhaling." She grabbed the cigarette and took a drag.

Laurel rubbed Bridget's back. "It's not her fault. It's her first cigarette."

"Go like this," Tidbit said. She gasped, then said, "My mom's home! That's how you do it." Gasp. "My mom's home! Like you just got caught."

Bridget tried. Gasp. "My mom's home!"

"Good, now try it with the cigarette." Tidbit took it from Carly and handed it to Bridget.

Bridget pressed the cigarette between her lips and inhaled the way she had just learned. She began coughing violently.

"Shhh," the girls whispered. Bridget's coughs sounded like a dog's bark echoing in the shower room.

"I'll get her some water," Laurel said, laughing. She ran out of the shower to the sinks, where she could see Bev asleep on the floor. The only cup she found was full of toothbrushes. Laurel dumped them in the sink and rinsed out the cup. She could hear that Bridget's cough-ing had calmed some. Laurel looked at herself in the mirror above the sink. She put down the cup of water and checked that the other girls were still in the shower. Then Laurel pulled up the leg of her pajama pants to make sure her cuts weren't bleeding.

At the sound of Bridget's coughing, Bev's eyes had popped open. She pretended to sleep again when Laurel walked out of the showers, but then had watched to see what Laurel was doing.

When Laurel pulled up the leg of her pants to look at her leg, Bev saw a series of long, irregular scabs covering her calf. She shut her eyes immediately.

For a second Laurel thought she had seen Bev move, but when she checked, Bev was still. She took the cup of water back to the girls in the shower. Bridget's eyes were red and watering, and she drank greedily.

When Carly lit up another cigarette, Bridget decided she would pass for the time being. To have something to talk about, she asked Tidbit, "So what's Alternative Girls like?"

"Pretty much what you'd expect. Everyone lying and saying they're following the process, and no one believing anyone."

"Yeah," Laurel said. "Tidbit really hates liars."

A while later Bridget asked, "Have any of you guys really seen the ghost in the Mansion?"

"Don't we ever get tired of talking about this?" Tidbit said.

"I've seen it," Laurel said. "I woke up one night, and she was standing over my bed, weeping. She was kind of like this star, light was shining out of her. And she still had the rope tied around her neck."

"What's her story again?" Bridget asked.

"She was this lady who worked here years ago. And she had nothing else in her life, not one single thing. She just came to work here, her office was one of the therapy rooms near the attic, she did like payroll or something. And one day for no reason at all she just walked into the attic and hung herself from one of the beams."

"Hanged herself," Carly said.

"What?"

"You said she hung herself. It's correct to say she hanged herself."

"That's not right," Tidbit said. "Does that sound right to you? 'She hanged herself?' That sounds stupid."

"That whole story sounds stupid," Carly said. "It's so made up.

If the Mansion's haunted it's haunted by the ghost of some kid who died here, not some made-up lady. I heard there was a boy who jumped over the banister on the fourth floor and died when he landed in the Great Hall."

"When was that?" Bridget asked.

"I don't know, a long time ago."

"Did anyone get killed since you guys've been here?"

Tidbit put the cigarette out by dipping it in a small puddle of standing water. "No," she said, "but when New Boys rioted this one time a faculty member got kicked so hard he lost a testicle."

The girls laughed. "Shut up," Carly said.

"No, it's true. And the poor guy had only been working here for like two weeks."

Carly lit up another cigarette and passed it. "What the hell does that have to do with anything, Tidbit?"

"I swear it happened. That's what *I* think might be haunting the Mansion. The ghost of that lost testicle."

The girls passed the cigarette around the circle quietly. They talked Bridget through taking another small drag, which she executed without incident. When the girls were quiet, they became aware of the sound of water running in the other room. Laurel stood up.

"I must have left the faucet on when I went to get water for Bridget." She walked out to shut it off but ran back into the shower and said, "Bev's gone."

"Oh, shit," Carly said. The girls ran out of the shower room to look.

"I'm sure she just went back to bed," Tidbit said.

"Yeah, but do you think she heard us?" Laurel asked. "I mean, do you think she realized that we dragged her out here so you guys could smoke? And do you think she knew I was with you? Fuck."

"Come on," Tidbit said, "this is Bev. We have to put her shoes on or she'd go out into the snow barefoot. She probably just thought she wandered in here and fell asleep. Who knows what she thought."

But the girls hurried to brush their teeth and wash their hands. Carly flushed the cigarette butts. Tidbit sprayed the shower with Lysol. Then Laurel went with them back to their room, where they found Bev, asleep atop her covers in her jeans.

"Good," Laurel said. "Good night, guys." She went back to her room and tried to go to sleep, vaguely worried that Bev saw what she had, in fact, seen. Laurel reassured herself: Even if she says something, no one will listen.

**In the girls'** room, the air was soft and sweet as overripe fruit. Bridget asked Tidbit to tell her again the story of the stables.

"It's late," Tidbit said. "I should get back upstairs."

"Come on, I got up so you guys could smoke."

"You smoked, too."

"Come on."

Tidbit sighed. "Well, I don't think anyone believes this anymore," she began, "but there used to be these stables where the gym is now." She sat on the floor, leaning back against Carly's bed.

"There are pictures," Bridget said. "I've seen them."

"I don't mean no one believes there were stables, I mean about the rest. They were the largest private stables in the country or the state or something. When the guy who built this place lived here. Grafflin, who the town's named after. And there was a fire in the stables, and a lot of the horses died. People used to say there were these ghosts of the horses that caused shit to happen at the school."

This was the ghost story Bridget had wanted to hear. The girls could see her getting excited, sitting up.

Tidbit continued, "The worst thing is that the horse ghosts are so powerful and so terrified that there's no way to deal with them. Human ghosts you can kind of talk to or negotiate with, because there's something they want, but these are just enraged and totally irrational. It's like the ghosts believe they're still on fire."

"And burning is the worst way to die," Bridget said.

"Yeah," Tidbit said, "just ask Burn Victim." She held him up for Bridget to see. Then she got up, said goodnight, and slipped quietly from the room.

**For the incident** with the ax on Parents' Sunday, my dorm voted to put me on Reciprocity Detail. I tried to be proud, to feel like a badass, but really I was embarrassed. After what happened, they felt better not having me around as much. For a few days there had been rain, so no work could be done, and I was stuck with New Boys avoiding me. But after breakfast on the first clear day I reported to Zbigniew's office in the equipment shed at the Farm, a corner of campus that in addition to the equipment shed included the pigpen and a Dumpster that held paper recycling. Tidbit was already waiting there.

"You have a watch?" Zbigniew asked.

"A watch?" I looked down at my wrist to see. "Yeah, I have a watch."

"Good. Tidbit has no watch. Every five minutes she comes to see is it time for lunch."

Zbigniew explained our work assignment for the day. It seemed that the hill that led down from the Mansion to Route 294 dipped back up before it reached the road near the small stand of old-growth white pines called the Enchanted Forest. This meant that the Enchanted Forest stood in a slight depression, which turned into a sizable puddle when it rained. Zbigniew had installed an underground pump that sent the water out to the road, but the pump had gotten clogged with fallen leaves and pine needles. He wanted us to get them out of the pump.

"That's it? Just clear dead leaves out of it?" I asked.

Zbigniew nodded and handed Tidbit a rake. "But first we have to put water to the pigpen."

We followed Zbigniew to the back of his office where there was a large sink. He handed us each a bucket to fill. He explained that we had to do this every day. On the wall next to the sink hung an embroidered sampler that read, THE PEN IS MIGHTIER . . . THAN THE PIGS. Tidbit pointed out two large barrels that held seeds for the birdfeeders.

Zbigniew led us down a narrow dirt path to the pen, a small enclosure that held a pig, a goat, and some chickens. Taking care of the animals used to be a part of the students' therapy, but Aubrey had since decided that relationships with animals were detrimental to the ability to form genuine relationships with other people. So the animals in the pen were left to be taken care of by Zbigniew and whoever else might remember.

After showing me where to put the water and where and when to put out the animals' food, Zbigniew sent us to clear the water pump. It wasn't until we had walked across campus and down to the Enchanted Forest that we understood it was *now* surrounded by an enormous puddle.

"Oh, bother," Tidbit said.

"How are we supposed to clear out the pump? We can't even see where it is."

"I know where it is," Tidbit said. She had walked to the edge of the puddle and was reaching with the rake toward a part of the pump that broke the surface of the water. It almost reached, but didn't quite.

"So what are we supposed to do?" I asked.

"Well, I think there's only one thing to do, but at least we can sit down here for a while before we do it." Tidbit sat on the grass and dropped the rake half in the water.

I sat down near her. It was strange. We knew each other, but we didn't. For a while we stared out past the rise in the lawn, toward the road. We could see the top edges of cars as they drove by. Each breeze that rose started an intricate ticking in the trees above as pine needles fell and knocked lightly against branches on their way down.

"I heard about you freaking out with the ax," Tidbit said. "I think we're the only two people who've gotten into trouble for acting out with axes."

"Yeah? What'd you do?"

"I was on Reciprocity Detail with this girl named Courtney, and we were chopping wood. We were fighting, and I just got so mad I hit her with an ax. In the arm. Zbigniew kicked me off RD and wouldn't talk to me for like three months."

"Did you hurt her?"

"Not really. I cut her jacket, but her arm just had a bruise."

"Hmm." I tapped the edge of the puddle with the tip of my sneaker, sending out ripples. They stretched out to bump against the trunks of trees and returned, circles crossing other circles. "I just was trying to get my parents to take me home. But they wouldn't listen to anything. It was like Aubrey put some sort of voodoo on them."

Tidbit nodded. "RO-bots," she said.

"Huh?"

"Roaring Orchards–bots." Tidbit rolled up her jeans and started untying her sneakers.

"Did your parents come up last Sunday?"

"My mom did. And my cat."

"What's her name?" Tidbit had pulled off her socks and stood up. Her feet were pale and looked soft.

"His name," she said. "Fatface." She waded a few paces into the puddle and gasped. She began swinging the rake underwater in the general vicinity of the pump, occasionally raking back and forth. "Come on," she said. "Help."

I hurried to take off my shoes and roll up my pants. When I walked into the water I could feel the chill grass beneath my feet, but the water was icy. I took two steps and stopped, concentrating on catching my breath. "You getting anything?" I asked.

"No. I don't think this is going to work." She handed me the rake and let me try. I swung the rake against something under the water. I couldn't manage to displace any leaves. Pulling my pants higher I stepped farther into the puddle. It was wide, but not very deep. "If it gets any colder this water's going to freeze."

"We'll be stuck in here until spring," Tidbit said.

I tried again with the rake, but still had no luck.

"I've seen that happen," Tidbit said. "To the ducks on the pond near my house."

"The ones you made your mask like?"

"What?"

"That's what you told Brenda. I'm in that class. You told her all about it in Expressions." I handed Tidbit the rake and began rolling up my sleeves.

"Oh, yeah, I forgot that. I was just bullshitting Brenda. But the ducks would sometimes get frozen into the pond if it got cold really early. My friend Eli used to go out on the ice with his hockey stick and try to decapitate them with a slap shot. Sometimes he just broke their necks, but when they came off it was crazy. You'd see these duck heads sliding across the ice or find them later in the weeds."

I reached down where the pump was to pull out handfuls of wet black leaves. I saw the scars on my forearms and was suddenly ashamed of them. I was not unaware of the perverse attraction they could have, especially at Roaring Orchards where pain took on an aspect of glamour. But I didn't want Tidbit to see them. I couldn't really stop pulling out leaves or roll down my sleeves now that I'd started, so I just moved and tried to turn my arms so that my forearms were hidden. The clumps of leaves I pulled up looked like seaweed. They were partially decomposed and torn to shreds. I tossed them onto the grass, then walked around to the other side of the pump and continued working there.

"Is this thing supposed to start working, or are we just supposed to stop once we get rid of all the leaves we can?" I asked.

"I don't know. I can't feel my feet."

"I know. My hands are getting numb, too."

"Hey, look." Tidbit pointed up the hill to where a wild turkey had stopped to watch us standing in the puddle.

"What the fuck?"

"You see them all the time on the other side of campus. We put food out for them by the bird feeders."

I threw a clump of leaves in the turkey's direction. It didn't move. "Get out of here," I shouted. "Hey, give me the rake."

"Why?"

I picked up the rake and waved it in the direction of the turkey, but that only made it come closer. "Shit." I threw the rake at it and missed. The turkey came closer still and began investigating the tines with its beak.

"You stay there and keep it occupied." Tidbit walked out of the puddle and in a wide arc circled behind the turkey. Then she started running. Waving her arms and yelling, she ran right at it. The turkey looked over its shoulder and scrambled for a second, and then it was running. I stared at its legs as it ran. They were like real legs, I thought, until I noticed it was running at me. I ran out of the water and turned to see the turkey working its wings. It cleared the puddle in an impossible leap. After two more long strides on the other side, it hopped the fence and was flying. It flew low at first, over Route 294, and then straight up, over the telephone wires on the other side of the road. It descended, and I lost it somewhere in the woods across the street.

"Holy shit! Did you see that?" I was jumping up and down.

"Fuck! Did you even know they could fly? I didn't know they could fly. Holy fuck!"

"Shh." Tidbit laughed. "Keep your voice down." She rubbed her right foot against her left shin to try to get the leaves and dead grass off. "That was pretty great."

"Yeah." I was still looking at where the turkey had disappeared. "Did you know they could fly?"

"I think I knew," she said, "but I forgot."

We grabbed our shoes and ran back to the Mansion barefoot. I followed Tidbit up the stairs and around a number of hallways to a small room where she found some fresh towels. I still had no idea where anything in that monstrous building was.

We collapsed onto the floor and began to rub our feet dry. "So what did you do to get sent here?" I asked.

"Huh?"

"To get sent here. You said you had a self-afflicting personality, but you must have done something."

"Oh." Tidbit put down her towel and brushed the hair out of her face. "I was doing a lot of drugs. Meth, mostly. There were these older guys who would always let me have some, and they were really sweet, I'd known all of them since I was little. They're the ones who gave me the tattoo on my neck. Of my name." She turned quickly and pulled back her hair to show me again. "And they'd let me hang out and get high, but they always made sure I'd gone to school that day; they wouldn't let me have any if I'd skipped. They would always ask me what I learned that day. And even if I'd gone, you know, I'd usually have to make up something that I learned because how often do you actually learn anything? But these guys didn't know the difference, it was kind of cute how dumb they were.

"But I started kind of dating one of them, and he'd give me some extra because I told him I couldn't get through a day at school without it. Which was kind of true. But I started doing this thing at school where I'd get into a fight every day. Fighting on that stuff feels amazing. At the beginning of the day, when it was still gray and foggy out and everyone's hanging out in the cafeteria waiting for the bell to ring, I'd decide who I was going to fight with later. Just any random kid. And then the rest of the day, it was like I was this superslick machine, you know? I'd look for that person and it was like I was on rails. And as soon as I found them, I'd start in on them like crazy. Can you imagine what it feels like to fight someone you hardly even know, and know you can't lose? That you can't even get hurt?" Tidbit's eyes were bright.

"You'd never lose?"

"Well, I might get beat up, but I couldn't feel a fucking thing. Of course that didn't last long. After about a week and a half of getting into a fight a day, the principal told me not to come to school anymore. So I'd just stay home and get high and play with my cat. And then they told me to come here, and my mom was driving me so nuts it sounded fine."

I put down my towel and started putting my socks and sneakers on. "Was that Fatface or another cat?"

"That was Fatface."

"D'you miss him?"

"Yeah, even though I just saw him Parents' Sunday. I hope my mom brings him next time. I'm gonna stuff his whole head in my mouth and just suck on it all day."

"What?" I laughed.

"I just love him so much. I want to cut him open and kiss him all over his slimy insides."

"Yeah, I bet he'd love that." I felt she was teasing me, but I didn't know why.

"I'm gonna make him give me a hug and tie his arms in a big bow right around my neck."

# 3

**A**ubrey stopped on the stairs to catch his breath. One hand
rested on the banister and the other on his knee. He hated
this. From where he stood he could hear the ladies in the office
typing and talking on the phones. Sun glinted off the polished
floor of the Great Hall. Through the windows in the Meditation
Room he saw a dorm of girls walking across campus together.
Aubrey stared at his hand clutching the banister. The black hairs
sprouting from his knuckles were like spiders' legs, he thought. He
shook himself loose and continued up to the therapy rooms.

He couldn't allow himself to think of these as things he would
miss. Aubrey felt very much that he was the only one holding
Roaring Orchards together, not so much in what he did, as in how
he thought about it. The school, he felt, existed in his head as much
as it existed in the world. Or, rather, it could only exist in the
world because it first existed in his head. If he began to indulge his
melancholy, to think of all these things as drifting away from him,
the school would indeed begin to spiral out of control. He could
already feel it pulling apart. He had to keep it together.

Aubrey paused outside the door, then walked in. Doris was
already sitting on the couch and talking with Frances, who was
also my therapist for a time. Frances was probably the kindest adult
I met at Roaring Orchards, if only intermittently attentive. She

would stare out the window as I spoke and twist one of her long curls around her finger, and with each twist it made whatever problem I was talking about seem less important. Aubrey sat down next to Doris. Frances was telling Doris about her youngest niece, who had just begun nursery school. The therapy rooms were simply furnished. A desk with a computer for the therapists, a couch that converted into a bed for when visitors to the school stayed over. This room had a framed print hanging on either side of the door. One was of a painting by Balthus, the other a Maxfield Parrish.

"Well, let's begin," Frances said.

Aubrey lay his head down in Doris's lap. With a jolt she slid away from him, and Aubrey sat back upright. "See, that's the problem," he said.

"What's the problem," Frances said.

"I have no partner. I am completely alone."

For a while they sat. He could feel Doris's anger but wouldn't be the first to speak.

Doris said, "You're not alone."

"I feel alone," he said. He turned to her. "When I hired you for this job it wasn't just to be an administrator. This campus is a family. We all act out family roles here for one another and for the children. And how are the children supposed to trust us to take care of them when we won't take care of one another?"

"I just don't want you to lie down on my lap is all," Doris said.

Aubrey sighed. "I'm not going to do anything to you."

"Do you hear what Doris is saying, Aubrey?" Frances leaned back in her chair. "She's claiming a boundary. You need to respect that."

"I'm not transgressing anyone's boundaries. I'm sitting here very nicely. But I think I have a right to discuss why that particular boundary. Why Doris refuses to allow any degree of intimacy to develop between us."

Doris began to stutter a response, but Frances held up a hand to stop her. "You said you felt alone, Aubrey. Why don't you say a little more. What do the doctors say?"

"I don't see what that has to do with this."

"Aubrey, you're sick. You should talk about how you're feeling."

"Sick isn't a feeling," he said. "Exhausted isn't a feeling, and dizzy isn't a feeling, and harried isn't a feeling either. It never stops around here. Everyone wants something and no one ever thinks about what I might need. I go to breakfast, I go to Campus Community meetings, to meetings with Regular Kids or whoever, it's always the same. The other day I thought it would be nice to read something to everyone in the Campus Community meeting. I wanted to share something that we could discuss, some way for me to give my own personal angle on what it is we're all trying to accomplish together. I thought maybe a passage about the proper and improper use of anger from Seneca's *De Ira* or Philodemus on the importance of confessing our failings. Just so the students can feel that they're part of a tradition of therapeutic thinking that goes back thousands of years. I spent the morning flipping through texts, and I found so many wonderful passages I couldn't decide. I was so excited. I brought a stack of books with me to breakfast, and I thought I would decide when I got there, when I saw how things felt in the room. But when I got to Campus Community, I looked around the room and I thought, Oh God, what's the point? No one wants to hear anything from me. They resent me, all they want are more reasons to justify their resentment. So you know what I did? I lectured on the rules. I was what they needed me to be: the father. It's not what I ever wanted to be. It's not why I built this place. Rules, rules, rules. But who's going to clarify the process when I'm gone? Her?" He nodded toward Doris.

"Well, that's a somewhat hurtful way to put it, don't you think?" Frances said. "Doris, what do you have to say to that?"

Doris said nothing. She just slowly shook her head.

"They're just waiting for me to die," Aubrey said.

**Because of the** ongoing case against Ellie and a number of other complaints and cases pending against Roaring Orchards, Aubrey's lawyers thought it would be a good idea for the staff to be trained in restraint techniques. They didn't want anyone to be able to claim that the school employed unqualified people.

The dorm parents had been trained first so that they could take over activities in the Classroom Building while the teachers took their turn. They would be substitute teachers for the day. The novelty of this had everyone a bit keyed up.

Aaron filled in for Dedrick, who had left him a desultory series of notes for each class. In Cooking with Butter, they were to discuss *Walden*. I wish I had been there instead of on Reciprocity Detail, but I only heard about how it went later. Aaron waited for everyone to sit down. "All right class, settle down," he said and waited. He smiled. "I'm Aaron and I'll be your teacher for today."

"We know who you are, Aaron," Pudding said.

"Good. Now everyone take out your books." So far, so good. Aaron looked at the page of notes Dedrick had left. He looked up to make sure that everyone had a book open. He read off the page, "Discuss the pond as a metaphor for the soul, especially in relation to the sounding of the pond in 'The Pond in Winter.'" Aaron looked out at the class and waited. There were about eight students staring back at him, most of whom he knew well. But Aaron couldn't tell if they were looking at him eagerly or anxiously.

"Anyone want to discuss that? Which pond do you think he's talking about?" The clock on the other side of the room clicked loudly, the minute hand slipping back and then jumping forward. "Pudding?"

"Walden Pond?"

"Okay. Does anybody else have any other ideas?" He looked back down at the sheet of notes. "Okay, good. Let's go to the next one. Discuss the classical allusions in 'The Bean-Field.'"

The students shifted in their seats and looked around. Aaron was beginning to get nervous. There were only a few more discussion questions left. He saw that Beverly Hess had her head down on her desk. At least this he knew how to deal with.

"Bev, could you stand up please?"

Bev stood. "Sorry," she said. She shook her head back and forth.

"What did you think of *Walden*? Did you like the book?" he asked.

Bev looked around. "I smell cookies."

Aaron nodded. "So the classical allusions. What do you guys think he means by 'classical allusions'?"

"I have a question," Carly Sibbons-Diaz said.

"Good," Aaron said. "Go ahead."

"What's the deal with the pumpkins? I mean"—she paused to flip through her copy of the book—"hold on. Here it is. Page one thirty-two. He says, 'I would rather sit on a pumpkin and have it all to myself than be crowded on a velvet cushion.' But later—." She went back to flipping through her copy of *Walden*. The other students watched her. Aaron had hurried to find the place on page 132. He left his thumb there as he now flipped ahead to find Carly's next citation. "On page one fifty-four," Carly said, "he says, 'None is so poor that he need sit on a pumpkin. This is shiftlessness.' So which is it? Is he in favor of sitting on pumpkins or not?"

Aaron was scanning page 154 to find the section she had read. "That's a good question," he said. "I guess it depends on what 'shiftlessness' means." He turned to check Dedrick's notes for anything about pumpkins. There was nothing. "What do you guys think about Carly's question?"

"Maybe somebody popped his furniture," Pudding said. "So he had to sit on fruits."

"Yeah, and then they popped his pumpkins," Bev said.

Aaron laughed. This was exciting. He hoped they would continue.

"Look," Eric Gold said. "After what you read on page hunnerd fifty-four. He said, 'Blah-blah, pumpkin. This is shiftlessness.' Then 'There is a plenty of such chairs as I like best in the village garrets to be had for taking them away. Furniture!' Is he talking about stealing furniture?"

"That's why it got popped," Pudding said.

"I think he's saying," Eric said, "that if you're really poor you could sit on a pumpkin but then you could always just go and steal a chair."

"Yeah," Pudding said, "he definitely likes chairs better than pumpkins."

"But he likes pumpkins better than velvet cushions," Carly said.

Aaron was amazed. He picked up a piece of chalk and wrote on the board,

Chair
Pumpkin
Cushion

He stepped back and looked at it. It seemed they had figured something out. "So that's his order of preference," he said.

"Then why doesn't he just come out and say it?" Carly asked.

They were all looking at him again. "I don't know," Aaron said. He looked again at the notes Dedrick had left. "That's a very good question."

**Our work project** for that day was to decorate the Christmas tree in the Cafetorium. Tidbit and I had spent the morning in the Mansion attic finding the boxes of lights and ornaments. Zbigniew had gone out to buy tinsel. We carried the boxes and got the aluminum ladder from the upper equipment shed, but when we got to the Cafetorium we saw the teachers and the man who had come to teach restraint techniques. We put down our things and helped them move some tables out of the way.

"We're supposed to decorate the tree," Tidbit said. "Are we not supposed to see what you guys are doing?"

Doris looked at the restraint trainer. He was short and muscular, dressed in track pants and a T-shirt. He had neatly parted blond hair and a face that initially looked young, but at a second glance was clearly an aging man's face, desperately preserved. He shrugged.

"We're not doing anything secret," Doris said. "You can go ahead."

We set up the aluminum ladder. Tidbit climbed to the top with some ornaments and tinsel and I climbed behind her, to decorate the middle part of the tree. Mostly, though, we watched the teachers.

The trainer, whose name was Lindsay, was showing them how to hold someone down by holding their clothes rather than their arms and legs. June was playing the student, and Lindsay had Spencer help him hold her down. Lindsay bunched the cuff of June's jeans near her ankle in one fist and did the same with the sleeve of her shirt. He had Spencer do the same and then insisted that June try to get up. Then he had everyone else take turns restraining and being restrained. Except for Doris, who said she couldn't participate in any strenuous activity.

Tidbit told me to climb down so we could wrap the lights around the tree. Lindsay was asking Doris what she would do in a crisis situation. Tidbit held one end of the string of lights, and I walked around the tree, squeezing between ladder and tree when I got to that side.

Later, Lindsay discussed the Diamond of Don't. He made his thumbs and forefingers into a diamond to demonstrate. It stood for "discuss options, notice the threat." Then he told them about standing in an L. "Stand sideways to an aggressive student," he said. He pointed at Dedrick. "You be the student." Lindsay stood so that the line of his shoulders was perpendicular to that of Dedrick's. He looked at Dedrick over his left shoulder. "See my feet?" The teachers looked down to see that Lindsay's left foot was pointed toward Dedrick while his right foot was at a ninety-degree angle. "That's the L. Standing like this gives them less of a target, and, try to hit me." He made Dedrick try to hit him and showed a number of intricate ways to take him down. "Don't fight them, *use* their momentum," he kept saying. "Plus, from here"—he pivoted his feet—"you can turn and run." To demonstrate the L he held up his left hand with his thumb perpendicular to the other fingers. "You can remember it if you remember me," he said. "Lindsay."

The training was still going on when it was time for Tidbit and me to break for lunch. Floyd had spaghetti for us.

I whispered to Tidbit, "Can you get him to put salsa on mine instead of tomato sauce?" I liked it better that way.

Tidbit asked. "Sure," Floyd said, and gave her a wink.

We sat down with our food and watched the training session. A few minutes into lunch, Jodi showed up with my meds. She poured the contents of the envelope onto my tongue and watched me drink a glass of water to wash them down. Then she checked my mouth. For a moment she stared silently at the training with Tidbit and me, shaking her head like it was the dumbest thing she'd ever seen.

"I don't know why they keep us on so many meds," I said when Jodi had left. "We're not sick, we're just sad."

"Speak for yourself," Tidbit said.

The restraint training was apparently done, but Lindsay refused to let the Teachers' Group go until Doris agreed to participate in a couple of the drills. She insisted that she couldn't. Now he was telling her that she needed to learn to walk without a cane. To demonstrate how easy it would be for a student to take it from her, he took it from her.

"Now I could use this as a weapon," Lindsay said.

"Could I please have that back?"

Lindsay walked over to where Tidbit and I were sitting. "Now what would you two do if you took this cane from Doris?"

"Lemme see?" Tidbit said. He handed her the cane, and she considered it for a moment before looking back up. "What's your name again? Lisa?"

"Lindsay."

"Oh yeah. First of all, Lindsay, I wouldn't take it from Doris, Lindsay, because I'm not an asshole." She got up and walked over to Doris. She gave her back her cane. "And secondly, I wouldn't act out around Doris because I only act out around assholes." She sat back down next to me.

"You kids are lucky I don't work here," Lindsay said.

"Yup," Tidbit said. "Say, Lindsay, are you such a tool because you've got a girl's name or because those steroids shriveled up all your special parts?"

"Tidbit," June said.

"You should tell your girlfriend to watch her mouth," Lindsay said to me.

"Thanks for the suggestion," I said. "I'll try to take it in."

# 4

The heat in the Mansion came on in late November. The thermostats didn't work, so when the heat was turned on, it stayed on until spring. This kept the Mansion and everyone inside it warm and dry, so dry that the students and faculty members who lived there got nosebleeds. Those who had been at Roaring Orchards since the previous winter or longer took this as a matter of course, but people new to the school reacted with some alarm. Soon, though, everyone got used to the fact that anyone at any point might start bleeding from the nose for no discernible reason: a teacher asking a question, a student raising her hand, a child serving as waiter in the Cafetorium. It wasn't unusual, late that fall and through the winter, to see people walking around campus with crimson tissues held against their noses, nodding to one another, carrying on as though there were nothing unusual about it. A layer of snow had descended that would remain through the winter, varying only in thickness. Lights came on earlier in the houses around the valley, and bare branches trembled in the wind above them.

Otherwise things proceeded apace. New faculty members came and went. Old students ran away and some were brought back. New students were enrolled and some ran away. Tidbit and I worked together on Reciprocity Detail. Despite the start of a new semester, we stayed in the same classes, as Doris was too overwhelmed with her other responsibilities to set up new ones. Dedrick added to his syllabus some more books that Spencer could reach from the couch; Spencer taught the next lessons in the math and history textbooks to those classes respectively; June came up with some more safe science projects and Brenda with some art projects. The most noticeable change that winter was that we all saw Aubrey less and less. We figured that he was busy, or visiting doctors or resting.

**Imagine dinner in** winter. The large glass windows of the Cafetorium give out onto the snowy lawn in the center of the campus. As they serve and eat, the students watch the blue light of evening fade to dark. Huddled shapes pass occasionally in the distance, teachers leaving the Classroom Building or students on their way to therapy in the upper reaches of the Mansion.

Student waiters ferry plastic trays of dry, salty pork chops and squash enchiladas from the kitchen to their tables. There are baskets with bags of bread. The salad is left over from some event that Floyd catered at his other job, with flowers in it that most everyone avoids, though it isn't lost on the students that these would have been a nice touch when they were fresh.

Roger and Ellie sit quietly with a few Regular Kids at the Admin Table. Some faculty members are off for the night, and Aubrey rarely eats dinner with the students. During announcements, Jenna, one of the Regular Kids sitting at the Admin Table, says that Aubrey has given permission for us to have a dance in the spring. Anyone who wants to volunteer to help organize it should let her know.

Throughout the short Campus Community meeting after dinner, Ellie keeps thinking how bare the room looks with so few people in it. Again and again she follows the eyes of students in the meeting to the people they watch through the windows, people passing beneath lights far across campus. She feels it herself, an almost physical need to be somewhere else. In the warm, bright room she feels abandoned by the souls loosed in the dark. The distances they move through seem endless.

After dinner she and Roger walk around the grounds. The top layer of snow has frozen to a crust that cracks and sinks underfoot as they walk. Roger has his beeper clipped to the waistband of his pants in case of emergencies. Conversation drags lazily between them. They walk aimlessly, past the supply shed, by the baseball backstop on the north side of the campus. Ellie pulls off a mitten and wraps her fingers around one of the metal bars of the backstop. She thrills with cold.

They watch TV in his apartment in the Paddock and eat Ritz crackers. His beeper starts going off around ten, when the dorm parents on duty have gotten their kids to sleep. Ellie says she'll go along to keep him company, to say hello to people on campus. She likes the walk across Route 294 and around the campus at night, she says. None of these reasons are false. But it would be just as true to say that she feels panicky in his apartment alone. She can never concentrate on anything there, other than listening for the sounds of his return. Alone she always ends up pacing around the apartment, opening and closing the darkly stained cabinets.

At the Mansion, everything seems to be in order. Laurel Pfaff went up to a meeting in Alternative Girls to ask what she had to do to get them all to consent to her being more appropriately placed into their dorm. Since she is still restricted to her room, it isn't clear whether she would actually become a part of their dorm or just move into a room in Alternative Girls. Alternative Boys had a good meeting, Spencer says. Eric and Pudding discussed their relationship and why they are always bickering. Ellie is sorry she missed that. They sound all right, her boys.

In one dorm after another, Ellie sits beside Roger in the various lounges and listens to the dorm parents report on the evening's events. Or she sits behind them on the stairs, her knees tucked under her chin. She sticks the tip of her tongue out of the corner of her mouth as she flips through a magazine or bites the side of a fingernail, waiting for them to finish. She feels very much like a student tonight. A privileged student who gets to travel from dorm to dorm with Roger and hear all the gossip.

Ellie likes that Roger isn't nervous when she watches him. He's usually an uncomfortable person, with a loud defensive laugh like the last bit of bathwater washing down the drain. But somehow his life has swallowed her up and he is no more aware of her than he is of himself when he's alone. She picks up her coat and follows him out of the Mansion.

The last dorm to check on is mine. Roger says it's the quietest dorm on campus because of Jodi. Roger attributes her ability to command New Boys' respect to the fact that she is over it.

"Over what?" Ellie asks.

"Everything. Whatever it is, Jodi's over it."

But that night Jodi was off, and Aaron was covering the dorm. He had watched us a couple of times since the ax incident on Parents' Sunday, and he just got worse and worse. He was wary of me, but for some reason assumed he could trust the rest of the dorm. So we'd had a lot of fun with him, especially about Alberto, a new intake from Mexico City who'd been placed in our dorm because he'd tried to run when his parents enrolled him.

When Roger came in, we were all still running around in our underwear, getting ready for bed. I headed into the bathroom to brush my teeth. I saw William Kay walk briskly into the kitchen, looking over his shoulder and stuffing the last bit of a tofu dog into his mouth.

"We're running a little late," Aaron told Roger, "but it's my fault." The microwave hummed loudly behind him and emitted four discreet beeps. Aaron headed toward the kitchen.

"Aaron, why are they all in different rooms? They're supposed to be grouped," Roger said.

Aaron didn't answer him; he just told William to get out of the kitchen and go use the bathroom. I was now listening by the bathroom door and heard Aaron open the microwave.

"What's that?" Roger asked.

"Tofu dogs. The boys were still hungry after dinner."

Ellie turned and went to the living room. She took a magazine off the bookshelf in the back of the room and sat down on the couch. Roger walked across the living room and leaned into the bathroom. "Into bed, guys. Now."

"But we just—," Han Quek began saying, but Roger cut him off.

"Now."

We rushed giggling to bed. Roger stayed with Aaron as he arranged the nighttime meds and filled cups of water. They both came into our bedroom, and Roger watched as Aaron gave us our meds. Aaron didn't seem at all bothered. Then Roger said that he wanted to speak with us and sent Aaron out of the room. He chewed us out for taking advantage. He told us how much this job meant to Aaron, and how hard he was working at trying to do well. And he said that if we felt let down that Aaron was doing such a poor job taking care of us, acting out was a dishonest way of dealing with it. In the living room, Aaron and Ellie were talking.

"So how's everything going?" Aaron asked.

"Okay. Good. It's my night off."

"Nice," Aaron said. "Jodi's too."

"Uh-huh."

"It's cold out."

"Yeah, very."

When Roger finished his lecture to us, he left us to sleep or eavesdrop and went into the living room. He looked at Ellie and rolled his eyes before sitting down next to Aaron. "So," he said, "we'll get to the tofu dogs, but first tell me about what kind of night you guys had."

"It was a good night. After dinner, they cleaned up and then did their homework. Brenda came by to talk to Gary about working his process, turning over his sexual fibs. Ross was just reading this one enormous book and not writing anything, but he said it was for a class, and the other guys said that was the truth, so I figured it was okay. I can show you the book if you—"

"No, that's fine," Roger said. "I think I've heard about that."

"Yeah, so homework was good. And in the meeting, Benjamin checked in, and Adalberto was talking about this book his father sent him—"

"You mean Alberto?"

"Who?"

"Who did you say was talking in the meeting?"

"Adalberto?"

"Yeah, there's no Adalberto in this dorm. There's an Alberto."

Aaron looked over his shoulder at the closed door of our bedroom. "The kid with really short dark hair?"

"And the accent. The new kid."

"Yeah, his name's not Adalberto?"

"No, it's Alberto."

"Oh. I'm sure he told me that was his name. I've been calling him that all night."

"Maybe you just heard him wrong," Roger said.

"No, 'cause first I called him Alberto, and they corrected me."

"Uh-huh. So he was talking about a book?"

"Yeah, he was talking about this book his father sent him. It was about being, you know, like a ninja of the spirit, he said, a sort of peaceful warrior? He said it had really been helping him. The other guys were making fun of it and, well, he, Alberto, he got pretty upset, but otherwise things went fine. They all seemed okay later. We finished a little before you came in."

Roger nodded. "Okay. And the deal with the tofu dogs?"

"Oh, well, when we were done with the meeting the boys said they were still hungry and was there anything else to eat because they didn't like the pork chops or the enchiladas. Plus, by the time we bring food back here from the kitchen, it really is sort of cold."

"Well, Aaron, if they want warm food they should get their shit together and move up to a dorm that's not always on restriction," Roger said. Aaron must have looked hurt or confused, but Roger was intent not to let him make this his fault. "I know it sounds harsh, but they're the ones manipulating you. Don't look at me."

"Is there some rule against tofu dogs?" Aaron asked. "I didn't think it'd be such a big problem."

"There's no specific rule against tofu dogs, Aaron, but you know the schedule by now, don't you? Dinner, cleanup, home-work, meeting, bed. I don't understand why you'd decide not to follow that."

As the two men talked Ellie watched Aaron play with the band of his watch, slipping the end of it in and out of the loop it went through after passing through the buckle.

"I just thought that it would be good to get them to enjoy some-thing healthy," Aaron said. "They didn't ask for the tofu dogs, they were sure they wouldn't even like them. So I told them to just try one. And they did like them. It was like they learned that you have to try things. If anything, it was me manipulating them."

"Yeah, but Aaron, kids don't get sent to New Boys to learn to try new foods. This is the lowest-functioning dorm on campus. It's not a slumber party. These are dangerous kids. You saw what Gary did to William Kay with that closet rod, didn't you? And what William would've done back if we'd let him. The only lesson they need to learn is to not get violent and not run away, to follow the rules. And here you're helping them break the rules."

"So I should have sent them to bed hungry?"

"No, they should learn to eat the food that's provided for them and to be grateful for it."

Aaron nodded, thinking. "Well, what if one of them kept kosher?"

"Kosher? Aaron, who in this dorm is kosher? Adalberto?"

The wind outside whipped through the bare branches.

Then Ellie said, "Aaron, I know you were just trying to take good care of them, but really the best thing you can do is to help them follow the process here. It's probably the most difficult thing you can do for them. Even if you disagree with how the school does things, and I do all the time, the kids can't really choose to reject it."

Aaron sighed. "I know. I *know* that. But I hate going through the same motions night after night. I mean, anybody can just follow the schedule, you know?"

"Look, Aaron," Roger said, "don't think I haven't had my problems with this place too. My elbows are so messed up from all the restraints I've held kids in that I think about suing Aubrey for workman's compensation all the time. But it really does give the kids a sense of security to stick to the process. It's what they want, even if they'll never say so."

"I thought I was! I mean, I knew there was nothing about tofu dogs in their schedule, but I thought I was making a connection with the boys, you know? We were all getting along and laughing. I mean, isn't that a part of the process too, relationships?" He tugged at a loose piece of rubber on the side of his sneaker, and it peeled slowly away.

■　■　■

**Later, when Roger** and Ellie are walking back to the Paddock, Roger tells her he thought she'd been great.

"When?"

"It was just great, both of us helping Aaron understand the process. I know you've had your doubts, and I guess I used to, too, but it was really nice both being on the same page like we were."

"I really meant what I said. A lot of it's bullshit. Those poor kids are trapped here, though, and it isn't fair to them to pretend that there's any other way out than doing what they're told."

"Yeah," he says, with an edge that might be disappointment or sarcasm or fear. He watches crystals glint in the frozen snow as he walks. "It's like they say. Fake it till you make it."

**Inside the Cottage,** we were still talking. The Christmas lights flashed on and off in different patterns. Jodi only let us plug the lights in for a few minutes before going to sleep, but Aaron didn't know that.

"Do you think Aaron's going to get into trouble?" Alberto asked.

"Faculty can't really get into trouble," William said.

"They can get probated."

"Yeah, but then they get unprobated in like a week," I said. "They can hardly get anybody to stay and work here, so they're never going to fire anyone."

"Remember bald Matt?" Ross said. "He used to fall asleep when he was watching us and he didn't get fired."

"He was an honorary gypsy," Gary said.

"What?"

"That's what he told us, that he got made an honorary gypsy. I don't remember how."

"Hey, what'd you tell Brenda tonight?" Ross asked Gary.

"I bet you want to know, you little homo. You're almost as bad as she is. Don't worry, I came up with some pretty sick stuff."

"Come on, what was it?" Ross asked.

"What are you guys talking about?" This was Alberto, hanging down from his top bunk.

Ross sat up in his bed. "Gary decided he's a sex addict. If you want to follow the process to get privileges and move up through the dorms and get out of here," he said, "you've got to be dealing with some problem. It can be like alcoholism or drug abuse, or like you're addicted to sugar or you act out sexually. So Gary decided that he's convalescing from a sexual addiction. Brenda said she'd be his commitment holder, which means he's got to tell her about all his sexual acting out, so he can learn not to be ashamed of it."

I was laughing so hard at this; I don't even know why.

"Except," Gary said, "when I told her true stories, she thought I wasn't telling her everything, so I started exaggerating. And the more I'd exaggerate, the happier she'd get about how much I trusted her. You know, that I'm telling her that kind of stuff? At least that's what she said. I kind of think she's just getting off on it. But anyway, the weirder the shit I come up with is, the more honest and brave she thinks I am. So I just keep making up crazier and crazier stuff to tell her I've done."

"So what'd you say?"

"Well, you know how last week I made up that thing about jerking off our family's mule?" He looked up at Alberto and explained, "She thinks everyone in Moscow's got a mule in their backyard. So anyway, today I told her that I once convinced the baker's daughter, who was semiretarded, to come over and take off her clothes and I made her jerk off the mule while I watched. Then I told her how guilty I felt about having done that, and Brenda gave me this real long hug."

"Brenda was always hugging people in that Expressions class I was in," I said.

"Eww," Ross said. "She's like thirty."

"Yeah, but she's got a nice rack," Han Quek said. "Speaking of which, Benjamin, are you gonna get any off of Tidbit? She's still on Reciprocity Detail, isn't she?"

"Just make sure you don't get bit," William said.

Ross laughed. "Yeah, that's no joke. Don't get bit."

"What are you guys talking about?"

"You don't know? That's what she got sent here for."

"She told me she got sent here for taking meth and getting into fights."

William bounced on his back and kicked the bunk above him. "Ha, sucker. She got sent here for biting people," he said. "When she was totally sober."

"And she's done it like twice since she's been here," Ross said, "so that's got to be true."

"What do you mean, biting people?" I asked.

"Like she gets into fights and totally loses her shit and bites people. On the arm or shoulder or whatever. And doesn't let go."

"Shit," I said. The boys were quiet for a while, watching the Christmas lights blink slowly, one bulb glowing brighter as the one beside it faded, my roommates' faces and quilts changing color along with them. I couldn't tell how much time had passed when I heard Ross ask, "Hey, Gary, is that true? About the baker's daughter?"

"There's no baker. We got our bread from a supermarket, you dipshit."

**Ken's eyes and** bald head shone as he leaned forward and listened intently to Aubrey. Their waitress had just brought him a mug of hot tea, and Ken wrapped his hands around it gladly as if to demonstrate his appreciation for all simple things. He was a tall, athletic man in his fifties with a fringe of bright white hair and a neatly trimmed white beard.

"I think of the school," Aubrey was saying, "as an enormous psychic mending workshop. There are any number of mother and father figures for the students' transference, and though they don't explicitly enroll and disenroll people the way they do in your sessions, I think it's something that goes on all the time, beneath the surface, unspoken. There are so many different relationships changing form spontaneously, there's no way to control it, but it works. If you trust the system, the whole thing works."

Ken nodded as he stirred sugar into his tea, watching the spoon go round. It was clear to him that Aubrey had something more serious than this to discuss with him, and Ken felt he knew what it was. It was also clear to him that Aubrey wouldn't get to it until he had said whatever it was he needed to say. If that meant his condescending to Ken, Ken was happy to wait through it. He felt he held all the cards.

"Although," Aubrey allowed, "I suppose there's no reason why we couldn't make things more explicit, the way you do. There's a great deal of opportunity in a position like mine. Did I ever tell you about founding Roaring Orchards? It really wasn't anything I had planned to do."

They made room on the table as their waitress arrived with their lunch. Patti's Pantry wasn't the sort of place where Aubrey had imagined having this sort of conversation, but then his life seemed to have become a series of disappointing compromises. Ken certainly wasn't who he had thought of leaving in charge of the school he had built, but Ken was who there was. Aubrey had hoped that Doris might grow into her role, but he had since given up on her. At least Ken understood the process. If he was a bit rigid, the day-to-day vagaries of running the school would cure him of that. If Ken was a bit calculating, Aubrey hoped that would subside as he understood that he didn't need to wrest the school from Aubrey's control.

"I was a Latinist, working at a small school in Pennsylvania," Aubrey said. He fiddled with his French fries. "I was just out of school and hadn't been there long, but through a number of strange occurrences that I don't even really remember the particulars of, I ended up as the assistant headmaster. Mostly, I'm sure, because no one else wanted the job." Ken laughed at this, looking up from his soup. Aubrey smiled.

"And there was an incident with a few students, seniors, who had brought their girlfriends onto campus. I can still see the look on those boys' faces as they were standing in my little office. And it just didn't make any sense to me to expel them, which would have been the penalty. I realized that that's what all these schools do. Their job is to teach the students, but instead of teaching them they just toss out anyone who has something to learn. All of a sudden it seemed absolutely crazy to me. So I said we aren't going to expel these students, and we aren't going to expel students for anything, ever. We would discipline them, we would teach them, we would help them heal, but we'd never kick anyone out. And as soon as I made that decision, everyone went nuts."

"I can imagine," Ken said.

"It was so interesting. I didn't understand at the time why that would upset everyone so much. But within a week, the school's executive board had met and not only relieved me of my administrative responsibilities, they fired me as a teacher. And I spent two nights sleeping on the floor of my therapist's apartment because I really had nowhere else to go. But do you know who immediately understood what I was up to?"

"Who?"

"The parents," Aubrey continued. "About a third of them withdrew their kids from the school and came up here with me, and we bought Roaring Orchards. There was a lot of work to do on the Mansion and Classroom Building, but we all worked on it together. And I guess we still are." He took a bite of his tuna melt.

Ken wondered how much longer this would go on. He told Aubrey a little about what he had been up to. He had been traveling a good deal, doing workshops. And they still did the twice-yearly sessions at the complex in Pownal.

"At the old dog track?"

"Yes, the old dog track."

"But you think you might be interested in being in one place for an extended period," Aubrey said.

"I'm beginning to understand what the pleasures of a life like that might be."

Aubrey nodded. "You know, the truth is I've never really thought of myself primarily as a headmaster. I tend to think of what I do as essentially the work of a political theorist."

Ken crushed a cracker in his fist and dropped it into his soup. "Go on," he said.

# 5

Laurel paced around her room a little bit before sitting down on the lower bunk. Marcy still insisted on waking her up at the same time as everyone else, even though she couldn't use the bathroom until the other girls had left for breakfast. She was tired and had to pee. She walked across the hall to get clean underwear and sweatpants to change into later, tossed them on her bed, and sat down. The sound of the girls in the showers only made her have to pee worse. It had been a long time since Laurel had anything else to do but look out the window and think.

The scent of mixed shampoos drifted down the hall on the steam from the showers. The fruity smells tickled the back of her throat. Laurel walked over to the window and imagined her unicorn. Her window had a view of the small back parking lot and the stand of pines behind it. The pines surrounded a small above-ground swimming pool covered by a blue tarp. The unicorn Laurel imagined stood by one of the pine trees chewing on grass. He looked up at her. His coat was white but had yellowed. It was an effort for her to remember to imagine his horn.

When Marcy took her books away Laurel thought she could entertain herself easily by making up stories. She had been so excited about it that she began right away. Laurel thought about it now, that first day with nothing to do. She had imagined the campus full of all these beautiful horses with colorful manes and iridescent horns; she thought about what they all might be up to. But by the time Marcy came by with her lunch that day, Laurel had run out of ideas. And the whole thing began to seem juvenile, clichéd and cartoony. She was embarrassed just thinking of it.

But this one old-looking unicorn, who never did anything but chew grass and stare at her, had stuck in her head. Laurel tried to think up adventures for him. She pictured him lifting the tarp off the pool with his horn. She imagined him bursting into Aubrey's rooms and chasing him out of the Mansion. She couldn't even come up with a name for him. Her unicorn kept her company, in a way, but he was always a disappointment. Her imagination was this dismal thing, a top-heavy flower always flopping over whenever she tried to grab it.

As soon as New Girls left the dorm Laurel went to use the bathroom. She took her time. There were plenty of disadvantages to her rooming, but at least she could go to the bathroom without a dozen other girls within arms' distance. In general Laurel tried not to take advantage of being alone in the dorm but there wasn't any reason to hurry back to the room she would be sitting in all day. She stood under the shower until the hot water ran out.

Laurel dried herself roughly and got dressed. She spun a handful of toilet paper off a roll and took it with her when she left the bathroom. Back in her room Laurel hung her towel on its hook behind the door. From her dresser she took a pair of white socks and the razor blade she kept hidden in a gap where the bottom and side of the drawer were loosely joined.

Laurel pulled on her socks. She didn't like using the razor on herself when her skin still had the poached, rubbery feel from the hot water. She lay down on the bottom bunk and swung her right leg up, resting her foot against the bottom of the bunk above her. She looked up at her foot in its sock. What Laurel hated most about her rooming was that no one was watching her. It was insulting. Everyone was so sure that she wouldn't run away, it was like they were daring her to. She reached up and pulled the right leg of her sweats up to expose her calf and knee. She passed her hand over the thin white scars that ran along her calf parallel to her shin.

She had others, too, nests of irregular lines left on her hip, her thigh, above her elbow. It was because of these that she couldn't rejoin the dorm. If she did she would have to start showering with the girls again. They would see that she'd been cutting, and they would find out that she'd had the razor blade since Beverly dropped it in the bushes. There would be no end of trouble. Laurel ran her hand over the scars. Faculty looked at her like she was crazy when she insisted that she still couldn't remember that stupid conversation with Aubrey. They never considered she might have another reason for staying roomed, never thought there was ever anything going on that they didn't know about. No matter how many times things blew up in their faces.

Laurel picked up the razor blade and sat up. She leaned over her leg. She pressed one corner of the blade into her calf and slowly pulled it up toward the inside of her knee. Everything slowly went dim except the gray thing dragging through her. The gravelly sting pressed her edges and cleansed her steady breath. Tense, she lifted the blade. Tiny beads of blood appeared along the line she had made. The beads grew but didn't move, though her leg trembled. Her blood looked greasy and bright.

When she went to dab the blood with the toilet paper, Laurel noticed she was still clutching the razor blade between her thumb and index and middle fingers, the top knuckles bent backward and gone white. She put it down on the bed and pressed the paper against her leg. The paper absorbed the blood in splotches. She pulled it back to watch blood seep again from the cut, this time into a thinner line of dots and dashes.

When the cut had stopped bleeding Laurel made another one parallel to it. The pain was less focused now. The first cut still throbbed some. The reason she thought cutting wasn't working was that she didn't really believe in it anymore. Even as she did it she wondered whether she really had a good-enough reason to be cutting herself. The other girls all had such strange, awful stories about why they were the way they were. But Laurel didn't have much wrong with her. She pressed the toilet paper against the second cut and left it there while she absently rocked the blade back and forth against her shin, making tiny diagonal slashes. When she thought of what made her do it, nothing much came to mind. She thought of the sickly color of the thick wall-to-wall carpeting they had at home. It was gray with a touch of purple to it. Their dinner table had a glass top that her dad's watch knocked against every time he forked something off his plate, over and over again, all through dinner.

Laurel used the razor to trim the nail of her big toe. It was like the cuts were supposed to be arrows pointing to the thing that made you upset enough to make them. But with her, there was nothing where the arrows were pointing, just a blank. If New Girls saw the scars she had left all over herself and asked her why she'd done it, she wouldn't have any reason to give them. It was just something she did, but never too deep. It was something anyone could do.

She imagined slashing herself all over, but she could only bring herself to make cuts deliberately, where they wouldn't be easily seen. If she cut herself badly enough no one would say she was just being needy. But with the delicate scars she had etched into herself they would say she was doing it for attention, which for all she knew might be true. The only way she could tell was to see if she let herself get caught. As long as she kept her cutting secret she couldn't be doing it for attention. Which was why she knew she had to run away.

Laurel put the razor back in its hiding place in her drawer. Her hands still trembled, and the thrill of fear she always got from cutting made her a bit dizzy. When she went to the bathroom a little later to flush the bloody toilet paper, she looked around to find the room where Marcy had stored her things. She found them in garbage bags in an open room. When Laurel finally did run away, she took the razor with her. No one but she and Beverly knew what she'd been doing.

**New Girls were** annoyed that they even had to have a candor meeting about Laurel running away, since she hadn't really been in their dorm for weeks. Marcy assured them that it was just a formality, but she made them write fibs anyway. No one wrote anything, which was fine with Marcy. But when she asked whether anyone knew of any fibs Laurel might have had, Bev began rubbing her face with her fists.

"Bev?" Marcy asked.

"I don't know."

"You don't know what?"

Bev looked at her over her fists. "I don't know if I know if she had fibs or not."

"Look," Marcy said, "we're not going to go through this with you again. Go stand in the corner until you figure out whether or not you know."

"Okay, okay," Bev said as she got up and walked toward the corner. She paused. She opened her mouth but said nothing. Then she said, "I think Laurel cut herself. With the razor I dropped by the school building."

The dorm erupted in moans.

"That was like months ago," someone shouted. "This is ridiculous."

"She's just trying to pin it on Laurel 'cause she's gone," Carly Sibbons-Diaz said. "She probably still has it."

Marcy told Bev to sit back down.

"Are you making this up because you have the razor?" she asked.

Bev felt it had been a mistake to say anything. She should have kept quiet like everyone else.

"Bev, do you still have that razor?" Marcy asked.

Now she had to answer this. The truth hadn't worked so far, but she was sure the right thing was to say that she didn't have it. "No."

"But you had to think about it," Marcy said.

Bev couldn't tell if this was a question or not. "Yes," she said.

"Oh God," someone said from the other side of the lounge.

New Girls all had to stay where they were while Marcy called a couple of Regular Kids to come down and search Bev's room. While they waited, they continued their meeting.

"Why did you say that about Laurel?" Marcy asked Bev.

"I don't know anymore. I just miss her so much."

"Are you guessing or are you telling me the truth?"

"I'm telling you the truth?"

Marcy threw up her hands. The meeting went on like this for some time.

Carly Sibbons-Diaz asked, "How is it that what started off as a meeting about Laurel running away is now focused on Bev?"

"Um, maybe because she's a needy suckbag?" someone said. "Who needs to be ghosted."

"No," Bev said.

Bridget Divola gave an impatient little jump in her seat. "You guys are being so sideways. I'm so tired of everyone being called needy, needy, needy. I never even heard that word before I came here. And now it's all anybody can say. You can't use ghosting as a punishment or just because you don't want to include Bev."

"No," Carly said, "but if Bev can't get by without being the center of attention, then maybe being ghosted could teach her to be okay just in herself. It would help her to, you know, not always be needing validation."

The Regular Kids finished searching Bev's room. They didn't find anything. Marcy thanked them, and they went, but not before suggesting that there should be some sort of consequence that might keep Bev from setting situations like this up in the future.

"I think," Marcy told the Regular Kids, "I think she's trying to do the right thing. I'm just not sure that she knows what that is."

"Well, she's not working on following the process," Jenna told her. "None of us would be able to think clearly if we didn't. But she should know that there are consequences for that."

In the end, and against Marcy's better judgment, the dorm decided that Bev should be ghosted. No one would be allowed to speak to her or make eye contact with her until the consequence was lifted.

**Crocodile Tears had** live music on Thursdays; the teachers had often talked about going, but they had never gone. This week Doris was determined. The bar was connected to the one nice hotel in town, the Lamb & Goose. The music wasn't much of a draw, but this was Webituck, New York, and it was something to do. More important for Doris's purposes, it was someplace to go, someplace where the teachers could sit down like adults and order drinks among people who had no idea what a wiggle was or what "popped" meant. It was what she felt she needed. With some degree of desperation she set about getting as many of the other teachers as she could to take their weekly evening off on Thursday and join her for a drink.

By the time they all piled into one of the vans and left campus, the teachers felt less like normal people going to get a drink than like parents anxiously leaving their children for a few short hours. The dorm parents had wanted to know why everyone was taking the same night off. They wondered, not necessarily to themselves, why the teachers got to do something like that when the dorm parents never did. These were questions the teachers couldn't quite answer, other than to say that it seemed important to Doris. But things were arranged; people traded their scheduled nights off, and the teachers, except for Brenda, were accommodated. They were excited to all be getting off campus together, but even the tinge of giddiness they felt was simultaneously a defeat: they were relatively sure that normal people didn't get this excited about drinks at Crocodile Tears.

As she drove them into town, Doris thought about how to tell everyone that she was leaving. Hopefully, once they got settled at the bar someone would ask why she had wanted them all to go out together, and then she could explain. But if they didn't ask she wasn't sure how she would bring it up. She had to tell them tonight because tomorrow she would start packing up. She planned to be gone by the end of the weekend. Aubrey had asked her to please leave in the least disruptive way possible. At Roaring Orchards, this generally meant simply disappearing. In the rearview mirror, Doris could see that June was leaning her head against the rattling window and watching the landscape sail past. She reminded Doris of a child on a school bus. Spencer cried out that he thought he saw a big bird in a tree, and they all began speculating as to what it might have been.

Doris parked in the large lot behind the Lamb & Goose, the farthest reaches of which hadn't been cleared of snow. The teachers got out and waited for Doris, who walked slowly with her cane, watching out for patches of ice. They had moved on from joking about the bird Spencer saw to talking about run-ins with large birds generally. Dedrick was telling them that once, on a fishing trip, he'd been quietly stalked for hours by a peahen. Nervous about what an odd group they must seem, they laughed too loudly in the cold.

The teachers entered through the main doors of the Lamb &
Goose and headed downstairs to the bar. As she carefully negoti-
ated the stairs, Doris was upset to hear how loud it was. When
they entered Crocodile Tears, they saw a pudgy, bearded man on a
small stage playing acoustic guitar and singing into a microphone.
People were shouting to be heard over the music. The teachers
found two small tables that they pushed together. Doris sat down
and draped her wool coat over the back of her chair. While Spencer went to get a pitcher and some glasses, the rest of the teachers
smiled at one another and looked around the bar.

Doris noticed that other than the people sitting at the bar,
everyone seemed to have come in groups of four or five people.
Some were tourists, she imagined, or people up for the skiing at
Holiday Hill. But mostly, she guessed, these were everyday people
from around here, regular people with jobs. She wondered what
they all did. She would have liked to guess with June and the other
teachers, but it seemed childish. It was strange to think that she'd
soon be joining them in the world, the world outside of Roaring
Orchards.

Spencer returned with a pitcher in one hand and his other arm
draped over Zbigniew's shoulder. "Look who I found!" he cried.

"Hi, Zbyszek," June and Dedrick said. Doris waved. As Zbigniew
placed two stacks of pint glasses on the table, she noticed a tired-
looking woman with yellow hair following behind him. She
looked to Doris like she had a serious job, maybe lawyer or real
estate agent.

They pulled up a couple of extra chairs, and Spencer poured
beers for everyone, then went to get another pitcher. Zbigniew
introduced his friend Della to everyone. He was friendly, but
antsy—it was clear he hadn't been expecting to run into people from school at Crocodile Tears. Doris wondered how often
he came here. Being in charge of maintenance and Reciprocity

Detail, he didn't have a dorm to cover. It seemed odd to Doris, it seemed a failing, that she had never given any thought to what Zbyszek did in the evenings.

Spencer returned with two more pitchers, and after a couple of beers, things around the table were more comfortable. It turned out that Doris hadn't been too far off about Della. She was a receptionist at a real estate office. After a while, they were joined by her friend Anne. Anne was a brunette with high cheekbones and short bangs. Doris didn't catch what it was that she did.

By now, Doris had given up on having the conversation she wanted to have. Maybe she would get a chance later to talk to everyone about leaving; maybe she wouldn't. But this was her last night with her friends, even if they didn't know it, and she decided to try to enjoy herself. Faculty who left the school on bad terms, as Doris was about to do, were not allowed to visit campus or have any contact with students. The teachers and dorm parents could see her on their nights off, but Doris knew how difficult that would be.

The bar quieted some. The bearded man had stopped playing guitar and was now setting up a small drum kit on the stage. The teachers were trying to explain to Della and Anne what it was like working at the school. Spencer began to tell them about Bald Matt and Crybaby Matt, and they all leaned over their beers to listen.

"Wait," Anne interrupted as soon as he'd started, "you've all got nicknames for each other?"

"No, no," Spencer said. "They worked at the school at different times, so when they were there, we just called them each Matt. But since they left, we needed a way to know which one we were talking about. So now they're Bald Matt and Crybaby Matt.

Spencer tried to pour himself another beer, but the little left in the pitcher only filled his glass halfway. "So Bald Matt got his name because he was bald. But he was such a freak. When he was watching the kids in the evening, you'd go down there to help with homework or whatever, and he'd be walking around in his underpants. And he would tell the kids these nutso stories about his life before he started working at the school. Like he said he'd been part owner of a brothel someplace, and he'd somehow been made an honorary gypsy. I don't remember how that happened—we didn't find out a lot of this until after he left. Because as soon as he was gone, the kids played up how awful he was to them and all that, but while he was there they loved him because he had these crazy stories and he'd let them get away with anything."

"Like what?" Della asked.

"Oh, I don't know. I just remember he used to end each meeting by making them hold hands and say the mystic sound of om."

"What did he finally get fired for?" June asked.

Spencer looked around the table. "You know," he said, "I have no idea." Everyone cracked up at that. Spencer got up to get another pitcher and said, "Dedrick, you tell them about Crybaby Matt. That story breaks my heart every time."

Dedrick raised his glass to Spencer, he wasn't sure why. When Spencer had left, he asked Doris, "Do you remember why Bald Matt got fired?"

Doris had been listening so long, she was surprised to be addressed. "Yes," she said, "but I won't say."

Dedrick laughed again. "Fair enough. You guys really want to hear about Crybaby Matt?" He looked at Della and Anne, who were nodding. "All right. So this is how he got his name. We were all really happy when we hired this guy, 'cause he seemed normal enough, and as you can probably tell by now, normal is at a premium where we work. And I guess he was pretty normal; he just wasn't cut out for Roaring Orchards. He'd been at the school for —I don't know—maybe a week, and I ran into him on campus and asked him what's up. It turns out that he had that night off, and so did I, so I said, 'Well, we should do something.' I said I'd come by his room when I got done with classes.

"So I go up to his room, which is on one of the upper floors of the Mansion. The door's not quite closed, and I can hear him inside. But he doesn't answer when I knock. So I open the door and peer in, and Matt's there, sprawled out on his bed just bawling his eyes out. Which is awkward. There aren't even any sheets on the bed. I feel for the guy, plus I'm hoping he'll stay, so I tried to be supportive, and I asked him, 'Matt, man, how're you doing?'"

Dedrick leaned his head on his fist for a second, laughing. "And then Matt looks up at me, his eyes all red and his hair all crazy, and he screams at me through his tears, 'How does it look like I'm doing?'"

When the teachers stopped laughing, Della asked, "Wait, but why was he crying?"

Dedrick was annoyed to have to explain. "Because he'd just moved to this place and found out it was totally nuts, or because he realized he'd have like no free time and be surrounded by lunatics and be totally cut off from the outside world." Dedrick swirled his beer in his glass, then smirked. "The real question," he said, "is why aren't the rest of us crying all the time. Anyway, then for Halloween, Crybaby Matt decided to dress up as our headmaster Aubrey. Aubrey lent him one of his suits, and when Matt inevitably bolted, he took it with him. Aubrey still yells at us about it sometimes."

**The teachers all** headed back to campus together. Spencer made a clumsy attempt to stay at the bar with Zbyszek, Della, and Anne and was a bit too drunk to pick up on their hints that he go. But Dedrick convinced him, and they all rode home in silence. They decided to go back to Dedrick's apartment to watch a movie. Doris parked the van in the lot by the Paddock.

Spencer found a bottle of wine that he tried to open while Dedrick and June looked through the tapes for something to watch. The cork in the wine bottle squeaked as Spencer turned it. It wasn't coming out, though he kept trying.

Doris imagined telling them she was going. She feared they would try to convince her to stay, and she was afraid she would let them succeed. But she knew that wouldn't happen. It couldn't— Aubrey had asked her to leave so that Ken could begin taking over. Maybe it was just a fantasy, that they would beg her to stay and convince Aubrey to let her.

Doris didn't want to go, she realized. These were some of the nicest people she knew. It was true that there was something strange about people who stayed at Roaring Orchards, something dependent and passive, but there was also something genuinely sweet about them. You couldn't stay at the school long if you were judgmental. You couldn't stay there long if you were selfish. Doris had never felt as accepted as she did there. She knew every inch of the campus, every uneven hallway and irregular corner in the Mansion, every preposterous sign on the grounds. She knew all the rules and the logic behind all the rules. Doris thought of her small apartment, of the room where she'd fallen asleep and woken up thousands of times.

She felt a tickle across her lips and heard June shout, "Doris, you're bleeding!"

Doris brushed her hand across her mouth and saw a bright string of blood dangle from her hand as more dripped down her face.

June was on her feet. "I'll get some towels."

"But what—"

"It's just a nosebleed, don't worry."

Doris pinched her nose and leaned forward, trying to catch the blood in her palms. She could hear the squeaking of the wine bottle resume as Spencer tried again to twist out the cork. June came and led Doris to the bathroom. She helped clean her up. When her nose had stopped bleeding and the shock had passed, Doris sat down on the edge of the tub and began to cry. No one understood why until she returned to Dedrick's living room and told her friends that she was leaving.

# 6

Tidbit and I were working behind the Cafetorium, flattening boxes. There was a shed where Floyd put all the cardboard boxes that food for the kitchen came in, and these had to be flattened and taken to the recycling Dumpster by the Farm. We tore the boxes at the corners or pulled off the packing tape and piled the flattened cardboard in a wheelbarrow.

"D'you hear about Laurel The Pfaff?" Tidbit asked.

"I don't hear about anything that you don't tell me. I'm in a restricted dorm. It's a fib to tell me anything."

"Well, she ran the other day."

"Which one was she again?"

"She'd been here forever. She was roomed."

"No one was watching her?"

Tidbit shrugged. "I guess Marcy didn't think she'd run. She'd been here forever."

I was struggling to collapse a box that had been wrapped in plastic tape. "What did you call her?"

"Laurel The Pfaff. That was her nickname that Aubrey popped, but I guess it's unpopped now. This is funny. She got it because she'd been at the school so long that one day a letter came saying that she had jury duty. And the computer that sends the letters includes your middle name, but just the first three letters. Her middle name is Theresa, so the envelope read 'Laurel The Pfaff.'"

I didn't really get it.

"I mean, it was really funny because she was so embarrassed that she was still here when she was old enough to be on jury duty. And everyone knew that Aubrey would never let her go. So we were joking about the police coming to get her. Sheldon, this guy who used to work here, could do really good helicopter sound effects, and he was like *ft-ft-ft-ft-ft-ft* and then said, like through a loudspeaker, 'Surrender The Pfaff immediately, we know The Pfaff is in there.' I think that's when she wrote Aubrey a letter and he popped the nickname."

I placed the last few boxes we'd flattened on the wheelbarrow. "We should take these to the Dumpster." I pushed the wheelbarrow toward the Farm, but it tottered and lurched over every bit of uneven ground, and it was impossible to keep the cardboard from slipping off the top of the pile. Finally, Tidbit held the pile steady as I carefully guided the wheelbarrow along.

"Any gossip in New Boys?" Tidbit asked.

"Not really. William Kay got moved up to Alt Boys."

"Really? He'll just get moved back. He's a complete menace."

"I know," I said. The campus was dusted lightly with snow. There were puddles in the tire tracks on the side of the path, lacy with ice at the edges. "Do you think she'll get far?"

"Who, Laurel? She can go wherever she wants. She's nineteen."

"Well, what's the farthest anyone's ever gotten?"

Tidbit lurched to catch some of the boxes that began to slide off the pile. "I never got very far," she said. "But there were these two girls, Kim Henry and Cerelle something or other, who ran away from here once. They were away a couple of days, I guess, and then it was Sunday morning. And they were kind of a mess, but they went to this church over in Bilston. And they gave these people at the church their whole story, about how they'd run away from their school, and they'd been having this horrible time and they wanted to go back and all that but they'd spent all their money. Except they said they'd run away from a school in California and that they'd hitched all the way across the country. And the people at this church actually put together a collection for them and bought them two tickets to California. As far as I know, that's the farthest."

"Wow." I had stopped the wheelbarrow.

"Yeah. But I don't think anyone could do that again. At least not with that church."

"What happened to them?"

"Cerelle got brought back here, but she ran again, and I think she ended up in a locked facility in like Wisconsin or someplace. Maybe Minnesota. I don't know what happened to Kim. Maybe she's still in California."

"Hmm."

"Yeah. She was nice."

On our way to the Dumpster we saw Zbigniew working on the fence to the pigpen. He waved hello. We waved back. Tidbit flipped open the lid of the Dumpster. When she tossed a cardboard box in, one of the campus's stray cats leaped out. It was a skinny orange thing and bolted into the pigpen. Zbigniew looked up and over at us. The cat disappeared into a pile of hay.

"I miss Fatface," Tidbit said.

We were quiet as we threw one flattened box after another into the Dumpster. This part was easy and went too fast. I turned the wheelbarrow to head back to the Cafetorium and break down more boxes, but Tidbit put her hand on my arm. "We should ask Zbyszek about where to leave the turpentine."

For the past couple of days Zbigniew had made us clean the windows of the Classroom Building that New Girls had painted over at the end of the summer. He had given us a couple of rags and an old can of turpentine. We hadn't been able to get the can closed right so we just left it in his office. Tidbit and I walked over to the pigpen to ask him about it, and he told us to bring him the can. So we headed to his office in the equipment shed to get it.

On the way, I asked Tidbit if she thought she would run away again. She didn't know. It was difficult to imagine that she would stay at the school until she graduated. But then she said that no, she wasn't going to run away again. We found the can and walked out, back down the narrow dirt path through a small copse of trees.

"Okay," Zbigniew said when we got back to the pen. "Leave the can. I'll take care with it when I finish the gate."

Tidbit and I leaned against the fence to watch the pig, the goat, and the few chickens. The goat was standing on the pig. That was how they spent their days, the pig lying on its side, the goat standing on it, scaring away the chickens. The goat was small, but its ears were long and hung down past its chin. Its brown coat was long as well, and two pale, thin horns grew out of its head. The pig was pale and very fat.

"We still haven't named them," I said.

"They have names," Tidbit said.

"It doesn't count if no one remembers what their names are." We had spoken about this before.

"They might remember," Tidbit said.

"They don't remember."

"What do you want to name them?"

"I don't know."

"We could name the pig Napoleon, like in that other book," Tidbit said.

"No," I said, "the goat should be Napoleon. He's small but he always stands on top."

"Then what do you want to name the pig?"

We were quiet for a moment, as a breeze sifted through the small woods. Then we heard Zbigniew call out slowly, as though enjoying the sound of it, "Elba."

**There was an** enormous fire already going in the fireplace as the faculty members wandered alone or in groups into the Great Hall for their weekly meeting. The first people began moving furniture, getting the low round table out of the center of the room, and dragging in mismatched armchairs from the Meditation Room and the Reception Room. When the seats were filled, teachers and dorm parents sat on the floor cross-legged or with their legs stretched out before them, completing the circle. Most had taken off their shoes, which was generally believed to facilitate more honest sharing. The Regular Kids were watching the dorms for the evening. Everyone began to quiet down.

"All right," Roger said. He was squashed into a corner of the long couch, his right leg crossed over his left knee. "I think Marcy said she wanted to check in tonight, and Aaron. Anyone else?" He looked around. "No one? Okay, who wants to start? Marcy, where are you? Do you want to start?"

"Thanks, Roger." Marcy settled herself in her chair. It was a black walnut armchair upholstered in light blue tartan. The legs ended in claw feet. "I just wanted to check in tonight to let everyone know how I'm doing. As some of you know"—Marcy smiled at a few faces around the circle that nodded in recognition—"as some of you know, the whole time I've worked here, I've continued seeing the therapist I was seeing in town before I took this job. I made an arrangement with Aubrey that I would have therapy on campus like everyone else, but I didn't want to stop seeing my therapist from before. Especially since when I started here Aubrey told me it would never work out, that I wouldn't last here, I shouldn't even bother, I'd end up quitting, and so on." Marcy laughed. "You know Aubrey. So I've been seeing two therapists, which hasn't always been easy." Marcy laughed yet again and rolled her eyes as if to say that she could tell some stories. She proceeded to tell a story.

Her old therapist had been working with her on learning to love herself. And the easiest way for Marcy to work toward this, he had explained, would be to begin by learning to love her inner child, whom he referred to as Little Marcy. The off-campus therapist even gave her a stuffed animal to represent Little Marcy, a kind of Raggedy Ann doll with brown hair like her own. And this had worked well for a while, Marcy said. She had felt a special type of affection for the doll, and she felt better generally as well. The idea was that if she could feel protective and compassionate toward Little Marcy, then why would adult Marcy deserve any less?

"I know this must all sound a little cuckoo. I mean, not just the doll and Little Marcy business, but I take care of a dorm *full* of Little Marcys every day! And that's what I said: I'm very nurturing, especially when it comes to empowering young women. This isn't something I particularly need to work on. But he was right—I started doing therapy with that doll, and suddenly I started feeling this change. I was so sad, but I was seeing things more clearly, I mean even visually I was noticing details and seeing distinctions more clearly. Honestly, I don't care if it sounds silly, because it was real and it was important, so I'm willing to risk whatever people might think. And emotionally it was like this great weepy clot in me was dissolving, and I was really feeling everything. I was so sad about how I had treated myself for so long and so excited about doing a better job from now on. Some nights before going to sleep I would just hug Little Marcy and cry.

"And then it stopped. The feeling just disappeared. It wasn't gradual, it was all at once, and I went back to feeling even worse than I had been before Doctor—before my therapist had given me Little Marcy. I didn't know if it just felt worse because I had a glimpse of how much better I could feel or be or what, but this doll went completely inert to me, I couldn't muster any sympathy for her or anything."

Marcy was sitting cross-legged in her armchair. She raised her knees so that she could hug them. "I didn't know what had happened, so I told Simon, who's my therapist on campus, the whole story I just told you. And he was, like, really annoyed. Like he was mad that I told him about it or that I hadn't told him about it till then, I don't know. But it upset me, and he wouldn't really talk about it, so I tried to talk about it with my other therapist, and that helped some, but now I'm like spending most my time, with either therapist, talking about the other one. And I don't know how to get out of it."

When it was clear to everyone that she was done, other faculty members began gently offering comments or asking questions, carefully avoiding making any suggestions about the problem with the two therapists. For reasons she couldn't articulate, Marcy became more and more frustrated.

"And this doll," Marcy said, "Little Marcy. Maybe I didn't make clear that that's still really a problem. I mean, I actually find her kind of chilling now. Wherever she is in my room I'm aware of her. I'll hide her in a drawer or something so I can sleep, but I know she's there. And I feel guilty, but if I go and try to take better care of her, as soon as I see her I'm disgusted or terrified or I don't know what."

Marcy looked out on a roomful of concerned, nodding heads. She was slightly out of breath. Dedrick was writing something down in the little notebook he kept with him. After a few people had said what they could to help, Roger thanked her and suggested they move on. Jodi fed the fire more logs. It's so strange to think that I'm older now than many of the faculty members were then.

The faculty shifted its attention toward Aaron, who sat in the middle of the long couch with other dorm parents on either side of him. He twisted his hips off the couch to retrieve a folded piece of loose leaf paper from his back pocket. He looked to be enduring a dull, obliterating pain.

"Thanks, Roger, everyone. Okay. I haven't done this before, and this isn't easy but. Well, this morning. Whoa." Aaron took a deep breath and rattled open his piece of paper. For a while he stared at it. "I had a meeting with all the dorm parents this morning and we talked about, I guess a lot of you know that I've been having a tough time lately with my job. Feeling overwhelmed. Messing up. And I admitted this morning that I had missed giving my dorm their meds a couple of times, and I hadn't filled out the med error reports, and we talked about that."

Aaron looked up upon hearing some hushed reaction but immediately looked back down at his page and continued.

"I wanted to probate myself for it, but we talked about it, and I guess I wasn't entirely clear about what had happened, and Roger said he thought, or it sounded like to him, that I had fibs. So we decided that I should spend the day writing down my fibs, and I want to read them and probate myself here with all of you to show that I'm really serious about fixing these things and doing a better job. And I want to thank the people who covered my dorm today while I was doing that. So, okay. Well, most of you know that I was the one who was covering New Boys on the Parents' Sunday when the ax didn't get put away. I probated myself for that with my dorm staff. But I thought I'd mention it here. And there are the missed meds I was talking about this morning."

As Aaron tried to be more clear than he had been in the morning about the circumstances under which he failed to administer medications, the rest of the faculty noticed that Aubrey had quietly entered the Great Hall and joined the circle. He stood standing next to Spencer who was sitting in a Windsor armchair with his back to the fire. When Spencer saw Aubrey he stood up and offered his chair. Aubrey nodded and sat down. Only then did Aaron become aware of him.

"No, please don't stop," Aubrey said. "I'm just joining the circle. Ignore me."

So Aaron did his best. He continued hesitantly, "Another fib is that one Saturday when I was covering Alternative Boys during cleanup I had the radio playing in the lounge and I turned it up so the kids could hear it. And then they started asking me to change it or put on this kind of music or that kind, and I did. Another fib I had wasn't exactly a broken rule but something I've felt guilty about. When I was first working here I was talking to Carly Sibbons-Diaz, and she was asking me about what kind of drugs I'd done, and when she asked me if I'd ever done heroin I told her I had, even though I never did. I just thought I'd have more authorit—"

"Enough, enough," Aubrey said. "Now I remember why I don't come to these meetings." He stood up. "Aaron, you poor thing, please, sit down over here by the fire." He tapped the short, spindled back of the armchair he had just been sitting in. Unsure whether it was some sort of trick, Aaron looked around and walked over and took the seat Aubrey offered. Aubrey motioned for someone to give him a chair facing Aaron.

"Now, I missed how you began. Why on earth is it that you were reading through this litany of nonsense?"

"I've been, you know, I've been making a lot of mistakes with my job. The responsibilities? And I talked about it with the dorm parents' group and we decided that if I got clean of all my intimacy blockers before probating myself—"

"Probate, schmobate, you're a wonderful man. How long have you been working here Aaron?"

"About five months."

"And in that time everyone here has taught you all the vocabulary, but they haven't taught you what any of it means, because apparently they have no goddamn idea. To see a fundamentally decent man struggling to do a better job here and then have a roomful of his colleagues sit and watch him flagellate himself . . . it wouldn't be any different if you were cutting yourself with a knife and they didn't do anything to stop it, or if they sat around and watched you put a needle in your arm, because you get the same rush from tearing yourself down, don't you?"

Aaron didn't know how to respond.

"Tell me what you're feeling, Aaron."

"I, uh, I'm a little confused right now."

"Good. That's an honest start."

"I guess why I'm confused is that I thought that if I turned over all my intimacy blockers then maybe I wouldn't screw up so much any—"

"My God," Aubrey said quietly. "He must've been a real bastard."

Aaron nodded, then asked, "Wait, who?"

"Your father. He must've been a real bastard. An impossible man to satisfy."

"I don't—"

"Aaron, let's start with something simple. Can you feel the fire behind you?"

"Sure."

"Tell me about it."

"About the fire?"

"Yes, do you feel the heat from the fire?"

"Sure."

"So talk about that for a minute."

"Well, my back is warm, especially my shoulders."

"Okay."

"Because there's just the wood bars. And the back of my neck, that's where the heat's strongest, I guess that's because my skin's not protected. I can feel the heat against the backs of my legs, my calves, too. But not as strong."

"All right, now let's move to something slightly more abstract. How are you feeling more generally, Aaron?"

Aaron sighed. "I just don't feel like I'm doing a very good job here, and I don't know—"

"But, Aaron, that isn't a feeling. You might be doing a good job, you might not be. Would you like to check that out?"

"How? You mean ask?"

"Yes. Go ahead."

"Uh, okay. Do you think I'm doing a good job?"

"No, I just keep you around because every month your parents send me a little of your Bar Mitzvah money." When Aaron saw that the rest of the faculty members were chuckling, he laughed, too.

"Aaron, you're exactly the sort of person the students can learn the most from, and they'll learn even more if you can role-model how to be honest about what you're feeling. As for the rest of you, I can't imagine what good you thought might come from humiliating this man. *This*, this is how you can do therapy with someone who's hurting, whether it's a member of your own group in this meeting or one of your students in a dorm meeting or in a classroom. Get them grounded, get them to live in the present, in the real. And then you can move their attention from what's going on around them to what's going on inside.

"Now, Aaron, let's move on to that. Tell me how you're feeling."

"Well, in general I'm feeling better, but I guess I'm a little upset about what you said about my dad."

"Very good. Go on."

For the rest of the meeting, Aubrey continued his demonstration with Aaron. When the meeting was over, everyone put the furniture back where it had been.

■ ■ ■

**There must have** been a morning when Roger's alarm clock buzzed through the silence, when Ellie slapped at it a few times before finally hitting the right button and was left staring up into the dark, her pulse raw and throbbing. Roger rubbed his face against his shoulder and slept. Ellie sat up and pulled the wool blanket around her. It was sickeningly cold. She groped along the cord of the bedside lamp to find the flimsy dial and turn it on. The window gave back to her a paler version of herself.

The windows were bare because window treatments were the school's responsibility, not Roger's. More than once now he had explained to her that this had been decided in a meeting with Aubrey and that he, Roger, was waiting for the school to take care of it. Ellie looked at him. He didn't have to be up for another hour and a half. In the lamplight Roger's back seemed a perfectly smooth white expanse, like cheese or uncooked dough. His shoulders were lightly dotted with freckles the same ginger color as his hair. Ellie caught herself thinking of something she had read once, that in Japan, ghosts have no feet. She had no idea why she thought of that. She climbed out of bed and gasped at the coldness of the floor against the soles of her own two feet.

Ellie took the shampoo from the wire basket hanging from the shower nozzle. She had an inclination to believe she was too good for him. She hated that about herself, but it wasn't something she could unthink. It was only by staying with Roger, by humbling herself, that she could wear away that ugliness in herself, Ellie thought. This was one of the things she could learn, as long as she had to stay at the school. The school's lawyers were dragging her case out the way Roger had told her they would. They assured her this was the best way. But she wondered whether she wouldn't rather accept the court's judgment than spend any more time at Roaring Orchards. Ellie stared at the water stains on the bottom of the shower. She twisted off the water and dried herself with a thick white towel she had brought from her parents' house. Her parents had found a lawyer they wanted her to talk to. Ellie went back to Roger's bedroom, where she sat on the floor to pull on her clothes so that she wouldn't be seen through the bare windows.

The first plum blush of dawn outlined the farthest mountains as Ellie crossed campus toward the Cafetorium. Phys ed was held there in the winter to save the cost of heating the Gym. The frost that tipped the grass disappeared as Ellie dragged her feet through it, leaving two crooked lines of darker green to mark where she passed across the silvered green of the lawn.

I and the rest of the students waiting outside in the cold pushed our fists deeper into our pockets, sleepily stomped our feet, and huddled together. It was one of the only activities I was required to attend while on Reciprocity Detail. Our stomping feet and the steam rising from our mouths and noses always made me think of a pack of animals. Which I suppose we were. Ellie pulled open the cold metal door and let us in. Our cheeks were flushed as we filed past. We bumped gently into her and one another, walked with small shuffling steps, our eyes closed. Our coats were bulky and soft. My eyes were tired and stung from the cold.

Ellie followed the last of us into the building. Inside it was dark except for the light from the kitchen, where Floyd was busy. The Cafetorium was full of the sluggish smells of breakfast and the ticks and scrapes of Floyd at work. After piling our heavy winter parkas and down jackets on one of the round wooden tables, some of us curled up on the floor for a few more minutes of sleep before Ellie brought the AV cart from the storage room. On her way she flipped on the lights, to our vain protests. She paused and looked back at us lying on the floor and shading our eyes, but only for a moment.

When Ellie got the thing into the Cafetorium and plugged it in she asked, "Which one do you guys want?"

There wasn't any answer from the students lying around the Cafetorium. We were intent on slowing things down. She read out loud from the stack of videocassettes piled on top of the VCR. "There's this *Oldies 'n' Aerobics* one, *Stretching to the Classics, Flexercise, Christmas Carol Ab-Workout*—"

"Not the ab workout," someone said from the carpet.

"Play the war one," Pudding said.

Ellie looked through the stack but didn't see anything like that.

"It's in the machine," Pudding said. "Dedrick played it yesterday."

She turned on the TV and hit PLAY. Creedence Clearwater Revival's "Run Through the Jungle" blared as a group of people in camouflage shorts and army fatigues flickered onto the screen behind the tracking lines. They ran in place and waved their hands over their heads. Some wore elastic headbands. Some had red handkerchiefs tied around their heads.

"No, let's do *Flexercise*," someone moaned from the floor.

"Everyone up," Ellie said. "Everyone up or I'm not signing your checksheets."

We slowly stood and arranged ourselves in front of the AV cart, mimicking the exercises in the video. Ellie dropped into a plastic chair to our side. She stared out at us while we aerobicized, but as the first song ended and the second began, Ellie noticed that Beverly Hess wasn't exercising. She just stood still in the crowd with her eyes closed.

"Bev, let's see you moving please."

"You can't talk to her," Carly Sibbons-Diaz called out. "She's ghosted."

"Excuse me?"

Carly stopped exercising and turned to Ellie. "Bev's neediness was getting beyond all proportion. The dorm voted to put her on a structure. We're not supposed to talk to her or look at her really."

"Until when?"

"Until she gets unghosted."

"But *you're* talking about her," Ellie said, sounding juvenile.

"Well, we can talk about her as long as we do it as if she's not here. We can't acknowledge her."

Other students had stopped to watch Ellie and Carly, but Bev was still facing the television with her eyes shut. "You know what," Ellie said, "everybody back to exercising. You too, Carly. If I need to talk to Bev to get her to behave, then that's what I'm going to do."

"Okay," Carly said, "but you're kind of splitting."

"Bev," Ellie said, standing up. "Bev." Bev didn't respond. Ellie walked over and leaned down so that her face was inches from Bev's. "*Bev.*" Bev kept her eyes closed.

Ellie sighed deeply and stepped behind Bev. She grabbed her forearms just below the elbows. As the pipes and drumrolls introducing "Billy Don't Be a Hero" came on she said, "Bev, you're going to do these exercises even if I have to do them with you. Do you understand?" When Bev didn't respond, she began.

She swung Bev's arms back and forth and then from side to side, like the people in the video were doing. She thought she felt Bev laughing. The rest of us began laughing as well. After a few moments Bev went limp and collapsed backward into Ellie's arms. Ellie caught her under the armpits and slowly let her down onto the ground. Leaning over her, Ellie watched to make sure she was breathing. She couldn't tell if she saw a slight smirk.

"Oh God," Carly said.

"Everyone leave her alone," Ellie said. She rolled the AV cart a few feet to the left. "Guys, move over here so you don't step on her. No, just leave her there."

Bev lay on the green carpet as we continued to exercise beside her. Ellie checked on her occasionally, less because she was worried than because she didn't want to let Bev go to sleep. Once or twice she pulled Bev's eyelids open and looked into her eyes as though she knew what she were doing. Bev continued to pretend that she was passed out. But when the tape was drawing to an end and we were cooling down to Donovan's "Universal Soldier" Bev began to shake and spit. She spun about on the carpet and opened her eyes wide. Ellie ran over and kneeled by her. Bev looked terrified. She looked over Ellie's shoulder and shook her head.

"No," Bev yelled. "No!"

Ellie looked back over her shoulder to see what Bev was looking at. She didn't see anything. Now Bev's eyes were squeezed shut and she was slapping at something a few inches in front of her face. And she was shouting. Ellie grabbed her by the wrists and pinned her hands to the ground.

"Bev," she said, "Bev. Look at me. What's wrong?" Bev only struggled to turn her face away.

Floyd had stepped out of the kitchen and was standing tentatively at the other side of the Cafetorium, wiping his hands on a kitchen towel. "Everything okay?" he called.

"I don't know," Ellie said. "Bev? Are you okay?"

"Don't let them get me," Bev said. She seemed genuinely frightened. Despite knowing better, I felt my skin go cold.

"Who's going to get you, Bev? No one's there."

"They're coming at me, from the vents. They're spirits!"

Ellie let go and stood up. She looked again at where Bev had been staring and noticed a heating vent high on the wall near the clock. Bev was still writhing on the floor and shrieking. Floyd walked over to better see what was going on. He stood next to Ellie with his hands on his hips.

"I see them, I'm seeing them," Bev said. "Help me!"

"Should we do something?" Floyd asked Ellie.

"I don't know. She's faking, I'm sure." Ellie didn't sound entirely sure. She turned to the rest of us. The exercise tape had finished and we were getting our coats on. "Wait there, everybody. You can't leave without Bev."

"We need you to sign our phys ed cards," Eric Gold said. "And we need to go back and shower so we can get to breakfast on time. Couldn't just New Girls stay?"

"We're supposed to ignore her," Carly said. "That's the whole point of her structure."

Ellie looked down at Bev, who seemed calmer. She was still staring at the heat vent and breathing heavily. "Has she done anything like this before?" Ellie asked.

"Not really like this," Carly said. "But she's said stuff about spirits."

"Recently?"

"Uh-huh."

Ellie kneeled next to Bev and helped her sit up. "Honey, are you all right?"

Bev blinked at her. "What happened?" she asked. "What am I doing on the floor?"

Ellie just looked at her. "Bev, do you think you can stand up?"

With Ellie's help she stood and looked around herself curiously. Ellie handed Bev her coat. Bev staggered to join her dorm and the rest of us. Ellie initialed the small squares of paper we each held out. "Could someone please put the AV cart back in the storage room?" Ellie called as we were hurrying out. No one did, and she was left to roll it back to its corner, over the tangle of extension cords and the long cords of old vacuum cleaners.

# 7

**I**t was at a Campus Community meeting that Aubrey broke the news that Doris had left and introduced Ken. The students were all shocked that Doris was gone—we were used to faculty members disappearing, but Doris in particular had seemed like someone without anyplace else to go. That, and her resigned oddness, had made her similar to a lot of us, and we'd grown to like her.

After Aubrey said a little bit about Ken, Ken took the opportunity to say he hoped no one would hold Doris's leaving against him. "I'm sure there are many of you who are going to miss—"

"Don't do that," Aubrey said.

"I'm sorry?"

"There's no need, Ken. Look," Aubrey said, turning to the students in the room. "No one here is more disappointed than I am that Doris couldn't handle her responsibilities. I hired her, and I relied on her, and I'm very hurt by her. But for those of you who were close to Doris, or those of you who have been abandoned in the past by women you relied on, this brings those feelings up and gives you the opportunity to deal with them. And that is a lot of what Ken's brand of therapy, psychic mending therapy, is about. It's very much like what goes on here every day, the way that different people on campus will take on different roles in their various relationships. And we observe how we react to one another, and we talk about what feelings that evokes and try to figure out why. Well, Ken's workshops do very much the same things but in a more formal way. Ken, you're laughing. Why are you laughing?"

"Because I'd forgotten quite what it's like around here, Aubrey. I hope you students understand what an exceptional teacher you have in this man. To take something like a headmistress's departure, and rather than seeing it the way I think we all did, as a negative, you manage to see what's healing about it. That's just wonderful."

Ken told the students and faculty members at the meeting that he was looking forward to getting to know us. That he wasn't going to jump right in with his system, but he was going to hang back and do a lot of listening and soon would hold some workshops so everyone could see what he was all about. Until then, he'd just be around. We could call him Ken or Dr. Ken, whichever we felt more comfortable with. As Aubrey went around the room, each member of the faculty and each Regular Kid took a turn at welcoming Ken to Roaring Orchards. Jenna also announced that on a Saturday in a few weeks' time, we would be having a square dance.

**Tidbit and I** got our schoolwork done early. It was our day to mop the floors in the Classroom Building, so when the other students finished classes we went to do our Reciprocity Detail. Roger had also asked that we dust the shelves in the library. It was one of the things he felt had slipped through the cracks when Doris had been in charge.

We were in the back corner of the library, cleaning the encyclopedias. Tidbit sprayed the books with cleaner, and I wiped them down.

"You have a zit," Tidbit said, "on your nose."

I kept cleaning. "So? I have one by my ear, too."

Tidbit stopped spraying books and looked at me. "I don't see it."

"My other ear." I nodded for Tidbit to move down the aisle so we could clean the books farther down. She slid a little way down the carpet, and I followed.

"Can I pop it?" she asked.

"No."

"Why not?"

"I don't pop them."

"What, never? Why not? That's the only good thing about having zits. Sometimes I put it off, to save them for later, but I always eventually pop mine." She was talking slowly, drawing this out to get a reaction. "And every night before bed, I squeeze out the blackheads around my nose."

I just looked at her and then back at the encyclopedias.

"C'mon, just let me pop the one by your ear. I'll let you do one of mine."

"No." I couldn't help laughing a little. "I don't want to pop any of yours. Besides, the one by my ear hurts."

"Oh, then you *have* to pop it." She dropped the spray bottle and crawled around to my other side. "Lemme see." She took my head in her hands. I squirmed some but let her look. Her hands felt cold against my face. "Oh yeah, this'll stop hurting if you pop it."

"Don't."

She pinched the zit above my ear, and I flinched.

"Stop moving," she said, sitting up on her knees and pushing my head against her thigh. I smelled the all-purpose cleaner we were using on the books and the detergent scent from her jeans. I felt her lean over me. She was humming some song.

"Ow, ow!" I said. "Quit it!" The pain was sharp. It didn't feel like a zit that was going to pop.

"Is it hurting less or hurting more?"

I twisted my head each time Tidbit pinched, rubbing against the texture of her jeans. "More, more, more." My right eye was closed and pressed against her thigh. My left was looking directly at one of her rivets. Under her breath, Tidbit sang the song she had been humming, "*Babe, your love's got me retarded, the way Heloise was Abelarded.*" It hurt enough where she was pinching me that I wondered whether she might actually do some serious damage.

"Oh, hold on," Tidbit said. She slid my head down her leg and onto the floor. I felt the carpet against my cheek and her breast against my shoulder.

"It's about to go," Tidbit said, more to herself than to me. She seemed almost out of breath.

"Stop it, it—"

But with a sudden rush it was over. My whole head stung. Tidbit said, "Ooh, that was a bad one," and wiped her hands on the carpet, letting me up.

"See? I bet it hurts less now."

I rubbed the side of my head. "It hurts less than when you were squeezing it."

"You'll see. It'll feel better."

"You didn't make it bleed, did you?" I took my hand off my ear and looked at my palm.

"No," she said, but she had to look to be sure.

Before we began mopping, Tidbit and I wandered around the Classroom Building to try to figure out what we had missed being on Reciprocity Detail. We didn't discover much, but we did find the masks we had made in Brenda's class, Expressions. We put them on. The empty rooms looked different through the eyeholes. I hadn't noticed before that the floor tiles were in a checkerboard pattern in maroon and black. There was chipping paint on bookcases. There was a door connecting two classrooms that I somehow hadn't known was there.

I was thinking to myself, *You go first, I'll follow you.* It didn't scare me, although I wondered if it should. I didn't know if I was saying it to myself exactly or if I was imagining saying it to Tidbit. But it was another decision I was trying to make. Or, rather, a decision I had made that I was trying to get myself to act on.

"Come on," I said. "We should start mopping."

Tidbit took her mask off. "We should put these away."

"No," I said. "Let's wear them." She put hers back on and placed her folded glasses in the pocket of her flannel shirt. We walked down to the atrium and into the small mop closet.

It was when we were filling up the bucket with soap and water that I told her, "I'm going to run away." I couldn't tell if she paused or not. "But I need you to come with me. I haven't done it before."

Tidbit lifted up her mask, but I touched her hand to stop her. She took it off anyway but left it on top of her head so the duck bill pointed straight up. "No," she said. "I told you, I'm not going to run away again."

"But you told me about the times you did, and someone always went with you. I don't have anyone else to go with me, and I don't want to do it alone."

"Well, that's your problem."

We took two mops and the mop bucket upstairs and began work on the landing. She put her glasses back on. We worked in silence. It had never occurred to me that working with Tidbit could be uncomfortable.

"Don't you want to get out of here? This place is so fucked up. I'm so bored I'm going crazy."

"You're not going crazy. And hell yes I want to get out of here. That's my point. If I keep running away I'll be here for fucking ever. And there's nothing more boring than acting out and getting cornered and acting out and getting cornered all over again. Everyone thinks they're doing their own thing and that they're the world's original badass, but it's just the same tired shit over and over. Following the process is the first really new thing I've done since I've been here."

"Well, that stuff isn't boring to me," I said, "not yet." But I didn't want to argue. I pulled off my mask and dropped it on one of the couches on the upper landing, where it rocked back and forth slightly before settling. I scrubbed at the floor with my mop. Tidbit did the same. Two days later she told me she would go with me.

**"Usually we would** just sit around during cleanup and talk," Bridget Divola explained to Claire King, who had been enrolled at the school a week before. "But today everyone's trying to get the dorm cleaned by seven so we can go to Cartoon Brunch tomorrow." Claire nodded. Bridget seemed satisfied. She pulled a long striped sock out of her pocket and sniffed it. "Cartoon Brunch is fun, but personally I find it insulting being manipulated like that. It's a gift from Aubrey, but you only get to go if your dorm gets checked out of cleanup on time. I'll do my part, but I won't jump through hoops."

Bridget had moved up from New Girls to Alternative Girls two weeks ago. Her refusal to return to campus on Parents' Sunday had been considered an attempt to run away, but Bridget claimed that she had learned a lot from that experience. It made her understand how much she needed to follow the process so that she wouldn't be that unclear again. It made her understand how much she needed to be at the school.

She and Claire were wiping down the long couch with wood polish. It had been upended so that Tidbit could vacuum underneath. Some other Alternative Girls had taken the cushions from the couch and were beating them with closet rods to get out the dust. Bridget and Claire polished the wooden frame, sitting in the shadow of the couch towering over them. When the square of paper towel Claire was using got dry and dusty, Bridget snatched it from her and stuffed it into the sock. She did the same with her own paper towel, took a long sniff of the sock, and stood up. She dropped the sock by the couch. "Come on," she said.

Claire followed Bridget to where June was sitting reading a magazine. Bridget picked up the roll of paper towels on the floor and tore off one square that she handed to Claire and another that she kept for herself. She held hers out, and June sprayed it with furniture polish, and then Claire did the same.

"Are you girls going to need more?" June asked. "I'm going to lock this stuff up and do the pipes in the bathroom."

"No," Bridget told her. "We're almost done."

"Anybody else need wood polish?" June called. No one answered. "I'll be in the bathroom, then," she said.

The girls walked back to where they had been working, on the side of the couch opposite June. "All this stuff with restricting our access to huffables has really gotten out of hand," Bridget said. She stuffed her square into the sock and took a sniff. She offered it to Claire, who took a sniff as well. Bridget took Claire's square of paper towel and began wiping the couch with it. "It's just begging us to act out."

Claire sat back and looked around the lounge. In the middle of the room Tidbit was yelling over the sound of the vacuum cleaner at the girls beating the cushions. Across the room, two girls had taken the long metal top and front off of the radiator that ran along the floor. They were using Q-tips to get dust and lint out from between the hundreds of thin metal squares that were attached, parallel to one another, down the length of the radiator.

"It's a matter of integrity," Bridget was saying. "Self-respect. That's what me and Frances usually talk about. She's my therapist. The therapists are Laura, Frances, and Simon. Who's yours? Claire? Hey!" Bridget swung the sock at her.

Claire turned. "What?"

"Who's your therapist?"

"I don't know yet."

"Oh. Well, there's Laura, Frances, and Simon. Frances is mine. I was just saying that what she and I are always trying to figure out about is self-respect, self-regard, self-consciousness, and self-esteem. Like, my self-esteem is really low, but I have a lot of self-regard. Frances says that I should try to have more self-esteem and maybe not so much self-regard. She thinks that each one of them should be at a specific level. But my theory that I always tell her about is that it doesn't matter how high or low any of them are, just so long as they're all equal. Like, if you have a lot of self-consciousness you need to have a lot of self-esteem, but if you have, like, low self-regard then you can have low self-esteem. See? My problem is that I can't ever decide—"

"Why isn't she working?" Tidbit was standing over them, holding the vacuum handle in one hand.

Bridget paused to look at her, then turned back to Claire. "I was saying, I can't—"

"I asked you why she isn't working," Tidbit said.

Bridget looked at her. "Yes. And you interrupted me and asked with a very obnoxious attitude."

"Thank you for the confrontation," Tidbit said. "I'll try to take it in."

"Well, you know her name. Why are you asking me?"

Tidbit looked at Claire. "Well? Claire?"

"My paper towel got used up. I'd get more, but June put the polish away. Anyway, we're almost done."

"But thanks for keeping an eye on us, Tidbit," Bridget added. "It makes me feel safe."

Tidbit sighed and walked away. She was trying to control her panic, and she knew she wasn't doing it well. Tidbit needed them to get the dorm clean so that she could see me. I only learned of this much later, but she had thought of a problem with our plan to run away, and Cartoon Brunch would be her only chance to tell me.

We had planned to meet in the woods first thing Monday morning, when we were supposed to be in Zbigniew's office. We figured that the earlier we left, the fewer things could go wrong. But Tidbit worried that we'd be missed immediately, since Zbigniew was one of the more competent adults at the school; someone would probably call the police before we had even gotten off campus. We'd have a better head start if we left around lunchtime. But she had no way to tell me unless both our dorms got checked out of cleanup by seven and were allowed to go to Cartoon Brunch. As far as New Boys went, she could only hope, but Tidbit wanted to make sure that Alternative Girls finished on time.

"Hey, Claire," she called, "you wanna vacuum so I can do the windows?"

Claire looked nervously to Bridget, then agreed. Bridget was the only girl in the dorm who'd been at all nice to her since she'd arrived. Claire was so scared of the school and the students that she'd been doing what she could to seem tougher than she was. When she introduced herself to the dorm, she told Alternative Girls that the reason she got sent to Roaring Orchards was that she got caught smoking acid.

"Wow," Tidbit had asked, "how much acid did you smoke?"

Now, as she took hold of the vacuum cleaner, Claire wanted to know what Tidbit had done to get sent to the school.

Tidbit smiled and patted Claire on the back. "Let's just say if you're ever stuck in a town as small as my hometown? Don't get caught having sex with the sheriff's daughter." Tidbit reached down and turned on the vacuum cleaner. She left it in Claire's hands and walked across the room to start on the windows. If they got checked out of cleanup on time, Tidbit thought, she'd start being nicer to Claire tomorrow.

■ ■ ■

**June propped the** bathroom door open and sat cross-legged beneath the sink. The bathroom held a hint of bleach and the sharp citrus smell of the cleaner the girls had used in cleaning the showers. Soon, though, the smell of the Brasso enveloped her completely. She squeezed a dollop of the white cream onto a sponge with which she began scrubbing the pipes that ran from the several sinks into the wall. The gray on the pipes turned darker in streaks as June began scrubbing, then became a chalky green that got thinner and thinner as she continued to work at it. The green finally melted away to reveal a bright color somewhere between gold and pink. June had cleaned about two inches of pipe. She bent to see where the pipes connected to the bottom of the sinks. She would be working at this a while.

And what color were the pipes, anyway? She squeezed some more Brasso onto the sponge. They were like a color you'd see on a dragonfly, she thought. A sunset at the North Pole. What was it about the North Pole? That the sun never set there? She coughed from the Brasso fumes. Did that mean the South Pole never saw the sun? She couldn't remember, and she couldn't think how to work it out. One moment it was like the pipes were made of white gold, the next they were the pinkish-tan feathers that covered a pigeon's throat.

June uncrossed her legs, pressed her sneakers against the wall in front of her, and pushed herself away from under the sink. She slid back across the tiles. Whoooo, she thought. She should get some fresh air; the fumes were getting to her. June stood up and shook her head. She leaned over a sink, threw some water on her face, and then headed around the corner of the bathroom into the open area where the showers were. She opened the small window high on the wall. That'll do it, she thought, still dizzy. The feel of the cool, wet weather outside was a relief. She would have to be careful not to be overwhelmed by the Brasso. What had she been thinking of? She had no idea and got back to work.

By the time Alternative Girls finished cleaning the lounge and kitchenette, June was well done with the pipes. The dorm regrouped and headed back down the hallway to clean the toilets and mop the bathroom floor. They left the toilets for last in case someone had to use them during the day. Outside the sun had not yet set, and no one said anything about the bathroom feeling particularly cold. When the bathroom was done, Alternative Girls all returned to the lounge where they sat down and discussed briefly whether they were finished.

"It is my consensus that the dorm is superclean," Bridget finally said.

"Agreed."

"Agreed."

"Agreed," the girls repeated around the circle.

June paged Roger to come and check. Usually it was Aubrey who inspected the dorms, but he was doing fewer and fewer things around campus. They tried to find things to talk about until Roger arrived. About forty-five minutes later he showed up, wearing a scarf wrapped around the bottom of his face.

"You're sure you're done?" he asked, tossing his scarf onto June's desk. "Everyone consented?"

June wasn't sure if he was asking her or the girls. "Well, girls?" she prompted. They all nodded.

"Then that's each of your commitment to me that this dorm is superclean. Let's see." He dug deep in one of the pockets of his coat and pulled out one white glove. This was exactly what Aubrey would have done. He put on the glove and tossed his coat onto June's desk. Roger looked at the girls with a grin and then pulled open the door between the lounge and hallway so that it was perpendicular to the wall. He stood on his tiptoes and ran one gloved finger across the top of the door. He looked at the finger and then showed it to the girls. Clean. He took the chair from June's desk and climbed up to run a finger across the top of the door frame and hopped down to show the girls again. This time his finger was black with dust.

"You girls aren't serious about this," Roger said, pulling off the glove and sticking it in the back pocket of his jeans. He grabbed his coat and hefted it under one arm. "Don't call again until the dorm's clean." He took his time wrapping himself in his scarf, then hustled out of the dorm.

**"Goddamnit," Tidbit said** when he was gone. "Who was supposed to dust that?"

"It doesn't matter," someone said. "I'm sure it's not the only place we missed."

"Really, Tidbit," Bridget added, "if you want to follow the process and you think that's going to make you better, fine. But this talking down to everyone really isn't going to help you develop your relationships in this dorm."

Tidbit's knee was bouncing up and down. "But if everyone would just—"

"He checked two places, and half of them were dirty," someone else said. "I mean, if you extrapolated that—"

"Oh, fuck it. Let's just finish cleaning."

June spoke up. "Well, now we can't until you pay for that f-word. What's going on with you, Tidbit?"

Tidbit fought back tears. "I don't want to have a whole meeting. Could you just take a dollar from my allowance?"

June looked at her. "All right," she said.

Tidbit didn't want to seem too anxious about getting to Cartoon Brunch, lest anyone became suspicious of why it was so important to her. She had hoped that simply doing her share and organizing things would get them checked out in time, but time was running out. It was already dark outside, and the girls had maybe half an hour.

"Here," Bridget said, holding up a roll of paper towels. "I have an idea. Everyone take a couple in each hand." She tossed the Formula 409 spray to Claire. "You spray them all. We'll make an assembly line. Everyone line up." The girls filed by, filling each fist with towels that Claire sprayed. The girls then dispersed to the various corners of the lounge to wipe down every exposed surface they could find.

"Come on, run," Bridget shouted when she had two handfuls of paper towels. She jogged in a circle around the lounge with her arms stretched out straight, canting like an airplane. She was try- ing to get the rest of the dorm to run in circles with her, but most of the girls just laughed and dusted where they were.

When everyone seemed to get tired of that, Bridget announced, "I'm running into the hallway in two seconds so anyone who doesn't want to get us hand-held better finish up and come with me." She circled the room once more and ran into the hall with the rest of Alternative Girls following, running up and down the cor- ridor jumping to dust the top of the door frames. One girl handed out fresh squares of paper towel. Girls bumped into one another; girls fell down laughing.

When they were done with the hall the girls entered the bath- room and set at once to wiping down the counters and the top edges of the stalls. "God, it's freezing in here," someone said. "Why's it so cold?"

"Did someone open the windows back here?" Claire walked around to the showers and the girls heard her scream.

Alternative Girls rounded the corner to see the white tile walls covered with moths, beetles, and caddis flies. More hovered near the fluorescent bulbs on the ceiling. Tidbit pushed by to see what was going on. What she saw made her sick. It was like the shower walls were breathing. She focused on one moth resting against the wall of the shower room, its gray wings folded back. It had bright orange markings near its head, and its abdomen was heaving as though the moth were out of breath. A bottle of shampoo sailed past Tidbit's ear and bounced against the shower wall, where it missed the bugs but sent some into flight toward the ceiling. But mostly the moths were still. Then Bridget pushed past holding the mop overhead, dripping dirty water as she swung it at the lights, shouting, "Kill them, kill them, we've got to get checked out."

Girls began pounding at the walls with balled-up paper towels, sponges, and plastic bottles. Tidbit watched dark stains blossom on the tiles, iridescent bits of wings and feelers stick to the bottom of a bottle of grapefruit hair conditioner, and all of it would have to be cleaned up. "Toward the window," someone shouted. "Push them toward the window."

Most of the bugs were flying now. Girls were running, laughing, and screaming as moths caught themselves in their hair and fluttered across their pursed lips. Tidbit yelled at everyone to stop. She told them to turn off the lights, they should just turn off the lights and let the bugs fly away, but Bridget was slapping the mop against the plastic light fixture above, streaking it gray, and no one could hear anything over all the shrieking.

Tidbit leaned against the wall beneath the window and slid to the floor. There was no way they could clean this up in time. They wouldn't go to Cartoon Brunch, and she and I would get caught and brought back to campus by Monday afternoon. She'd be cornered for a week, and all the work she'd done over the past months would be wasted. Tidbit pulled her hair in front of her face. She wouldn't let that happen. She would have to let me end up alone in the woods on Monday morning, where I'd assume she'd changed her mind again. Girls were screaming, bumping into her and stepping on her. Tidbit cried. She rested her elbows on her knees, letting snot get into her hair. Girls were running into one another, running into her. She could drown out all of it except the stepping on her feet.

Tidbit ran her hands over her wet face and kept saying, "Stop stepping on my feet, stop stepping on my feet," but they kept stepping on her, laughing. Tidbit had no idea if she was saying it loud enough for anyone to hear or if she was screaming it. She grabbed the last girl to step on her and bit her leg below the knee. Tidbit didn't unclamp her teeth until the girl, whoever she was, had crumpled and fallen to the ground. Then Tidbit was on top of her, throwing punches. Blood splattered the tiles. No one was laughing now; they were all trying to pull Tidbit off of Claire. When they did, Claire was left writhing on the floor, holding her leg.

The rest of the night they let Tidbit sit on a couch in the lounge and shout and cry as loud as she wanted. No one listened to a word. June called Roger to help figure out what to do. When he saw her he didn't even bother yelling. He just let her bawl until bedtime. They let her use the bathroom after the rest of the dorm was done with it. Then they told her to sleep by herself in the room closest to the lounge.

Tidbit climbed to the top bunk of the one bunk bed in the room. At the far end of the bed was a window that looked out on the woods behind the Mansion. Tidbit crawled to it and slammed her head against the window, over and over. She felt the glass bend beneath her forehead and slammed harder. June was screaming somewhere far away. Then there was a rough hand around her ankle that yanked her at once away from the window and off the side of the bed. Tidbit fell through the air face-first, flat off the top bunk until the frame of the bottom bunk caught her square across the cheekbone below her right eye. At first, it was the sound that surprised her, like a green fruit being split. The pain came after.

Everyone scared her by crowding around until she told them that it just stung a little and that she would go to sleep. It felt strange to hear herself talk. They discussed whether or not it was a good idea to let her sleep. Tidbit felt this had nothing to do with her. She was finally calm, having gotten what she felt she deserved.

**Sunday there was** snow. Ripples of white spread around the Mansion and across the bare branches. In New Boys we were quick out of bed and into the showers, then back in our pajamas pulling on boots and coats.

The cold stung my eyeballs and made chilly tears pool in the corners of my eyes. Loose snow spun around everyone's shins and flew easily from our shovels. To make sure that no fights arose that would keep us from brunch, we kept quiet as much as possible. When there was something to say, we all employed a careful excess of politeness, which quickly became a joke. Snow continued to fall as we worked. The rectangular swaths of macadam I cleared were soon covered with a layer of fuzz pocked with footprints.

I leaned on my shovel and looked out over the snow-covered hills, the gray trees, and the wet, black road. My face had gone numb. The sky was like a white wool blanket. Deep folds of silence lay everywhere. On the way into the Cottage, we bumped into one another softly just to create occasions to apologize decorously.

"Oh, terribly sorry, didn't see you."

"Not at all, not at all. Quite all right."

Back inside the Cottage we rushed to grab our blankets. We slowed on our way back outside and did our best to look sleepy and bored as we walked to the Mansion. The brunch was a gift from Aubrey, and racing to the Great Hall would make our compliance seem too cheaply bought. I had my own reason to seem aloof. I expected Tidbit to be there, and people might notice if we seemed too excited or spent too much time together. I had to be careful not to look for her, to ignore her if I saw her. I would be treacherous and true.

In the Great Hall, neither brunch nor the cartoons had yet arrived. I kept my head down and then very casually, as I walked, stole quick glimpses around the room. New Girls and Alternative Boys were arrayed around the Great Hall, draped across the long couch with blankets spread over their legs or sitting in groups on the rug. I didn't see Alternative Girls anywhere. A fire glowed in the huge fireplace to one side of the couch. A group of girls lay in front of it flipping through a large book.

I saw Pudding marching through the Great Hall calling for a staff member. Ellie was in the Reception Room, where the teachers and dorm parents generally spent time when their students were in the Great Hall for an event. "Ellie," he said, finding her with Marcy and Spencer. "This is a really dishonest Cartoon Brunch, wouldn't you say? No cartoons and no brunch? I think we might need to have a meeting."

I hadn't seen Pudding in months. It was nice to see nothing had changed.

Some of the New Boys tried to convince the girls lying on the couch to let them squeeze in. There wasn't anyplace for me to sit other than on the rug. I sat down by the girls near the fireplace, who were looking at what I now saw was an old photo album. I just stared at the fire and ignored them. I figured Alternative Girls were either still out doing their snow job or that they hadn't gotten checked out of cleanup in time. It wouldn't do any good to ask. I had to keep our plan hidden.

"Where are Alternative Girls?" I asked.

The girls looked at one another. "You're Benjamin. You're new, right?" one of them asked.

"Not really. Not anymore."

The girl had large dark eyes and long blond hair with the ends dyed black. She looked at me like one of those dolls with weighted eyelids. "I'm Carly," she said.

"I know."

"This is Torrin. She's new."

"Hi." New Boys had seen Torrin before, but no one knew her name. She was pretty in a perfect, absolute way. In front of girls like her, I found myself acting as though they didn't actually exist. It was rude of me, but I don't think I could really help it. Girls like her seemed to exist in a world different than mine. I wondered why Carly didn't introduce Bev, who was sitting right beside her.

"How come you want to know about Alternative Girls?" Carly asked.

I shrugged. I turned to watch Pudding, who was arguing with Ellie about whether he could ride the oversize rocking horse. "You're only saying no because I'm fat," Pudding said. "You can't discriminate just because I'm fat." He held the wooden dowel that went through the horse's head and rocked the horse back and forth on its rails.

"It's for decoration," Ellie said. "Do you see anyone else riding it? Any skinny people? Stop rocking it."

"What's with Pudding?" Carly asked.

I shrugged again. "He's needy."

"That horse is technically off campus," Carly said. "Touching it is just the same thing as running away. Someone should tell him." Bev was staring at me. I wondered what she was thinking. "Don't you think Torrin's pretty?" Carly asked.

I looked at Torrin. She was staring at the carpet and didn't react. Was Carly teasing me or trying to cheer her up? "I guess. Can I see that album? What is it?"

Carly turned it so that I could see. There was a black-and-white photo of a room that took me a moment to recognize as the Great Hall, the room we were in. The furniture was different, and there was some kind of bunting hanging from the landing on the second floor. "It's pictures of this place from before it was a school," she told me. "From when the family that built it lived here." In the picture everything seemed to fit better. I wasn't sure if there was more furniture or what.

"The girl's dead," Bev said.

"What girl?" I asked.

"The girl who lived—"

"Um, I know you didn't know this," Carly interrupted, "but Bev's ghosted, so no one's really supposed to talk to her."

"Really?"

"Yeah."

I looked at Bev. She nodded. "I am."

Carly opened her mouth to say something, but caught herself in time. She sighed.

I looked around the Great Hall. In comparison with the photograph in the album, everything looked simultaneously too big for people and too small for the room. The large couch seemed to swallow up all the people sitting on it. William Kay and Eric Gold had squeezed between the girls on the couch. The furniture seemed thin, as if it were made of plywood. The couches and chairs in the photograph had big buttons sunk deep in their cushions.

On the next page there were two more black-and-white photographs. There was one of the back garden, with the same stone path leading to and then circling the fountain. But instead of the shrubs on either side of it there were trees whose branches reached out to one another high above the path. A corner of the gazebo could be seen beyond the trees. The other showed a young couple. The woman sat in a chair and held hands with the man, who stood beside her. She had long dark hair that fell in ringlets over her shoulders. He wore a tie, and his collar came all the way up to his chin.

Floyd pushed open the doors to the Mansion dining room, where he had set up the brunch bar. On the long dark table there were warmed trays of scrambled eggs, mozzarella sticks, sausages, and jalapeño poppers. "You all must have kissed the old man's ass till it was good and shiny," Floyd shouted as the students filed into the dining room. "I got a note to bring the hot chocolate machine over, too."

Marcy and Spencer left to get the AV cart from the Cafetorium. We all got food and sat back down. Torrin rushed to get a seat on the couch, leaving Carly, Bev, and me alone with our plates on the rug. We sat quietly, watching the burned logs turn white with ash and letting the heat sting our faces.

It was then that Aubrey first walked through the Great Hall. No one noticed him until he was halfway through the room, and it was only when we all stiffened, as if we had been caught doing something wrong, that Aubrey seemed to realize that the hall was full of people. He was unshaven. He clearly hadn't expected anyone to be in the Great Hall. He muttered something, then continued. When he had almost made it across the hall, he turned and hurried back across the room and out through the Office, the way he had come. It was the first time I'd seen him in a long while.

Marcy and Spencer arrived with the AV cart and plugged it in. Snow had stuck to the wheels of the cart and was melting into puddles on the hardwood floor. Marcy popped in a tape of cartoons, and Ellie dimmed the lights so the students could better see the television. The tape was a mix of Woody Woodpecker and Tom and Jerry episodes, but they were recorded off of television and the best parts were the old commercials. Ellie and Marcy went around the room administering morning meds, checking the students' mouths in the flickering light of the TV or, in Bev's and my case, of the fire. When they were done with meds, the faculty left us alone to go sit in the Reception Room.

By that time most of the students sitting on the couch had finished eating. They passed their empty plates to be stacked on the floor. When they were sure the faculty members were gone they sank down and slid against one another, resting heads on each other's shoulders or chests. Some pulled their blankets up to their chins so their hands could move unseen.

This was the primary attraction of Cartoon Brunch. Spencer, Marcy, and Ellie chose not to worry about it. The faculty members always felt they were due a break, and they would have felt hypocritical trying to keep us from doing what they thought was only natural. And brunch was also a gift from Aubrey, so there was probably a certain vicarious satisfaction in letting the students abuse his generosity. Instead of watching us, they sat back in the deep couches of the Reception Room and made fun of us.

Spencer told a story about a fight that New Girls had once gotten into in the bathroom while he was covering the dorm. "I didn't know if I should go in to break it up or what because, you know, it's the girls' bathroom. But then I heard a mirror break. Just shatter. So I tell them I'm coming in, and when I enter I see these two girls wrestling on the floor. But before I can try to get them apart I notice all the girls who weren't even involved in the fight. They're all so anxious about what's going on right in front of them, the two girls pulling hair out and everything, that they've all picked up broken shards of the mirror and they're all cutting away at themselves like crazy." He laughed. "Every one of them."

**I figured that** Alternative Girls wouldn't be coming. It actually made things easier. This way Tidbit and I wouldn't have to avoid each other. I'd just see her in the morning, and then we'd be gone. Carly went back to flipping through the old pictures in the album. I watched the kids on the couch.

Suffused with sugar and fried food, they didn't say much as they began grabbing at one another, slipping hands under flannel tops and past elasticized waistbands. William grabbed the thin wrist of the girl beside him and directed it toward his arcing erection. He turned to see that it was Torrin, her face turned away from him so all he could see was the corner of her jaw and strands of hair that curled behind her pink ear. She pulled her hand back.

"C'mon," he said, "touch it."

Torrin laughed. He grabbed her arm again and she slapped his hand.

"Come on," he whispered now. He wrapped his arm around her waist. "If you don't I'll have to sneak into your dorm later and rape you."

She smiled. "That's gross. Then I'd have to have a little rape baby. No way."

William didn't let go. "C'mon, it'd be adorable. And you could knit it mittens and things." Torrin laughed and slapped him again.

Aubrey walked through the Great Hall for the second time and everyone stopped. This time we recognized his shuffling gait immediately. He paused as if he were waiting for us to so much as acknowledge him. He could feel that he had interrupted us, the students on the couch in front of the TV or on the floor by his fireplace, the faculty members lounging in the Reception Room. We were clearly having a fine time without him, and we were just as clearly waiting for him to be gone.

Aubrey wouldn't say anything, but he didn't leave us alone either. He opened the door that led down to the basement and walked down the stairs. But just as everyone in the Great Hall had relaxed and returned to whatever it was we'd been doing, he came back in through another door.

This is what Aubrey did for the rest of the afternoon. He wandered back and forth across the Mansion, up stairs and through the Office, looking distracted but intent on vexing all of us. He would disappear for a time, then return. At one point he must have exited and walked around the outside of the building, so that he crossed the Great Hall twice in the same direction. When it became clear that he would continue doing this, we weren't particularly bothered. We watched the cartoons and ate more brunch. I wondered whether Aubrey had initially been looking for something he had lost or what else might have been the matter with him. But no one said anything about it. Certainly no one said anything to him.

At some point, though, I became aware that Aubrey had ceased his perambulations and was standing quietly at the edge of the room opposite the TV, rocking slightly, as though waiting. "'And these mine enemies,'" he finally said, and everyone quieted down. A slide whistle sound came from the television, and someone jumped up to turn off the volume. Aubrey stood silhouetted, with his back to a window. Nacreous light poured in over his shoulder as he began a speech that I find I can recall to this day. Slowly my eyes adjusted to the light, and although Aubrey stood still he seemed to emerge from a darkness.

"'And these mine enemies,'" Aubrey said, "'all knit up in their distractions.' 'Their distractions'? 'My distractions' is more like it. The TV, the food, the fire. And you sitting and staring and staring and staring in your pajamas. You're like initiates in some tribal ritual where the body's left behind while the soul goes walking. And what do your souls witness on this vision quest? A hideous bird, devoid of character, and a smug, murderous mouse. As you'd say, whatever. It makes time pass, I guess. For me time hardly passes at all anymore; for me the day just drags and drags. It drags from the windows and it drags from the woods, and the walls, to be honest, I don't want to talk about the walls. It does give me a chance to think, though—the dragging does. Today I've been thinking about all the things I know and you don't, trying to understand what they are and whether any of them are worth the trouble I take trying to get them across. Across what? Now there's a question. Maybe that's something that you know and I don't, how could I tell?" Aubrey said. "You know, Erasmus said that 'every definition is a misfortune.' No you don't know that, why would any of you know that? Well, he said it, and I think that must make you some of the most fortunate ignoramuses anywhere. Because there are so many words that mean nothing to you, precisely nothing, probably the majority of words in the English language may as well be foreign to you. Like 'perspicacity,' for example. Or 'decorum.' Or 'gratitude,' certainly gratitude. The word 'immensity, to choose another, leaves you all completely baffled, I can tell, no matter how loudly I say it you simply cannot understand it. In fact, the louder I say it, the more perplexed you get, immensity, immensity! Whereas I have such a deep understanding of the word that I have no need to give voice to it at all." He paused and squeezed his eyes shut. "See?" He opened them again. "While you've all been so raptly sitting here, I've been walking around the Mansion and down to the basement and outside, through the garden and past the fountain, across the Ornamental Pond, into the Enchanted Forest and out again, off to the Farm and back to the garden, through the gazebo, where I sat for a time, thinking about what, I've forgotten already, back to the Office, and so on and so on. And every time I stepped inside the Mansion, the building seemed larger to me than the entire outdoors, the entire valley. And then I step from the Office into the Great Hall, I see its enormity and sense with absolute clarity that this one room dwarfs the entire Mansion," Aubrey said. "What is more, when I look into my own mind, I find it even vaster than the Great Hall we're in at this very moment. Isn't that something? On a science program I once saw on television I learned that a black hole the size of a snowball would be almost entirely empty, just a point at the center that would weigh ten times as much as the

Earth. I think it was on *NOVA*. So maybe it's not so surprising. Of course, this would be true of your minds as much as mine, God help us. The human brain is so complex. About three pounds, and so powerful that a child, if you halved his brain or hers, would grow up fine. No problems to speak of. Never tried it, but maybe some of you have. Worse than devils, some of you, and yet I let you live right here in my own home, an awful thought. Not that I expect your thanks or need any. You know, most schools hound their alumni for years after graduation, asking for donations. Maybe you don't know, why would you? We've never done that here, I've never done that. When you're done, you're done. That's the way it goes. That's what Reciprocity Detail is all about, that's what Regular Kids working in the lower-functioning dorms is all about. I make sure that you don't leave until you've given back as much as you've taken, and then we're finished, even-steven. No, my fondest wish is that this place leave no traces, that it disappear into your lives like a pharaoh sealed inside his tomb. If you so much as remember ever having been here, I will have failed," Aubrey said. "Is that extreme? Who can tell anymore. I don't ask you for anything, and it's lucky for me I don't, ingrates that you are. Just 'a pot of cheese so I can feast when I like.' Maybe one of those jalapeño poppers there." Aubrey walked into the dining room and came back with one. "You know what's like fielding a ground ball?" he asked, still chewing. "Working on the margins of wisdom. That's where I try to stay—if you're on the margins, on the perimeter, you can keep all of wisdom there in front of you, quite a thing to see, wisdom hopping like a grounder but then again also like an enormous lake shining in the sun, and me sitting on the shore watching it lap against the stones. Not that any of you would know what I'm talking about. I try to bring you all with me, there to the stony shore, but you just turn your backs on all that great wet wisdom sloshing about, you turn around and, like mules, wait to be led back home. And then you lift your tails and it's a good trip ruined. Never field a grounder that way. It breaks my heart. It absolutely does, the trouble you all have. You simply can't seem to come to terms with life's ordinary happiness. Or even for that matter with life's ordinary unhappiness. No, you all seem to be after a rather extraordinary unhappiness. It's heroic, really, if something pointless and infantile can be called heroic. But most things called heroic are pointless and infantile. Another definition, more misfortune. Well, so what? The point is, you pursue the legend of your outrageous unhappiness unrelentingly," Aubrey said. "Nothing and no one can get in your way, least of all me. No, no, nothing can get between you and your beloved unhappiness and I, for one, am too smart to try. You all imagine that you're rebelling against me, that somewhere there exist rules that for whatever reason are important to me and that you simply cannot accept. But that's not right, that's not right at all. The rules aren't important to me, very little is. I could pen you up like barnyard animals and go about my day. No, you're the ones who start it. You show up here so angry, you don't know what to do. So I give you something to expend your energy on. I build a little house, and I let you tear it down. Then I build another house, and I let you tear it down. Another house, tear it down. Then I build, you understand, this goes on for a while. What I wouldn't give to have someone do that for me, someone to give shape to all the chaos. I'd keep her on retainer. As it is, every day I have to decide anew what's allowed and what forbidden, what to ignore and what to jump up and down about, where the lines lie between one thing and another, what constitutes an idea, and, in the complete absence of criteria, I must determine who can rest and who must suffer. Every day I put a face on that which has no face, no face. Goodness, it's frightening, why must I repeat it? No face, no face, no face. Speaking of which," Aubrey said, "I saw some wonderfully terrifying masks on my trip through the Classroom Building earlier. Also, an amazing fantasy mansion constructed entirely out of Popsicle sticks. The things you all get up to in your classes, it made me sorry I haven't paid more attention to what goes on. But really. And I picked up this Popsicle palace and turned it in my hands because more than anything I wanted to look into its dark, inscrutable interiors. But I couldn't see inside, and the more this tiny fort frustrated my attempts, the more curious I was to see what it withheld. Surely there must be something there, why else would it be hidden? But I knew that if I cracked open its little rooms, if I even had the strength to, what I wanted most to see would be gone. Only in sleep can the eye embrace its goblin. I put down the wooden playhouse and I felt, when I saw it there before me, that this, this was the real world. Sticks, string, and glue. Compared to these, my thoughts seemed vague apparitions. This Mansion we're in, the Cafetorium, the Classroom Building: sticks, string, and glue. The process I invented for you all to follow: sticks, string, and glue. And each of you, even me, I thought, looking at this strange little Popsicle world that had somehow invaded our own, what are we but a band of puppets dancing foolishly, or dragging listlessly, no need to exaggerate, things are falling to pieces fast enough, dancing or dragging through the hours? And what are puppets but sticks, string, and glue? And sometimes pieces of felt and, what's it called, foam rubber? There are so many types of puppets: hand puppets and shadow puppets and finger puppets and rod puppets, dummies and marionettes, shoulder puppets and glove puppets, singing puppets and dancing puppets and automatons and Javanese puppets, animal puppets and people puppets, puppets with soft rope for hair and puppets with bald wooden heads, miscreated puppets and sock puppets and demi-puppets, parade puppets and articulated puppets, Vietnamese water puppets, a profusion and embarrassment of puppets, you wouldn't think we had time to do anything else. But then no, we really aren't much like puppets at all; they don't melt away like we do, like I am," Aubrey said. "I'm so disgusted with myself, really, every word out of my mouth's a lie. It's shameful going on like I do, and ridiculous. I fear it sometimes, no, always, how it must seem, parents leaving their children with me to be raised, and me with none of my own, a barren nurse. But I had a son once, it's true in a way. He was one of you, an absolute terror, a monster, really, and his parents finally wanted no more part of him. So I adopted him, signed the forms, and paid the fee or whatever it was. And he lived here like any of you do except that when he wanted the school to have a basketball team for him to play on, I put together a basketball team, and when he wanted to learn to play guitar I bought him a guitar, because he was my son, and that's what you do. And I loved him. It's pathetic, really. The lengths I go to and no one cares, not for me, not the least bit. And of course my son, one morning he was gone, had drifted away through the tall grass, along with the two girls who were in the band I'd let him put together after he'd gotten his guitar. How hurt and humiliated I was, was that it, yes, humiliated, and I missed him so much. Too sad even to be furious, though I put on a show as you can imagine. And after some days had passed, Floyd from the kitchen told me that things had begun to disappear from the refrigerators overnight, and I felt a faint glimmer, it was almost too much to hope for, that it might be him, my son, nearby and stealing from my kitchen. So one night I skulked by the kitchen's back entrance, hidden, and waited. Skulked and saw nothing, though hope sprung anew when Floyd told me the next morning that nothing had been stolen. So I skulked about another night and another. And then I saw him, I saw him, it thrills me now just to say it, I saw my son enter the kitchen, that cruel clever boy, and then leave with a bag full of stolen food. I followed him to the gym and stayed outside into the early hours, standing in the chill grass near the school vans, waiting to see if he would leave, where he would go, waited until the birds in the woods awoke with a cry just before sunrise, and I was sure he wouldn't come out. On subsequent nights I snuck back, to discover that he and the girls were living in the gym, behind the stage where the costumes are kept. I guess because they couldn't do laundry, they had taken to wearing the costumes, and the few times I saw them they looked like something out of Perrault. I didn't dare confront them lest they leave, though I knew I should, and I told no one. When Floyd suggested putting locks on the refrigerators to stop the thefts I told him to ignore them and order extra food. Because it was good to know my boy was safe and good to have him near. And soon I lost even that, soon he was gone for good; of course, he couldn't live behind the stage in costume forever, and he must've known it, I didn't raise any fools. I haven't seen or spoken to him since. Oh, it's true, it's true, I'm a fool and a sad old man. And those poor girls, I just let them disappear, they were my responsibility, too, but who knows what happened to them? Who knows what happens to any of us. You children think you'll have plenty of time, that life will be lenient and filled with second chances because you're so adorable. And you are, but you won't always be. Time moves in one direction, and each time you fuck up, you've fucked up forever. And you," Aubrey said, raising his voice and turning to the Reception Room where the faculty members were sitting, "you think there's time to repair the damage you're doing to your personalities, which weren't wonderful to begin with. I hear the way you laugh at these kids, the way you laugh and belittle them, make them the butts of your stories and jokes. Someone who'd just arrived here might have the illusion that you're just blowing off a little steam, but I didn't just arrive here and I don't have any illusions. If only I did, good heavens. Don't you realize how much more you laugh than they do, doesn't it startle you? You get nervous and you laugh; you get

the picture of the young couple. I looked more closely. The girl had dimples, and her fingers were entwined with the man's. She wasn't especially pretty but she seemed happy.

"That's the daughter of the guy who built the Mansion," Carly said. "Her name was Letitia or Lucretia or something like that. Lucretia, I think. Grafflin."

"Who the town's named after?" I asked. "Down the road?"

"Yeah, I guess. I don't know. Lucretia's dad was a chocolate manufacturer. Here he is." She flipped some pages, smoothed the book open, and slid it in front of me. The photograph showed a short round man in a dark suit proudly holding a large birdcage in front of him. In the cage was nothing but a blur, a swirl of dark and light. At the bottom of the page someone had carefully printed his name, Cubit C. Grafflin. "The bird must have been flying around when they took the picture," Carly said.

"She died at her wedding," Bev whispered.

"The bird?"

"Lucretia," Carly said. "Actually, it's true. The story is that she wanted to get married in winter and to have the ceremony out on the lake. And the lake was frozen over well enough, but she insisted on having the altar lit with all these candles they put on the lake and that made the ice weak. And it cracked and she drowned with her groom and the minister."

"No," Bev said, "she did *not* want to get married in winter." Her faint frizz of curls looked orange in the light of the fire. "She had to because she was pregnant. And now she haunts the lake and the baby haunts the Mansion. And the groom didn't die either, they saved him out of the frozen lake. But he never could get warm again."

"Did you hear something?" Carly asked. "There must be a draft or something, because I thought I heard someone talking."

Bev leaned toward me. "Your girlfriend's in the corner."

"Bev! You're not allowed to tell him that."

"Well, you're not supposed to be listening to me."

"She's not my girlfriend."

"Please," Carly said, "we're not supposed to talk to her."

# 8

Over the next few days, Tidbit's black eye blossomed grotesquely. The dark bruise stretched down to her cheekbone and swelled around her eyeball. The color was a pearly blue-black, which faded to lighter shades of purple and red around the edges.

Aaron was watching her in the corner. He had spent days doing this and was still amazed, minute by minute, that nothing happened. Tidbit sat, facing the corner. He sat in a chair behind her. That was it, hour after hour. By now his anxiety had waned, and he was used to the idea that all he had to do was sit here and wait for his shift to end.

Tidbit studied her eye carefully during her short bathroom breaks, standing on her toes and leaning against the sink to get a closer look at the mirror. She noticed that the part of the bruise covering her cheek had faded to a kind of gray-green. At the bottom of the swollen bag under her eye, a poorly delineated crescent of jaundiced yellow had appeared. Tidbit would occasionally pull her lower eyelid down to look at the bright blot of blood that had congealed at the bottom of her eyeball. But the dull ache this caused was sickening and kept her from doing it too often.

She had no way of knowing that I'd abandoned our plan to run when I found out she was in the corner. As far as she knew, I might have tried and gotten caught, or I might have run on my own.

Tidbit knew she should feel bad, but she didn't. She told me later that she was relieved to still be on campus; she didn't even mind sitting in the corner all day. And she thought it was funny picturing me waiting in the woods, trying to figure out what to do.

There was no word on how long Aubrey would make Tidbit stay in the corner, but Aaron was hoping it would be a while. The idea of going back to another dorm made him more and more anxious the longer he spent watching Tidbit. He liked how peaceful it was in the girls' wing when no one was around, how he could just watch the sunlight coming through the window change direction as the morning and then the afternoon went on. And people seemed to appreciate and sympathize with him when they passed through the dorm.

It was on his sixth day of watching her sit in the corner that Tidbit turned around in her chair. "Do you think you're going to stay here?" she asked him. "To work, I mean."

Something pleading in the tone of her voice made him feel like he could reply. She didn't seem to be testing him; she sounded worried that he would leave. "Yeah, I think so," he said, although he didn't know if he would.

"You should leave," Tidbit said. "You're still young. Nobody who works here has a life. You should get out and enjoy yourself."

Aaron couldn't think of anything to say in response, but it was nice of her, he thought, to think of him like that. "I like working here," he said, surprised at how much he meant it. "And I didn't have much of a life before, anyway." This he meant as a joke, so he laughed. Tidbit didn't.

She crossed her arms over the back of the chair. "What did you do before?" Her bruised eye looked shiny. Aaron thought her eyeball was a little yellow.

"I was a bike messenger. Actually, I rode a scooter."

"Why'd you leave a wicked job like that?"

Aaron laughed. "It didn't pay too well, so I was thinking about quitting anyway, but then my boss figured out that I had been driving around town for two months completely stoned. So I didn't really get a chance to quit."

"That sounds fun, though. Just don't tell any of the RO-bots."

Figuring this was something critical of the school, Aaron didn't ask her what she meant. He was already talking to her when he shouldn't be. "So what did you do to get sent here?" he asked instead.

"Me?"

"Uh, yeah."

"Well, at home I used to be in this band. I played bass and my best friend Eli was in it. We called ourselves the Broad Strokes. Anyway, we'd entered this Battle of the Bands they had at my high school every year. We were spending all this time practicing in Eli's garage, not so much because we wanted to win, but Battle of the Bands was really fun, and we'd been going since we were in like fifth grade. But then out of nowhere one day at school, the principal calls us all into his office. And he's like 'I can't let your band into this competition,' and we're all like, 'Why not?' And he says it's because of our name, like that explains it. But I was like 'What's wrong with our name?' And he looked at me like I was full of shit.

"But then Eli and our singer, Donna, were like 'No, really, what are you talking about?' The principal looked a little uncomfortable and started saying it was a double entendre, and we knew just what he meant, but we really didn't. So he explains that 'broad' could mean a woman, and 'strokes' was like, well, basically he accused us of our name being a reference to a handjob. Which none of us had even thought of, but this pervert had. And that's what I said, I said he was a pervert for thinking of that when we hadn't even meant it. And I wouldn't take it back, and he was like—"

Tidbit stopped at the sound of someone opening the front door of the dorm. She continued in a whisper, "Anyway, I wouldn't take it back and got kicked out. You should probably tell me to turn around and face the corner."

"Yeah, you should do that," Aaron said. "Thanks."

"You're welcome," she said as Kavita entered the room. Nurse Kavita was a nervous, pretty Indian woman who was perpetually overwhelmed by the extent of her responsibilities. She had to pour meds for every student on campus, most of whom took a heavy mixture three times a day, the exact proportions of which were constantly being adjusted by Dr. Wahl, the school's psychopharmacologist.

"Oh, what is that you're reading?" she asked Aaron.

It took him a moment to realize what she was talking about. Over the past few days, whenever a faculty member had seen him just sitting there by the corner, they reminded him that it was okay for him to read a book or magazine while he was watching Tidbit. They looked at him strangely when he said he was fine just sitting there, so this morning on his way to the dorm, he had stopped by the Teachers' Lounge and grabbed something off the shelf. He read to Nurse Kavita from the cover: *She Stoops to Conquer.*

"Oh. Is it any good?"

"I haven't really started it yet. It looks good."

"Well," she said, "I just came up to take a look at the eye. You can take a little break if you like." But Aaron said he was fine and watched as Tidbit turned in her chair and Nurse Kavita took a little white flashlight out of her jacket pocket. She looked at the swollen eye carefully, pressing and pulling gently and pausing whenever Tidbit sucked air through her teeth in pain. When she was done, Kavita told Aaron, "I'd like to have her go to the clinic. I'm afraid the swelling is putting pressure on the eyeball."

"You have to talk to Aubrey about that, right? Marcy said that none of the kids can have a doctor's appointment unless you tell him they need one."

"Yes," Kavita said, putting away her flashlight. "And sometimes not even then."

**Aaron leaned forward** over his steering wheel and looked both ways. The Webituck Medical Clinic was located in an expanse of fields interrupted only by large wooden signs offering plots for sale. But after what had just happened, he didn't want any more trouble. He pulled slowly out of the gravel parking lot and turned right. He accelerated evenly down the road, glad to be gone from the clinic.

Tidbit was next to him with her feet up on the dashboard. She stared out the window and watched the telephone poles sail by. Her eye followed the rise and fall of the wires between them.

"We missed lunch," Tidbit said.

"They'll have saved you something."

"Did you ask them to when you called?"

"No."

"Then they won't save either of us anything. We should stop somewhere."

"Yeah?" Aaron said, smiling. "Where do you think we should stop?" She wasn't crying anymore, but he hoped he could get her to smile.

"There's a Sugar Burger on the way back," she said. "You can't make me miss lunch. No matter what I did."

"I didn't say no. We can get Sugar Burger."

It had been drizzling on and off all morning, but that had stopped. Fog still clung to the hills that rose behind the fields. The road ran past some houses, and then they were following the shore of the lake to their left.

"Are you going a different way?" Tidbit asked.

"No," Aaron said. "What?"

"This isn't the way we came. I think you turned the wrong way out of the clinic."

Aaron didn't say anything for a time. He just drove. The lake's surface was like lead. "I think this'll turn out somewhere along where we want to go."

Tidbit had refused to be given a shot at the clinic. They had looked at her eye and said that she would be all right, but she was also supposed to get a tetanus shot because she had bitten someone again. There was nothing Aaron could do to make her. He had been uncomfortable enough walking in there escorting a sixteen-year-old girl with an enormous black eye. He called the school from the clinic phone, but Tidbit refused even to talk to anyone. She'd been bawling and yelling. Now, though, she seemed fine.

"Can we listen to some music?" she asked.

"Not now that you asked we can't."

"Why?"

"You know why. Alternative Girls don't have music privileges."

"But you're allowed to play music if you want when you're driving, even if a kid's in the car."

Aaron drew to a stop where the road ended in an intersection. He thought about it for a moment, then turned left. The road led up into thickening woods. Tidbit sloped down in her seat to get a better look at the branches spotted with buds. The wet branches were black against the pale, quilted sky.

"Aaron? So you don't want to listen to music?"

"Actually, I do. But we can't now that you asked me to because you'll never know whether we were listening to it because I wanted to or because you'd manipulated me into it. Which is what the rule is there to keep from happening. Shit, I think I better turn around." The car shuddered as he turned too quickly onto the gravel and made a wide U-turn.

"Maybe what I really wanted was no music," Tidbit said, "and I just manipulated you into not playing any."

"Maybe."

"You'll never know."

"I'll never know."

Aaron sped into the turns as the road exited the woods and rejoined the contours of the lake. The sky had cleared some, and Tidbit rolled her window down. She hummed to herself in the seat next to him and seemed very little. The school philosophy, as Aaron understood it, was that strictly enforcing the rules made students feel safe. He wondered whether she felt safe. Tidbit was playing with the door lock, pulling it up and pushing it down. She started singing, "*The owl of Minerva's on the windowsill, At midnight she gets restless, steals a Coupe de Ville, Romeo was pumping gas, got in without a fuss, And said, Darling it's late, who's gonna entertain us?* What?" she asked. "I'm allowed to sing, aren't I?"

"You're allowed to sing."

"It's from *Worries Are Wishes*. The Kinky Lincolns?"

"Yeah?"

"God, you're old."

Aaron laughed and turned back to the road. They passed the clinic again, and Aaron suddenly remembered that in all the confusion he had forgotten Tidbit's lunchtime meds when they had left. He could picture right where they were, sitting on an old copy of *Backwoods Boating* in the lobby. But he didn't stop. If he went to get them now, Tidbit would know he'd left them behind, and he would have to fill out another med error report. He watched the clinic drift away in the rearview mirror. He could only hope that Tidbit would forget about her lunchtime meds. He could come back here to get them later. Aaron was sure she'd be fine without them.

In Webituck they rolled past shopping centers sunk back from the road behind empty parking lots. Then Tidbit sat up and said, "There it is."

Sugar Burger was a plain cement box, painted white, except for the front, which was made up of large plate-glass windows. Above the windows hung a banner announcing a special: SWEET DEAL WITH MAPLE FRIES ONLY $3.99.

Aaron and Tidbit got out of the car and crossed the parking lot. Long puddles lay across the asphalt, but the sun was out, and the smell of rainwater evaporating from the pavement was thick in the air. Inside, beneath fluorescent lights and surrounded by plastic furniture, things felt even more delightfully ordinary. They got in a short line behind the only open register. In front of them was a man with two young girls who looked like sisters. As Tidbit looked around, she noticed that the restaurant was full of young girls sitting with their parents. It was eerie. She pointed it out to Aaron.

"Probably a ballet class just got out. A recital or something," he said.

"Why d'you say that?"

"Tight buns."

"Aaron! They're just kids."

"Their hair, Tidbit," he said. "Look at their hair."

He was right; the girls in line ahead of them also had their hair up tightly. They were whispering, the taller one occasionally looking up at Tidbit. At first Tidbit thought the girl was checking to see if she was listening in on their conversation, but then she remembered her eye. She's probably scared of me, Tidbit thought. The girl tugged on the man's pants.

"What is it, Ashley?" he said.

"Daddy, how much is thirty-five?"

"Thirty-five what?"

"Thirty-five. Is it a lot?"

"Thirty-five?" The man scratched at the stubble on his cheek. "It depends."

"Oh. What about . . . seventeen?"

"That's not a lot."

The girl looked at her sister. "A thousand?"

"Yeah, that's a lot."

Tidbit ordered a Sugar Burger with no meat, which took some explaining, an extra-large Sunkist soda, and an ApplePocket. Aaron got the Sweet Deal with maple fries. When they sat down, she waited a moment to see if he was going to give her her meds.

"You know it's funny," Aaron said. "I was pretty worried walking into the clinic with you. I mean, if you saw the two of us walking in someplace, with that eye, wouldn't you think I'd beat up my girlfriend?"

"Or your daughter," Tidbit said. She began eating.

"No. You think? I'm not that much older than you." He took a bite of his burger.

Tidbit laughed. "How can you eat that thing? Don't you know how they breed them?"

"What are you talking about?"

"You know how they're breeding cows bigger and bigger so they have more meat? Well, at one point, they made them so big that their hearts started to explode from trying to get blood to their whole huge bodies. So then they tried breeding cows with no bones that were just these sacks of meat, but their lungs kept collapsing under all the weight."

"Tidbit."

"What? You're the one eating it."

"Yeah. Did that occur to you at all? About your eye and walking into the clinic with me?"

Tidbit leaned forward to take a sip off the top of her orange soda. "Well, yeah. That's why I kept asking you if I could do things like sit across the room from you or use the pay phone. So you'd have to say no, and you'd look like some psycho control freak. I thought it was funny."

"I didn't realize that," Aaron said. "I was just worried that you were going to make up some story so you wouldn't have to go back to the school."

"Like what?"

"I don't know. Like saying that it wasn't an accident."

"It wasn't an accident. Roger pulled me off the bed."

Aaron was finishing his fries. "You could have made up something worse. How come you didn't?"

"We're not always trying to get away, you know. We could pretty much run whenever if we wanted. You guys aren't that smart." She slid the orange soda closer. Beads of condensation rolled down the waxed-paper cup when she touched it. "Why don't *you* leave?"

"I guess because there's always something interesting going on."

"Yeah, everyone says that. Everyone the interesting stuff isn't happening *to*."

"But you're happy staying there?"

"No," Tidbit said. She was half standing so she could suck on her soda straw without tipping the enormous cup. "But if I wanted to leave, I wouldn't have to wait for some dumb nurse to save me. For a while I thought I'd stay and try to be good and graduate, but now I'm okay just being there. I'll probably be in a ton of trouble when I get back, huh?"

"For refusing to get the shot?"

"Yeah."

"Probably."

"You think people will be mad?"

"The people you bit? Wouldn't you be?" Aaron started cleaning the table, piling the empty wrappers onto their tray.

"The *people* I bit? I only bit one person." Tidbit felt a sudden surge of resentment. They were sitting here like two normal people, but when they got back to the school she was going to get grief thrown at her while he had nothing to worry about.

Aaron was nice as far as faculty went, but didn't seem to get that he was dealing with real people. Over the course of the three weeks Tidbit had sat in the corner, her sixteenth birthday had passed. Aaron had asked her what she wanted, and she said vanilla pudding. So he got her a box of Jell-O pudding mix. He let her eat it in the corner. Tidbit had licked her finger and dipped it into the mix, over and over. That was really nice of him, she knew. Still, he didn't seem to understand. No one in Tidbit's dorm had even talked to her since she bit Claire, but she could hear what they said when they passed by her room.

As they cleared the table, Tidbit had trouble maneuvering the orange soda. It was too full, and the waxed-paper cup was weak and sweating condensation. However she grabbed it, the soda overflowed. Tidbit considered reminding Aaron about her lunch meds but didn't.

Both Tidbit and Aaron were increasingly anxious as they drove back to the school. Aaron wanted to drop Tidbit off and get back to the clinic to grab the meds as soon as possible. Tidbit wondered if her panic was worse because she had missed her meds. She knew she couldn't possibly feel a difference but it was something to focus on. Aaron rattled through the front gates of Roaring Orchards a touch too fast. Tidbit felt sick. He drove up past the weeping beech trees, tiny leaves budding along the length of their wands, and parked in the Mansion's carport.

They ran into Alternative Girls coming out of the Classroom Building. They were with June. Aaron began to tell her about what had happened at the clinic, but she had already heard. The girls in the dorm had as well, he thought, by the way they were looking at Tidbit.

"Is there any way," Aaron asked, "that I could leave her with you? There's one more thing I need to take care of off campus."

"Well, sure, she's out of the corner," June said. "They called from the clinic and said they'd found some meds you left behind."

"Oh. I'll stop by there, too, when I'm out."

"Roger already went and got them. Did Tidbit get her lunch meds?"

"You know, she didn't. Those, those must be the meds left at the clinic."

June nodded and checked her watch. "Don't forget to fill out a med error report," she told Aaron as he left. She pulled a small yellow med envelope out of her pocket. "Come on," she said to Tidbit, "it's not too late for you to take these. Do you need water?"

Tidbit shook her head.

June poured the contents of the package onto Tidbit's tongue. Tidbit swallowed and let June check her mouth. Alternative Girls were on their way to drop Claire off at therapy. As they continued toward the back entrance to the Mansion, the girls were being so cold to Tidbit that June had to remind them to stay within arms' distance. When Claire rolled her eyes, June told her that she and Tidbit would be holding hands for the rest of the afternoon if she didn't adjust her attitude.

Before the girls got to the Mansion, the back door opened, and I walked out with New Boys. June had her girls step to the side of the road and face away so that they wouldn't make eye contact with a restricted dorm. I saw Tidbit, but she couldn't see me. I watched her run her hands through her hair a couple of times. At this point no one outside her dorm had seen her black eye. "Oh my God," I heard her say to Claire, "do I look busted?"

"Do you look busted? You fucking bitch, you haven't even apologized for biting me, you won't get your shots, and you're worried about how you look?" Claire was shaking as she shouted, and it seemed it was only fear that kept her from hitting Tidbit. "Do I look busted with the bruises you gave me all over my face? Or the bite scars on my leg? I'd rather have been bit by a dog than you, you selfish, trashy whore."

Tidbit turned and ran. She slammed into some of the New Boys, and for a moment was face-to-face with me. She pushed past and ran into the Mansion. Claire called after her, "At least real bitches get their shots."

"Claire," June said. "Shit."

"Aren't we going to chase her?" Bridget asked.

"She's not going anywhere. We'll find her. But first we've got to pay for Claire's f-word and get you to therapy."

My dorm just stood still. Both Jodi and Spencer were watching us, and June waved Spencer over to ask him for help. "We can check the therapy rooms and the girls' wing. Could you look in the boys' wing and see if she's in Aubrey's apartment?"

"I'll check the boys' wing, but that's it. Last time I was up in Aubrey's rooms, he was in a nightshirt and Regular Kids were chasing him around the apartment trying to pinch his nipples."

**Tidbit did go** up to Aubrey's apartment, but not before hiding in a closet on the second floor to catch her breath. She kept expecting to cry, but she couldn't cry. Tidbit listened to hear if anyone was coming, then left the closet and climbed to Aubrey's rooms. She knocked gently and let herself in.

"Aubrey?" She took her shoes off and placed them on the pink carpet, by the door.

"Miss Lasker?" Aubrey's voice came from his bedroom in the back. Walking across the pink deep-pile carpet in her white socks felt fantastic. She dragged her feet some, to feel the carpet better.

"How'd you know it was me?" Tidbit asked when she entered Aubrey's room.

"I'm magic."

Aubrey was in bed, covered in sheets and a comforter so thick that his shape beneath them was completely obscured. He seemed to be only a head and arms propped up on pillows. He wore blue pajamas. Tidbit sat down in a chair by the bed.

"You don't seem to be so upset," he said.

"Should I be?"

Aubrey had shut his eyes. "When they called from the clinic about the shot, I could hear you wailing in the background. Like a wounded wombat, my mother would have said. Broke my heart."

Tidbit didn't know what to say. She looked around Aubrey's bedroom. The best part was the wallpaper. It was white with tan vertical stripes. The stripes were interrupted by pink medallions, which had designs painted on them in red. But the designs had faded with time. Tidbit had heard the wallpaper was a hundred years old.

"I'm sorry," she said. "But I didn't want the shot, and it felt like it was punitive. I mean, I only need it if I'm going to bite someone again, and I swear I won't. I swear."

Aubrey didn't respond. Tidbit waited. She couldn't tell whether, beneath all his covers, he was breathing. After waiting a little longer, she called, "Aubrey," and he stirred, his eyebrows moving first and then his large eyes opening.

"Dear, would you make me a cup of tea? The infuser's in the sink."

"Sure."

Tidbit had never made tea from loose leaves before, so she called out questions from the kitchen, and he told her what to do.

Once Tidbit managed to get the infuser open, he called, "You only want to fill it halfway with tea. That's so the leaves can expand. That makes more of the surface of each leaf exposed to water. It brews better that way. If you fill it all the way, the leaves press out of the perforations when they expand and get in your tea. Make yourself a cup, too."

"No thanks."

"You don't like tea?"

"I'm not, like, ninety."

Aubrey told her which cup and saucer he wanted, which she thought was funny. "Are you always that specific," she asked as she brought him his tea, "or are you just showing off?"

He nodded toward the chair for her to sit back down, and Tidbit wondered if maybe she'd overstepped. He took a sip of his tea and placed the saucer next to him on his comforter. "Thank you."

Tidbit nodded.

"Shouldn't I have gotten a phone call or a knock on the door by now? Shouldn't someone be looking for you? Who was watching your dorm when you ran up here?"

"June."

Aubrey rolled his eyes. "I'll be long dead before she gets the nerve to come looking in here for you. You should call her and tell her you're with me. Or, actually, no, don't call her. It's her job to find you."

"Okay."

"How's your mother? You heard from her lately?"

"I got a letter a couple of weeks ago. She seems good."

"Good. Did your mother drink, Tidbit? Was that a problem she had?"

"Not really, no. No. Unless you count tea." Tidbit smiled. "She drinks a lot of tea."

Aubrey raised his teacup and took a sip. "My mother drank. Not tea. And you know, I was thinking about things, and I realized the other day that two of my favorite passages in the world are about mothers and drinking. There's that part in the *Confessions* where Monica and August—do they have you read Saint Augustine here?"

"I don't think so," Tidbit said.

"God, it's like they're raising barnyard animals."

"We read *The Decameron*."

Tidbit had never actually seen someone's jaw drop before, and she giggled when Aubrey's did. "Saint Augustine was traveling with his mother, Monica," he said after a moment. "And she was dying, but there's this beautiful moment that comes a few days before she passes. She and her son are standing by a window, and they share a vision. Augustine says that they drank from the spring of life, with the mouths of their hearts wide open."

Tidbit leaned back and put her feet up on the edge of the bed. Aubrey patted them and continued, "The other bit I thought of is from the *Odyssey*. I'm just going to assume you haven't read that so you don't have to assure me that you read *The Sea-Wolf* or some such thing instead. Odysseus was lost in the land of the Cimmerians, I think, and to find his way needs to talk to a particular ghost named Tiresias. So he digs a pit and slaughters a sheep and fills the pit with the sheep's blood. And a crowd of hungry ghosts begins to crowd around the blood, but Odysseus won't let them have any until Tiresias arrives and answers his questions. After that, Odysseus lets the other ghosts in, and one of them is the ghost of his mother. He didn't even know she had died until he saw her ghost. And there's this moment when he stands there and watches his mother's ghost crawl up to the pit and drink this blood. It's one of the strangest things I've ever read."

Tidbit didn't know why he was telling her this. She wasn't even sure what he was trying to tell her or if he was just talking. But they seemed to be things he wanted to talk about, and it was nice sitting in an armchair in a quiet room with no one calling her names or trying to stick a needle into her.

"My favorite memory of my mother," Tidbit said, "was when we used to go to temple on Friday nights. I had these two velour pullovers that were this really, really dark blue. One was a crew neck, and one was a V-neck, and I used to sit on the floor of my room looking into the bottom drawer of my dresser, where I kept them, trying to decide which one to wear. I remember running my hand over them, just staring. I always wore my pink skirt, which I loved. Although now that I'm picturing it, it was really more peach than pink." Tidbit shifted in her chair. Aubrey patted her feet for her to continue.

"This was when my dad was still living with us, but he would come to services from work, so when we went home afterward I'd have to choose who to go home with. I don't know if it upset my dad, but I always went home with my mom. Mostly because she drove the Beetle, which was so much more fun. She would play these old Patti Smith cassettes, and I'd sing with her. But the best part was she'd let me put on the dome light, so it felt like we were in this little space capsule, just the two of us. That's my favorite memory, me and my mom going home from temple Friday nights. That car was like a lit-up igloo rolling through the dark."

Aubrey's eyes were shut, but he nodded and smiled. That memory had actually been of her father driving her home, and he never listened to music. But Tidbit knew what Aubrey was looking for, and she was happy to make him happy. The truth was, I never really knew how much of what Tidbit said was made up, and when she told me about this conversation with Aubrey, she said that she wasn't sure either. Her dad did drive a Beetle, she said. And the pullovers and skirt were real, she was certain. She remembered them.

She sat there quietly for a while. Aubrey fell back to sleep. His face looked like a little fire that had just been doused. Tidbit knew she should go back, and going back on her own made it seem easier. No one could say anything to her, because she'd been with

# 9

**K**en was anxious to hold his first workshop. He had spent plenty of time getting to know the students, the faculty, and Aubrey's system. He had sat in on meetings. He had gone out on Reciprocity Details. He and Aubrey had even put on a performance during dinner one night, a duet with Aubrey playing piano and Ken on the clarinet.

**But now things** were set. It was Friday, and classes were letting out early so those who wanted to could attend. He had found two students whom he thought he could help a great deal. Anyone could benefit from psychic mending, Ken believed, but there was a particular workshop that had truly astounding results, and he wanted that to be people's first impression of him here.

People were beginning to arrive. He was doing this workshop in the Campus Community room because it required space. He didn't want too many watching, because that could disrupt the session. But most of the Regular Kids would be there, and the therapists, and some of the dorm parents. Ken and Aubrey had had a long talk about whether Aubrey should be there. Ken very much wanted him to be. Aubrey thought it better that Ken have the room all to himself—to help people get used to the idea of his being in charge. Ken wondered, though, whether Aubrey was maybe just too tired. He checked to make sure the right equipment was there. The cushions, the camera.

Ken was anxious to begin, but teachers and dorm parents were trickling in, and he knew that he should give everyone time to relax, for the energy in the room to settle. He went over and talked to Jenna, the Regular Kid who was going to be filming the session. Ken stepped outside for a moment to see if any others were still on their way. He didn't see anyone. He returned to the room and began.

"All right, hello, everyone, and welcome. I've met you all, I know, but I'll start by saying that I'm Ken, and I want to thank you very much for being here. I think that this is going to be an interesting and eye-opening experience for many of you, and hopefully also a helpful one for our subjects, but also on a personal level"—here he smiled and ran his hand over the bald part of his head—"it's really very gratifying to feel so much support and interest.

"What we're all going to be taking part in this morning is a psychic mending workshop, of course, but of a very specific nature. This is a ReBirthing session that I've organized, and before we begin I want to explain how it differs from a typical psychic mending exercise. ReBirthing involves only two figures: the subject"—and here he pointed to Beverly Hess and William Kay, who were seated with their dorm parents—"and the Ideal Mother, whom the subject will choose and who will enroll at the appropriate time.

"Generally in psychic mending, many more figures are enlisted. For example, if we were dealing with the repercussions of, say, a divorce, we might have various members of the workshop enroll as the Real Father, the Ideal Father, the Real Mother, and the Ideal Mother, as well as, possibly, the Voice of Loyalty to Past Pain or the Voice of Hyperbolic Disappointment. But today there will just be the two figures, as I said.

"Now, ReBirthing is used specifically in cases where we suspect that a subject's difficulties result from an attachment disorder.

The theory goes that individuals experience attachment disorder, which is the inability to form strong, reliable connections with other people, especially with people in positions of authority, the theory is that this results from the failure to bond properly with the mother at birth. Some experts tell us that the absence of bonding even just during the first *fifteen minutes* of life can have lifelong repercussions. And of course the fear is then, the question is, that if it happens, if this bonding fails to happen, what can you do? Because how could you go back?"

Ken had been pacing back and forth across the front of the room as he was talking, but now he stopped and looked at the group assembled before him, his arms at his sides, his long fingers splayed. He sat down cross-legged on the carpet.

"That question, how could you go back, always seemed to me like such a failure of the imagination. You know, like a lot of you kids, I was very imaginative as a young person. Back in my day it was what the teachers used to call woolgathering, I was always off somewhere in my head. It's part of what gets us into so much trouble, right?" He looked around the room, smiling and nodding at the students. "And it always drove me bonkers when someone, usually some grown-up, would say, 'Oh, that's just imaginary,' or 'That's not real.' Because to me, what I imagined was more real than most of the so-called real things they were talking about. And when I became a therapist I discovered that there's a whole body of research that supports this, that says that for us as humans"—he made a gesture to encompass the whole room—"what we imagine has profound and measurable consequences.

"So all that ReBirthing does is it applies this insight to the problem of attachment disorder. If bonding has failed to occur, rather than simply saying 'Oh, well, what can we do,' what we do is to *imaginatively* re-create the experience of birth, so that this time bonding *can* occur."

Ken hopped up and grabbed two of the cushions from the large pile that lay on the floor. "How do we do it? We use a bunch of cushions like these to represent the birth canal, and Beverly and William will, one at a time, have to fight their way through a kind of gauntlet, just like a baby trying to be born. And when they get through, they'll have the opportunity to bond with the Ideal Mother of their choice.

"Now, it's important that no one improvise during this session, because it is delicate. You need to imagine that we're dealing with actual newborns, since that is essentially what William and Beverly will become. And it's important that while they are bonding, which will go on for ten minutes, that everyone is silent. Please. So before we begin, are there any questions?"

There were none. Ken arranged things to his satisfaction. He placed the cushions in a line at the front of the room, and he made sure the camera was in position to get the best possible shot. "Whenever possible, I like psychic mending sessions to be videotaped," he explained as he did this. "That way, the subject can go over them again, with a therapist or alone, and gain further insights.

"Now, of our two subjects, who wants to go first? Beverly? William? No? Beverly, why don't you come up here. I want to talk to you for a moment before we begin."

Bev looked at Marcy to see if it was all right, and when she nodded, Bev got up and stood next to Ken. She felt as though she were onstage. She looked back and forth from Ken to the rest of the group, her eyes wide open, nervous laughter bubbling through her wild smile.

"Beverly, your dorm parent explained to me that right now you're on a structure called ghosting because members of your dorm found you to be too needy. Well, that neediness is a sign that you don't trust that your needs are going to be met. You're constantly agitating for attention because you fear that you'll be forgotten, isn't that right?"

"Okay," Bev said, the tone of her laughter deeper now, incredulous.

"I'd like you now to choose someone from the group assembled here to be your Ideal Mother. If you could choose anyone here to be your mother, whom would you choose?"

"Marcy?"

"Are you asking me or telling me?"

"Telling you?"

"Good. Marcy, would you please sit at the end of the birth canal? No, the other end. Good, thank you. Now say, 'I enroll as the figure of your Ideal Mother.'"

Marcy tucked a lock of hair behind her ear. "I enroll as the figure of your Ideal Mother."

"Excellent. When Beverly emerges from the birth canal, I'd like you to hold her and look her in the eyes for ten minutes. Don't worry, I'll keep time. It's important that you look each other in the eye for as long as possible. I know Beverly isn't a baby, so you can't exactly hold her like one, but find the closest position that feels comfortable.

"Beverly, you come here with me." He walked to the other end of the line of cushions. "Excuse me—Aaron, is it? I'll need your help with this if you don't mind. Beverly is going to try to crawl from this point to where Marcy is sitting, and we are going to surround her tightly with cushions and make that journey as difficult as possible. Do you understand? Beverly, are you ready?"

As soon as Beverly began crawling, Ken and Aaron pressed the cushions against her from either side. Bev stopped and sat still until Ken explained that she should continue fighting until she got to Marcy. So she pushed against the cushions and giggled when she got pushed back. She ducked her head and pressed forward again, squeezed between the cushions. Bev breathed in the chemical smell of the stuffing. The rough wool covers scraped her face. She tried to get some traction, leaning forward and pressing her feet against the carpet. But she wasn't wearing shoes, and her feet slipped. She burrowed down, beneath where Ken and Aaron were pressing, and crawled on her elbows. A zipper cut her over one eye, but she crawled on. She saw a small triangle of carpet in front of her, where the pile of cushions ended. When she emerged, her, face was red and she was panting. Marcy was smiling down at her, and Bev smiled back. Bev climbed into Marcy's lap, and they stared at each other, Bev giggling intermittently. Marcy wiped a small drop of blood from above Bev's eye.

For ten minutes they sat there, the only distraction Ken's palpable excitement at how well his session was going. When ten minutes were up he exhaled loudly and told Bev that he would set up a time for them to talk later. For now she should just feel what she was feeling. Then it was William's turn. He chose Ellie to be his Ideal Mother. He said it with a note of triumph, as though he were making her do something she didn't want to. And the kids all laughed, because Ellie was gorgeous, and they knew William was taking advantage of the chance to lie in her lap and stare at her.

Ellie made an effort not to roll her eyes. "I enroll as the figure of your Ideal Mother," she said. Ken motioned for her to move to where Marcy had been sitting. She did and wondered if he would expect her to hold William in her lap.

"We're going to make this a difficult journey, William," Ken told him. "Because the most difficult journeys are the most valuable. Now I'll need another volunteer or two to help me and Aaron." Most of the boys at the session raised their hands while Ken rolled up his sleeves. He chose Tyler and Eric Gold. "A couple of big boys," he said. "We'll make this a real challenge."

William took a few steps back to get a running start. Ken

nodded at him, and William ran at the cushions he and Aaron were holding. Ken knocked him to the ground and pressed him with the cushions. "Now move, move, William! Move to the end of the canal!"

Aaron leaned down on a bunch of cushions and pillows he piled on top of William. Eric kneeled on the cushions near William's head.

"You fuckers are smothering me," William called out.

"Remember, you're a baby now. You can't talk."

William worked his legs and crawled on his elbows, trying to move under the cushions. Aaron laughed as he felt William lurch forward. Tyler called out to Eric to stop him, and from opposite sides of the canal they pressed the cushions together.

"I think we've got his face," Eric said as William punched against the pillows around him.

"Hold him," Tyler said. The boys laughed together, kneeling on the floor. Aaron was enjoying this. He imagined what he might say if they had a meeting later to discuss how the session had gone. He would say that what he liked was that Ken showed that you could deal with your issues but that it could also be fun. William twisted under the cushions. The boys had let go of his head, and he tried to find a place between the cushions where he could get a breath. But everything pressed down all over, and there wasn't any air anywhere. He felt an enormous pressure welling up inside him. He struggled to find some release, scraped at the carpet with his fingers. Aaron felt William's shoulder jerk forward and pushed him back, only to feel William lurch again.

About halfway through the canal, William stopped the way Bev had and lay there. Ken told him to go on, but William didn't. "Come on now, no giving up," he called. A few moments went by, and Ken told him again. The he lifted up the cushion and saw William's upper lip covered in blood. William was still. The students watching drew back instinctively. Purple spots were spread across his cheek and neck.

"Oh, goddamn it, goddamn it. We need to call an ambulance right away," Ken said. "Right away. Who knows where there's a phone? Could someone go?" He seemed calm, but what he felt was an overwhelming exhaustion laced with fear.

Aaron moved to check for a pulse at William's throat, but Ken knocked his arm away. "We shouldn't touch him. We need to get an ambulance. They know what to do."

"But we could give him CPR, couldn't we?"

"We need to tell Aubrey," someone said.

"Yes, fine, but first call the ambulance. Has somebody gone to call? It's important that we all remain calm." A few feet from him, Ellie was crying, and children were already running from the room.

**When Ellie got** back to her apartment after speaking with the police, there were three messages waiting on her answering machine. She had the unsettling impression that they were all, impossibly, about William. Then she realized that it had been four days since she had been back to her room. She had spent the last two nights at Roger's and before that had been on duty in the dorm. The red LED 3 flashed up at her again and again.

Things could not possibly be more fucked, Ellie thought as she sat down on the corner of her bed. The EMTs had taken William's body away, and the officers had only taken some preliminary statements, but even those were a disaster. Ken had tried to suggest that the students helping with the session got a little out of hand, that he had tried to tell them not to be so rough. The officers didn't question his account, and Ellie didn't contradict him. They just asked for the names of all the students who had been at the session. Then they asked about the video camera in the back of the room.

Ellie stared at the answering machine for a moment, then pressed PLAY. "Hi, honey," the tape played. "It's Dad. I wanted you to know that Mom and I ran into Mr. Fonseca, the lawyer Uncle Carson recommended, when we were having dinner at the Grouper the other night, and he mentioned that you hadn't called him." Ellie balled the edge of her comforter in her fist as she listened. "He'd be happy to talk to you about the case, honey. He thinks you're getting some very bad advice from the people up there." The second message was also from her father, asking whether she had received the first. On the third he said simply, "Sweetie, we can't help you if you don't call us."

It seemed like forever since Han Quek ran away. Ellie doubted any lawyer would want to help her now that she had also been present at the death of a student. She remembered thinking once, when she first got together with Roger, that her real life was waiting for her somewhere. Ellie had thought she would one day simply step back into it. The idea seemed worse than idiotic to her now. But she saw how someone who thought like that would have gotten herself where she was.

Ellie picked up the answering machine and slammed it down on the milk crate it rested on, then threw it on the floor. There was a soft pop when the phone plug tore out of the wall. She stomped on the machine until bits of plastic flew around the floor. Ellie pulled the minicassette tape out of the machine and ground it beneath her heel. Then she sat back down on her bed.

Later, Roger came in to see how she was. He turned on the light, which felt harsh, and made her sit up and drink some water. Ellie didn't feel at all like talking, but she listened.

"You can't blame yourself for this," he said. "Ken was running a delicate therapeutic intervention, and it would have been dangerous for you to interrupt. You trusted him. There's no way you could have known what would happen."

He sat down on the bed next to her and put an arm around her. She noticed the freckles on his forehead and registered the concern in his voice. "The thing about these kids," he said, "is, you have to remember, these are not healthy kids. William, if he had kept going the way he was at home, he would have ended up dead. One way or another. That's the direction he was heading in, the stuff he was getting into. We're trying to save these kids' lives, Ellie. Don't ever forget that. We're trying to save their lives, and it doesn't always work."

**Aaron spent the** next day in his apartment. It wasn't that he was afraid to go outside; the thought didn't even occur to him. It was only when he realized that he'd been there all day that the thought of going out made him at all uncomfortable. There wasn't really anywhere to go anyway. It was a Saturday, and they didn't need him on campus. They'd told him to get some rest. Surprisingly, he'd been able to. He actually was embarrassed he'd slept so well last night. Today, he'd even taken a nap.

Aaron felt that if he didn't force himself to remember that William was dead, he would be allowed to forget all about it. Maybe not forever—somewhere, he was sure papers were being filled out and shuffled that would drag him back to revisit what had happened. But right now William was just gone, and today wasn't much different than Saturday last week. That was the worst part. No, he had to keep reminding himself. That wasn't the worst part.

He heard music coming from somewhere, but he couldn't tell where. It wasn't from Zbigniew's room or anywhere close by. Aaron half stumbled out of his apartment, curious to find out if he was just hearing things or if it was real. It was lovely, whatever it was. He could only catch wisps of it, the melody intermittently drowned out by the rhythm. It was dark out, but the moon was bright enough that the tree trunks cast shadows on the grass.

Aaron followed the sound across campus, up the hill toward the opposite side of the Mansion. The closer he got, the more brash the music seemed. By the time he got to the Cafetorium, where the music was coming from, it had resolved itself into shrill strings dutifully climbing up and down the scale. Aaron peered in. The students were having their square dance.

Aaron walked in and poured himself a cup of store-brand caffeine-free soda. He sat down next to Spencer, who patted him on the shoulder.

"How you doing?"

Aaron took some pretzels from a Styrofoam bowl. "What is this?"

"They had it planned weeks ago and forgot about it. These guys just showed up, so we figured we might as well. Weird being a chaperone, I'll tell you that."

Two lines of students skipped along parallel to one another, then peeled away and circled around to meet up again. Then the guy with the microphone started telling them to do something else. Aaron felt himself filled with a rage so intense that for a moment he couldn't see. In that brief darkness he only knew that this was wrong, that it had to stop. He didn't know quite what that meant, and he wasn't going to do anything about it, but he knew it was so. Slowly, through pools of black, his sight returned, and Aaron was left with that knowledge. The man's microphone was hooked up to an amp. There was a woman working a record player. It was amazing how much noise they were making.

I was back by the table with the sodas, eating chips and hating the whole scene. Tidbit caught my eye and came over. We spoke without looking at each other, slowly filling our plastic cups, me with cola, she with lemon–lime. "You want to get out of here?" she asked me.

"Hi, Tidbit."

"Don't fuck around. Do you?"

"Just like that. Walk out. Right now?"

"You want to hang out here, after what happened?"

"Why, what happened?" I asked, and we looked at each other. "Statistically, there's *less* chance now that one of us will get smothered, since it just happened." I couldn't tell whether Tidbit was a bit shocked, but I hoped she was.

"Personally," she said, "I'm less worried about getting suffocated than about having to listen to any more of this music."

"I'm allowed to feel how I feel."

"God, you're a freak." She crouched down behind the table, veiled by the paper tablecloth draped from it. "Come down here." She tugged at the leg of my pants. It was stupid, but I ducked under the table. "See, we've done it."

"We haven't done anything."

"Follow me." She crawled to the back door and slipped out, me right behind.

Outside we stood up. "I want to grab some stuff from the Mansion," I said.

"What for?"

"Just like a change of clothes. And I've still got some money hidden."

"You want to *run*? I just meant let's get out of the fucking square dance."

I looked at her. "Well, yeah, I meant let's run. Do you still want to stay here? *After what happened?*"

Tidbit wasn't sure why I was making fun of her. I watched as she thought about it. I remembered how I had kept my eyes on her face the first time I had seen her, when she had walked into New Girls' lounge naked and introduced herself.

Tidbit was aware of me watching. She always wanted to be simple, to think just one thing, but her mind was always too many things. "Meet me by the Farm in like five minutes, and we'll talk about it," she said. "I'll get my cigarettes."

"All right." We circled around behind the Cafetorium and made our way to the back of the Mansion.

**It was dark,** but we could still see Napoleon and Elba back in the covered part of the pigpen. Elba lying down, Napoleon standing on her. "Do they stay like that all night?" Tidbit asked. She said she'd always assumed that Napoleon would climb down to sleep. The goat bent to scratch his nose against his leg. He lifted his head back up and flicked an ear. "Maybe he sleeps standing up," she said.

"I really don't want to argue," I said. "If you want to stay, that's fine, but I think I'm going to go." I had brought my backpack.

We were leaning against the fence. Tidbit didn't say anything. She knew it wasn't that big a decision. I'd be gone a few days and then I'd be back, probably.

She dragged on her cigarette. "Where do you think you're gonna go?"

"I hadn't thought about it. I wasn't planning on running until you said something."

"You should go down to January Lake. It's nice around there."

I nodded. I asked Tidbit for a cigarette. When she struck the match for me, it threw uneven light across the planes of her face. "So, which way is January Lake?" I asked.

Tidbit probably assumed I knew and was just playing stupid but she told me the way to go. I asked what she did for food when she had run.

"It depends. Once I made it to the Alexander Academy in Bilston and hid in these guys' dorm room, and they brought me food. And one time I ended up in this cornfield and just ate ears of corn, but it's too early for that now. But you said you've got money, right?"

"And I took Spencer's ID."

"Really?"

"Yup." I patted the backpack that hung from my right shoulder.

"Well, I was going to say," Tidbit said. She couldn't help laughing.

"What?"

"You could just get food at the mini-mart on the way to the lake. You can get booze there, too."

I nodded. "Yeah, well, bye, Tidbit," I said. But I didn't go anywhere. I flicked my cigarette into the pigpen, where it landed in the loose pile of hay. A few bits of hay flared up. We watched to see what would happen. The embers shifted some. In the dark, I could just barely make out a thin, twisting line of smoke. There were no more flames, though the pile of hay shifted and shifted again. Then one of the stray cats shot out from under the hay, burning embers caught in her coat. She tumbled and turned, skidding and rolling over her shoulders in the dirt until she knocked over the can of turpentine and went up like a torch.

Tidbit backed away from the pen. The cat was running straight into the wall of the shed, over and over, as the burning turpentine spilled across the pen and the wooden wall caught fire. I was just saying, "Oh, oh, oh." She took my hand and pulled me toward the woods, though I continued to look over my shoulder to watch the fire burn. Then I turned and ran, too.

The goat looked up briefly at the rising flames. It shifted its feet slightly on the pig's side and shook its coat. Lying on the ground, the pig stretched its neck to look, too. As the heat increased and smoke rolled around it, the goat kneeled and laid its head down on its front legs. Neither the pig nor the goat moved or seemed to particularly notice the fire, other than to blink in the heat and flinch as parts of the burning roof fell down.

# 10

**W**e ran alongside a ditch scattered with stones, weeds, and bits of litter. No one from the school would chase us, but the police would be notified, and they might actually try to track us down. Especially, Tidbit said, if they were told there was a pair of arsonists on the loose. I breathed deeply and took large strides, holding her hand, terrified of what I'd done. Tidbit pulled her hand from my grip, hurrying to get away from the school. She kicked me in the leg.

"Come on," she said.

We followed Route 294 until we saw the twenty-four-hour mini-mart. Tidbit stopped under some trees across the street, and we both sat down to catch our breath. Tidbit let her hair down and then fixed it again in a purple rubber band.

"How much've you got?" she asked.

"Eighteen, I think." I rifled through my stash. My bag was packed tightly, and it took a minute to find the money.

"What's that?" Tidbit asked, pointing.

"What's what? That? Oh, that's a bottle of fabric softener." The answer didn't seem to satisfy her. "Pure 'n' Gentle. I get a rash if I use any other brand. So I thought I should bring it."

"Where do you think you'll use it?"

"I don't know. Where do you wash your clothes when you run away?"

"I don't think I washed my clothes any of the times I've run away." She looked at the blue bottle for a long moment. "You've got the money?"

"Yeah, eighteen dollars. And Spencer's ID. What should I get?"

"Cigarettes, booze, and, like, some apples. And some water."

"And I'll get peanut butter."

"Okay."

I started toward the store, but Tidbit grabbed my arm. "No, wait. It'll look strange if you just walk in there this late without a car having pulled up. The guy'll know. Let's just wait for someone to pull in, so it'll look like you're with them."

We sat back in the sparse woods and watched the gas station. Strings of colorful plastic flags hanging in front of the store window popped loudly in the wind. Sitting on the ridge of a small hill, I could see behind the gas station to January Lake, although it was late enough that all I really saw were the lights of the houses around it reflected across the dark water. I listened for sirens heading toward the school; I didn't hear any.

I was scraping bits of bark from a stick I'd found when Tidbit let out a little laugh. She rested her head on my shoulder. "At least you didn't bring a washing machine." I liked her leaning against me like that and did my best not to move. The shoulder she was leaning on began to shake slightly but uncontrollably. An old mint-green Cadillac pulled into the gas station. Tidbit leaned back in the pine needles, and we watched and waited.

A woman got out of the passenger seat, stood up and stretched in the wind. She was old, and thin, and was wearing a summer dress and sandals. The driver's-side door opened, and an old man sitting there turned so that his legs pointed out of the car. He leaned forward, his elbows on his knees, and took a white sporting cap off his head. They seemed to have been driving for a long time. The old man got out of his car to pump gas. His wife dabbed at the windshield with a squeegee. The man looked at the Cadillac and called out, "Margaret, did you do this? When did this happen, Margaret?"

"What?" she said.

"The back fender, what happened to the back fender?"

"Nothing."

"Nothing. I'm not blind, I can see that something happened to the fender." The old man had his cap in his hand and was peering down at his car.

The woman sighed. She turned to her husband and said sharply, "Well, if you're not blind, you can see what happened to the fender."

Tidbit tapped my arm and nodded for me to go to the store. I crossed the street, and the couple looked at me as I passed through the parking lot. Drops of soapy water dripped from the squeegee in the woman's hand. The scene reminded me of something, but I couldn't quite place it. I headed into the mini-mart, hands in my pockets.

"Whadja get?" Tidbit asked when I returned to the woods.

I poked around in the bag and pulled out a pack of cigarettes. "These," I said, handing them to her. "And this." I pulled out a flask-sized bottle.

"Blackberry brandy?"

"It sounded good, and I thought it would keep us warm. I didn't really know what to get."

Tidbit shrugged. She lit one of her cigarettes. "They didn't give you a problem about the ID?"

"They didn't even check it. I also got apples and peanut butter some water and these." I removed a clear plastic bag of chocolates, each wrapped in colored foil. "They were on sale. My bag's kinda full. Could you take some of this?"

"No."

I looked at her a second, then shrugged and pulled the bottle of Pure 'n' Gentle out of my bag to make room for the groceries.

"At least take these then," I said, handing Tidbit the brandy and chocolates. The rest fit snugly in my bag. I swung the bag onto my shoulders, grabbed my fabric softener, and followed Tidbit back to the road. We passed the chocolates and the bottle of brandy back and forth, dropping the pastel foil wrappers behind us.

Tidbit stopped suddenly. "Look at that," she whispered, pointing up. Under a streetlight, I saw shadows flickering in midair, shifting blocks of darkness cut from the night sky and shooting back and forth erratically. It took me a moment to focus my eyes before I realized that there were two bats flying high above us.

"Watch this," Tidbit said. She grabbed a small stone from the ground and tossed it into the air. Both bats swooped at it and veered away just before touching it. "They think it's a bug to eat until they get close," she said. She tossed another stone up so that the top of its arc was just a few feet above our heads. The bats' bodies were larger than I would have thought. The brandy was quickly going to my head. Tidbit threw another stone that would have hit me if I hadn't ducked.

"Hey," I said, but she was already heading down the road. I knew she was angry about the fire and about having to run when she hadn't wanted to. I wanted to tell her it wasn't my fault, but it was my fault. Maybe the brandy was getting to her, too. I looked up at the bats one last time before following her. Their wings were shaped like oak leaves.

What the old lady reminded me of, I realized as I hurried to catch up, was my mom, just a few months before I'd been sent to Roaring Orchards. Her "days," when she wouldn't—couldn't—move from the white couch in the living room, watching television and smoking cigarettes. My dad just went to work and came back late, and after a while didn't even try to talk to her; he just went to their bedroom and slept. My mom stayed on the couch, except for when, late at night, she would roam around the house doing chores. That whole time was odd to think about. I imagine something similar was going on when she got burned after sending me to the school. I couldn't hold all the pieces of it in my head at once.

There was one night I remembered clearly. I'd gotten into the habit of waking up in the middle of the night to check on my mom, and when I got up I couldn't find her anywhere. I went all through the house twice, faster and faster, beginning to panic but too scared to wake my father or call the police, when I heard a faint scratching by the living room window. I looked out and saw my mother down in the yard, in her bathrobe, raking the leaves, slowly, beneath the streetlight. I came closer to the window. She wasn't accomplishing much: just dragging the rake through the leaves. Then she stopped and looked up at me as if she had known I was there the whole time. I stood perfectly still, watching her look at me, and she was still, too, seeing me watch her. I could feel my pulse in my fingertips. I felt something stretch between us, and I felt it snap. I blinked, then bored of standing there, turned and went to bed.

**Tidbit and I** left the road about a quarter mile from January Lake and headed straight through the woods toward the water. Thin branches and vines stretched across the ground, and in the absence of streetlamps we walked through shadows. Trees loomed up in front of us from out of nowhere. We bumped and tripped through the dim shapes until the sloshing, glittery expanse of water spread out before us. It lapped against the mud shore and emitted a deep hiss that echoed in the leaves and stones all around.

"Shit," said Tidbit, "where's the boats?"

"I don't know." I caught my breath. "Are there boats?"

"Yeah, there's a whole bunch of them someplace. Didn't you think about this at all? Fuck. We'll find them." She grabbed my hand and pulled me after her along the shore, which we followed around the lake. It soon thinned to a narrow strip of dirt and rocks, so that we were walking along with the lake to our right and the dark woods to our left. I felt my face flush, and my footsteps were heavy. We each slipped repeatedly, on stones or mud, and kept from falling by stomping into the water. She was determined to keep moving away from the school, but it felt like it was me she was trying to get away from. I struggled to keep up.

I slipped on a wet rock and landed in a puddle of loose silt, my leg sinking into the mud up to my knee. Tidbit had to help pull me out, yanking on both my arms, after taking the blue bottle of liquid fabric softener from me and tossing it near a fallen tree. Pulling my leg out, I lost a shoe in the muck. Tidbit went back to fish it out while I hopped up the shore and sat down on the tree where she'd thrown the bottle.

Sitting there, squeezing the water out of my muddy sock, I felt my throat tighten and my chest swell. A hot, fat tear sat poised on the pink shelf of my eyelid, trembling. I thought about getting caught for setting the fire and about Tidbit ending up back in the corner. I wasn't going to fall apart, I decided. If this was what it was like, then fine. I dragged my forearm across my cheek, crushing the tear. I pulled on my sock and twisted my foot into the soggy sneaker Tidbit handed me. She looked surprised to see me produce a clean towel from my stuffed book bag and begin drying the leg of my pants.

"I know it's not your fault we had to run," she said. "I'm just worried. And I left Burn Victim behind."

"Burn Victim?"

"I'll tell you later. He's my silent witness."

When we got going again, we stayed farther up in the woods and moved slowly, stumbling and feeling around. Tidbit fell over a huge bump that gave out a muffled knell. A boat. We started to crawl around to see if there were more, and there were boats everywhere, each one turned upside down, covering the hill like scales on a fish.

"Try to find one that's not locked to a tree," Tidbit said. This was difficult in the dark. I felt around for chains or cables, or just tried to pull the boats away, but locks kept stopping me. Tidbit found a loose rowboat at the top of the hill, and we flipped it over and dragged it toward the lake. The metal hull amplified every noise as it slid across pine needles and scraped against stones. When we got it to the shore, we could see it was dark green, or had been. The paint was faded where it hadn't chipped, and the name LINDA was stenciled across the stern in white.

The boat bounced lightly on the waves as I pushed it backward into the water.

"Get in," I said, leaning on the bow to keep it steady. Tidbit hunched down and scurried to the back. I put one foot into the boat and pushed off the shore with the other. I dropped my book bag and the blue bottle of Pure 'n' Gentle at my feet, fitted the oars into the oarlocks, and, jerking and tilting, we floated away from shore.

**"You know what's** amazing?" Tidbit was leaning back against the side of the rowboat and dragging her fingers through the water. "We were just killing ourselves to climb and crawl over the ground, to get from here to there, but now we're just sailing way above it. The ground's all the way down there and all that's between us and it"—she lifted her wrist and let water drip from her fingers—"is this." Tidbit had the brandy and the chocolates. I didn't mention that we weren't quite sailing.

"You know what's at the bottom of this lake?" she asked.

"What? Hold on, just tell me if I get us off course." My back was to the front of the boat, and my rowing was getting clumsy. Rather than plying through the water, one or the other of the oars kept skipping across the surface, causing me to turn the boat erratically and lose my balance. "We should be heading toward that light." I pointed to a light across the lake. We were almost halfway there. I rotated the oars so that they rested in the boat; I wanted a rest. Tidbit passed me the brandy. "What's at the bottom of the lake?"

"This is where Cubit Grafflin's daughter had her wedding, on the ice. She's still down there somewhere, in her dress, along with the minister and one of her guests."

"Could we please not have any more bullshit stories? I'm so sick of that."

"What are you talking about?"

"Every single fucking thing anyone says at that school is a complete lie. No one's stories make any sense."

"Like whose?"

"Pudding says he stole ten thousand dollars from his dad and spent it taking cabs. Gary makes up shit about jerking off mules to tell Brenda, or else he just lies to us about what he told her. That story you told me about the girls who ran away and got to California? The people at the church wouldn't check before they bought a plane ticket? Right."

"What's that about Gary?"

"It's like all the stories *almost* work, but none of them really do."

"Maybe that story didn't really happen," Tidbit said. "But what do you care if it's true or not?"

"I don't care. I just don't want to hear any more bullshit."

For a while we listened to the sound of the water lapping against the sides of the boat. Then Tidbit said, "You're right. A lot of people make things up. But a lot of people have pretty weird stories, too."

"Yeah. So what'd you do to get sent here?"

"What do you mean? I told you, didn't I?"

"I guess I forgot. Tell me again?"

Tidbit looked at me. "I don't want to talk about it."

"Uh-huh." I watched her take a drink of the brandy. She handed me the bottle, and I drank some. "Do you think they think we set the fire on purpose?" I asked.

"What, because of William? They might not even know we're gone yet."

I took another long pull from the bottle of brandy and then looked at it. "I bet they know. I bet they think we set the fire on purpose."

We passed the bottle back and forth. Tidbit lit a cigarette. "My dorm's probably in a candor meeting right now. Yours, too. I can just see it."

"This stuff is really sweet. It's making my tongue feel heavy."

"June's probably half asleep and mumbling to people to let go of their fibs. And they're all going to have to sit there staring at their feet until someone starts to cry about how angry she is at me." The boat was spinning slowly in the breeze.

"I think this stuff is making my teeth hurt."

"Give me that. Are you even listening? Your dorm's probably in the same spot right now. Ellie's not any different, even if she's cute."

"Well," I said, "I'm in Jodi's dorm now, not Ellie's. Jodi is not cute. And Ellie's problem is that she's got her own problems."

"You don't feel bad about taking off?" Tidbit tapped her feet in the water in the bottom of the boat.

"No. I feel great about taking off, actually. That place is a fucking gulag." I paused to take a drink. "Gu-lag." The bottle was almost empty. "We're not supposed to feel bad for acting out. We're children, and they're supposed to be taking care of us. Isn't that what Aubrey says? Who I feel bad about is Ed and Naoko."

"Who?"

"No one. Never mind."

Tidbit folded a candy wrapper into a little boat and set it out on the water. She leaned back again and dipped her fingers into the lake, which seemed higher than it had before. "I think the boat's leaking," she said.

"No, why would anyone leave a leaky boat out by a lake?"

"Look." Tidbit kicked her feet around in the water at the bottom of the boat, which was a few inches deep.

I looked around my feet for a moment. "Do you think that's why this one wasn't locked up?" I took the oars and started rowing. "Where's the light we're heading to?"

"Over there, I think," Tidbit said, pointing. "What should I do?" She cupped her hands and splashed handfuls of water out of the boat. As I rowed, the water sloshed all around, soaking everything.

"Get rid of whatever you can," I told her. She threw the empty brandy bottle and the chocolates that were left overboard. Then she picked up the bottle of Pure 'n' Gentle that had floated toward her feet.

"Wait."

"Benjamin."

"Okay, but just dump it out and use the bottle to bail out the boat." Tidbit poured the contents into the lake. The liquid was pale blue and left a brilliant slick along the surface that rose and fell in our wake. She pushed the empty bottle under the water in the boat and waited for it to fill up before pouring it out again over the side.

The water we had taken on weighed the boat down enough that with every tilt caused by my clumsy rowing, more water poured in over the gunwales. Before long, the boat was too heavy to row, so the two of us sat there, sinking.

"Just pour the bottle out and put the top back on tight. It'll float," I suggested without much enthusiasm. The bow sank below the water, and the boat began to slip away beneath us.

"Let's go," Tidbit said.

I was surprised as I leaned into the lake and started swimming that I didn't get wet, at least not all at once. The cold water took its time, trickling down my back and up my legs after seeping through my sleeves, collar, and cuffs.

I let my book bag sink. Tidbit held the empty bottle of liquid fabric softener under her chin. She kicked and moved smoothly along. I swam a nervous kind of breaststroke but tired quickly. I dunked under to see how far the bottom was, and realized that the lake was very shallow; I could just keep my head up if I hopped along on my toes.

Which is how we proceeded, two heads disembodied in the dark water, hers gliding slowly across the surface, mine bobbing up and down, moving along in slow, distended arcs. Tidbit took in a mouthful of lake water and spat it at me. I splashed back.

Climbing out of the water was awful. My clothes clung heavy and tight and in the wind chilled mercilessly. Tidbit and I dragged ourselves up the shore and toward the houses, our lips blue and teeth chattering.

On that side of the lake, the woods were cleared all the way down to the shore to make room for lakefront homes. We walked through the wide yards, looking into the windows and garages of one house after another, trying to find one where no one was home. It took us a long while before we found a yellow clapboard house that was a good possibility, and by the time we got there, both Tidbit and I were cold and uncomfortable enough to take our chances.

"Break the window by the back door," Tidbit said, looking around the edges of the lawn for a good-sized rock. "I'll tell you if any lights go on."

"I don't think that's a very good idea."

"Benjamin, how else will we know if anyone's inside?"

"We could ring the bell."

"No, that's not how you do it."

"Well, why not? We could just run if anyone answers."

"Fine, I'll break it. Just tell me if any lights go on." Tidbit found two rocks and walked around to the bottom of the back steps, which were wooden and painted gray. She took a breath and hurled one rock through a window in the back door, winced at the noise it made, and waited. She looked back at me. I shook my head. Tidbit climbed the steps and used the other rock to clear shards of glass from the window, reached in, and unlocked the door. She motioned for me to follow her.

Inside, when the darkness resolved into shapes, we found ourselves in front of an umbrella rack, next to a line of pegs on the wall hung with raincoats and jackets. There was a woven rug on the floor. We crept forward, through a space with a washer and dryer. Board games were piled on the dryer, a cardboard box with a checkers set on top. The box was missing its lid, and I could see the folded, beat-up board and pieces scattered around. With a laugh, Tidbit pointed to a shelf above the washer, where there was a bottle of Pure 'n' Gentle, identical to the one I'd been carrying.

Carefully, we rounded a corner and walked into the kitchen. The stove was on an island in the middle, over which hung all kinds of enormous pots and utensils. Tidbit wandered in to take a closer look in the cabinets, while I walked through to the living room. There wasn't a lot of furniture—a couch, three chairs, a table—but it seemed solid and comfortable. I had the sense I often had at home, moving around my house at night. The furniture seemed to be different at night, as if it didn't exist for human purposes then. It felt like I had intruded on a den of large, quiet animals breathing softly in their sleep.

There was a tremendous noise in the kitchen, and I looked back at Tidbit. She had knocked down some of the pots and was standing frozen. She mouthed *Sorry*, and we waited. When there was no reaction, we relaxed.

I found a couple of bathrobes and some towels in an upstairs closet. I changed in the bathroom and took a quick shower while Tidbit got out of her clothes and into a robe and warmed up under the covers in the big bedroom. When I was done in the shower, Tidbit went in. She had left on the TV in the bedroom, and it was showing a submarine adventure movie. The crew had just narrowly escaped from the enemy fleet, only to be mistaken for an enemy ship by their own navy. "We can't return fire, for God's sake!" shouted the captain.

I looked around the bedroom. There was a fireplace, and the mantel was arranged with decorative things—a candlestick on one end, some dried flowers and a cowbell on the other. On the dresser, a hairbrush lay next to a lacquered wooden box. I opened the box and picked through the jewelry inside. I assumed that none of it was real, although I couldn't be sure. I played with the links of a chunky gold necklace and ran a string of pearls through my fingers. There were framed photographs standing next to the jewelry box. There was one with a man and a woman, a boy and girl, really, next to a car. They were both facing the camera and laughing. The boy was hugging the girl around the waist, from behind, and holding her up in the air a little. The car was a black Trans Am. The girl's hair was straight, light brown, and she had bangs that hung down in front of her face; her hands were on the boy's wiry forearm. I ran my finger along the girl's tanned left leg. Tidbit was done in the shower, and she was leaning her head against my back. Behind the boy, the black car looked dusty and hot, parked in the grass. I felt the steam still rising off Tidbit, and the smell of shampoo.

I was surprised, when I turned around, to see that she was naked. I doubled the string of pearls, trying not to seem nervous or strange, and put them on her. I let her lead me to the bed.

Tidbit kissed me. Just when I'd relaxed enough to enjoy the feel of her tongue around mine, she rolled on top of me and looked down. "You're weird," she said.

"So," I said. "Why?"

"I don't know why, but you are. I came out of the shower and was talking to you, but you just kept looking at that picture."

"I didn't hear." I didn't really like being called weird. "You still like me, though?"

Tidbit pretended to think about it. "I like you enough to sleep with you."

"That's a good answer. Very clear. Your therapist would be proud."

Tidbit lay down looking at me. She drew her fingertip along the line of my cheek and said, "You're so cute when you're condescending."

**I woke up** before Tidbit did and went downstairs to wash our clothes. I was starving, and as the clothes were washing, I hunted through the kitchen for food. I found a box of Froot Loops but no milk, so I wandered around the living room with the box, eating. Lines of sunlight shot through the blinds on the windows and swelled on the floor. I remembered my mother telling me that when I was a baby, I would try to pick up the sunlight as it lay on the floor of my playroom. When I heard the washing machine finish, I put our things in the dryer and went back to roaming the house. About fifteen minutes had passed before I realized that I'd forgotten to add the fabric softener. But when I went to put it in, there was an older woman standing in the back doorway, staring at the machine. She looked up.

It was the woman from the picture upstairs. I could tell, although she was older. Her face had changed. It continued to change as I stood there.

"I'll call the police," she said.

I was overwhelmed by pity. This woman was an adult, she probably owned the house, but seemed so scared. I knew I should run, but I was curious about this feeling. It wasn't unpleasant. Somehow I felt okay as long as I kept her from entering the house, her house.

"I'm sorry," I said, "I'll just be a second." I opened the door of the dryer, which blocked her from walking in. The woman gasped. I fished out my jeans and slowly pulled them on. "You're the lady from the picture upstairs, right? With the Trans Am?"

"Get out," she said. Her voice had hooks in it, was real. "Just get out."

"Who was that guy? I mean, it's a really nice car."

"Please."

Suddenly, I knew exactly what she meant. I looked back over my shoulder, at the steps that went upstairs. I grabbed my shirt from the dryer and kept my eyes on her as I buttoned it. "Sorry about all this," I said, vaguely waving behind me. I pushed past her, and began to run.

**Upstairs, Tidbit was** having a dream. She dreamed that she was in a movie theater and that it was crowded and something was wrong, she didn't know what. She was trying to watch the movie, a movie about horses, but she couldn't concentrate. It was full of close-up shots of horses running, lots of them, sprinting. Their legs were like ax handles and pounded the earth, moving so fast they blurred. Tidbit was tossing in her seat, upset, and then she remembered her own horse. Seeing the movie reminded her—she had completely forgotten she had a horse. Tidbit panicked. She tried to remember when she had last fed her horse and realized with a sickening certainty that she couldn't remember ever feeding it. She never had, not once. She sat stuck in her seat in the theater in the dream, her horse starving somewhere and nothing she could do for it.

Tidbit woke to see a woman's face peering at her from under a sharp, blue hat. Officer Sotelo was as surprised when Tidbit opened her eyes as Tidbit was, and jumped back. Another policeman was standing in the doorway to the bedroom. "Sarah Lasker?" he said. "Come with us."

I wandered through the woods and tried to imagine what might be happening. Probably the woman would call the police, and they would find Tidbit. Or the woman would find Tidbit and then call the police. Either way, there didn't seem to be anything I could do about it. I had my pants and shirt, but I was still walking around barefoot.

The morning was cool and a mist from the lake drifted through the trees. I could move through the mist, I thought, because I was more dense than the mist. And the mist could move through the forest because it was more dense than the forest. But the mist couldn't go through a tree. A tree could move through the mist, if a tree could move. If it were dense enough, I thought, a tree could move through me like I was a cloud.

I had to go back to find Tidbit, I couldn't just leave her, but I didn't know if I should go back to the house or back to the school. Maybe she was still at the house. Maybe Tidbit had talked to the lady. Maybe the lady bought her a ticket to California.

A birch tree lay on the ground, its wood all rotted out. But the bark was still there, wrapped around nothing like scrolls of parchment. The farther I walked from the house, the more it made sense to head back to the school, though I wasn't sure exactly which way that was. I thought I could wander until I ended up somewhere that looked familiar and then just go back the way we had come. But then I remembered we had taken a boat and that the boat sank. So I would have to walk around the lake. At least that gave me a direction to move in, around the lake.

I paced quickly through the trees and tried to avoid stepping on any twigs with my bare feet. This was the first of several times that I would find myself returning to Roaring Orchards. I stayed at the school for about three years, during which I ran away three or four more times, and I came back each time, voluntarily, except the last. There was always a sense that I'd miss out if I didn't, that if I failed to return something would remain unfinished. But once I got back, I never had any idea what it was.

My most recent return was just a few months ago, when I ended up sitting on the floor of the Teachers' Lounge and began to write this recollection. Aubrey had long since passed, and the school itself been shuttered. Due to numerous complaints and violations, Roaring Orchards had been forbidden by the Office of Children and Family Services from accepting new students until a series of improvements was implemented. Because the usual number of students were still running away or being withdrawn by their parents, the population dwindled until the handful of children and faculty members left on campus could no longer afford to stay. I followed the story in the *Mohawk County Gazette*, which covered the legal case against the school and its fallout, and whose archives I would occasionally read online. I could never find out what happened to the last few people living at Roaring Orchards; they seemed to just disappear.

I did once come across a picture of Pudding, though, or at least I thought I did. There was an article about a new men's shelter that had opened not far from where the school was, and the article was accompanied by a photograph of a man reclining across a bed, watching television. He looked just like Pudding and seemed to be the right age. But when I wrote a letter, addressed to Andrew Pudding, care of the men's shelter mentioned in the article, I heard nothing back.

My last visit to the school was occasioned by something I saw in the *Gazette*. A place named the West Glen Country School, which was waiting to buy the property, had withdrawn its offer because the physical plant was in such disrepair. At that point, the campus had been empty for two and a half years. After the last students from Roaring Orchards left, to wherever it was they went, it was discovered that tanks beneath the Mansion had been leaking heating oil, for how long no one knew. It was Roaring Orchards' responsibility, or the responsibility of whoever now represented Roaring Orchards, or what was left of it, to pay for the cleanup before the property was sold. While they raised the money or fought the decision or decided what to do, the buildings began to fall apart, and the West Glen Country School decided it would be impossible to move their operations to the campus in Webituck.

I took a train up through the Hudson River valley, past Golden's Bridge and Tenmile River, and got off at the old stone station in Bilston. The train was noisy and crowded at first, but the farther north we went, the fewer passengers remained. The last part of the trip I shared with only a few souls who sat quietly on the cracked leather seats as the train rolled past marshes or followed along the thruway, and whose silence and distant politeness, by the time I disembarked, made me feel like I'd known them my entire life. I walked the eight miles to the campus unsure of what I would find.

When I first passed through the gates, neither the Mansion in the distance nor the other buildings I could see appeared to have changed much. The driveway buckled at points, cracked by the roots of the trees growing on either side, and the grass on the hill had gone wild. But that seemed to be the worst of it. Only as I got closer did I recognize the extent of the devastation. The porch that wrapped around the Mansion had collapsed, and ferns and weeds grew all the way to the front steps. The gingerbreading above the entrance had begun to rot and was augmented by a vast expanse of cobwebs. When I stepped inside, the smell hit me before anything else—the walls and ceiling were in the process of being devoured by mold. All that was left in the Office were filing cabinets, their empty drawers lying open. Trash had collected in the corners. Phone jacks sprouted cords that lay coiled or stretched across the hardwood floor. I passed into the Great Hall, which, emptied of its furniture, seemed immense. The marble mantle of the fireplace had cracked, and in the fireplace itself lay a dead animal that I didn't look at closely enough to identify. Part of the Great Hall's ceiling had fallen, and through the hole I could see the wooden beams that supported the floor above. Tufts of dirty pink insulation hung down. The wide stairway that twisted its way up to the higher floors was covered in small, desiccated animal droppings. I only made it halfway to the second floor before I had to turn around—the stairs became soft and the banister wobbled when I touched it. In one of the bedrooms on the first floor, a suitcase lay open on a bed, dusty men's clothing piled high inside it.

The enormous windows in the Cafetorium were broken, and the carpeting was ruined by weather and scattered with dead leaves. In the Cottage, the kitchen fixtures were covered in rust. Part of the carpet was torn up—by what, I can only imagine—and spread across the walls were hundreds of small black and larger gray mold spots, with occasional fuzzy patches of dark blue and blurred orange rings. I leaned in to look at the little bathroom, which was much as I remembered it, and at the bedroom I once shared, where the mattresses still lay on the bunk beds, sagging in their frames. The walls of the Classroom Building were cracked down to their foundations, and the rooms scattered with fallen acoustic tiles; the ceiling's grid of aluminum beams held only fire alarms whose frayed wires wound into space. The linoleum floor tiles in the atrium were warped and uneven. And among the yellowed paperbacks and brittle hardcover books in the Teachers' Lounge, I found that strange notebook with the teachers' speculations about which of us might grow up to be killers.

When I put down my pencil and went outside again, the sunset was an orange pall that traced the silhouettes of the trees. In the half-light, the garden behind the Mansion was barely recognizable. I had trouble finding the path that led to the fountain, it was so overgrown with weeds and with the box bushes that I had once helped to keep trimmed. The small gazebo to the side of the garden looked as if it had been built in a wilderness. As I rounded the Mansion I saw a fallen window box, sitting upright, in which rainwater had collected. A waterbug dimpled the surface of the water as it swam endlessly back and forth from one side to the other and back again, and I felt a shiver from my spine to the very roots of my hair. Crows called from the ancient beeches.

On the day I abandoned Tidbit and circled the lake to return to Roaring Orchards for the first time, it occurred to me that if there were anything inside of me, it would have to be denser than I was; if a self or soul were a gauzy, misty thing, I would just pass right through it. When I thought I had gotten close to the school, I was amazed to see another fallen birch trunk, perfectly hollowed out just like the one I had seen on the other side of the lake. I was afraid that maybe I had somehow walked in a circle.

But it was only a corrugated metal pipe, half buried in the dirt.

**The school-wide restriction** had been Ken's decision. After what happened to William, and then the fire and the runaways, he must have been scared of things spinning any further out of control. When the students argued that they were being punished for things they hadn't even done, Ken ordered that all the students, every one of them, be sheeted. At first they thought this was funny, but then their clothes were locked away and the students realized the other faculty members weren't going to stop him. Resentment grew. They began talking and laughing too loudly as they passed through the Mansion in underwear and bedsheets, shouting as they chased one another up the stairs.

On the way to drop off Ross Salazar at therapy, New Boys ran in circles around the big field in front of the Mansion and, despite Jodi's entreaties, didn't stop until they felt like it. Alternative Girls refused to go to classes that morning and just sat around their lounge reading magazines. When Ellie was leading Alternative Boys back from picking up their breakfast, they hadn't even pretended to avert their eyes when they passed New Girls dressed in sheets. The few students who could usually be relied on to police the others kept quiet.

Ken called an emergency faculty meeting in Doris's old office. He sprawled, exhausted, in a rolling armchair while the rest of the faculty crowded on the other side of the huge oak desk. No one knew why he was having the meeting there, whether he didn't realize that emergency meetings generally took place in the Campus Community room or if he was showing that things would be done differently now. Ken sat upright and stroked his white beard. He said that no New or Alternative kids were to leave their dorms for any reason. Classes were canceled so that teachers could help out the dorm parents. Therapists would go to the dorms and meet with students in their bedrooms; meals would be delivered by Regular Kids and eaten in the lounges. This was a crisis, Ken said, the first of what he assumed would be many challenges that they would face together. For Aubrey's sake and for the sake of the students, he was confident that they could weather the storm. Ken's insistence on their shared future made the faculty assume he was thinking about leaving. But no one asked. Ellie had been sent to inform the cooks of the changes.

She didn't know their names. The head cook ran a dish towel through his hand again and again as she explained things to him. The emergency had imbued her with a clarity and purpose she hadn't felt before. The students were in danger, and there was no one but the faculty to take charge. She was willing to be honest and forceful and clear. A cold fire had burned away all her doubts. She knew packing up the meals would mean more work for the cooks. She tried to be understanding, but she did not apologize.

When Ellie left the Cafetorium, the sight of a police cruiser parked outside the Mansion brought her up short, but only for a moment. Whatever the police were here for, she would handle it. She would try to keep them in the Office. If they wanted to interview more people about what happened to William, she would tell them this wasn't a good time. They could call tomorrow and schedule a meeting. She just hoped she wouldn't be interrupted by any students dressed in sheets.

Ellie entered the Mansion and saw Tidbit and two officers standing in the Office. She ran to give Tidbit a hug. Ellie was genuinely thankful to see her; she had completely forgotten about her. She brushed the hair out of Tidbit's eyes and asked, "Are you all right? Where's Benjamin?"

"I don't know," Tidbit said.

"He ran from the house they had broken into when the home owner returned," one of the officers said. Ellie looked up to see Officer Sotelo, the woman who had charged her with assault and reckless endangerment when Han Quek had run away. She felt a thrill that she couldn't quite account for.

Ellie stood up straight and shook Officer Sotelo's hand. "Thank you for bringing her back."

"Well, we're required to. The young man, Benjamin, hasn't returned?"

"No."

"Well, we'd appreciate if you'd let us know if he does." The officer looked down at Tidbit and then asked Ellie, "Could I speak to you alone for a minute?"

Ellie nodded and gestured toward the Great Hall. She felt equal to this woman in a way she hadn't all those months ago. She wondered if Officer Sotelo even recognized her. They left Tidbit with the other officer.

"Sarah told me that she was a little worried about the other students yelling at her," Officer Sotelo began. "She mentioned something about being made to stay in a corner while her dorm mates screamed things."

"That's a bit of an exaggeration. We'll have a meeting with the dorm, and the students will be encouraged to be honest about how they felt when Ti—, when Sarah ran away. Also, there were some animals that died, which has been very upsetting. But there's no need for anyone to yell at her, and certainly no one will say anything mean or abusive."

"But she'll be left in a corner?"

Ellie looked the officer in the eye. "Usually after a student's been on the road, we'll keep them separate from the dorm for a bit, to get readjusted. And also to make sure that any drugs or alcohol they might have taken are out of their system. Tidbit knew that was the procedure when she decided to run away."

"So, what, she just stands there, facing a corner?"

"Well, we give her a chair, but, yes, basically, that's the idea. If it's something you're concerned about, I could ask her to come in here, and we could talk about it."

"No, I guess that's all right." Officer Sotelo and Ellie both knew there was very little the police could do about what took place on campus, even now. "If we find the boy, we'll bring him by."

As the police were leaving, Officer Sotelo turned and told Ellie, "The lady's okay, by the way."

"I'm sorry?"

"The woman whose house they broke into, who found them. She's fine, in case you were wondering."

"I'm glad to hear that," Ellie said.

When they were gone, she called Aubrey to let him know Tidbit was back. He asked for her to be sent up to his rooms. Ellie took her upstairs and stopped at the threshold to Aubrey's apartment. She had to give Tidbit a little push, then closed the door behind her.

**On her way** across the Mansion to return to her boys, Ellie found Roger outside of Alternative Girls' dorm, sitting on the floor and crying.

"God, honey, what happened? Are you okay?" She sat down beside him.

"No," Roger said, and leaned his head against her shoulder for a moment before sitting up suddenly. Above his ginger beard, his cheeks and eyes were red. "Well first, I find out Aaron's leaving," he said. "On my way up here I saw him packing up, and he wouldn't say a word to me. I ended up yelling at him like a crazy person." More tears rolled down his face.

"Are you serious? That son of a bitch. He was at our meeting and didn't say a thing." Ellie rubbed Roger's back. "But you're sad that he's leaving? That's very sweet."

"No, I'm furious that he's leaving! I'm crying because after that I came up here, and Alt Girls were totally tearing up their lounge. A couple of girls, Claire and Bridget and someone, came at me swinging socks with bars of soap or something in them, but before they even hit me, I just collapsed on the floor crying. I was so upset and scared and disappointed. They laughed and left me alone, and I crawled out here onto the landing."

Ellie leaned back to look at him. "Oh, Roger, think for a second how that must have made those girls feel. Are they still in there now? They must feel completely out of control. Just when they most needed you to stay. . . . I understand you're disappointed and scared, but we're the adults, we've got to act like it."

Roger started crying again and pressed his face to Ellie's shoulder. She hugged him. Ellie thought she could understand how exhausting it must be for Aubrey, trying to keep the school from going to pieces. She used to think that he simply had his job and they all had theirs, but this wasn't quite so. Everyone pulled in his or her own direction, and it was only Aubrey who kept it all in his head, who could see through everyone's evasions. That much clarity was excruciating, she realized.

Roger sounded like he was choking on his tears. "Okay, okay, hon," Ellie said, and squeezed his arm. "We're not doing them any good sitting out here. Let's go, Roger. Come on, now, get it together."

**Tidbit made her** way to Aubrey's bedroom, and when he saw her he just nodded toward the chair by his bed, and she sat down. Tidbit kicked off her shoes and put her feet up on the edge of his bed again.

"You had a little adventure?" he asked, and Tidbit nodded. His voice was raspy.

"But you're back?"

Tidbit nodded again. That was all he said for a long time. Throughout the morning and early afternoon, Tidbit stayed in his apartment and looked after things. People called occasionally, and if Aubrey was awake he would answer his phone and listen but not say much. When he was asleep, Tidbit answered. The calls were from faculty members letting Aubrey know what was happening elsewhere on campus. As the afternoon went on, Tidbit heard strange noises from around the Mansion—creaking on the stairs, doors being pulled open and slammed shut, quick, pounding footfalls as though people were sprinting down the hallways. But eventually the phone calls stopped.

Tidbit napped in the chair by Aubrey's bed, and when she woke up she warmed up some soup she found in the refrigerator. She made a bowl for Aubrey and one for herself. She found some stale bread on the counter but toasted it, and it was all right. As they ate, Aubrey told her about his plan to write a book that would tell the history of Roaring Orchards and explain his philosophy. It would be, he said, a kind of intellectual autobiography. He talked about some things she didn't follow, about the Garden of Epicurus and about the tragedies of Seneca. He said that maybe she could help him, that he could dictate parts and she could write them down.

After Aubrey fell back asleep, Tidbit pulled one book off of his shelves and then another. She paged through one by someone called Procopius, but she couldn't really concentrate. She walked around the room looking at the medallions on the wallpaper, trying to figure out what the designs on them had once been. Some looked like they were paintings of flowers, but others seemed to be abstract designs, like paisley.

**Aaron hadn't said** much to anyone the past two days. Yesterday he had waited for someone to come and talk to him, but no one had. In the evening, he sat at the square dance and had become aware of how angry he was. He watched the kids dance, then watched the caller and his assistant break down the speakers and record player and pack their things and leave. Since then, every time he tried to say anything more than a few words, his breath failed him.

He squeezed the black garbage bag stuffed with his comforter into the backseat of his car. Aaron's things fit easily into a few trash bags and the cheap plastic bins he had used when he moved in. He went in to see if he'd forgotten anything. His room looked just as it had when he'd arrived: yellow walls, bare mattress. Aaron had grown attached to this weird room, to the strange view of tree trunks immediately outside his window. He thought of taking something as a souvenir. There were a couple of empty med envelopes lying around, and the paperback he had borrowed from the school library lay in the corner. Aaron picked it up and saw that it was stamped PROPERTY OF ROARING ORCHARDS SCHOOL FOR TROUBLED TEENS, WEBITUCK, NEW YORK. He put it in his back pocket, began thinking about the students he would miss, then made himself stop.

When Ken called his emergency meeting this morning, Aaron had hoped there would be a chance to talk about what had happened. He wanted to find a way to tell everyone that the school, the program, all of it, had to stop, the kids be sent home. Or at least he wanted to make someone explain to him why it should continue. But the meeting hadn't been for that. Ken took the opportunity to announce that they were in crisis and to suspend all reflection in favor of panic. The emergency absolved them of any responsibility; they had only to regain control.

Again, Aaron's breath had failed him. He felt like he should call a meeting, but they were already in a meeting. As he tried to speak he saw images of himself standing in front of the room screaming, knocking people off their chairs; he saw himself crouched behind the desk. If he began, he didn't know where it would end. Then the meeting was over, and Aaron went to his apartment and began packing. When Roger caught him loading up his car, Aaron had hardly been able to look at him, let alone explain.

Aaron opened the driver's-side door and looked around one last time. It was embarrassing that the only place he had to go was back to his parents' house. He took the book from his pocket and tossed it onto the backseat. As he drove past the Mansion, Aaron told himself that he didn't bear the place any ill will, though he knew that wasn't true. Sunlight glinted across the windshield, and Aaron rolled his window down. The school was what it was, and he knew that even if he stayed, the system made it impossible for him to do anyone any good. As he drove through the gates and away down Route 294, Aaron knew that, too, was a lie.

**No one noticed** that Bev had left. Students were everywhere, doing what they wanted. The sight of people wrapped in sheets running up and down the Mansion stairs unnerved her. It made her think of the demons she used to pretend to see, and she wondered whether this was some sort of punishment for lying. Or maybe her lies had made this happen? Anyway, it would be much funnier if they all were running around in the woods instead. She told a few of the other girls her idea, but no one wanted to go. So she left to do that herself. She was sure that everyone else would follow in a minute. It was too funny.

That's what I saw when I finally made it back to the school: Bev wrapped in a sheet running in figure eights around trees. She stopped when she saw me. "You're not wearing any shoes," she said.

"You're not wearing any clothes."

Bev looked down and then back at me, laughing. "Everyone else is coming, too. We're all running."

I looked but didn't see anyone else. "Where?" I asked.

"They'll be right here in a minute." And then she whispered, "You shouldn't talk to me, I'm a ghost."

"Is Tidbit here? Did she get brought back?"

"I don't know, she's not in my dorm. Everything's crazy inside."

"You didn't see a police car or anything?"

Bev stopped. "Are the police coming?"

"I don't know." I wasn't sure how much I could believe what Bev told me.

As loud as she could, she shouted, "Yeesterday we are reading a turgee!"

**From the window** of Aubrey's apartment, Tidbit thought she saw something in the woods. Just a tiny movement, a flash of white. But she had no idea if it was anything and, if it were, what it might be. She was vaguely anxious that people were running. It made her feel that she was being left behind.

Aubrey was swimming just beneath the surface of himself. Opening his eyes was an immense task. But there were things he wanted to say and to see. He had an idea, a bright, simple thing he wanted to tell someone before he forgot. He focused, and slowly his eyes opened. Tidbit sat looking out the window. There didn't seem to be anything to say. Whatever it was he had been thinking of was lost in the intricacy of the things around him. The curtains, the complicated bit of sky he could see, and this incomprehensible child, her face in the sunlight. Aubrey squinted. There was too much and he didn't want to know anything about any of it. Tired and cranky, Aubrey rolled onto his side and faced the wall. He shut his eyes, not for the last time, on the fading designs on the marvelous wallpaper.

## ACKNOWLEDGMENTS

I am happy to have this opportunity to thank the Fulbright Program and the International Institute for Modern Letters, now part of the Black Mountain Institute, for grants that aided in the completion of this novel.

For their often baffling confidence in me and my work, my deepest thanks to my parents, and to Jami and Avi Josefson, Mali and Stephen Reimer, Henny, Amy, and Constantine Iliescu, and Lilly Ionascu; to Jim Shepard, Doug Unger, Richard Wiley, and Dave Hickey; to the late David Foster Wallace, whose generosity and whose body of work will always mean such a tremendous amount to me; to Julia Kohn, Andrew Miller, Tom Bissell, Jeff Alexander, Amber Hoover, Matthew McGough, Kim Henry, Dan Polsby, Vanessa Wruble, Karen Savir, Forrest Cole, Nathalie Chicha, and Michael Joseph Gross; and especially to Mark Doten, Bronwen Hruska, Scott Cain, and all the other wonderful people at Soho Press.

## TOM BISSELL ON DAN JOSEFSON, THE STATE OF PUBLISHING, AND DAVID FOSTER WALLACE

When the manuscript of *That's Not a Feeling* landed on my desk, one of the first things I was curious about was the David Foster Wallace blurb. I went to Dan's friend, Tom Bissell (*Chasing the Sea* and *Extra Lives: Why Video Games Matter*) for the full story.

—**Mark Doten, editor**

**MD: When did you meet Dan?**

TB: I've known Dan for almost ten years now. He's part of a group of guys who went to Williams together, and who became my closest friends in New York City, but I met Dan last of all of them. I knew of Dan, of course, and that he wanted to be a writer, but he was away in Romania for a long time, and we didn't really talk much until he got back. Once he did, the first thing he told me was how much he had liked *Chasing the Sea*, my first book. So, obviously, I loved him. After that, we became incredibly close incredibly quickly. We had very different writing styles but very similar ideas about what writing was for and what it should do. And we'd read a lot of the same books. Pretty soon we were spending just about every weekend hanging out together. I'd say I'm as close to Dan as I am to any other man or writer on this planet.

When Dan finished *That's Not a Feeling*, things in publishing weren't great. They were not as bad as they are now, obviously, but they were really, really bad, and at the time it didn't seem possible things could get much worse.

MD: I started working at Soho in August 2008, the very moment of the big economic downturn, and quite a rough time in publishing, with layoffs at all the big places—so I feel like in some sense the current lay of the land is all I've known. Do you think Dan's book would have been picked up by a big house if it had been completed, say, ten years earlier?

TB: It's a mug's game to pretend to know the answer to these hypotheticals, but everything in my heart says yes, I think it would have, especially with what Dan brings to the table with his connections and blurbs and talent. No one ten years ago would have read the book and thought, This is gonna sell a million copies. But ten years ago they might have been more sanguine about the career Dan has before him. And it will be a great career, filled with tremendously fine books. Franzen's second book sold 2,200 copies in paperback. I know, because I used to work for the publisher who did it. It seems to me that the big houses today are much more content to poach writers like Dan after their third or fourth book rather than nurture them from the start, as FSG did with Franzen. And maybe that even makes sound financial sense. But it doesn't make much cultural or artistic sense. Which is my two cents.

MD: It's certainly a great opportunity for independent press editors like myself, as agents and authors find some of the old doors closed to them. As dire as things may be in some corners, I think we're in the middle of a very exciting time for independents like Soho, Coffeehouse, Other, Melville, Graywolf and so on. And there are new presses emerging all the time—Dzanc and Tyrant and Featherproof, to name just three—that have been publishing some really tremendous fiction.

TB: I agree, wholeheartedly. The bigger houses will always get the chance to publish amazing stuff, but a certain brand of amazing book seems increasingly beyond their capacity to pursue. And that's where you and Graywolf and Melville come in. Don't freak out or anything, but you're increasingly holding nothing less than the fate of serious American writing in your collective hands.

**MD: The shift certainly has created some changes in terms of gate-keepers. On the side of authors connecting with publishers, we have diffusion—more and more presses and venues for authors to target, even as fewer agents feel they are able to take on fiction that seems risky.**

TB: But that's where these questions get so ridiculous and frustrating: risky to whom? Think of something like *House of Leaves* or *Cloud Atlas* or other densely literary, "difficult" books that have done extremely well. There is an appetite out there for work that's unusual in some way, but agents pretend not to see that. Because they've had their hearts broken, so many agents back off from ever being hurt again. And that really gets my goat. Agents have to braver than writers, even, in some ways. So while I thought Dan's book was astoundingly good, its unusual aspects and emotional subtlety, I feared, would make it a hard sell to agents who didn't bother to read it carefully and slowly. I provided it with a blurb, but I wanted to give Dan's book a real attention-getting shot with agents, using what little power I had. Thinking cap was on.

**MD: And so we come to that amazing David Foster Wallace blurb.**

TB: At the time I was living in Las Vegas. It was the spring of 2008. Dave Wallace and I had just reignited a correspondence after several years of not being in touch. I didn't know, at the time, that he was in the middle of a terrible depressive tailspin (he alluded to being sick in his letters, but attributed it to a gastric illness), but we got the idea of my then-girlfriend and me driving over from Vegas to Claremont, CA, to spend a weekend with him and his wife, Karen. Right after we settled on this plan, I asked Dave if he would consent to reading Dan's book, which I described to him, and told him of my fears. Dave said he could imagine exactly the kind of book it was, because he had friends he'd done the same thing for, for the same reason. He asked me to send it to him, and I did.

When we got to Claremont, Dave told me he'd just finished Dan's book, that he admired it, and that he wanted to dictate his blurb while he played chess. I wrote down about seven versions of the blurb while we played, which he fiddled with and changed after each move. He said he hated writing blurbs, because he was always aware that the truth of what he felt about books always seemed so plainspoken, while the blurby part of him wanted to say something smart and original. We had a long conversation about what blurbs were even for, and why they were so important. I wished I'd kept the piece of paper on which Dave and I worked out Dan's blurb—written in my handwriting with Dave's notational corrections on it—but I didn't. I had no idea what was to come.

I'm pretty sure Dan's book was the last thing Dave blurbed. It may have even been one of the last novels he read. A couple weeks after we left, Dave tried to kill himself. Five months later, he succeeded.

The irony is that not even with Dave's blurb did Dan's book get the careful, sensitive read it deserves and needs—that is, not until you. Dave blurbed Dan's book as a favor to me, but also because he knew that certain types of novels are quote-unquote hard sells in the minds of many agents and editors. But I'd like to think Dave recognized something in Dan's book—the way it cuts right to the heart of human longing and disappointment, and speaks to the quieter, less flashy parts of ourselves. Its honesty. Its integrity. Dave did see that in Dan's book, I know. May it have given him some respite from his own horror at the time he read it. And may Dave's truthful, unflashy blurb convince people of what so many of Dan's earliest readers knew all along: Dan Josefson is a great writer and his novel is beautiful.

## DAN JOSEFSON ON THE THE PLACES HE LIVED WHEN WRITING
### *TNAF*, AND HOW THEY INFLUENCED HIM

**Where I Wrote It**

Of the many things that confuse me as a writer, the question of where to live is at once the most pressing and the most trivial. Pressing because I am, of course, always living someplace, so even a failure to decide is itself a kind of decision. And trivial because writing novels seems to be such exclusively mental work that it could just as well be done in one place as anywhere else. I began this book in Las Vegas, NV, and continued to work on it in Constanta, Romania, and in New Marlborough, MA, before finally finishing it in Brooklyn, NY.

In Las Vegas, teaching assistantships at the university provided enough money for a classmate and me to rent a two-bedroom apartment around the corner from the Liberace Museum. Wall-to-wall carpeting, central air, a swimming pool, and a mimosa tree right outside the door; the peaked ceilings must have been twenty feet high. Our neighbor in the adjacent apartment was an electrician who was working on the city's new monorail. He was partially deaf, which meant we could play our music as loud as we wanted. It also meant the action movies he watched with his son most nights were turned up high enough to make our shared wall shake. My room was on the opposite side of the apartment; I did most of my reading and writing in a La-Z-Boy recliner I bought at the Goodwill, and many nights, a notebook open on my chest, I fell asleep to the muffled sounds of explosions, car crashes, and laser cannons pounding away like the desert's heartbeat.

Tuesday nights I'd walk across the UNLV campus, past the aloe plants, desert willows, and red bottlebrush. If the sprinklers were on, the sharp scent of sage would rise as I walked to the art department classrooms, where Dave Hickey let me sit in on his art criticism seminars. Dave taught us history and theory and what he could about making good art, but mostly he coached us to make more art.

He also did his best to prepare us to continue working once we graduated. One Tuesday he told us a kind of parable, about a man visiting family in Texas: The man went with his brother-in-law one evening to feed the cattle at the small ranch where the brother-in-law worked part-time. As the pickup turned into the parking lot, gravel crunching beneath its tires, the cattle began to head toward where the alfalfa hay was kept. Impressed, the visitor asked, "They're pretty smart, then, the cows?" The brother-in-law thought for a moment, then said, "They're smart enough to know that when I show up I'm going to feed them. But they're not smart enough to wonder why I'm feeding them." In that, Dave suggested, the cattle were like graduate students: they can think, but they don't think things through.

So I was in school, writing about a school, and plotting, in both senses, an escape. From the Mojave Desert, I made it as far as the Black Sea coast, where I rented a furnished apartment from a woman I called Doamna Rodica. I wrote at the dining room table, surrounded by icons hanging on the walls and glass-fronted display cases filled with Doamna Rodica's collection of ceramics from around the Eastern Bloc. When I wasn't writing I'd wander through the old parts of town, past the statue of Ovid and down to the marina, or watch chess games in the park. Sometimes I'd see movies in a cavernous, mostly empty theater—Turkish movies, American movies, German movies, Romanian movies. Most evenings I stood on my small balcony, which overlooked a grape arbor, as the sky darkened and the sun set.

After I'd been in Romania six or seven months, the American military arrived, out of nowhere it seemed, thousands of troops.

I'd see them in the restaurants or jogging on the beach. Most were stationed at the airport north of town or had taken over the pastel colored resort hotels on the seashore. They were there to prepare for and participate in the invasion of Iraq. I enjoyed getting to know the few soldiers and airmen I met, but remained as baffled by their sudden appearance as they did to find me in Constanta. Our mutual surprise wasn't at all allayed by our smug SecDef's observation that we were, all evidence to the contrary notwithstanding, in the New Europe.

Doamna Rodica would show up unannounced some mornings, to see how I was doing or to retrieve a frozen chicken from her icebox. It was her apartment I was living in—she had simply moved in with her daughter and grandchildren for a year to make some extra money by renting the place. In her shoes, I would probably have checked on me too. We did our best to make small talk. Once she told me that she had been waiting fifty years for the Americans to arrive. "And now here you are." It was easier when I had the news on and we could simply watch TV and shake our heads. I remember us both standing slack-jawed as live reports were broadcast from a school in Beslan, North Ossetia, where 1,100 children and adults were being held hostage. My work was slowed somewhat by that rare gift, an idea for another novel. But little by little, in fits and starts, both books progressed, like two cars being driven across the country by one driver.

I returned to the States and to a series of short residencies on couches and in spare bedrooms, including a longer stay in the Berkshires taking care of a large, energetic poodle. The landscape was familiar, and inescapably literary. Edith Wharton's house and gardens were nearby, as was Melville's Arrowhead. And Mount Graylock wasn't far away. Melville had called the mountain his sovereign lord and king, and there, Hawthorne saw through the darkness once the light of a burning kiln that would find its way into his story about

Ethan Brand, "who had mused to such strange purpose, in days gone by." And I found myself close to an odd school where, for a year and a half after graduating college. I had taught English and History and Math. My time at the school was the impetus and catalyst for the novel I was writing. I worked with increasing speed as I realized—with some exasperation and disbelief—that it *still* wasn't done.

Caught in Brooklyn's tractor beam, I moved to the city and wrote until my money ran out, then freelanced until the assignments dried up, and finally found another dubious gift, a day job. The morning commute and lunch break were novelties; this book eventually wound toward its end. I don't know how much one's immediate surroundings influence one's work, or how much they should. Jean Rhys wrote about the Caribbean fifty years after she had left Dominica; Mark Twain wrote about the Mississippi in Hartford, CT. I don't know how experience is transformed into memory, or memory into remembrance, although it's a question that arises in this novel. It does seem to me that things impress themselves on my eye and mind more strongly as they're disappearing. Outside the manager's office at the apartment complex where I lived in Las Vegas, there were two parking spaces reserved for visitors. In front of each stood a sign that read "If You Lived Here, You'd Be Home Now."

1. Early in the book, Benjamin quotes Aubrey as saying of the students, "They all stay except the ones that don't." Why do so many stay at Roaring Orchards when it seems so easy to leave? Why did Benjamin stay for so long? What makes him and Tidbit later decide to run away?

2. What words would you use to describe the therapy regimen at Roaring Orchards? Does it make sense? Do you think it benefits the students?

3. Benjamin often describes scenes that he could not have witnessed. How do you account for this?

4. How do the teachers and dorm parents feel about their roles at the school? To what degree do you think they are complicit in treatment that they disapprove of?

5. There are descriptions of many animals in the book, including deer, ducks, a caterpillar, a turkey, an owl, a cat, and Napoleon and Elba, the goat and pig at the Farm. What might be the significance of this?

6. How do things at the school change once Aubrey gets sick? Why does his illness have such an effect on the students and faculty?

7. Do parents play an important role in their children's therapy regimen at Roaring Orchards? Do you think they should be more involved or less, or does their level of involvement seem appropriate?

8. Over the course of the book, some faculty members grow more critical of the school while others begin to embrace the school's philosophy. For example, by the end Aaron has left while Ellie seems more committed than ever. What do you think accounts for this difference?

9. What is Benjamin's attitude toward the school as he is looking back? Has his way of thinking changed since he was a student? Why does he return to the school years after having left?

10. In Aubrey's monologue during the Cartoon Brunch, he chastises the faculty for laughing at the students. What part does humor play in the various relationships at the school? Who laughs at whom? Is Aubrey right in his criticism?

11. There are several inanimate representations of people or animals in the book: dolls, masks, and puppets. What purpose do these serve? What feeling do you get when they are described?

12. At several points, Tidbit dismisses the idea that Roaring Orchards is an exciting place. How does the form of the book, the pace and development of the plot, support her contention that "everyone thinks . . . they're the world's original badass but it's just the same tired shit over and over"?